P9-DGX-352

Praise for #1 bestselling author
Lee Child and his Reacher series

"Lee Child [is] the current poster-boy of American crime fiction." —*Los Angeles Times*

"Jack Reacher is a tough guy's tough guy." —*Santa Monica Mirror*

"Like his hero, Jack Reacher, Lee Child seems to make no wrong steps." —The Associated Press

"Jack Reacher is one of the best thriller characters at work today." —*Newsweek*

"Reacher is Marlowe's literary descendant, and a twenty-first-century knight—only tougher." —*Star Tribune* (MN)

"Child has long been one of the best contemporary thriller writers." —The Daily Beast

"That this Reacher is so effortlessly larger than life is evidence of how intense the overall series has become." —Janet Maslin, *The New York Times*

"No one kicks butt as entertainingly as Reacher." —*Kirkus Reviews*

By Lee Child

Ebooks

RUNNING BLIND

LEE CHILD

JOVE BOOKS, NEW YORK

A JOVE BOOK
Published by Berkley
An imprint of Penguin Random House LLC
375 Hudson Street, New York, New York 10014

Copyright © 2000 by Lee Child
Excerpt from *Echo Burning* copyright © 2001 by Lee Child
Excerpt from *Make Me* copyright © 2015 by Lee Child
Penguin Random House supports copyright. Copyright fuels creativity, encourages diverse voices, promotes free speech, and creates a vibrant culture. Thank you for buying an authorized edition of this book and for complying with copyright laws by not reproducing, scanning, or distributing any part of it in any form without permission. You are supporting writers and allowing Penguin Random House to continue to publish books for every reader.

A JOVE BOOK and BERKLEY are registered trademarks and the B colophon is a trademark of Penguin Random House LLC.

ISBN: 9780515143508

G. P. Putnam's Sons hardcover edition / July 2000
First Jove mass-market edition / July 2001
Berkley trade paperback edition / September 2005
Jove premium edition / July 2009

Printed in the United States of America
51 53 55 57 59 58 56 54 52 50

Cover photos: snowy road © antos777/Shutterstock;
old plastic © isaravut/Shutterstock
Cover design by Judith Lagerman

For Edith and Norman,
after twenty-six years of good times

1

PEOPLE SAY THAT knowledge is power. The more knowledge, the more power. Suppose you knew the winning numbers for the lottery? All of them? Not guessed them, not dreamed them, but really knew them? What would you do? You would run to the store. You would mark those numbers on the play card. And you would win.

Same for the stock market. Suppose you really knew what was going to go way up? You're not talking about a hunch or a gut feeling. You're not talking about a trend or a percentage game or a whisper or a tip. You're talking about knowledge. Real, hard knowledge. Suppose you had it? What would you do? You would call your broker. You would buy. Then later you'd sell, and you'd be rich.

Same for basketball, same for the horses, whatever. Football, hockey, next year's World Series, any kind of sports at all, if you could predict the future, you'd be home free. No *question. Same for the Oscars, same for the Nobel Prize, same for the first snowfall of winter. Same for anything.*

Same for killing people.

Suppose you wanted to kill people. You would need to know ahead of time how to do it. That part is not too difficult. There are many ways. Some of them are better than others. Most of them have drawbacks. So you use what knowledge you've got, and you invent a new way. You think, and you think, and you think, and you come up with the perfect method.

You pay a lot of attention to the setup. Because the perfect method is not an easy method, and careful preparation is very important. But that stuff is meat and potatoes to you. You have no problem with careful preparation. No problem at all. How could you, with your intelligence? After all your training?

You know the big problems will come afterward. How do you make sure you get away with it? You use your knowledge. You know more than most people about how the cops work. You've seen them on duty, many times, sometimes close-up. You know what they look for. So you don't leave anything for them to find. You go through it all in your head, very precisely and very exactly and very carefully. Just as carefully as you would mark the play card you knew for sure was going to win you a fortune.

People say that knowledge is power. The more knowledge, the more power. Which makes you just about the most powerful person on earth. When it comes to killing people. And then getting away with it.

LIFE IS FULL of decisions and judgments and guesses, and it gets to the point where you're so accustomed to making them you keep right on making them even when you don't strictly need to. You get into a *what if* thing, and you start speculating about what you would do if some problem was yours instead of somebody else's. It gets to be a habit. It was a habit Jack Reacher had in spades. Which was why he was sitting alone at a restaurant table and gazing at the backs of two guys twenty feet away and wondering if it would be enough just to warn them off or if he would have to go the extra mile and break their arms.

It was a question of dynamics. From the start the dynamics of the city meant that a brand-new Italian place in Tribeca like the one Reacher was in was going to stay pretty empty until the food guy from the *New York Times* wrote it up or an *Observer* columnist spotted some celebrity in there two nights in a row. But neither thing had happened yet and the place was still uncrowded, which made it the perfect choice for a lonely guy looking to eat dinner near his girlfriend's apartment while she worked late at the office. The dynamics of the city. They made it inevitable Reacher would be in there. They made it inevitable the two guys he was watching would be in there, too. Because the dynamics of the city meant any bright new commercial venture would sooner or later get a visit on behalf of somebody wanting a steady three hundred bucks a week in exchange for not sending his boys in to smash it up with baseball bats and ax handles.

The two guys Reacher was watching were standing close to the bar, talking quietly to the owner. The bar was a token affair built across the corner of the room. It made a neat sharp triangle about seven or eight feet on a side. It was not really a bar in the sense that anybody was ever going to sit there and drink anything. It was just a focal point. It was somewhere to keep the liquor bottles. They were crowded three-deep on glass shelves in front of sandblasted mirrors. The register and the credit card machine were on the bottom shelf. The owner was a small nervous guy and he had backed away into the point of the triangle and was standing with his backside jammed against the cash drawer. His arms were folded tight across his chest, defensively. Reacher could see his eyes. They were showing something halfway between disbelief and panic and they were darting all around the room.

It was a large room, easily sixty feet by sixty, exactly square. The ceiling was high, maybe twenty or twenty-five feet. It was made of pressed tin, sandblasted back to a dull glow. The building was more than a hundred years old, and the room had probably been used for everything, one time or another. Maybe it had started out as a factory. The windows were certainly large enough and numerous enough to illuminate some kind of an industrial operation back when the city was only five stories tall. Then maybe it had become a store. Maybe even an automobile showroom. It was big enough. Now it was an Italian restaurant. Not a checked-red-tablecloth and Mama's-sauce type of Italian restaurant, but the type of place which has three hundred thousand dollars invested up front in bleached avant-garde decor and which gives you seven or eight handmade ravioli parcels on a large plate and calls them a meal. Reacher had eaten there ten times in the four weeks it had been open and he always left feeling hungry. But the quality was so good he was telling people about it, which really had to mean something, because Reacher was no kind of a gourmet. The place was named Mostro's, which as far as he understood Italian translated as *monster's*. He wasn't sure what the name referred to. Certainly not the size of the portions. But it had some kind of a resonance, and the whole place with its pale maple and white walls and dull aluminum accents was an attractive space. The people who worked there were amiable and confident. There were whole operas played beginning to end through excellent loudspeakers placed high on the walls. In Reacher's inexpert opinion he was watching the start of a big reputation.

But the big reputation was obviously slow to spread. The spare avant-garde decor made it OK to have only twenty tables in a sixty-by-sixty space, but in four weeks he had never seen more than three of them occupied. Once he had been the only customer during the whole ninety-minute span he spent in the place. Tonight there was just one other couple eating, five tables away. They were sitting face-to-face across from each other, side-on to him. The guy was medium-sized and sandy. Short sandy hair, fair mustache, light brown suit, brown shoes. The woman was thin and dark, in a skirt and a jacket. There was an imitation-leather briefcase resting against the table leg next to her right foot. They were both maybe thirty-five and looked tired and worn and slightly dowdy. They were comfortable enough together, but they weren't talking much.

The two guys at the bar were talking. That was for sure. They were leaning over, bending forward from the waist, talking fast and persuading hard. The owner was against the register, bending backward by an equal amount. It was like the three of them were trapped in a powerful gale blowing through the room. The two guys were a lot bigger than medium-sized. They were dressed in identical dark wool coats which gave them breadth and bulk. Reacher could see their faces in the dull mirrors behind the liquor bottles. Olive skin, dark eyes. Not Italians. Syrians or Lebanese maybe, with their Arab scrappiness bred out of them by a generation of living in America. They were busy making one point after another. The guy on the right was making a sweeping gesture with his hand. It was easy to see it represented a bat plowing through the bottles on the shelf. Then the hand was chopping up and down. The guy was demonstrating how the shelves could be smashed. *One blow could smash them all, top to bottom*, he was suggesting. The owner was going pale. He was glancing sideways at his shelves.

Then the guy on the left shot his cuff and tapped the face of his watch and turned to leave. His partner straightened up and followed him. He trailed his hand over the nearest table and knocked a plate to the floor. It shattered on the tile, loud and dissonant against the opera floating in the air. The sandy guy and the dark woman sat still and looked away. The two guys walked slowly to the door, heads up, confident. Reacher watched them all the way out to the sidewalk. Then the owner came out from behind the bar and knelt down and raked through the fragments of the broken plate with his fingertips.

"You OK?" Reacher called to him.

Soon as the words were out, he knew it was a dumb thing to say. The guy just shrugged and put an all-purpose miserable look on his face. He cupped his hands on the floor and started butting the shards into a pile. Reacher slid out of his chair and stepped away from the table and squared his napkin on the tile next to him and started collecting the debris into it. The couple five tables away was watching him.

"When are they coming back?" Reacher asked.

"An hour," the guy said.

"How much do they want?"

The guy shrugged again and smiled a bitter smile.

"I get a start-up discount," he said. "Two hundred a week, goes to four when the place picks up."

"You want to pay?"

The guy made another sad face. "I want to stay in business, I guess. But paying out two bills a week ain't exactly going to help me do that."

The sandy guy and the dark woman were looking at the opposite wall, but they were listening. The opera fell away to a minor-key aria and the diva started in on it with a low mournful note.

"Who were they?" Reacher asked quietly.

"Not Italians," the guy said. "Just some punks."

"Can I use your phone?"

The guy nodded.

"You know an office-supply store open late?" Reacher asked.

"Broadway, two blocks over," the guy said. "Why? You got business to attend to?"

Reacher nodded.

"Yeah, business," he said.

He stood up and slid around behind the bar. There was a new telephone next to a new reservations book.

The book looked like it had never been opened. He picked up the phone and dialed a number and waited two beats until it was answered a mile away and forty floors up.

"Hello?" she said.

"Hey, Jodie," he said.

"Hey, Reacher, what's new?"

"You going to be finished anytime soon?"

He heard her sigh.

"No, this is an all-nighter," she said. "Complex law, and they need an opinion like yesterday. I'm real sorry."

"Don't worry about it," he said. "I've got something to do. Then I guess I'll head back on up to Garrison."

"OK, take care of yourself," she said. "I love you."

He heard the crackle of legal documents and the phone went down. He hung up and came out from behind the bar and stepped back to his table. He left forty dollars trapped under his espresso saucer and headed for the door.

"Good luck," he called.

The guy crouched on the floor nodded vaguely and the couple at the distant table watched him go. He turned his collar up and shrugged down into his coat and left the opera behind him and stepped out to the sidewalk. It was dark and the air was chill with fall. Small haloes of fog were starting up around the lights. He walked east to Broadway and scanned through the neon for the office store. It was a narrow place packed with items marked with prices on large pieces of fluorescent card cut in the shape of stars. Everything was a bargain, which suited Reacher fine. He bought a small labeling machine and a tube of superglue. Then he hunched back down in his coat and headed north to Jodie's apartment.

His four-wheel-drive was parked in the garage under her building. He drove it up the ramp and turned south on Broadway and west back to the restaurant. He slowed on the street and glanced in through the big windows. The place gleamed with halogen light on white walls and pale wood. No patrons. Every single table was empty and the owner was sitting on a stool behind the bar. Reacher glanced away and came around the block and parked illegally at the mouth of the alley that ran down toward the kitchen doors. He killed the motor and the lights and settled down to wait.

The dynamics of the city. The strong terrorize the weak. They keep on at it, like they always have, until they come up against somebody stronger with some arbitrary humane reason for stopping them. Somebody like Reacher. He had no real reason to help a guy he hardly knew. There was no logic involved. No agenda. Right then in a city of eight million souls there must be hundreds of strong people hurting weak people, maybe even thousands. Right then, at that exact moment. He wasn't going to seek them all out. He wasn't mounting any kind of a big campaign. But equally he wasn't about to let anything happen right under his nose. He couldn't just walk away. He never had.

He fumbled the label machine out of his pocket. Scaring the two guys away was only half the job. What mattered was *who* they thought was doing the scaring. A concerned citizen standing up alone for some restaurant owner's rights was going to cut no ice at all, no matter how effective that concerned citizen might be at the outset. Nobody is afraid of a lone individual, because a lone individual can be overwhelmed by sheer numbers, and anyway sooner or later a lone individual dies or moves away or loses interest. What makes a big impression is an *organization*. He smiled and looked down at the machine and started to figure out how it worked. He printed his own name as a test and pinched the tape off and inspected it. *Reacher.* Seven letters punched through in white on a blue plastic ribbon, a hair over an inch long. That was going to make the first guy's label about five inches long. And then about four, maybe four and a half for the second guy. Ideal. He smiled again and clicked and printed and laid the finished ribbons on the seat next to him. They had adhesive on the back under a peel-off paper strip, but he needed something better than that, which is why he had bought the superglue. He unscrewed the cap off the tiny tube and pierced the metal foil with the plastic spike and filled the nozzle ready for action. He put the cap back on and dropped the tube and the labels into his pocket. Then he got out of the car into the chill air and stood in the shadows, waiting.

The dynamics of the city. His mother had been scared of cities. It had been part of his education. She had told him *cities are dangerous places. They're full of tough, scary guys.* He was a tough boy himself but he had walked around as a teenager ready and willing to believe her. And he had seen that she was right. People on city streets were fearful and furtive and defensive. They kept their distance and crossed to the opposite sidewalk to avoid coming near him. They made it so obvious he became convinced the scary guys were always right behind him, at his shoulder. Then he suddenly realized *no, I'm the scary guy. They're scared of me.* It was a revelation. He saw himself reflected in store windows and understood how it could happen. He had stopped growing at fifteen when he was already six feet five and two hundred and twenty pounds. A giant. Like most teenagers in those days he was dressed like a bum. The caution his mother had drummed into him was showing up in his face as a blank-eyed, impassive stare. *They're scared of me.* It amused him and he smiled and then people stayed even farther away. From that point onward he knew cities were just the same as every other place, and for every city person he needed to be scared of there were nine hundred and ninety-nine others a lot more scared of him. He used the knowledge like a tactic, and the calm confidence it put in his walk and his gaze redoubled the effect he had on people. The dynamics of the city.

Fifty-five minutes into the hour he moved out of the shadows and stood on the corner, leaning back against the brick wall of the restaurant building, still waiting. He could hear the opera, just a faint breath of sound coming through the glass next to him. The traffic thumped and banged through potholes on the street. There was a bar on the opposite corner with an extractor roaring and steam drifting outward through the neon glare. It was cold and the people on the sidewalk were hurrying past with their faces ducked deep into scarves. He kept his hands in his pockets and leaned on one shoulder and watched the traffic flow coming toward him.

The two guys came back right on time in a black Mercedes sedan. It parked a block away with one tire hard against the curb and the lights went out and the two front doors opened in unison. The guys stepped out with their long coats flowing and reached back and opened the rear doors and pulled ball bats off the rear seat. They slipped the bats under their coats and slammed the doors and glanced around once and started moving. They had ten yards of sidewalk, then the cross street, then ten more yards. They moved easily. Big, confident guys, moving easily, striding long. Reacher pushed off the wall and met them as they stepped up onto his curb.

"In the alley, guys," he said.

Up close, they were impressive enough. As a pair, they certainly looked the part. They were young, some way short of thirty. They were heavy, padded with that dense flesh which isn't quite pure muscle but which works nearly as well. Wide necks, silk ties, shirts and suits that didn't come out of a catalog. The bats were upright under the left side of their coats, gripped around the meat of the wood with their left hands through their pocket linings.

"Who the hell are you?" the right-hand guy said.

Reacher glanced at him. The first guy to speak is the dominant half of any partnership, and in a one-on-two situation you put the dominant one down first.

"The hell are you?" the guy said again.

Reacher stepped to his left and turned a fraction, blocking the sidewalk, channeling them toward the alley.

"Business manager," he said. "You want to get paid, I'm the guy who can do it for you."

The guy paused. Then he nodded. "OK, but screw the alley. We'll do it inside."

Reacher shook his head. "Not logical, my friend.

We're paying you to stay out of the restaurant, starting from now, right?"

"You got the money?"

"Sure," Reacher said. "Two hundred bucks."

He stepped in front of them and walked into the alley. Steam was drifting up to meet him from the kitchen vents. It smelled of Italian food. There was trash and grit underfoot and the crunch of his steps echoed off the old brick. He stopped and turned and stood like an impatient man bemused by their reluctance to follow him. They were silhouetted against the red glare of traffic waiting at the light behind them. They looked at him and looked at each other and stepped forward shoulder to shoulder. Walked into the alley. They were happy enough. Big confident guys, bats under their coats, two on one. Reacher waited a beat and moved through the sharp diagonal division between the light and the shadow. Then he paused again. Stepped back like he wanted them to precede him. Like a courtesy. They shuffled forward. Came close.

He hit the right-hand guy in the side of the head with his elbow. Lots of good biological reasons for doing that. Generally speaking the human skull is harder than the human hand. A hand-to-skull impact, the hand gets damaged first. The elbow is better. And the side of the head is better than the front or the back. The human brain can withstand front-to-back displacement maybe ten times better than side-to-side displacement. Some kind of a complicated evolutionary reason. So it was the elbow, and the side of the head. It was a short hard blow, well delivered, but the guy stayed upright on rubber

knees for a long second. Then he let the bat go. It slid
down inside his coat and hit the ground end-on with a
loud wooden *clonk*. Then Reacher hit him again. Same
elbow. Same side of the head. Same snap. The guy went
down like a trapdoor had opened up under his feet.

The second guy was almost on the ball. He got his
right hand on the bat handle, then his left. He got it
clear of his coat and swung it ready, but he made the
same mistake most people make. He swung it way too
far back, and he swung it way too low. He went for a
massive blow aimed at the middle of Reacher's body.
Two things wrong with that. A big backswing takes time
to get into. And a blow aimed at the middle of the body
is too easy to defend against. Better to aim high at the
head or low at the knees.

The way to take a blow from a bat is to get near, and
get near early. The force of the blow comes from the
weight of the bat multiplied by the speed of the swing. A
mathematical thing. *Mass times velocity equals momentum.* Nothing you can do about the mass of the bat. The
bat is going to weigh exactly the same wherever the hell
it is. So you need to kill the speed. You need to get close
and take it as it comes off the backswing. While it's still
in the first split second of acceleration. While it's still
slow. That's why a big backswing is a bad idea. The farther back you swing it, the later it is before you can get it
moving forward again. The more time you give away.

Reacher was a foot from it before the swing came in.
He watched the arc and caught the bat in both hands,
low down in front of his gut. A foot of swing, there's no
power there at all. Just a harmless smack in the palms.
Then all the momentum the guy is trying to put into it

becomes a weapon to use against him. Reacher swung with him and jacked the handle up and hurled the guy off balance. Kicked out at his ankles and tore the bat free and jabbed him with it. The jab is the move to use. No backswing. The guy went down on his knees and butted his head into the restaurant wall. Reacher kicked him over on his back and squatted down and jammed the bat across his throat, with the handle trapped under his foot and his right hand leaning hard on the business end. He used his left hand to go into each pocket in turn. He came out with an automatic handgun, a thick wallet, and a mobile phone.

"Who are you from?" he asked.

"Mr. Petrosian," the guy gasped.

The name meant nothing to Reacher. He had heard of a Soviet chess champion called Petrosian. And a Nazi tank general of the same name. But neither of them was running protection rackets in New York City. He smiled incredulously.

"Petrosian?" he said. "You have *got* to be kidding."

He put a lot of sneer in his voice, like out of all the whole spectrum of worrisome rivals his bosses could possibly think of, Petrosian was so far down the list he was just about totally invisible.

"You're kidding us, right?" he said. "Petrosian? What is he, crazy?"

The first guy was moving. His arms and legs were starting a slow-motion scrabble for grip. Reacher crunched the bat for a second and then jerked it away from the second guy's neck and used it to tap the first guy on the top of the head. He had it back in place within a second and a half. The second guy started gagging under the force of the wood on his throat. The first guy was limp on the floor. Not like in the movies. Three blows to the head, nobody keeps on fighting. Instead, they're sick and dizzy and nauseous for a week. Barely able to stand.

"We've got a message for Petrosian," Reacher said softly.

"What's the message?" the second guy gasped. Reacher smiled again.

"You are," he said.

He went into his pocket for the labels and the glue.

"Now lie real still," he said.

The guy lay real still. He moved his hand to feel his throat, but that was all. Reacher tore the backing strip off the label and eased a thick worm of glue onto the plastic and pressed the label hard on the guy's forehead. He ran his finger side to side across it, twice. The label read *Mostro's has protection already.*

"Lie still," he said again.

He took the bat with him and turned the other guy face upward with a hand in his hair. Used plenty of glue and smoothed the other label into place on his brow. This one read *don't start a turf war with us.* He checked the pockets and came out with an identical haul. An automatic handgun, a wallet, and a telephone. Plus a key for the Benz. He waited until the guy started moving again. Then he glanced back at the second guy. He was crawling up to his hands and knees, picking at the label on his head.

"It won't come off," Reacher called. "Not without taking a bunch of skin with it. Go give our best regards to Mr. Petrosian, and then go to the hospital."

He turned back. Emptied the tube of glue into the

first guy's palms and crushed them together and counted to ten. Chemical handcuffs. He hauled the guy upright by his collar and held him while he relearned how to stand. Then he tossed the car key to the second guy.

"I guess you're the designated driver," he said. "Now beat it."

The guy just stood there, eyes jerking left and right. Reacher shook his head.

"Don't even think about it," he said. "Or I'll rip your ears off and make you eat them. And don't come back here either. Not ever. Or we'll send somebody a lot worse than me. Right now I'm the best friend you got, OK? You clear on that?"

The guy stared. Then he nodded, cautiously.

"So beat it," Reacher said.

The guy with the glued hands had a problem moving. He was out of it. The other guy had a problem helping him. There was no free arm to hold. He puzzled over it for a second and then ducked down in front of him and came back up between the glued hands, piggybacking him. He staggered away and paused in the mouth of the alley, silhouetted against the glare of the street. He bent forward and jacked the weight onto his shoulders and turned out of sight.

The handguns were M9 Berettas, military-issue nine-millimeters. Reacher had carried an identical gun for thirteen long years. The serial number on an M9 is etched into the aluminum frame, right underneath where *Pietro Beretta* is engraved on the slide. The numbers on both guns had been erased. Somebody had used a round-tipped file, rubbing from the muzzle toward the trigger guard. Not a very elegant job of work. Both magazines

were full of shiny copper Parabellums. Reacher stripped
the guns in the dark and pitched the barrels and the
slides and the bullets into the Dumpster outside the
kitchen door. Then he laid the frames on the ground
and scooped grit into the firing mechanisms and worked
the triggers in and out until the grit jammed the mechanisms. Then he pitched them into the Dumpster and
smashed the phones with the bats and left the pieces
where they lay.

The wallets held cards and licenses and cash. Maybe
three hundred bucks in total. He rolled the cash into his
pocket and kicked the wallets away into a corner. Then
he straightened and turned and walked back to the sidewalk, smiling. Glanced up the street. No sign of the
black Mercedes. It was gone. He walked back into the
deserted restaurant. The orchestra was blazing away and
some tenor was winding up to a heroic high note. The
owner was behind the bar, lost in thought. He looked
up. The tenor hit the note and the violins and cellos and
basses swarmed in behind him. Reacher peeled a ten
from the stolen wad and dropped it on the bar.

"For the plate they broke," he said. "They had a change
of heart."

The guy just looked at the ten and said nothing.
Reacher turned again and walked back out to the sidewalk. Across the street, he saw the couple from the restaurant. They were standing on the opposite sidewalk,
watching him. The sandy guy with the mustache and
the dark woman with the briefcase. They were standing
there, muffled up in coats, watching him. He walked to
his four-wheel-drive and opened the door. Climbed in
and fired it up. Glanced over his shoulder at the traffic

stream. They were still watching him. He pulled out into the traffic and gunned the motor. A block away, he used the mirror and saw the dark woman with the briefcase stepping out to the curb, craning her head, watching him go. Then the neon wash closed over her and she was lost to sight.

2

GARRISON IS A place on the east bank of the Hudson
River, up in Putnam County, about fifty-eight road
miles north from Tribeca. Late on a fall evening, traffic
is not a problem. One toll plaza, empty parkways, average speed can be as high as you dare to make it. But
Reacher drove cautiously. He was new to the concept of
driving a regular journey from A to B. He was new to
even *having* an A or a B. He felt like an alien in a settled
landscape. And like any alien, he was anxious to stay out
of trouble. So he drove slow enough not to be noticed
and let the late commuters in their fast sedans scurry
past him on the left and the right. The fifty-eight miles
took him an hour and seventeen minutes.

His street was very dark, because it was buried deep in
an underpopulated rural area. The contrast with the
brassy glow of the city was total. He turned into his

driveway and watched his headlight beams bounce and flick over the massed plantings crowding the asphalt. The leaves were turning dry brown and they looked vivid and unreal in the electric light. He rounded the last curve and the beams swung toward the garage door and washed over two cars waiting nose-out in front of it. He jammed to a panic stop and their lights came on and blazed in his face and blinded him just as his mirror filled with bright light from behind. He ducked his head away from the glare and saw people running at him from the side with powerful flashlight beams bouncing in front of them through the dark. He swiveled and saw two sedans crunching to a stop behind him, headlights swinging and blazing. People were spilling out and running toward him. His car was pinned motionless in a bright matrix of light. People were flashing through light and darkness, coming at him. They had guns and dark vests over their coats. They were surrounding his car. He saw that some of the flashlights were strapped to shotgun barrels. The crowding people were lit from behind by the harsh beams from their cars. Fog was drifting up from the river and hanging in the air. The lights were cutting through the fog and the beams were crisscrossing in crazy moving horizontal patterns.

A figure stepped close to his car. A hand came up and rapped on the glass next to his head. The hand opened. It was a small hand, pale and slim. A woman's hand. A flashlight beam turned directly on it and showed it was cupping a badge. The badge was shaped like a shield. It was bright gold. There was a gold eagle perched on the top of the shield with its head cocked to the left. The flashlight moved closer and Reacher saw raised lettering on the shield, gold on gold. He stared at it. It said *Federal Bureau of Investigation. U.S. Department of Justice.* The woman pressed the shield against the window. It touched the glass with a cold metallic click. She shouted in at him. He heard her voice coming at him out of the darkness.

"Turn off the engine," she was shouting.

He could see nothing except beams of light aimed at him. He killed the motor and heard nothing but fog hanging in the air and the crunch of restless boots on his driveway.

"Place both hands on the wheel," the woman's voice shouted.

He placed both hands on the wheel and sat still, head turned, watching the door. It was opened from the outside and the light clicked on and spilled out over the dark woman from the restaurant. The sandy guy with the fair mustache was at her shoulder. She had the FBI badge in one hand and a gun in the other. The gun was pointed at his head.

"Out of the vehicle," she said. "Nice and slow."

She stepped back, with the gun tracking the movement of his head. He twisted and swung his legs out of the footwell and paused, one hand on the seatback, the other on the wheel, his weight ready to slide his feet to the ground. He could see a half-dozen men in front of him caught in the glare of headlights. There would be more behind him. Maybe more near the house. Maybe more at the mouth of the driveway. The woman stepped back another pace. He stepped down to the ground in front of her.

"Turn around," she said. "Place your hands on the vehicle."

He did as he was told. The sheet metal was cold to the touch and slimy with night dew. He felt hands on every inch of his body. They took his wallet from his coat and the stolen cash from his pants pocket. Somebody pushed past his shoulder and leaned in and took his keys from the ignition.

"Now walk to the car," the woman called.

She pointed with the badge. He half turned and saw headlight beams trapped in the fog, missing his legs by a yard. One of the sedans near the garage. He walked toward it. He heard a voice behind him shouting *search his vehicle*. A guy in a dark blue Kevlar vest was waiting at the car near the garage. He opened the rear door and stepped back. The woman's briefcase was upright on the rear seat. Imitation leather, with a clumsy coarse grain stamped into its surface. He folded himself inside next to it. The guy in the vest slammed the door on him and simultaneously the opposite door opened up and the woman slid in alongside him. Her coat was open and he saw her blouse and her suit. The skirt was dusty black and short. He heard the whisper of nylon and saw the gun again, still pointing at his head. The front door opened and the sandy guy knelt in on the seat and stretched back for the briefcase. Reacher saw pale hairs on his wrist. The strap of a watch. The guy flipped the case open and pulled out a sheaf of papers. He juggled a flashlight and played the beam over them. Reacher saw dense print and his own name in bold letters near the top of the first page.

"Search warrant," the woman said to him. "For your house."

The sandy guy ducked back out and slammed the door. The car went silent. Reacher heard footsteps through the fog. They grew faint. For a second the woman was backlit by the glare outside. Then she reached up and forward and clicked on the dome light. It was hot and yellow. She was sitting sideways, her back against the door, her knees toward him, resting her gun arm along the seatback. The arm was bent, with the elbow on the parcel shelf so the gun was canted comfortably forward, pointing at him. It was a SIG-Sauer, big and efficient and expensive.

"Keep your feet flat on the floor," she said.

He nodded. He knew what she wanted. He kept his back against his own door and shoved his feet underneath the front seat. It put an awkward sideways twist in his body that meant if he wanted to start moving he would be slow enough at it to get his head blown off before he got anywhere.

"Hands where I can see them," she said.

He straightened his arms and cupped his palms around the headrest on the seat in front of him and rested his chin on his shoulder. He was looking sideways at the SIG-Sauer's muzzle. It was rock-steady. Beyond it her finger was tight on the trigger. Beyond that was her face.

"OK, now sit still," she said.

Her face was impassive.

"You're not asking what this is about," she said.

It's not about what happened an hour and seventeen

minutes ago, he said to himself. *No way was this all organized in an hour and seventeen minutes.* He kept quiet
and absolutely still. He was worried about the whiteness
in the woman's knuckle where it wrapped around the
SIG-Sauer's trigger. *Accidents can happen.*

"You don't want to know what this is about?" she
asked.

He looked at her, blankly. *No handcuffs,* he thought.
Why not? The woman shrugged at him. *OK, have it your
own way,* she was saying. Her face settled to a stare. It
was not a pretty face, but it was interesting. Some character there. She was about thirty-five, which is not old,
but there were lines in her skin, like she spent time making animated expressions. *Probably more frowns than
smiles,* he thought. Her hair was jet-black but thin. He
could see her scalp. It was white. It gave her a tired,
sickly look. But her eyes were bright. She glanced beyond him, out into the darkness through the car window, out to where her men were doing things in his
house.

She smiled. Her front teeth were crossed. The right
one was canted sideways and it overlaid the left one by a
fraction. An interesting mouth. It implied some kind of
a decision. Her parents hadn't had the flaw corrected,
and later neither had she. She must have had the opportunity. But she had decided to stick with nature. Probably the right choice. It made her face distinctive. Gave it
character.

She was slim under her bulky coat. There was a black
jacket that matched the skirt, and a cream blouse loose
over small breasts. The blouse looked like polyester that

had been washed many times. It spiraled down into the waistband of the skirt. She was twisted sideways and the skirt was halfway up her thighs. Her legs were thin and hard under black nylon. Her knees were pressed together, but there was a gap between her thighs.

"Would you stop doing that, please?" she said.

Her voice had gone cold, and the gun moved.

"Doing what?" Reacher asked.

"Looking at my legs."

He switched his gaze up to her face. "Somebody points a gun at me, I'm entitled to check them out head to toe, wouldn't you say?"

"You like doing that?"

"Doing what?"

"Looking at women."

He shrugged. "Better than I like looking at some things, I guess."

The gun moved closer. "This isn't funny, asshole. I don't like the way you're looking at me."

He stared at her.

"What way am I looking at you?" he asked.

"You know what way."

He shook his head.

"No, I don't," he said.

"Like you're making advances," she said. "You're disgusting, you know that?"

He listened to the contempt in her voice and stared at her thin hair, her frown, her crooked tooth, her hard dried-up body in its ludicrous cheap businesswoman's uniform.

"You think I'm making advances to you?"

"Aren't you? Wouldn't you like to?"

He shook his head again.

"Not while there are dogs on the street," he said.

THEY SAT IN crackling hostile silence for the best part of twenty minutes. Then the sandy guy with the mustache came back to the car and slid into the front passenger seat. The driver's door opened and a second man got in. He had keys in his hand. He watched the mirror until the woman nodded and then fired up the motor and eased past Reacher's parked truck and headed out toward the road.

"Do I get to make a phone call?" Reacher asked. "Or doesn't the FBI believe in stuff like that?"

The sandy guy was staring straight ahead, at the windshield.

"At some point within the first twenty-four hours," he said. "We'll make sure you're not denied your constitutional rights."

The woman kept the SIG-Sauer's muzzle close to Reacher's head all the way back to Manhattan, fifty-eight fast miles through the dark and the fog.

3

They parked underground someplace south of midtown and forced him out of the car into a white-painted garage full of bright light and dark sedans. The woman turned a full circle on the concrete floor with her shoes scraping in the silence. She was examining the whole crowded space. A cautious approach. Then she pointed toward a single black elevator door located in a distant corner. There were two more guys waiting there. Dark suits, white shirts, quiet ties. They watched the woman and the sandy guy all the way in across the diagonal. There was deference in their faces. They were junior guys. But they were also comfortable, and a little proud. Like they were some kind of *hosts*. Reacher suddenly understood the woman and the sandy guy were not New York agents. They were visitors from somewhere else. They were on somebody else's turf. The woman hadn't examined the whole garage simply because she was cautious. She had done it because she didn't know where the elevator was.

They put Reacher in the center of the elevator car and crowded in around him. The woman, the sandy guy, the driver, the two local boys. Five people, five weapons. The four men took a corner each and the woman stood in the center, close to Reacher, like she was claiming him as hers. One of the local boys touched a button and the door rolled shut and the elevator took off.

It traveled upward for a long time and stopped hard with *21* showing on the floor indicator. The door thumped back and the local boys led the way out into a blank corridor. It was gray. Thin gray carpet, gray paint, gray light. It was quiet, like everyone except the hardcore enthusiasts had gone home hours before. There were closed doors spaced along the corridor wall. The guy who had driven the sedan down from Garrison paused in front of the third and opened it up. Reacher was maneuvered to the doorway and looked in at a bare space, maybe twelve by sixteen, concrete floor, cinderblock walls, all covered in thick gray paint like the side of a battleship. The ceiling was unfinished, and the ducting was all visible, square trunking made from thin flecked metal. Fluorescent fittings hung from chains and threw a flat glare across the gray. There was a single plastic garden chair in the corner. It was the only thing in the room.

"Sit down," the woman said.

Reacher walked away from the chair to the opposite corner and sat on the floor, wedged into the angle of the cinder-block walls. The cinder block was cold and the paint was slick. He folded his arms over his chest and stretched his legs out straight and crossed his ankles. Rested his head on the wall, forty-five degrees to his shoulders, so he was gazing straight at the people standing by the door. They backed out into the corridor and closed the door on him. There was no sound of a lock turning, but there didn't need to be, because there was no handle on the inside.

He felt the faint shudder of footsteps receding through the concrete floor. Then he was left with nothing but silence floating on a whisper of air from the vents above his head. He sat in the silence for maybe five minutes and then he felt more footsteps outside and the door opened again and a man stuck his face inside the room and stared straight in at him. It was an older face, big and red and bloated with strain and puffy with blood pressure, full of hostility, and its frank stare said *So you're the guy, huh?* The stare lasted three or four long seconds and then the face ducked back out and the door slammed and the silence came back again.

The same thing happened over again five minutes later. Footsteps in the corridor, a face around the door, the same frank stare. *So you're the guy.* This time the face was leaner and darker. Younger. Shirt and tie below it, no jacket. Reacher stared back, three or four seconds. The face disappeared and the door slammed.

This time the silence lasted longer, somewhere around twenty minutes. Then a third face came to stare. Footsteps, the rattle of the handle, the door opening, the stare. *This is the guy, huh?* This third face was older again, a man somewhere in his fifties, a competent expression, a thatch of gray hair. He wore thick glasses and behind them his eyes were calm. Serious speculation in both of them. He looked like a guy with responsibilities. Maybe some kind of a Bureau chief. Reacher stared back at him, wearily. No words were spoken. No communication took place. The guy just stared for a spell and then his face disappeared and the door closed again.

Whatever was happening outside kept on happening for the best part of an hour. Reacher was left alone in the room, sitting comfortably on the floor, just waiting. Then the waiting was over. A whole crowd of people came back together, noisy in the corridor, like an anxious herd. Reacher felt the stamp and shuffle of footsteps. Then the door opened and the gray-haired guy with the eyeglasses stepped into the room. He kept his trailing foot near the threshold and leaned his weight inside at an angle.

"Time to talk," he said.

The two junior agents pushed in behind him and took up station like an escort. Reacher waited a beat and then he jacked himself upright and stepped away from his corner.

"I want to make a call," he said.

The gray-haired guy shook his head.

"Calling comes later," he said. "Talking comes first, OK?"

Reacher shrugged. The problem with getting your rights abused was that somebody had to witness it for it to mean anything. Somebody had to see it happen. And the two young agents were seeing nothing. Or maybe they were seeing Moses himself coming down and reading the whole Constitution off of big tablets of stone. Maybe that's what they would swear to later.

"So let's go," the gray-haired guy said.

Reacher was crowded out into the gray corridor and into a big knot of people. The woman was there, and the sandy guy with the mustache, and the older guy with the blood pressure, and the younger guy with the lean face and the shirtsleeves. They were buzzing. It was late in the evening, but they were all pumped up with excitement. They were up on their toes, weightless with the intoxication of *progress*. It was a feeling Reacher recognized. It was a feeling he had experienced, more times than he cared to remember.

But they were divided. There were two clear teams. There was tension between them. It became obvious as they walked. The woman stuck close to his left shoulder, and the sandy guy and the blood pressure guy stuck close to her. That was one team. On his right shoulder was the guy with the lean face. He was the second team, alone and outnumbered and unhappy about it. Reacher felt his hand near his elbow, like he was ready to make a grab for his prize.

They walked down a narrow gray corridor like the bowels of a battleship and spilled into a gray room with a long table filling most of the floor space. The table was curved on both long edges and chopped off straight at the ends. On one long side, backs to the door, were seven plastic chairs in a line, well spaced out, with the curve of the table edge focusing them all across toward a single identical chair placed in the exact center of the opposite side.

Reacher paused in the doorway. Not too difficult to work out which chair was his. He looped around the end of the table and sat down in it. It was flimsy. The legs squirmed under his weight and the plastic dug into the muscle under his shoulder blades. The room was cinder block, painted gray like the first one, but this ceiling was finished. There was stained acoustic tile in warped framing. There was track lighting bolted to it, with large can-shaped fixtures angled down and toward him. The tabletop was cheap mahogany, thickly lacquered with shiny varnish. The light bounced off the varnish and came up into his eyes from below.

The two junior agents had taken up position against the walls at opposite ends of the table, like sentries. Their jackets were open and their shoulder holsters were visible. Their hands were folded comfortably at their waists. Their heads were turned, watching him. Opposite him, the two teams were forming up. Seven chairs, five people. The gray-haired guy took the center chair. The light caught his eyeglasses and turned them into blank mirrors. Next to him on his right-hand side was the guy with the blood pressure, and next to him was the woman, and next to her was the sandy guy. The guy with the lean face and the shirtsleeves was alone in the middle chair of the left-hand three. A lopsided inquisition, hunching toward him, indistinct through the glare of the lights.

The gray-haired guy leaned forward, sliding his forearms onto the shiny wood, claiming authority. And subconsciously separating the factions to his left and right.

"We've been squabbling over you," he said.

"Am I in custody?" Reacher asked.

The guy shook his head. "No, not yet."

"So I'm free to go?"

The guy looked over the top of his eyeglasses. "Well,

we'd rather you stayed right here, so we can keep this whole thing civilized for a spell."

There was silence for a long moment.

"So make it civilized," Reacher said. "I'm Jack Reacher. Who the hell are you?"

"What?"

"Let's have some introductions. That's what civilized people do, right? They introduce themselves. Then they chat politely about the Yankees or the stock market or something."

More silence. Then the guy nodded.

"I'm Alan Deerfield," he said. "Assistant Director, FBI. I run the New York Field Office."

Then he turned his head to his right and stared at the sandy guy on the end of the line and waited.

"Special Agent Tony Poulton," the sandy guy said, and glanced to his left.

"Special Agent Julia Lamarr," the woman said, and glanced to her left.

"Agent-in-Charge Nelson Blake," the guy with the blood pressure said. "The three of us are up here from Quantico. I run the Serial Crimes Unit. Special Agents Lamarr and Poulton work for me there. We came up here to talk to you."

There was a pause and the guy called Deerfield turned the other way and looked toward the man on his left.

"Agent-in-Charge James Cozo," the guy said. "Organized Crime, here in New York City, working on the protection rackets."

More silence.

"OK now?" Deerfield asked.

Reacher squinted through the glare. They were all

looking at him. The sandy guy, Poulton. The woman, Lamarr. The hypertensive, Blake. All three of them from Serial Crimes down in Quantico. *Up here to talk to him.* Then Deerfield, the New York Bureau chief, a heavyweight. Then the lean guy, Cozo, from Organized Crime, *working on the protection rackets.* He glanced slowly left to right, and right to left, and finished up back on Deerfield. Then he nodded.

"OK," he said. "Pleased to meet you all. So what about those Yankees? You think they need to trade?"

Five different people facing him, five different expressions of annoyance. Poulton turned his head like he had been slapped. Lamarr snorted, a contemptuous sound in her nose. Blake tightened his mouth and got redder. Deerfield stared and sighed. Cozo glanced sideways at Deerfield, lobbying for intervention.

"We're not going to talk about the Yankees," Deerfield said.

"So what about the Dow? We going to see a big crash anytime soon?"

Deerfield shook his head. "Don't mess with me, Reacher. Right now I'm the best friend you got."

"No, Ernesto A. Miranda is the best friend I got," Reacher said. "Miranda versus Arizona, Supreme Court decision in June of 1966. They said his Fifth Amendment rights were infringed because the cops didn't warn him he could stay silent and get himself a lawyer."

"So?"

"So you can't talk to me until you read me my Miranda rights. Whereupon you can't talk to me anyway because my lawyer could take some time to get here and then she won't let me talk to you even when she does."

The three agents from Serial Crime were smiling broadly. Like Reacher was busy proving something to them.

"Your lawyer is Jodie Jacob, right?" Deerfield asked. "Your girlfriend?"

"What do you know about my girlfriend?"

"We know everything about your girlfriend," Deerfield said. "Just like we know everything about you, too."

"So why do you need to talk to me?"

"She's at Spencer Gutman, right?" Deerfield said. "Big reputation as an associate. They're talking about a partnership for her, you know that?"

"So I heard."

"Maybe real soon."

"So I heard," Reacher said again.

"Knowing you isn't going to help her, though. You're not exactly the ideal corporate husband, are you?"

"I'm not any kind of a husband."

Deerfield smiled. "Figure of speech, is all. But Spencer Gutman is a real white-shoe operation. They consider stuff like that, you know. And it's a financial firm, right? Real big in the world of banking, we all know that. But not much expertise in the field of criminal law. You sure you want her for your attorney? Situation like this?"

"Situation like what?"

"Situation you're in."

"What situation am I in?"

"Ernesto A. Miranda was a moron, you know that?" Deerfield said. "A couple of smokes short of a pack? That's why the damn court was so soft on him. He was a subnormal guy. He needed the protection. You a moron, Reacher? You a subnormal guy?"

"Probably, to be putting up with this shit."

"Rights are for guilty people, anyway. You already saying you're guilty of something?"

Reacher shook his head. "I'm not saying anything. I've got nothing to say."

"Old Ernesto went to jail anyhow, you know that? People tend to forget that fact. They retried him and convicted him just the same. He was in jail five years. Then you know what happened to him?"

Reacher shrugged. Said nothing.

"I was working in Phoenix at the time," Deerfield said. "Down in Arizona. Homicide detective, for the city. Just before I made it to the Bureau. January of 1976, we get a call to a bar. Some piece of shit lying on the floor, big knife handle sticking up out of him. The famous Ernesto A. Miranda himself, bleeding all over the place. Nobody fell over themselves rushing to call any medics. Guy died a couple minutes after we got there."

"So?"

"So stop wasting my time. I already wasted an hour stopping these guys fighting over you. So now you owe me. So you'll answer their questions, and I'll tell you when and if you need a damn lawyer."

"What are the questions about?"

Deerfield smiled. "What are any questions about? Stuff we need to know, is what."

"What stuff do you need to know?"

"We need to know if we're interested in you."

"Why would you be interested in me?"

"Answer the questions and we'll find out."

Reacher thought about it. Laid his hands palms up on the table.

"OK," he said. "What are the questions?"

"You know Brewer versus Williams, too?" the guy called Blake said. He was old and overweight and unfit, but his mouth worked fast enough.

"Or Duckworth versus Eagan?" Poulton asked.

Reacher glanced across at him. He was maybe thirty-five, but he looked younger, like one of those guys who stay looking young forever. Like some kind of a graduate student, preserved. His suit was an awful color in the orange light, and his mustache looked false, like it was stuck on with glue.

"You know Illinois and Perkins?" Lamarr asked.

Reacher stared at them both. "What the hell is this? Law school?"

"What about Minnick versus Mississippi?" Blake asked.

Poulton smiled. "McNeil and Wisconsin?"

"Arizona and Fulminante?" Lamarr said.

"You know what those cases are?" Blake asked.

Reacher looked for the trick, but he couldn't see it.

"More Supreme Court decisions," he said. "Following on from Miranda. Brewer was 1977, Duckworth 1989, Perkins 1990, Minnick 1990, McNeil 1991, Fulminante 1991, all of them modifying and restating the original Miranda decision."

Blake nodded. "Very good."

Lamarr leaned forward. The light scatter off the shiny tabletop lit her face from below, like a skull.

"You knew Amy Callan pretty well, didn't you?" she asked.

"Who?" Reacher said.

"You heard, you son of a bitch."

Reacher stared at her. Then a woman called Amy Callan came back at him from the past and slowed him just enough to allow a contented smile to settle on Lamarr's bony face.

"But you didn't like her much, did you?" she said.

There was silence. It built around him.

"OK, my turn," Cozo said. "Who are you working for?"

Reacher swung his gaze slowly to his right and rested it on Cozo.

"I'm not working for anybody," he said.

"'Don't start a turf war with us,'" Cozo quoted. "Us is a plural word. More than one person. Who is us, Reacher?"

"There is no us."

"Bullshit, Reacher. Petrosian put the arm on that restaurant, but you were already there. So who sent you?"

Reacher said nothing.

"What about Caroline Cooke?" Lamarr called. "You knew her too, right?"

Reacher turned slowly back to face her. She was still smiling.

"But you didn't like her either, did you?" she said.

"Callan and Cooke," Blake repeated. "Give it up, Reacher, from the beginning, OK?"

Reacher looked at him. "Give what up?"

More silence.

"Who sent you to the restaurant?" Cozo asked again. "Tell me right now, and maybe I can cut you a deal."

Reacher turned back the other way. "Nobody sent me anywhere."

Cozo shook his head. "Bullshit, Reacher. You live in

a half-million-dollar house on the river in Garrison and you drive a six-month-old forty-five-thousand-dollar sport-utility vehicle. And as far as the IRS knows, you haven't earned a cent in nearly three years. And when somebody wanted Petrosian's best boys in the hospital, they sent you to do it. Put all that together, you're working for somebody, and I want to know who the hell it is."

"I'm not working for anybody," Reacher said again.

"You're a loner, right?" Blake asked. "Is that what you're saying?"

Reacher nodded. "I guess."

He turned his head. Blake was smiling, satisfied.

"I thought so," he said. "When did you come out of the Army?"

Reacher shrugged. "About three years ago."

"How long were you in?"

"All my life. Officer's kid, then an officer myself."

"Military policeman, right?"

"Right."

"Several promotions, right?"

"I was a major."

"Medals?"

"Some."

"Silver Star?"

"One."

"First-rate record, right?"

Reacher said nothing.

"Don't be modest," Blake said. "Tell us."

"Yes, my record was good."

"So why did you muster out?"

"That's my business."

"Something to hide?"

"You wouldn't understand."

Blake smiled. "So, three years. What have you been doing?"

Reacher shrugged again. "Nothing much. Having fun, I guess."

"Working?"

"Not often."

"Just bumming around, right?"

"I guess."

"Doing what for money?"

"Savings."

"They ran out three months ago. We checked with your bank."

"Well, that happens with savings, doesn't it?"

"So now you're living off of Ms. Jacob, right? Your girlfriend, who's also your lawyer. How do you feel about that?"

Reacher glanced through the glare at the worn wedding band crushing Blake's fat pink finger.

"No worse than your wife does, living off of you, I expect," he said.

Blake grunted and paused. "So you came out of the Army, and since then you've done nothing much, right?"

"Right."

"Mostly on your own."

"Mostly."

"Happy with that?"

"Happy enough."

"Because you're a loner."

"Bullshit, he's working for somebody," Cozo said.

"The man says he's a loner, damn it," Blake snarled.

Deerfield's head was turning left and right between them, like a spectator at a tennis game. The reflected light was flashing in the lenses of his glasses. He held up his hands for silence and fixed Reacher with a quiet gaze.

"Tell me about Amy Callan and Caroline Cooke," he said.

"What's to tell?" Reacher asked.

"You knew them, right?"

"Sure, way back. In the Army."

"So tell me about them."

"Callan was small and dark, Cooke was tall and blond. Callan was a sergeant, Cooke was a lieutenant. Callan was a clerk in Ordnance, Cooke was in War Plans."

"Where was this?"

"Callan was at Fort Withe near Chicago, Cooke was at NATO headquarters in Belgium."

"Did you have sex with either of them?" Lamarr asked.

Reacher turned to stare at her. "What kind of a question is that?"

"A straightforward one."

"Well, no, I didn't."

"They were both pretty, right?"

Reacher nodded. "Prettier than you, that's for damn sure."

Lamarr looked away and went quiet. Blake turned dark red and stepped into the silence. "Did they know each other?"

"I doubt it. There's a million people in the Army, and

they were serving four thousand miles apart at different times."

"And there was no sexual relationship between you and either of them?"

"No, there wasn't."

"Did you attempt one? With either of them?"

"No, I didn't."

"Why not? Afraid they'd rebuff you?"

Reacher shook his head. "I was with somebody else on both occasions, if you really want to know, and one at a time is usually enough for me."

"Would you like to have had sex with them?"

Reacher smiled, briefly. "I can think of worse things."

"Would they have said yes to you?"

"Maybe, maybe not."

"What's your best guess?"

"Were you ever in the Army?"

Blake shook his head.

"Then you don't know how it is," Reacher said. "Most people in the Army would have sex with anything that moves."

"So you don't think they'd have rebuffed you?"

Reacher kept his gaze tight on Blake's eyes. "No, I don't think it would have been a serious worry."

There was a long pause.

"Do you approve of women in the military?" Deerfield asked.

Reacher's eyes moved across to him. "What?"

"Answer the question, Reacher. You approve of women in the military?"

"What's not to approve?"

"You think they make good fighters?"

"Stupid question," Reacher said. "You already know they do."

"I do?"

"You were in 'Nam, right?"

"I was?"

"Sure you were," Reacher said. "Homicide detective in Arizona in 1976? Made it to the Bureau shortly afterward? Not too many draft dodgers could have managed that, not there, not back then. So you did your tour, maybe 1970, 1971. Eyesight like that, you weren't a pilot. Those eyeglasses probably put you right in the infantry. In which case you spent a year getting your ass kicked all over the jungle, and a good third of the people kicking it were women. Good snipers, right? Very committed, the way I heard it."

Deerfield nodded slowly. "So you like women fighters?"

Reacher shrugged. "You need fighters, women can do it the same as anybody else. Russian front, World War Two? Women did pretty well there. You ever been to Israel? Women in the front line there too, and I wouldn't want to put too many U.S. units up against the Israeli defenses, at least not if it was going to be critical who won."

"So, you got no problems at all?"

"Personally, no."

"You got problems otherwise than personally?"

"There are military problems, I guess," Reacher said. "Evidence from Israel shows an infantryman is ten times more likely to stop his advance and help a wounded buddy if the buddy is a woman rather than a man. Slows the advance right down. It needs training out of them."

"You don't think people should help each other?" Lamarr asked.

"Sure," Reacher said. "But not if there's an objective to capture first."

"So if you and I were advancing together, you'd just leave me if I got wounded?"

Reacher smiled. "In your case, without a second thought."

"How did you meet Amy Callan?" Deerfield asked.

"I'm sure you already know," Reacher said.

"Tell me anyway. For the record."

"Are we on the record?"

"Sure we are."

"Without reading me my rights?"

"The record will show you had your rights, any old time I say you had them."

Reacher was silent.

"Tell me about Amy Callan," Deerfield said again.

"She came to me with a problem she was having in her unit," Reacher said.

"What problem?"

"Sexual harassment."

"Were you sympathetic?"

"Yes, I was."

"Why?"

"Because I was never abused because of my gender. I didn't see why she should have to be."

"So what did you do?"

"I arrested the officer she was accusing."

"And what did you do then?"

"Nothing. I was a policeman, not a prosecutor. It was out of my hands."

"And what happened?"

"The officer won his case. Amy Callan left the service."

"But the officer's career was ruined anyway."

Reacher nodded. "Yes, it was."

"How did you feel about that?"

Reacher shrugged. "Confused, I guess. As far as I knew, he was an OK guy. But in the end I believed Callan, not him. My opinion was he was guilty. So I guess I was happy he was gone. But it shouldn't work that way, ideally. A not-guilty verdict shouldn't ruin a career."

"So you felt sorry for him?"

"No, I felt sorry for Callan. And I felt sorry for the Army. The whole thing was a mess. Two careers were ruined, where either way only one should have been."

"What about Caroline Cooke?"

"Cooke was different."

"Different how?"

"Different time, different place. It was overseas. She was having sex with some colonel. Had been for a year. It looked consensual to me. She only called it harassment later, when she didn't get promoted."

"How is that different?"

"Because it was unconnected. The guy was screwing her because she was happy to let him, and he didn't promote her because she wasn't good enough at her job. The two things weren't connected."

"Maybe she saw the year in bed as an implied bargain."

"Then it was a contractual issue. Like a hooker who gets bilked. That's not harassment."

"So you did nothing?"

Reacher shook his head. "No, I arrested the colonel, because by then there were rules. Sex between people of different rank was effectively outlawed."

"And?"

"And he was dishonorably discharged and his wife dumped him and he killed himself. And Cooke quit anyway."

"And what happened to you?"

"I transferred out of NATO HQ."

"Why? Upset?"

"No, I was needed someplace else."

"You were needed? Why you?"

"Because I was a good investigator. I was wasted in Belgium. Nothing much happens in Belgium."

"You see much sexual harassment after that?"

"Sure. It became a very big thing."

"Lots of good men getting their careers ruined?" Lamarr asked.

Reacher turned to face her. "Some. It became a witch-hunt. Most of the cases were genuine, in my opinion, but some innocent people were caught up. Plenty of normal relationships were suddenly exposed. The rules had suddenly changed on them. Some of the innocent victims were men. But some were women, too."

"A mess, right?" Blake said. "All started by pesky little women like Callan and Cooke?"

Reacher said nothing. Cozo was drumming his fingers on the mahogany.

"I want to get back to the business with Petrosian," he said.

Reacher swiveled his gaze the other way. "There is no business with Petrosian. I never heard of anybody called Petrosian."

Deerfield yawned and looked at his watch. He pushed his glasses up onto his forehead and rubbed his eyes with his knuckles.

"It's past midnight, you know that?" he said.

"Did you treat Callan and Cooke with courtesy?" Blake asked.

Reacher squinted through the glare at Cozo and then turned back to Blake. The hot yellow light from the ceiling was bouncing off the red tint of the mahogany and making his bloated face crimson.

"Yes, I treated them with courtesy."

"Did you see them again after you turned their cases over to the prosecutor?"

"Once or twice, I guess, in passing."

"Did they trust you?"

Reacher shrugged. "I guess so. It was my job to make them trust me. I had to get all kinds of intimate details from them."

"You had to do that kind of thing with many women?"

"There were hundreds of cases. I handled a couple dozen, I guess, before they set up special units to deal with them all."

"So give me a name of another woman whose case you handled."

Reacher shrugged again and scanned back through a succession of offices in hot climates, cold climates, big desks, small desks, sun outside the window, cloud outside, hurt and outraged women stammering out the details of their betrayal.

"Rita Scimeca," he said. "She would be a random example."

Blake paused and Lamarr reached down to the floor and came up with a thick file from her briefcase. She slid it sideways. Blake opened it and turned pages. Traced down a long list with a thick finger and nodded.

"OK," he said. "What happened with Ms. Scimeca?"

"She was Lieutenant Scimeca," Reacher said. "Fort Bragg, North Carolina. The guys called it hazing, she called it gang rape."

"And what was the outcome?"

"She won her case. Three men spent time in military prison and were dishonorably discharged."

"And what happened to Lieutenant Scimeca?"

Reacher shrugged again. "At first she was happy enough. She felt vindicated. Then she felt the Army had been ruined for her. So she mustered out."

"Where is she now?"

"I have no idea."

"Suppose you saw her again someplace? Suppose you were in some town somewhere and you saw her in a store or a restaurant? What would she do?"

"I have no idea. She'd probably say hello, I guess. Maybe we'd talk awhile, have a drink or something."

"She'd be pleased to see you?"

"Pleased enough, I guess."

"Because she would remember you as a nice guy?"

Reacher nodded. "It's a hell of an ordeal. Not just the event itself, but the process afterward, too. So the investigator has to build up a bond. The investigator has to be a friend and a supporter."

"So the victim becomes your friend?"

"If you do it right, yes."

"What would happen if you knocked on Lieutenant Scimeca's door?"

"I don't know where she lives."

"Suppose you did. Would she let you in?"

"I don't know."

"Would she recognize you?"

"Probably."

"And she'd remember you as a friend?"

"I guess."

"So you knock on her door, she'd let you in, right? She'd open up the door and see this old friend of hers, so she'd let you right in, offer you coffee or something. Talk a while, catch up on old times."

"Maybe," Reacher said. "Probably."

Blake nodded and stopped talking. Lamarr put her hand on his arm and he bent to listen as she whispered in his ear. He nodded again and turned to Deerfield and whispered in turn. Deerfield glanced at Cozo. The three agents from Quantico sat back as he did so, just an imperceptible movement, but with enough body language in it to say *OK, we're interested.* Cozo stared back at Deerfield in alarm. Deerfield leaned forward, staring straight through his glasses at Reacher.

"This is a very confusing situation," he said.

Reacher said nothing back. Just sat and waited.

"Exactly what happened at the restaurant?" Deerfield asked.

"Nothing happened," Reacher said.

Deerfield shook his head. "You were under surveillance. My people have been following you for a week.

Special Agents Poulton and Lamarr joined them tonight. They saw the whole thing."

Reacher stared at him. "You've been following me for
a week?"

Deerfield nodded. "Eight days, actually."

"Why?"

"We'll get to that later."

Lamarr stirred and reached down again to her briefcase. She pulled out another file. Opened it and took out
a sheaf of papers. There were four or five sheets clipped
together. They were covered in dense type. She smiled
icily at Reacher and reversed the sheets and slid them
across the table to him. The air caught them and riffed
them apart. The clip dragged on the wood and stopped
them exactly in front of him. In them Reacher was referred to as *the subject*. They were a list of everything he
had done and everywhere he had been in the previous
eight days. They were complete to the last second. And
they were accurate to the last detail. Reacher glanced
from them to Lamarr's smiling face and nodded.

"Well, FBI tails are obviously pretty good," he said.
"I never noticed."

There was silence.

"So what happened in the restaurant?" Deerfield asked
again.

Reacher paused. *Honesty is the best policy,* he thought.
He scoped it out. Swallowed. Then he nodded toward
Blake and Lamarr and Poulton. "These law school buffs
would call it *imperfect necessity,* I guess. I committed a
small crime to stop a bigger one happening."

"You were acting alone?" Cozo asked.

Reacher nodded. "Yes, I was."

"So what was *don't start a turf war with us* all about?"

"I wanted it to look convincing. I wanted Petrosian to take it seriously, whoever the hell he is. Like he was dealing with another organization."

Deerfield leaned all the way over the table and retrieved Lamarr's surveillance log. He reversed it and riffed through it.

"This shows no contact with anybody at all except Ms. Jodie Jacob. She's not running protection rackets. What about the phone log?"

"You're tapping my phone?" Reacher asked.

Deerfield nodded. "We've been through your garbage, too."

"Phone log is clear," Poulton said. "He spoke to nobody except Ms. Jacob. He lives a quiet life."

"That right, Reacher?" Deerfield asked. "You live a quiet life?"

"Usually," Reacher said.

"So you were acting alone," Deerfield said. "Just a concerned citizen. No contact with gangsters, no instructions by phone."

He turned to Cozo, a question in his eyes. "You comfortable with that, James?"

Cozo shrugged and nodded. "I'll have to be, I guess."

"Concerned citizen, right, Reacher?" Deerfield said.

Reacher nodded. Said nothing.

"Can you prove that to us?" Deerfield asked.

Reacher shrugged. "I could have taken their guns. If I was connected, I would have. But I didn't."

"No, you left them in the Dumpster."

"I disabled them first."

"With grit in the mechanisms. Why did you do that?"

"So nobody could find them and use them."

Deerfield nodded. "A concerned citizen. You saw an injustice, you wanted to set it straight."

Reacher nodded back. "I guess."

"Somebody's got to do it, right?"

"I guess," Reacher said again.

"You don't like injustice, right?"

"I guess not."

"And you can tell the difference between right and wrong."

"I hope so."

"You don't need the intervention of the proper authorities, because you can make your own decisions."

"Usually."

"Confident with your own moral code."

"I guess."

There was silence. Deerfield looked through the glare.

"So why did you steal their money?" he asked.

Reacher shrugged. "Spoils of battle, I guess. Like a trophy."

Deerfield nodded. "Part of the code, right?"

"I guess."

"You play to your own rules, right?"

"Usually."

"You wouldn't mug an old lady, but it was OK to take money off of a couple of hard men."

"I guess."

"When they step outside what's acceptable to you, they get what they get, right?"

"Right."

"A personal code."

Reacher said nothing. The silence built.

"You know anything about criminal profiling?" Deerfield asked suddenly.

Reacher paused. "Only what I read in the newspaper."

"It's a science," Blake said. "We developed it at Quantico, over many years. Special Agent Lamarr here is currently our leading exponent. Special Agent Poulton is her assistant."

"We look at crime scenes," Lamarr said. "We look at the underlying psychological indicators, and we work out the type of personality which could have committed the crime."

"We study the victims," Poulton said. "We figure out to whom they could have been especially vulnerable."

"What crimes?" Reacher asked. "What scenes?"

"You son of a bitch," Lamarr said.

"Amy Callan and Caroline Cooke," Blake said. "Both homicide victims."

Reacher stared at him.

"Callan was first," Blake said. "Very distinctive MO, but one homicide is just one homicide, right? Then Cooke was hit. With the exact same MO. That made it a serial situation."

"We looked for a link," Poulton said. "Between the victims. Not hard to find. Army harassment complainants who subsequently quit."

"Extreme organization at the crime scene," Lamarr said. "Indicative of military precision, maybe. A bizarre, coded MO. Nothing left behind. No clues of any kind. The perpetrator was clearly a precise person, and clearly a person familiar with investigative procedures. Possibly a good investigator himself."

"No forced entry at either abode," Poulton said. "The killer was admitted to the house in both cases, by the victims, no questions asked."

"So the killer was somebody they both knew," Blake said.

"Somebody they both trusted," Poulton said.

"Like a friendly visitor," Lamarr said.

There was silence in the room.

"That's what he was," Blake said. "A visitor. Somebody they regarded as a friend. Somebody they felt a bond with."

"A friend, visiting," Poulton said. "He knocks on the door, they open it up, they say hi, so nice to see you again."

"He walks in," Lamarr said. "Just like that."

There was silence in the room.

"We explored the crime, psychologically," Lamarr said. "Why were those women making somebody mad enough to kill them? So we looked for an Army guy with a score to settle. Maybe somebody outraged by the idea of pesky women ruining good soldiers' careers, and then quitting anyway. Frivolous women, driving good men to suicide?"

"Somebody with a clear sense of right and wrong," Poulton said. "Somebody confident enough in his own code to set these injustices right by his own hand.

Somebody happy to act without the proper authorities getting in the way, you know?"

"Somebody both women knew," Blake said. "Somebody they knew well enough to let right in the house, no questions asked, like an old friend or something."

"Somebody decisive," Lamarr said. "Maybe like somebody organized enough to think for a second and then go buy a label machine and a tube of glue, just to take care of a little *ad hoc* problem."

More silence.

"The Army ran them through their computers," Lamarr said. "You're right, they never knew each other. They had very few mutual acquaintances. Very few. But you were one of them."

"You want to know an interesting fact?" Blake said. "Perpetrators of serial homicide used to drive Volkswagen Bugs. Almost all of them. It was uncanny. Then they switched to minivans. Then they switched to sport-utilities. Big four-wheel-drives, exactly like yours. It's a hell of an indicator."

Lamarr leaned across and pulled the sheaf of papers back from Deerfield's place at the table. She tapped them with a finger.

"They live solitary lives," she said. "They interact with one other person at most. They live off other people, often relatives or friends, often women. They don't do much normal stuff. Don't talk much on the phone, they're quiet and furtive."

"They're law enforcement buffs," Poulton said. "They know all kinds of stuff. Like all kinds of obscure legal cases defining their rights."

More silence.

"Profiling," Blake said. "It's an exact science. It's regarded as good enough evidence to get an arrest warrant in most states of the Union."

"It never fails," Lamarr said. She stared at Reacher and then she sat back with her crooked teeth showing in a satisfied smile. Silence settled over the room.

"So?" Reacher said.

"So somebody killed two women," Deerfield said.

"And?"

Deerfield nodded to his right, toward Blake and Lamarr and Poulton. "And these agents think it was somebody exactly like you."

"So?"

"So we asked you all those questions."

"And?"

"And I think they're absolutely right. It was somebody exactly like you. Maybe it even *was* you."

4

"No, it wasn't me," Reacher said.

Blake smiled. "That's what they all say."

Reacher stared at him. "You're full of shit, Blake. You've got two women, is all. The Army thing is probably a coincidence. There are hundreds of women out there, harassed out of the Army, maybe thousands. Why jump on that connection?"

Blake said nothing.

"And why a guy like me?" Reacher asked. "That's just a guess, too. And that's what this profiling crap comes down to, right? You say a guy like me did it because you *think* a guy like me did it. No evidence or anything."

"There is no evidence," Blake said.

"The guy didn't leave any behind," Lamarr said. "And that's how we work. The perpetrator was obviously a smart guy, so we looked for a smart guy. You saying you're not a smart guy?"

Reacher stared at her. "There are thousands of guys as smart as me."

"No, there are millions, you conceited son of a bitch," she said. "But then we started narrowing it down some. A smart guy, a loner, Army, knew both victims, movements unaccounted for, a brutal vigilante personality. That narrowed it down from millions to thousands to hundreds to tens, maybe all the way on down to you."

There was silence.

"Me?" Reacher said to her. "You're crazy."

He turned to Deerfield, who was sitting silent and impassive.

"*You* think I did it?"

Deerfield shrugged. "Well, if you didn't, it was somebody exactly like you. And I *know* you put two guys in the hospital. You're already in big trouble for that. This other matter, I'm not familiar with the case. But the Bureau trusts its experts. That's why we hire them, after all."

"They're wrong," Reacher said.

"But can you prove that?"

Reacher stared at him. "Do I have to? What about innocent until proven guilty?"

Deerfield just smiled. "Please, let's stay in the real world, OK?"

There was silence.

"Dates," Reacher said. "Give me dates, and places."

More silence. Deerfield stared into space.

"Callan was seven weeks ago," Blake said. "Cooke was four."

Reacher scanned back in time. Four weeks was the start of fall, seven took him into late summer. Late summer, he had done nothing at all. He had been battling the yard. Three months of unchecked growth had seen him outdoors every day with scythes and hoes and other unaccustomed tools in his hands. He had gone days at a time without even seeing Jodie. She had been tied up with legal cases. She had spent a week overseas, in England. He couldn't recall for sure which week it had been. It was a lonely spell, his time absorbed with beating back rampant nature, a foot at a time.

The start of fall, he'd transferred his energies inside the house. There were things to be done. But he'd done them all alone. Jodie had stayed in the city, working her way up the greasy pole. There were random nights together. But that was all. No trips anywhere, no ticket stubs, no hotel registers, no stamps in his passport. No alibis. He looked at the seven agents ranged against him.

"I want my lawyer now," he said.

THE TWO LOCAL sentries took him back to the first room. His status had changed. This time they stayed inside with him, one standing on each side of the closed door. Reacher sat in the plastic garden chair and ignored them. He listened to the tireless fluttering of the ventilation inside the exposed trunking in the ceiling, and waited, thinking about nothing.

He waited almost two hours. The two sentries stood patiently by the door, not looking at him, not speaking, never moving. He stayed in his chair, leaning back, staring at the ducts above his head. There were twin systems up there. One blew fresh air into the room and the other sucked stale air out. The layout was clear. He traced the flow with his eyes and imagined big lazy fans outside on the roof, turning slowly in opposite directions, making the building breathe like a lung. He imagined the spent breath from his body floating away into the Manhattan night sky and out toward the Atlantic. He imagined the damp molecules drifting and diffusing in the atmosphere, catching in the breeze. Two hours, they could be twenty miles offshore. Or thirty. Or forty. It would depend on the conditions. He couldn't remember if it had been a windy night. He guessed not. He recalled the fog. Fog would blow away if there was a decent wind. So it was a still night, and therefore his spent breath was probably hanging sullenly in the air right above the lazy fans.

Then there were people in the corridor outside and the door opened and the sentries stepped out and Jodie walked in. She blazed against the gray walls. She was wearing a pastel peach dress with a wool coat over it, a couple of shades darker. Her hair was still lightened from the summer sun. Her eyes were bright blue, and her skin was the color of honey. It was the middle of the night, and she looked as fresh as morning.

"Hey, Reacher," she said.

He nodded and said nothing. He could see worry in her face. She stepped close and bent down and kissed him on the lips. She smelled like a flower.

"You talk to them?" he asked her.

"I'm not the right person to deal with this," she said. "Financial law, yes, but criminal law, I've got no idea."

She waited in front of his chair, tall and slim, head

cocked to one side, all her weight on one foot. Every new time he saw her, she looked more beautiful. He stood up and stretched, wearily.

"There's nothing to deal with," he said.

She shook her head. "Yes, there damn well is."

"I didn't kill any women."

She stared at him. "Of course you didn't. I know that. And *they* know that, or they'd have put you in handcuffs and leg irons and taken you straight down to Quantico, not dumped you in here. This must be about the other thing. They *saw* you do that. You put two guys in the hospital, with them watching."

"It's not about that. They reacted too fast. This was set up before I even *did* the other thing. And they don't care about the other thing. I'm not working the rackets. That's all Cozo's interested in, organized crime."

She nodded. "Cozo's happy. Maybe more than happy. He's got two punks off the street, no cost to himself. But it's turned into a catch-22, don't you see that? To convince Cozo, you had to make yourself out as a vigilante loner, and the more you made yourself out as a vigilante loner, the more you pushed yourself into this profile from Quantico. So whatever reason they brought you in for, you're starting to confuse them."

"The profile is bullshit."

"They don't think so."

"It has to be bullshit. It came up with me."

She shook her head. "No, it came up with somebody like you."

"Whatever, I should just walk out of here."

"You can't do that. You're in big trouble. Whatever

else, they *saw* you beat on those guys, Reacher. FBI agents, on *duty*, for Christ's sake."

"Those guys deserved it."

"Why?"

"Because they were picking on somebody who didn't need picking on."

"See? Now you're making their case for them. A vigilante, with his own code."

He shrugged and looked away.

"I'm not the right person for this," she said again. "I don't do criminal law. You need a better lawyer."

"I don't need any lawyer," he said.

"Yes, Reacher, you need a lawyer. That's for damn sure. This is for real. This is the *FBI*, for God's sake."

He was silent for a long moment.

"You have to take this seriously," she said.

"I can't," he said. "It's bullshit. I didn't kill any women."

"But you made yourself fit the profile. And now proving them wrong is going to be tough. Proving a negative always is. So you need a proper lawyer."

"They said I'm damaging your career. They said I'm not an ideal corporate husband."

"Well, that's bullshit too. And even if it was true, I wouldn't care. I'm not saying get a different lawyer for my sake. I'm saying it for yours."

"I don't want *any* lawyer."

"So why did you call me?"

He smiled. "I thought you might cheer me up."

She stepped into his arms and stretched up and kissed him, hard.

"I love you, Reacher," she said. "I really do, you know that, right? But you need a better lawyer. I don't even understand what this is *about*."

There was a long silence. Just ventilation flutter above their heads, the faint noise of air against metal, the quiet sound of time passing. He listened to it.

"They gave me a copy of the surveillance report," she said.

He nodded. "I thought they would."

"Why?"

"Because it eliminates me from the investigation," he said.

"How?"

"Because this is not about two women," he said.

"It isn't?"

"No, it's about *three* women. Has to be."

"Why?"

"Because whoever's killing them, he's working to a timetable. You see that? He's on a three-week cycle. Seven weeks ago, four weeks ago, so the next one has already happened, this past week. They put me under surveillance to eliminate me from the investigation."

"So why did they haul you in? If you're eliminated?"

"I don't know," he said.

"Maybe the timetable fell apart. Maybe he stopped at two."

"Nobody stops at two. You do more than one, you do more than two."

"Maybe he fell ill and took a break. Could be months before the next one."

He was silent.

"Maybe he was arrested for something else," she said.

"That happens, time to time. Something unconnected, you know? He could be in jail ten years. They'll never know it was him. You need a good lawyer, Reacher. Somebody better than me. This isn't going to be easy."

"You were supposed to cheer me up, you know that?"

"No, I was supposed to give you advice."

He stared at her, suddenly uncertain.

"There's the other thing too," she said. "The two guys. You're in trouble for that, whatever."

"They should thank me for that."

"Doesn't work that way," she said.

He was silent.

"This is not the Army, Reacher," she said. "You can't just drag a couple of guys behind the motor pool and beat some sense into them anymore. This is New York. This is civilian stuff now. They're looking at you for something bad and you can't just pretend they're not."

"I didn't do anything."

"Wrong, Reacher. You put two guys in the hospital. *They watched you do it.* Bad guys, for sure, but there are *rules* here. You broke them."

Then there were footsteps in the corridor outside, loud and heavy. Maybe three men, hurrying. The door opened. Deerfield stepped into the room. The two local boys crowded his shoulder. Deerfield ignored Reacher and spoke directly to Jodie.

"Your client conference is over, Ms. Jacob," he said.

Deerfield led the way back to the room with the long table. The two local agents sandwiched Reacher between them and followed him. Jodie trailed the four of them through the door. She blinked in the glare of the lights. A second chair had been placed over on the far side.

Deerfield stood and pointed at it, silently. Jodie glanced at him and moved around the end of the table and sat down with Reacher. He squeezed her hand under the cover of the shiny mahogany slab.

The two local boys took up station against the walls. Reacher stared forward through the glare. The same lineup was ranged against him. Poulton, Lamarr, Blake, Deerfield, and then Cozo, sitting isolated between two empty chairs. Now there was a squat black audio recorder on the table. Deerfield leaned forward and pressed a red button. He announced the date and the time and the place. He identified the nine occupants of the room. He placed his hands in front of him.

"This is Alan Deerfield speaking to the suspect Jack Reacher," he said. "You are now under arrest on the following two counts."

He paused.

"One, for aggravated assault and robbery," he said. "Against two persons yet to be definitively identified."

James Cozo leaned forward. "Two, for aiding and abetting a criminal organization engaged in the practice of extortion."

Deerfield smiled. "You are not obliged to say anything. If you do say anything, it will be recorded and may be used as evidence against you in a court of law. You are entitled to be represented by an attorney. If you cannot afford an attorney, one will be provided for you by the state of New York."

He leaned forward to the recording machine and pressed the stop button.

"So did I get it right? Seeing as how you're the big expert on Miranda?"

Reacher said nothing. Deerfield smiled again and pressed the red button and the machine hummed back into life.

"Do you understand your rights?" he asked.

"Yes," Reacher said.

"Do you have anything to say at this point?"

"No."

"That it?" Deerfield asked.

"Yes," Reacher said.

Deerfield nodded. "Noted."

He reached forward and clicked the recording machine to off.

"I want a bail hearing," Jodie said.

Deerfield shook his head.

"No need," he said. "We'll release him on his own recognizance."

Silence in the room.

"What about the other matter?" Jodie asked. "The women?"

"That investigation is continuing," Deerfield said. "Your client is free to go."

5

HE WAS OUT of there just after three in the morning. Jodie was agitated, torn between staying with him and getting back to the office to finish her all-nighter. He convinced her to calm down and go do her work. One of the local guys drove her down to Wall Street. They gave him back his possessions, except for the wad of stolen cash. Then the other local guy drove him back to Garrison, hustling hard, fifty-eight miles in forty-seven minutes. He had a red beacon on the dash connected to the cigar lighter with a cord, and he kept it flashing the whole way. The beam swept through the fog. It was the middle of the night, dark and cold, and the roads were damp and slick. The guy said nothing. Just drove and then jammed to a stop at the end of Reacher's driveway in Garrison and took off again as soon as the passenger door slammed shut. Reacher watched the flashing light disappear into the river mist and turned to walk down to his house.

He had inherited the house from Leon Garber, who was Jodie's father and his old commanding officer. It had been a week of big surprises, both good and bad, back at the start of the summer. Meeting Jodie again, finding out she'd been married and divorced, finding out old Leon was dead, finding out the house was his. He had been in love with Jodie for fifteen years, since he first met her, on a base in the Philippines. She had been fifteen herself then, right on the cusp of spectacular womanhood, and she was his CO's daughter, and he had crushed his feelings down like a guilty secret and never let them see the light of day. He felt they would have been a betrayal of her, and of Leon, and betraying Leon was the last thing he would have ever done, because Leon was a rough-and-ready prince among men, and he loved him like a father. Which made him feel Jodie was his sister, and you don't feel that way about your sister.

Then chance had brought him to Leon's funeral, and he had met Jodie again, and they had sparred uneasily for a couple of days before she admitted she felt the exact same things and was concealing her feelings for the exact same reasons. It was a thunderclap, a glorious sunburst of happiness in a summer week of big surprises.

So meeting Jodie again was the good surprise and Leon dying was the bad one, no doubt about it. But inheriting the house was both good *and* bad. It was a half-million-dollar slice of prime real estate standing proudly on the Hudson opposite West Point, and it was a comfortable building, but it represented a big problem. It *anchored* him in a way which made him profoundly uncomfortable. Being static disconcerted him. He had moved around so often in his life it confused him to spend time in any one particular place. And he had never lived in a house before. Bunkhouses and service bungalows and motels were his habitat. It was ingrained.

And the idea of property worried him. His whole life, he had never owned more than would fit into his pockets. As a boy he had owned a baseball and not much else. As an adult he had once gone seven whole years without owning anything at all except a pair of shoes he preferred to the Defense Department issue. Then a woman bought him a wallet with a clear plastic window with her photograph in it. He lost touch with the woman and junked the photograph, but kept the wallet. Then he went the remaining six years of his service life with just the shoes and the wallet. After mustering out he added a toothbrush. It was a plastic thing that folded in half and clipped into his pocket like a pen. He had a wristwatch. It was Army issue, so it started out theirs and became his when they didn't ask for it back. And that was it. Shoes on his feet, clothes on his back, small bills in his pants, big bills in his wallet, a toothbrush in his pocket, and a watch on his wrist.

Now he had a house. And a house is a complicated thing. A big, complicated, physical thing. It started with the basement. The basement was a huge dark space with a concrete floor and concrete walls and floor joists exposed overhead like bones. There were pipes and wires and machines down there. A furnace. Buried outside somewhere was an oil tank. There was a well for the water. Big round pipes ran through the wall to the septic system. It was a complex interdependent machine, and he didn't know how it worked.

Upstairs looked more normal. There was a warren of rooms, all of them amiably shabby and unkempt. But they all had secrets. Some of the light switches didn't work. One of the windows was jammed shut. The range in the kitchen was too complicated to use. The whole place creaked and cracked at night, reminding him it was real and there and needed thinking about.

And a house has an existence beyond the physical. It's also a bureaucratic thing. Something had come in the mail about *title*. There was insurance to consider. Taxes. Town tax, school tax, inspection, assessment. There was a bill to pay for garbage collection. And something about a scheduled propane delivery. He kept all that kind of mail in a drawer in the kitchen.

The only thing he had bought for the house was a gold-colored filter cone for Leon's old coffee machine. He figured it was easier than always running to the store to buy the paper kind. Ten past four that morning, he filled it with coffee from a can and added water and set the machine going. Rinsed out a mug at the sink and set it on the counter, ready. Sat on a stool and leaned on his elbows, and watched the dark liquid sputtering into the flask. It was an old machine, inefficient, maybe a little furred up inside. It generally took five minutes to finish. Somewhere during the fourth of those five minutes, he heard a car slowing on the road outside. The hiss of damp pavement. The crunch of tires on his asphalt drive. *Jodie couldn't stand to stay at work*, he thought. That hope endured about a second and a half, until the car came around the curve and the flashing red beam started sweeping over his kitchen window. It washed left to right, left to right, cutting through the river mist, and then it died into darkness and the motor noise died into silence. Doors opened and feet touched the ground. Two people. Doors slammed shut. He stood up and killed the kitchen light. Looked out of the window and saw the vague shapes of two people peering into the fog, looking for the path that led up to his front door. He ducked back to the stool and listened to their steps on the gravel. They paused. The doorbell rang.

There were two light switches in the hallway. One of them operated a porch light. He wasn't sure which one. He gambled and got it right and saw a glow through the fanlight. He opened the door. The bulb out there was a spotlight made of thick glass tinted yellow. It threw a narrow beam downward from high on the right. The beam caught Nelson Blake first, and then the parts of Julia Lamarr that weren't in his shadow. Blake's face was showing nothing except strain. Lamarr's face was still full of hostility and contempt.

"You're still up," Blake said. A statement, not a question.

Reacher nodded.

"Come on in, I guess," he said.

Lamarr shook her head. The yellow light caught her hair.

"We'd rather not," she said.

Blake moved his feet. "There someplace we can go? Get some breakfast?"

"Four thirty in the morning?" Reacher said. "Not around here."

"Can we talk in the car?" Lamarr asked.

"No," Reacher said.

Impasse. Lamarr looked away and Blake shuffled his feet.

"Come on in," Reacher said again. "I just made coffee."

He walked away, back to the kitchen. Pulled a cupboard door and found two more mugs. Rinsed the dust out of them at the sink and listened to the creak of the hallway floor as Blake stepped inside. Then he heard Lamarr's lighter tread, and the sound of the door closing behind her.

"Black is all I got," he called. "No milk or sugar in the house, I'm afraid."

"Black is fine," Blake said.

He was in the kitchen doorway, moving sideways, staying close to the hallway, unwilling to trespass. Lamarr was moving alongside him, looking around the kitchen with undisguised curiosity.

"Nothing for me," she said.

"Drink some coffee, Julia," Blake said. "It's been a long night."

The way he said it was halfway between an order and paternalistic concern. Reacher glanced at him, surprised, and filled three mugs. He took his own and leaned back on the counter, waiting.

"We need to talk," Blake said.

"Who was the third woman?" Reacher asked.

"Lorraine Stanley. She was a quartermaster sergeant."

"Where?"

"She served in Utah someplace. They found her dead in California, this morning."

"Same MO?"

Blake nodded. "Identical in every respect."

"Same history?"

Blake nodded again. "Harassment complainant, won her case, but quit anyway."

"When?"

"The harassment thing was two years ago, she quit a year ago. So that's three out of three. So the Army thing is not a coincidence, believe me."

Reacher sipped his coffee. It tasted weak and stale. The machine was obviously all furred up with mineral deposits. There was probably a procedure for cleaning it out.

"I never heard of her," he said. "I never served in Utah."

Blake nodded. "Somewhere we can talk?"

"We're talking here, right?"

"Somewhere we can sit?"

Reacher nodded and pushed off the counter and led the way into the living room. He set his mug on the side table and pulled up the blinds to reveal pitch dark outside. The windows faced west over the river. It would be hours until the sun got high enough to lighten the sky out there.

There were three sofas in a rectangle around a cold fireplace full of last winter's ash. The last cheery blazes Jodie's father had ever enjoyed. Blake sat facing the window and Reacher sat opposite and watched Lamarr as she fought her short skirt and sat down facing the hearth. Her skin was the same color as the ash.

"We stand by our profile," she said.

"Well, good for you."

"It was somebody exactly like you."

"You think that's plausible?" Blake asked.

"Is what plausible?" Reacher asked back.

"That this could be a soldier?"

"You're asking me if a soldier could be a killer?"

Blake nodded. "You got an opinion on that?"

"My opinion is it's a really stupid question. Like asking me if I thought a jockey could ride a horse."

There was silence. Just a muffled *whump* from the basement as the furnace caught, and then rapid creaking as the steam pipes heated through and expanded and rubbed against the floor joists under their feet.

"So you were a plausible suspect," Blake said. "As far as the first two went."

Reacher said nothing.

"Hence the surveillance," Blake said.

"Is that an apology?" Reacher asked.

Blake nodded. "I guess so."

"So why did you haul me in? When you already proved it wasn't me?"

Blake looked embarrassed. "We wanted to show some progress, I guess."

"You show progress by hauling the wrong guy in? I don't buy that."

"I already apologized," Blake said.

More silence.

"You got anybody who knew all three?" Reacher asked.

"Not yet," Lamarr said.

"We're thinking maybe previous personal contact isn't too significant," Blake said.

"You were thinking it *was*, couple of hours ago. You

were telling me how I was this big friend of theirs, I knock on the door, they let me right in."

"Not you," Blake said. "Somebody like you, is all. And now we're thinking maybe we were wrong. This guy is killing by category, right? Female harassment complainants who quit afterward? So maybe he's not personally known to them, maybe he's just in a *category* known to them. Like the military police."

Reacher smiled. "So now you think it was me again?"

Blake shook his head. "No, you weren't in California."

"Wrong answer, Blake. It wasn't me because I'm not a killer."

"You never killed anybody?" Lamarr said, like she knew the answer.

"Only those who needed it."

She smiled in turn. "Like I said, we stand by our profile. Some self-righteous son of a bitch just like you."

Reacher saw Blake glance at her, half supportive, half disapproving. The light from the kitchen was coming through the hallway behind her, turning her thin hair to a wispy halo, making her look like a death's-head. Blake sat forward, trying to force Reacher's attention his way. "What we're saying is, it's possible this guy is or was a military policeman."

Reacher looked away from Lamarr and shrugged.

"Anything's possible," he said.

Blake nodded. "And, you know, we kind of understand that maybe your loyalty to the service makes that hard to accept."

"Actually, common sense makes that hard to accept."

"In what way?"

"Because you seem to think trust and friendship are important to the MO in some way. And nobody in the service trusts an MP. Or likes them much, in my experience."

"You told us Rita Scimeca would remember you as a friend."

"I was different. I put the effort in. Not many of the guys did."

Silence again. The fog outside was dulling sound, like a blanket over the house. The water forcing through the radiators was loud.

"There's an *agenda* here," Blake said. "Like Julia says, we stand behind our techniques, and the way we read it, there's an Army involvement. The victim category is way too narrow for this to be random."

"So?"

"As a rule, the Bureau and the military don't get along too well."

"Well, there's a big surprise. Who the hell *do* you guys get along with?"

Blake nodded. He was in an expensive suit. It made him look uncomfortable, like a college football coach on alumni day.

"Nobody gets on with anybody," he said. "You know how it is, with all the rivalries. When you were serving, did you ever cooperate with civilian agencies?"

Reacher said nothing.

"So you know how it is," Blake said again. "Military hates the Bureau, the Bureau hates CIA, everybody hates everybody else."

There was silence.

"So we need a go-between," Blake said.

"A what?"

"An adviser. Somebody to help us."

Reacher shrugged. "I don't know anybody like that. I've been out too long."

Silence. Reacher drained his coffee and set the empty mug back on the table.

"You could do it," Blake said.

"Me?"

"Yes, you. You still know your way around, right?"

"No way."

"Why not?"

Reacher shook his head. "Because I don't want to."

"But you *could* do it."

"I could, but I won't."

"We got your record. You were a hell of an investigator, in the service."

"That's history."

"Maybe you still got friends there, people who remember you. Maybe people who still owe you favors."

"Maybe, maybe not."

"You could help us."

"Maybe I could, but I won't."

He leaned back into his sofa and spread his arms wide across the tops of the cushions and straightened his legs.

"Don't you feel anything?" Blake asked. "For these women getting killed? Shouldn't be happening, right?"

"There's a million people in the service," Reacher said. "I was in thirteen years. Turnover during that period was what? Maybe twice over? So there's two million people out there who used to be in with me. Stands to reason a few of them will be getting killed, just like a few of them will be winning the lottery. I can't worry about all of them."

"You knew Callan and Cooke. You liked them."

"I liked Callan."

"So help us catch her killer."

"No."

"Without somebody like you, we're just running blind."

"No."

"I'm asking for your help here."

"No."

"You son of a bitch," Lamarr said.

Reacher looked at Blake. "You seriously think I would want to work with her? And can't she think of anything else to call me except *son of a bitch*?"

"Julia, go fix some more coffee," Blake said.

She colored red and her mouth set tight, but she struggled up out of the sofa and walked through to the kitchen. Blake sat forward and talked low.

"She's real uptight," he said. "You need to cut her a little slack."

"I do?" Reacher said. "Why the hell should I? She's sitting here drinking my coffee, calling me names."

"Victim category is pretty specific here, right? And maybe smaller than you think. Female harassment complainants who subsequently quit the service? You said hundreds, maybe thousands, but Defense Department says there's only ninety-one women who fit those parameters."

"So?"

"We figure the guy might want to work his way through all of them. So we have to assume he's going to, until he's caught. If he's caught. And he's done three already."

"So?"

"Julia's sister is one of the other eighty-eight."

Silence again, apart from domestic noises in the kitchen.

"So she's worried," Blake said. "Not really panicked, I guess, because one in eighty-eight isn't bad odds, but it's bad enough for her to be taking it real personal."

Reacher nodded, slowly.

"Then she shouldn't be working the case," he said. "She's too involved."

Blake shrugged. "She insisted. It was my judgment call. I'm happy with it. Pressure can produce results."

"Not for her. She's a loose cannon."

"She's my lead profiler. She's effectively driving this case. So I need her, involved or not. And she needs you as a go-between, and I need results, so you need to cut her a little slack."

He sat back and stared at Reacher. A fat old man, uncomfortable in his suit, sweating in the nighttime chill, with something uncompromising in his face. *I need results.* Reacher had no problem with people who needed results. But he said nothing. There was a long silence. Then Lamarr came back into the room, carrying the pot from the machine. Her face was pale again. She had recovered her composure.

"I'm standing by my profile," she said. "The guy's somebody exactly like you. Maybe somebody you used to know. Maybe somebody you worked with."

Reacher looked up at her. "I'm sorry about your personal situation."

"I don't need your sympathy. I need to catch the guy."

"Well, good luck."

She bent and poured coffee into Blake's mug, and then walked over to Reacher's.

"Thank you," he said.

"You going to help us?" she asked.

He shook his head. "No."

"What about an advisory role?" Blake asked. "Purely consultative? Deep background?"

Reacher shook his head again. "No, not interested."

"What about something entirely passive?" Blake asked. "Just brainstorming? We feel you could be close to the guy. At least maybe close to the *type* of guy."

"Not my bag," Reacher said.

There was silence.

"Would you agree to be hypnotized?" Blake asked.

"Hypnotized? Why?"

"Maybe you could recall something buried. You know, some guy making some threats, some adverse comments. Something you didn't pay too much attention to at the time. Might come back to you. Might help us piece something together."

"You still do hypnotism?"

"Sometimes," Blake said. "It can help. Julia's an expert. She'd do it."

"In that case, no thanks. She might make me walk down Fifth Avenue naked."

Silence again. Blake looked away, then he turned back.

"Last time, Reacher," he said. "The Bureau is asking for your help. We employ advisers all the time. You'd get paid and everything. Yes or no?"

"This is what hauling me in was all about, right?"

Blake nodded. "Sometimes it works."

"How?"

Blake paused, and then he decided to answer. Reacher saw a guy prepared to be frank, in the interests of being persuasive.

"It shakes people up," Blake said. "You know, make them feel they're the prime suspect, then tell them they're not, the emotional flip-flop can make them feel a sort of gratitude toward us. Makes them want to help us out."

"That's your experience?"

Blake nodded again. "It works, more often than not."

Reacher shrugged. "I never studied much psychology."

"Psychology is our trade, manner of speaking," Blake said.

"Kind of cruel, don't you think?"

"The Bureau does what it has to do."

"Evidently."

"So, yes or no?"

"No."

Silence in the room.

"Why not?"

"Because your emotional flip-flop didn't work on me, I guess."

"Can we have a formal reason, for the record?"

"Ms. Lamarr is the formal reason. She pisses me off."

Blake spread his hands, helplessly. "But she's only pissing you off to make the flip-flop work. It's a technique."

Reacher made a face.

"Well, she's a little too convincing," he said. "Take her off the case and I might consider it."

Lamarr glowered and Blake shook his head.

"I won't do that," he said. "That's my call and I won't be dictated to."

"Then my answer is no."

Silence. Blake turned the corners of his mouth down.

"We talked with Deerfield before we came up here," he said. "You can understand we'd do that, right? As a courtesy? He authorized us to tell you Cozo will drop the racketeering charge if you play ball."

"I'm not worried about the racketeering charge."

"You should be. Protection rackets stink, you know that? They ruin businesses, they ruin lives. If Cozo scripts it right, some local jury of Tribeca traders is going to hate your guts."

"I'm not worried about it," Reacher said again. "I'll beat it in a second. I stopped it, remember? I didn't start it. Jury of Tribeca merchants, I'll look like Robin Hood."

Blake nodded and ducked his head and wiped his lips with his fingers.

"Problem is it could be more than a racketeering charge. One of those guys is critical. We just heard from Bellevue. Broken skull. He dies, it's a homicide charge."

Reacher laughed. "Good try, Blake. But nobody got a broken skull tonight. Believe me, I want to break somebody's skull, I know how to do it. It wouldn't happen by accident. So let's hear the rest of them."

"The rest of what?"

"The big threats. Bureau does what it has to do, right? You're willing to move right on into the gray areas. So let's hear what other big threats you've got lined up for me."

"We just want you to play ball here."

"I know that. And I want to hear how far you're prepared to go."

"We'll go as far as we have to. We're the Bureau, Reacher. We're under pressure here. We're not going to waste time. We got none to waste."

Reacher sipped his coffee. It tasted better than when he made it. Maybe she used more grounds. Or less. "So give me the bad news."

"IRS audit."

"You think I'm worried about an IRS audit? I've got nothing to hide. They find some income I've forgotten about, I'll be extremely grateful, is all. I could use the cash."

"Your girlfriend, too."

Reacher laughed again. "Jodie's a Wall Street lawyer, for God's sake. Big firm, nearly a partner. She'll tie the IRS in a knot without even thinking about it."

"We're serious, Reacher."

"Not so far, you're not."

Blake looked at the floor. "Cozo's got guys on the street, working undercover. Petrosian's going to be asking who did his boys last night. Cozo's guys could let your name slip."

"So?"

"They could tell him where you live."

"And that's supposed to scare me? Look at me, Blake. Get real. There's maybe ten people on the planet I need to be scared of. Extremely unlikely this guy Petrosian happens to be one of them. So he wants to come up here for me, I'll float him back to town in a box, all the way down the river."

"He's a hard guy, is what I hear."

"I'm sure he's real hard. But is he hard enough?"

"Cozo says he's a sexual deviant. His executions always involve some sexual element. And the corpses are always explicitly displayed, naked, mutilated, really bizarre. Men or women, he doesn't care. Deerfield told us all about that. We talked to him about it."

"I'll take my chances."

Blake nodded. "We thought you'd say that. We're good judges of character. That's our trade, in a manner of speaking. So we asked ourselves how you'd react to something else. Suppose it's not *your* name and address Cozo leaks to Petrosian? What if it's your girlfriend's name and address?"

6

"WHAT ARE YOU going to do?" Jodie asked.

"I don't know," Reacher said.

"I can't believe they're acting like this."

They were in Jodie's kitchen, four floors above lower Broadway in Manhattan. Blake and Lamarr had left him in Garrison and twenty restless minutes later he had driven south to the city. Jodie came home at six in the morning looking for breakfast and a shower and found him waiting in her living room.

"Are they serious?"

"I don't know. Probably."

"Shit, I can't believe it."

"They're desperate," he said. "And they're arrogant. And they like to win. And they're an elite group. Put it all together, this is how they behave. I've seen it before.

Some of our guys were exactly the same. They did what it takes."

"How long have you got?"

"I have to call them by eight. With a decision."

"So what are you going to do?"

"I don't know," he said again.

Her coat was over the back of a kitchen chair. She was pacing nervously, back and forth in her peach dress. She had been awake and alert for twenty-three straight hours, but there was nothing to prove it except a faint blue tinge at the inside corners of her eyes.

"They can't get away with this, can they?" she said. "Maybe they're not serious."

"Maybe they're not," he said. "But it's a game, right? A gamble? One way or the other, we're going to worry about it. Forever."

She dropped into a chair and crossed her legs. Put her head back and shook her hair until it fell behind her shoulders. She was everything Julia Lamarr was not. A visitor from outer space would categorize them both as *women*, with the same parts in the same quantities, hair and eyes and mouths and arms and legs, but one was a dream and the other was a nightmare.

"It just went too far," he said. "My fault, absolutely. I was jerking them around, because I just didn't like her at all, from the start. So I figured I'd tease them a little, keep it going, and then eventually say yes. But they dropped this on me, before I could get around to it."

"So get them to take it back. Start over. Cooperate."

He shook his head. "No, threatening me is one thing.

You, that's way over the line. They're prepared to even *think* a thing like that, then to hell with them."

"But were they really serious?" she said again.

"Safest strategy is assume they might be."

She nodded. "So I'm scared. And I guess I'd still be a little scared, even if they took it back."

"Exactly," he said. "What's done is done."

"But why? Why are they so desperate? Why the threats?"

"History," he said. "You know what it's like. Everybody hates everybody else. Blake said that to me. And it's true. MPs wouldn't piss on Quantico if it was on fire. Because of Vietnam. Your dad could have told you all about it. He's an example."

"What happened about Vietnam?"

"There was a rule of thumb, draft dodgers were the Bureau's business, and deserters were ours. Different categories, right? And we knew how to handle deserters. Some of them went to the slammer, but some of them got a little TLC. The jungle wasn't a lot of fun for the grunts, and the recruiting depots weren't exactly bulging at the seams, remember? So the MPs would calm the good ones down and send them back, but nine times out of ten the Bureau would arrest them again anyway, on the way to the airport. Drove the MPs crazy. Hoover was unbearable. It was a turf war like you never saw. Result was a perfectly reasonable guy like Leon would hardly even speak to the FBI ever again. Wouldn't take calls, didn't bust a gut answering the mail."

"And it's still the same?"

He nodded. "Institutions have long memories. That stuff is like yesterday. Never forgive, never forget."

"Even though women are in danger?"

He shrugged. "Nobody ever said institutional thinking is rational."

"So they really need somebody?"

"If they want to get anywhere."

"But why you?"

"Lots of reasons. I was involved with a couple of the cases, they could find me, I was senior enough to know where to look for things, senior enough that the current generation probably still owes me a few favors."

She nodded. "So put it all together, they probably *are* serious."

He said nothing.

"So what are we going to do?"

He paused.

"We could think laterally," he said into the silence.

"How?"

"You could come with me."

She shook her head. "They wouldn't *let* me come with you. And I can't, anyway. Could be weeks, right? I have to work. The partnership decision is coming up."

He nodded. "We could do it another way."

"OK, how?"

"I could go take Petrosian out."

She stared at him. Said nothing.

"No more threat," he said. "Like trumping their ace."

She turned her stare to the ceiling, and then she shook her head again, slowly.

"We have a thing at the firm," she said. "We call it the *so what else* rule. Suppose we've got some bankrupt guy we're looking after. Sometimes we dig around and find he's got some funds stashed away that he's not telling us about. He's hiding them from us. He's cheating. First thing we do, we say *so what else*? What else is he doing? What else has he got?"

"So?"

"So what are they really doing here? Maybe this is not about the women at all. Maybe this is about Petrosian. He's presumably a smart, slippery guy. Maybe there's nothing to pin on him. No evidence, no witnesses. So maybe Cozo is using Blake and Lamarr to get you to get Petrosian. They profiled you, right? Psychologically? They know how you think. They know how you'll react. They know if they use Petrosian to threaten me, your very first thought will be to go get Petrosian. Then he's off the street without a trial, which they probably couldn't win anyway. And nothing is traceable back to the Bureau. Maybe they're using you as an assassin. Like a guided missile or something. They wind you up, and off you go."

He said nothing.

"Or maybe it's something else," she said. "This guy killing these women sounds pretty smart too, right? No evidence anywhere? Sounds like it's going to be a difficult case to prove. So maybe the idea is you eliminate him. There might not be enough proof to satisfy the courts, but there might be enough to satisfy you. In which case you fix him, on behalf of the women you knew. Job done, cheap and quick, nothing traceable back. They're using you like a magic bullet. They fire it here in New York, and it hits home wherever and whenever."

Reacher was silent.

"Maybe you were never a suspect at all," she said.

"Maybe they weren't looking for a killer. Maybe they were looking for somebody who would *kill* a killer."

There was silence in the room. Outside, the street sounds of early morning were starting up. It was dark gray dawn, and traffic was building.

"Could be both things," Reacher said. "Petrosian and this other guy."

"They're smart people," Jodie said.

He nodded. "They sure as hell are."

"So what are you going to do?"

"I don't know. All I know is I can't go to Quantico and leave you here alone in the same city as Petrosian. I just can't do that."

"But maybe they're not serious. Would the FBI really do something like that?"

"You're going around in a circle. The answer is, we just don't know. And that's the whole point. That's the effect they wanted. Just *not knowing* is enough, isn't it?"

"And if you don't go?"

"Then I stay here and guard you every minute of every day until we get fed up with it to the point where I go after Petrosian anyway, irrespective of whether they were kidding in the first place or not."

"And if you do go?"

"Then they keep me on the ball with the threat against you. And in their opinion *on the ball* means what? Can I stop after I find the guy? Or do they make me go all the way and rub him out?"

"Smart people," she said again.

"Why didn't they just ask me straight?"

"They can't just *ask* you. It would be a hundred percent illegal. And you mustn't do it, anyway."

"I can't?"

"No, not Petrosian or the killer. You mustn't do either thing they want."

"Why not?"

"Because then they own you, Reacher. Two vigilante homicides, with their *knowledge*? Right under their noses? The Bureau would *own* you, the whole rest of your life."

He leaned his hands on the window frame and stared at the street below.

"You're in a hell of a spot," she said. "We both are."

He said nothing.

"So what are you going to do?" she asked again.

"I'm going to think," he said. "I've got until eight o'clock."

She nodded. "Think carefully."

JODIE WENT BACK to work. The partnership track beckoned. Reacher sat alone in her apartment and thought hard for thirty minutes, and then he was on the phone for twenty. Blake had said *maybe there are people who still owe you favors*. Then at five minutes to eight he called the number Lamarr had given him. She answered, first ring.

"I'm in," he said. "I'm not happy about it, but I'll do it."

There was a brief pause. He imagined the crooked teeth, revealed in a smile.

"Go home and pack a bag," she said. "I'll pick you up in two hours exactly."

"No, I'm going to see Jodie. I'll meet you at the airport."

"We're not going by plane."

"We're not?"

"No, I never fly. We're driving."

"To Virginia? How long will that take?"

"Five, six hours."

"Six hours? In a car with you? Shit, I'm not doing that."

"You're doing what you're told, Reacher. Garrison, in two hours."

JODIE'S OFFICE WAS on the fortieth floor of a sixty-floor tower on Wall Street. The lobby had twenty-four-hour security and Reacher had a pass from Jodie's firm that let him through, day or night. She was alone at her desk, reviewing morning information from the markets in London.

"You OK?" he asked her.

"Tired," she said.

"You should go back home."

"Right, like I'm really going to sleep."

He moved to the window and looked out at a sliver of lightening sky.

"Relax," he said. "There's nothing to worry about."

She made no reply.

"I decided what to do," he said.

She shook her head. "Well, don't tell me about it. I don't need to know."

"It'll work out. I promise."

She sat still for a second, and then she joined him at the window. Nuzzled into his chest and held him tight, her cheek against his shirt.

"Take care," she said.

"I'll take care," he said. "Don't worry about it."

"Don't do anything stupid."

"Don't worry about it," he said again.

She turned her face up and they kissed. He kept it going, long and hard, figuring the feeling was going to have to last him into the foreseeable future.

H E DROVE FASTER than usual and was back at his house ten minutes before Lamarr's two hours were up. He took his folding toothbrush from the bathroom and clipped it into his inside pocket. He bolted the basement door and turned the thermostat down. Turned all the faucets off hard and locked the front door. Unplugged the phone in the den and went outside through the kitchen.

He walked to the end of the yard through the trees and looked down at the river. It was gray and sluggish, lined with morning mist like a quilt. On the opposite bank, the leaves were starting to turn, shading from tired green to brown and pale orange. The buildings of West Point were barely visible.

The sun was coming over the ridge of his roof, but it was watery, with no warmth in it. He walked back to the house and skirted the garage and came out on his driveway. Hunched into his coat and walked out to the street. He didn't look back at the house. *Out of sight, out of mind*. That was the way he wanted it. He crossed the shoulder and leaned on his mailbox, watching the road, waiting.

7

LAMARR ARRIVED EXACTLY on time in a new Buick Park Avenue with shined paint and Virginia plates. She was alone and looked small in it. She eased to a stop and pressed a button and the trunk lid opened. There was a chrome *supercharged* label on the lip. Reacher closed the trunk again and opened the passenger door and slid inside.

"Where's your bag?" she asked.

"I don't have a bag," he said.

She looked blank for a second. Then she looked away from him like she was dealing with a social difficulty and eased away down the street. She paused at the first junction, unsure.

"What's the best way south?" she asked.

"On a plane," he said.

She looked away again and made a left, away from the river. Then another, which set her heading north on Route 9.

"I'll pick up I-84 in Fishkill," she said. "Go west to the Thruway, south to the Palisades, pick up the Garden State."

He was silent. She glanced at him.

"Whatever," he said.

"Just making conversation."

"No need."

"You're not being very cooperative."

He shrugged. "You told me you wanted my help with the Army. Not with the basic geography of the United States."

She raised her eyebrows and made a shape with her mouth like she was disappointed, but not surprised. He looked away and watched the scenery from his window. It was warm in the car. She had the heater on high. He leaned over and turned his side down by five degrees.

"Too hot," he said.

She made no comment. Just drove on in silence. I-84 took them across the Hudson River and through New-burgh. Then she turned south on the Thruway and squirmed back in her seat, like she was settling in for the trip.

"You never fly?" he asked.

"I used to, years ago," she said. "But I can't now."

"Why not?"

"Phobia," she said simply. "I'm terrified, is all."

"You carrying your gun?" he asked.

She lifted a hand from the wheel and pulled back the

flap of her jacket. He saw the straps of a shoulder holster, stiff and brown and shiny, curving next to her breast.

"Would you use it?"

"Of course, if I had to."

"Then you're dumb to be scared of flying. Driving a car and getting in gunfights are a million times more likely to kill you."

She nodded. "I guess I understand that, statistically."

"So your fear is irrational," he said.

"I guess," she said.

There was silence. Just the hum of the motor.

"The Bureau got many irrational agents?" he asked.

She made no reply. Just reddened slightly under the pallor. He sat in the silence, watching the road reel in ahead. Then he started to feel bad for riding her. She was under pressure, from more than one direction.

"I'm sorry about your sister," he said.

"Why?" she asked.

"Well, I know you're worried about her."

She kept her eyes on the road. "Blake tell you that? While I was making the coffee?"

"He mentioned it."

"She's my stepsister, actually," she said. "And any worrying I do about her situation is strictly professional, OK?"

"Sounds like you don't get along."

"Does it? Why should it? Should I care more just because I'm close to one of the potential victims?"

"You expected *me* to. You expected me to be ready to avenge Amy Callan, just because I knew her and liked her."

She shook her head. "That was Blake. I would have

expected you to care anyway, as a human being, except in your case I wouldn't, actually, because you match the killer himself for profile."

"Your profile is wrong. Sooner you face up to that, sooner you'll catch the guy."

"What do *you* know about profiling?"

"Nothing at all. But I didn't kill those women, and I wouldn't have, either. Therefore you're wasting your time looking for a guy like me, because I'm exactly the wrong type of a guy to be looking for. Stands to reason, right? Borne out by the facts."

"You like facts?"

He nodded. "A lot better than I like bullshit."

"OK, try these facts," she said. "I just caught a killer in Colorado, without ever even being there. A woman was raped and murdered in her house, blows to the head with a blunt instrument, left posed on her back with her face covered by a cloth. A violent sexual crime, spontaneously committed, no forced entry, no damage or disruption to the house. The woman was smart and young and pretty. I reasoned the perpetrator was a local man, older, lived within walking distance, knew the victim, had been in the house many times before, was sexually attracted to the victim, but was either inadequate or repressed as to communicating it to her appropriately."

"And?"

"I issued that profile and the local police department made an arrest within an hour. The guy confessed immediately."

Reacher nodded. "He was a handyman. He killed her with his hammer."

For the first time in thirty minutes, her eyes left the

road. She stared at him. "You can't possibly know that. It hasn't been in the paper here."

"Educated guess. The cloth over her face means she knew him and he knew her, and he was ashamed to leave her uncovered. Probably made him feel remorseful, maybe like she was watching him from beyond the grave or something. That kind of semifunctional thinking is indicative of a low IQ. The lack of forced entry and the lack of disruption to the house both mean he was familiar with the place. He'd been there many times before. Easy enough to figure."

"Why easy?"

"Because what kind of a guy with a low IQ has been visiting with a smart and pretty girl many times before? Got to be a gardener or a handyman. Probably not a gardener, because they work outside and they tend to come at least in pairs. So I figured a handyman, probably tormented by how young and cute she was. One day he can't stand it anymore, he makes some kind of a clumsy advance, she's embarrassed by it, she rejects it, maybe even laughs at it, he freaks out and rapes her and kills her. He's a handyman, got his tools with him, he's accustomed to using them, he'd use a hammer for a thing like that."

Lamarr was silent. Reddening again, under the pallor.

"And you call that profiling?" Reacher asked. "It's just common sense."

"That was a very simple case," she said quietly.

He laughed. "You guys get paid for this? You study it in college and all?"

They entered New Jersey. The blacktop improved and the shoulder plantings got tidier, like they always do. Every state puts a lot of effort into the first mile of its highways, to make you feel you're entering a better place from a worse one. Reacher wondered why they didn't put the effort into the *last* mile instead. That way, you'd miss the place you were leaving.

"We need to talk," Lamarr said.

"So talk. Tell me about college."

"We're not going to talk about college."

"Why not? Tell me about Profiling 101. You pass?"

"We need to discuss the cases."

He smiled. "You did go to college, right?"

She nodded. "Indiana State."

"Psychology major?"

She shook her head.

"So what was it? Criminology?"

"Landscape gardening, if you must know. My professional training is from the FBI Academy at Quantico."

"Landscape gardening? No wonder the Bureau snapped you up in a big hurry."

"It was relevant. It teaches you to see the big picture, and to be patient."

"And how to grow things. That could be useful, killing time while your bullshit profiles are getting you nowhere."

She was silent again.

"So are there many irrational phobic landscape gardeners at Quantico? Any bonsai enthusiasts scared of spiders? Orchid growers who won't step on the cracks in the sidewalk?"

Her pallor was whitening. "I hope you're real proud of yourself, Reacher, making jokes while women are dying."

He went quiet and looked out of the window. She was

driving fast. The road was wet and there were gray clouds ahead. They were chasing a rainstorm south.

"So tell me about the cases," he said.

She gripped the wheel and used the leverage to adjust her position in the seat.

"You know the victim group," she said. "Very specific, right?"

He nodded. "Apparently."

"Locations are obviously random. He's chasing particular victims, and he goes where he has to. Crime scenes have all been the victim's residence, so far. Residences have been basically various. Single-family housing in all cases, but varying degrees of isolation."

"Nice places, though."

She glanced at him. He smiled. "The Army paid them all off, right? When they quit? Scandal avoidance, they call it. A big chunk of money like that, a chance to settle down after a few footloose years, they probably bought nice houses."

She nodded as she drove. "Yes, and all in neighborhoods, so far."

"Makes sense," he said. "They want community. What about husbands and families?"

"Callan was separated, no kids. Cooke had boyfriends, no kids. Stanley was a loner, no attachments."

"You look at Callan's husband?"

"Obviously. Any homicide, first thing we do is look at family. Any married woman, we look at the husband. But he was alibied, nothing suspicious. And then with Cooke, the pattern became clear. So we knew it wasn't a husband or a boyfriend."

"No, I guess it wasn't."

"First problem is how he gets in. No forced entry. He just walks in the door."

"You think there was surveillance first?"

She shrugged. "Three victims is not a large number, so I'm wary of drawing conclusions. But yes, I think he must have been watching them. He needed them to be alone. He's efficient and organized. I don't think he would have left anything to chance. But don't overestimate the surveillance. It would be pretty obvious pretty quickly that they were alone during the day."

"Any evidence of a stakeout? Cigarette butts and soda cans piled up under a nearby tree?"

She shook her head. "This guy is leaving no evidence of anything."

"Neighbors see anything?"

"Not so far."

"And all three were done during the day?"

"Different times, but all during daylight hours."

"None of the women worked?"

"Like you don't. Very few of you ex-Army people seem to work. It's a snippet I'm going to file away."

He nodded and glanced at the weather. The roadway was streaming. The rain was a mile ahead.

"Why don't you people work?" she asked.

"Us *people*?" he repeated. "In my case because I can't find anything I want to do. I thought about landscape gardening, but I wanted a challenge, not something that would take me a second and a half to master."

She went silent again and the car hissed into a wall of rain. She set the wipers going and switched on the headlights and backed off the speed a little.

"Are you going to insult me all the time?" she asked.

"Making a little fun of you is a pretty small insult compared to how you're threatening my girlfriend. And how you're so ready and willing to believe I'm the type of guy who could kill two women."

"So was that a yes or a no?"

"It was a maybe. I guess an apology from you would help turn it into a no."

"An apology? Forget about it, Reacher. I stand by my profile. If it wasn't you, it was some scumbag just like you."

The sky was turning black and the rain was intense. Up ahead, brake lights were shining red through the deluge on the windshield. The traffic was slowing to a crawl. Lamarr sat forward and braked sharply.

"Shit," she said.

Reacher smiled. "Fun, right? And right now your risk of death or injury is ten thousand times higher than flying, conditions like these."

She made no reply. She was watching her mirror, anxious the people behind her should slow down as smartly as she had. Ahead, the brake lights made a red chain as far as the eye could see. Reacher found the electric switch on the side of his seat and racked it back. He stretched out and got comfortable.

"I'm going to take a nap," he said. "Wake me up when we get someplace."

"We're not through talking," Lamarr said. "We have a deal, remember? Think about Petrosian. I wonder what he's doing right now."

Reacher glanced to his left, looking across her and out her window. Manhattan lay in that direction, but he could barely see the far shoulder of the highway.

"OK, we'll keep on talking," he said.

She was concentrating on riding the brake, crawling forward into the deluge.

"Where were we?" she said.

"He's staked them out sufficient to know they're alone, it's daylight, somehow he walks right in. Then what?"

"Then he kills them."

"In the house?"

"We think so."

"You *think* so? Can't you tell?"

"There's a lot we can't tell, unfortunately."

"Well, that's wonderful."

"He leaves no evidence," she said. "It's a hell of a problem."

He nodded. "So describe the scenes for me. Start with the plantings in their front yards."

"Why? You think that's important?"

He laughed. "No, I just thought you'd feel better telling me something you *did* know a little about."

"You son of a bitch."

The car was crawling forward. The wipers beat slowly across the glass, back and forth, back and forth. There were flashing red and blue lights up ahead.

"Accident," he said.

"He leaves no evidence," she said again. "Absolutely nothing. No trace evidence, no fibers, no blood, no saliva, no hair, no prints, no DNA, no nothing."

Reacher locked his arms behind his head and yawned. "That's pretty hard to do."

Lamarr nodded, eyes fixed on the windshield. "It sure is. We've got lab tests now like you wouldn't believe, and he's beating all of them."

"How would a person do that?"

"We don't really know. How long have you been in this car?"

He shrugged. "Feels like most of my life."

"It's been about an hour. By now, your prints are all over everything, the door handles, the dash, the seat-belt buckle, the seat switch. There could be a dozen of your hairs on the headrest. A ton of fiber from your pants and your jacket all over the seat. Dirt from your backyard coming off your shoes onto the carpet. Maybe old fibers from your rugs at home."

He nodded. "And I'm just sitting here."

"Exactly. The violence associated with homicide, all that stuff would be spraying all over the place, plus blood maybe, saliva too."

"So maybe he's not killing them in the house."

"He leaves the bodies in there."

"So at least he'd have to drag them back inside."

She nodded. "We know for sure he spends time in the house. There's proof of that."

"Where does he leave the bodies?"

"In the bathroom. In the tub."

The Buick inched past the accident. An old station wagon was crumpled nose-first into the back of a sport-utility exactly like Reacher's own. The station wagon's windshield had two head-shaped holes broken through it. The front doors had been crowbarred open. An ambulance was waiting to U-turn through the divider. Reacher turned his head and stared at the sport-utility. It wasn't his. Not that he thought it could be. Jodie wouldn't be driving anywhere. Not if she had any sense.

"In the tub?" he repeated.

Lamarr nodded at the wheel. "In the tub."

"All three of them?" he asked.

Lamarr nodded again. "All three of them."

"Like a signature?"

"Right," she said.

"How does he know they've all got tubs?"

"You live in a house, you've got a tub."

"How does he know they all live in houses? He's not selecting them on the basis of where they live. It's random, right? They could live anyplace. Like I live in motels. And some of them just have showers."

She glanced across at him. "You don't live in motels. You live in a house in Garrison."

He glanced down, like he had forgotten.

"Well, now I do, I guess," he said. "But I was on the road, before. How does he know these women weren't?"

"That's a catch-22," she said. "If they were homeless, they wouldn't be on his list. I mean, to be on his list, they need to live somewhere, so he can find them."

"But how does he know they all have tubs?"

She shrugged. "You live somewhere, you've got a tub. Takes a pretty small studio to have just a shower stall."

Reacher nodded. This was not his area of expertise. Real estate was pretty much foreign terrain to him. "OK, they're in the tub."

"Naked. And their clothes are missing."

She was clear of the crash site and was accelerating into the rain. She put the windshield wipers on high.

"He takes their clothes with him?" he asked. "Why?"

"Probably as a trophy. Taking trophies is a very common phenomenon in serial crimes like these. Maybe it's symbolic. Maybe he thinks they should still be in uniform, so he robs them of their civilian gear. As well as their lives."

"He take anything else?"

She shook her head. "Not as far as we can tell. There was nothing obviously removed. No big spaces anywhere. Cash and cards were all still where they should be."

"So he takes their clothes and leaves nothing behind."

She was quiet for a beat.

"He does leave something behind," she said. "He leaves paint."

"Paint?"

"Army camouflage green. Gallons of it."

"Where?"

"In the tub. He puts the body in there, naked, and then he fills the tub with paint."

Reacher stared past the beating wipers into the rain. "He drowns them? In paint?"

She shook her head again. "He doesn't drown them. They're already dead. He just covers them with paint afterward."

"How? Like he paints them all over?"

She was gunning it hard, making up for lost time. "No, he doesn't paint them. He just fills the tub with the paint, right up to the rim. Obviously it covers the bodies."

"So they're floating in a tub full of green paint?"

She nodded. "That's how they were all found."

He fell silent. He turned away and stared through his window and stayed silent for a long time. To the west, the weather was clearer. It was brighter. The car was moving fast. Rain hissed under the tires and beat on the underbody. He stared blankly at the brightness in the west and watched the endless road reel in and realized he was *happy*. He was heading somewhere. He was on the move. His blood was stirring like an animal at the end of winter. The old hobo demon was talking to him, quietly, whispering in his head. *You're happy now,* it was saying. *You're happy, aren't you? You even forgot for a moment you're stuck in Garrison, didn't you?*

"You OK?" Lamarr asked.

He turned toward her and tried to fill his mind with her face, the white pallor, the thin hair, the sneering teeth.

"Tell me about the paint," he said quietly.

She looked at him, oddly.

"It's Army camouflage basecoat," she said. "Flat green. Manufactured in Illinois by the hundred thousand gallons. Produced sometime within the last eleven years, because it's new process. Beyond that, we can't trace it."

He nodded, vaguely. He had never used it, but he had seen a million square yards of stuff daubed with it.

"It's messy," he said.

"But the crime scenes are immaculate. He doesn't spill a drop anywhere."

"The women were already dead," he said. "Nobody was fighting. No reason to spill any. But it means he must carry it into the house. How much does it take to fill a tub?"

"Somewhere between twenty and thirty gallons."

"That's a lot of paint. It must mean a hell of a lot to him. You figured out any significance to it?"

She shrugged. "Not really, not beyond the obvious military significance. Maybe removing the civilian clothes and covering the body with Army paint is some kind of reclamation, you know, putting them back where he thinks they belong, in the military, where they should have stayed. It traps them, you see. Couple of hours, the surface is skinning over. It goes hard, and the stuff underneath jellifies. Leave it long enough, I guess the whole tub might dry solid, with them inside. Like people put their baby's shoe in a Perspex cube?"

Reacher stared ahead through the windshield. The horizon was bright. They were leaving the weather behind. On his right, Pennsylvania looked green and sunny.

"The paint is a hell of a thing," he said. "Twenty or thirty gallons? That's a major load to haul around. It implies a big vehicle. A lot of exposure obtaining it. Exposure just carrying it into the house. Very visible. Nobody saw anything?"

"We canvassed, door to door. Nobody reported anything."

He nodded, slowly. "The paint is the key. Where's he getting it from?"

"We have no idea. The Army is not being especially helpful."

"I'm not surprised. The Army hates you. And it's embarrassing. Makes it likely it's a serving soldier. Who else could get that much camouflage paint?"

She made no reply. She just drove, south. The rain was gone and the wipers were squealing over dry glass. She switched them off with a small definite movement of her wrist. He fell to thinking about a soldier somewhere, loading cans of paint. Ninety-one women on his list, some skewed mental process reserving twenty or thirty gallons for each one of them. A potential total of two,

two and a half thousand gallons. Tons of it. Truckloads of it. Maybe he was a quartermaster.

"How is he killing them?" he asked.

She slid her hands to a firmer grip on the wheel. Swallowed hard and kept her eyes on the road.

"We don't know," she said.

"You don't *know*?" he repeated.

She shook her head. "They're just dead. We can't figure out how."

8

THERE ARE NINETY-ONE altogether, and you need to do exactly six of them in total, which is three more, so what do you do now? You keep on thinking and planning, is what. Think, think, think, that's what you do. Because it's all based on thinking. You need to outwit them all. The victims, and the investigators. Layers and layers of investigators. More and more investigators all the time. Local cops, state cops, the FBI, the specialists the FBI brings in. New angles, new approaches. You know they're there. They're looking for you. They'll find you if they can.

The investigators are tough, but the women are easy. Just about as easy as you expected them to be. There was no overconfidence there. None at all. The victims go down exactly as you imagined. You planned long and hard, and the planning was perfect. They answer the door, they let you in, they fall for it. They're so damn keen to fall for it,

their tongues are practically hanging out. They're so stu-
pid, they deserve it. And it's not difficult. No, not difficult
at all. It's meticulous, is what it is. It's like everything else.
If you plan it properly, if you think it through, if you pre-
pare correctly, if you rehearse, then it's easy. It's a technical
process, just like you knew it would be. Like a science. It
can't be anything else. You do this, and then you do this,
and then you do this, and then you're done, home free.
Three more. That's all. That'll do it. The hard part is over.
But you keep on thinking. Think, think, think. It worked
once, it worked twice, it worked three times, but you know
there are no guarantees in life. You know that, better than
anybody. So you keep on thinking, because the only thing
that can get you now is your own complacency.

"YOU DON'T KNOW?" Reacher said again.

Lamarr was startled. She was staring straight ahead, tired, concentrating, gripping the wheel, driving like a machine.

"Know what?" she said.

"How they died."

She sighed and shook her head. "No, not really."

He glanced across at her. "You OK?"

"Don't I look OK?"

"You look exhausted."

She yawned. "I'm a little weary, I guess. It was a long night."

"Well, take care."

"You worrying about me now?"

He shook his head. "No, I'm worrying about myself. You could fall asleep, run us off the road."

She yawned again. "Never happened before."

He looked away. Found himself fingering the airbag lid in front of him.

"I'm OK," she said again. "Don't worry about it."

"Why don't you know how they died?"

She shrugged. "You were an investigator. You saw dead people."

"So?"

"So what did you look for?"

"Wounds, injuries."

"Right," she said. "Somebody's full of bullet holes, you conclude they've been shot to death. Somebody's got their head smashed in, you call it trauma with a blunt object."

"But?"

"These three were in bathtubs full of drying paint, right? The crime scene guys take the bodies out, and the pathologists clean them up, and they don't find anything."

"Nothing at all?"

"Nothing obvious, not at first. So then naturally they look harder. They still don't find anything. They know they didn't drown. When they open them up, they find no water or paint in the lungs. So then they search for external injuries, microscopically. They can't find anything."

"No hypodermic marks? Bruising?"

She shook her head. "Nothing at all. But remember, they've been coated in paint. And that military stuff wouldn't pass too many HUD regulations. Full of all kinds of chemicals, and fairly corrosive. It damages the skin, postmortem. It's conceivable the paint damage might be obscuring some tiny marks. But whatever killed them was very subtle. Nothing gross."

"What about internal damage?"

She shook her head again. "Nothing. No subcutaneous bruising, no organ damage, no nothing."

"Poison?"

"No. Stomach contents were OK. They hadn't ingested the paint. Toxicology was completely clear."

Reacher nodded, slowly. "No sexual interference either, I guess, because Blake was happy both Callan and Cooke would have slept with me if I'd wanted them to. Which means the perpetrator was feeling no sexual resentment, therefore no rape, or else you'd be looking for somebody who'd been rebuffed by them, one time or another."

Lamarr nodded. "That's our profile. Sexuality wasn't an issue. The nakedness is about humiliation, we think. Punishment. The whole thing was about punishment. Retribution, or something."

"Weird," Reacher said. "That definitely makes the guy a soldier. But it's a very unsoldierly way to kill somebody. Soldiers shoot or stab or hit or strangle. They don't do subtle things."

"We don't know exactly what he did."

"But there's no *anger* there, right? If this guy is into some retribution thing, where's the anger? It sounds too clinical."

Lamarr yawned and nodded, all at once. "That troubles me too. But look at the victim category. What else can the motive be? And if we agree on the motive, what else can the perp be except an angry soldier?"

They lapsed into silence. The miles rolled by. Lamarr held the wheel, thin tendons in her wrists standing out like cords. Reacher watched the road reeling in, and tried not to feel happy about it. Then Lamarr yawned again, and she saw him glance sharply at her.

"I'm OK," she said.

He looked at her, long and hard.

"I'm OK," she said again.

"I'm going to sleep for an hour," he said. "Try not to kill me."

WHEN HE WOKE up, they were still in New Jersey. The car was quiet and comfortable. The motor was a faraway hum and there was a faint tenor rumble from the tires. A faint rustle of wind. The weather was gray. Lamarr was rigid with exhaustion, gripping the wheel, staring down the road with red unblinking eyes.

"We should stop for lunch," he said.

"Too early."

He checked his watch. It was one o'clock. "Don't be such a damn hero. You should get a pint of coffee inside you."

She hesitated, ready to argue. Then she gave it up. Her body suddenly went slack and she yawned again.

"OK," she said. "So let's stop."

She drove on for a mile and coasted into a rest area in a clearing in the trees behind the shoulder. She put the car in a slot and turned the motor off and they sat in the sudden silence. The place was the same as a hundred others Reacher had seen, low-profile Federal architecture of the fifties colonized by fast-food operations that lodged behind discreet counters and spread their messages outward with gaudy advertisements.

He got out first and stretched his cramped frame in

the cold, damp air. The highway traffic was roaring behind him. Lamarr was inert in the car, so he strolled away to the bathroom. Then she was nowhere to be seen, so he walked inside the building and lined up for a sandwich. She joined him within a minute.

"You're not supposed to do that," she said.

"Do what?"

"Stray out of my sight."

"Why not?"

"Because we have rules for people like you."

She said it without any trace of softness or humor. He shrugged. "OK, next time I go to the bathroom I'll invite you right inside with me."

She didn't smile. "Just tell me, and I'll wait at the door."

The line shuffled forward and he changed his selection from cheese to crabmeat, because he figured it was more expensive and he assumed she was paying. He added a twenty-ounce cup of black coffee and a plain doughnut. He found a table while she fiddled with her purse. Then she joined him and he raised his coffee in an ironic toast.

"Here's to a few fun days together," he said.

"It'll be more than a few days," she said. "It'll be as long as it takes."

He sipped his coffee and thought about time.

"What's the significance of the three-week cycle?" he asked.

She had chosen cheese on whole-wheat and was pecking a crumb from the corner of her mouth with her little finger.

"We're not entirely sure," she said. "Three weeks is an

odd interval. It's not lunar. There's no calendar significance to three weeks."

He did the math in his head. "Ninety-one targets, one every three weeks, it would take him five and a quarter years to get through. That's a hell of a long project."

She nodded. "We think that proves the cycle is imposed by something external. Presumably he'd work faster if he could. So we think he's on a three-week work pattern. Maybe he works two weeks on, one week off. He spends the week off staking them out, organizing it, and then doing it."

Reacher saw his chance. Nodded.

"Possible," he said.

"So what kind of soldier works that kind of pattern?"

"That regular? Maybe a rapid-response guy, two weeks on readiness, one week stood down."

"Who's on rapid response?"

"Marines, some infantry," he said.

Then he swallowed. "And some Special Forces."

Then he waited to see if she'd take the bait.

She nodded. "Special Forces would know subtle ways to kill, right?"

He started on the sandwich. The crabmeat could have been tuna fish. "Silent ways, unarmed ways, improvised ways, I guess. But I don't know about *subtle* ways. This is about concealment, right? Special Forces are interested in getting people dead, for sure, but they don't care about leaving anybody puzzled afterward about how they did it."

"So what are you saying?"

He put his sandwich down. "I'm saying I don't have a clue about who's doing what, or why, or how. And I don't see how I should. You're the big expert here. You're the one studied landscape gardening in school."

She paused, with her sandwich in midair. "We need more from you than this, Reacher. And you know what we'll do if we don't get it."

"I know what you *say* you'll do."

"You going to take the chance we won't?"

"She gets hurt, you know what I'll do to you, right?"

She smiled. "Threatening me, Reacher? Threatening a federal agent? You just broke the law again. Title 18, paragraph A-3, section 4702. Now you're *really* stacking up the charges against yourself, that's for sure."

He looked away and made no reply.

"Stay on the ball, and everything will be OK," she said.

He drained his cup, and looked at her over the rim. A steady, neutral gaze. "The ethics bothering you here?" she asked.

"Are there ethics involved?" he asked back.

Then her face changed. A hint of embarrassment crept into it. A hint of softening. She nodded. "I know, it used to bother me too. I couldn't believe it, when I got out of the Academy. But the Bureau knows what it's doing. I learned that, pretty quick. It's a practical thing. It's about the greatest good for the greatest number. We need co-operation, we ask for it first, but you better believe we make damn sure we get it."

Reacher said nothing.

"It's a policy I believe in, now," Lamarr said. "But I want you to know using your girlfriend as a threat wasn't my idea."

Reacher said nothing.

"That was Blake," she said. "I'm not about to criticize him for it, but I wouldn't have gone down that road myself."

"Why not?"

"Because we don't need *more* women in danger here."

"So why did you let him do it?"

"Let him? He's my boss. And this is law enforcement. Emphasis on the *enforcement*. But I need you to know it wouldn't have been my way. Because we need to be able to work together."

"Is this an apology?"

She said nothing.

"Is it? Finally?"

She made a face. "Close as you'll get from me, I guess."

Reacher shrugged. "OK, whatever."

"Friends now?" she said.

"We'll never be friends," Reacher said. "You can forget about that."

"You don't like me," she said.

"You want me to be honest with you?"

She shrugged. "Not really, I guess. I just want you to help me out."

"I'll be a go-between," he said. "That's what I agreed to. But you need to tell me what you want."

She nodded. "Special Forces sound promising to me. First thing you'll do is check them out."

He looked away, and clenched his teeth to keep himself from smiling.

THEY SPENT A whole hour at the rest stop. Toward the end of it Lamarr started to relax. Then she seemed reluctant to get back on the road.

"You want me to drive?" Reacher asked.

"It's a Bureau car," she said. "You're not permitted."

But the question jogged her back on track. She gathered her purse and stood up from the table. Reacher took the trash to the receptacle and joined her at the door. They walked back to the Buick in silence. She fired it up and eased it out of the slot and merged onto the highway.

The hum of the motor came back, and the faint noise from the road and the muted rush of the air, and within a minute it was like they had never stopped at all. Lamarr was in the same position, upright and tense behind the wheel, and Reacher was sprawled on her right, watching the view flash by.

"Tell me about your sister," he said.

"My stepsister."

"Whatever, tell me about her."

"Why?"

He shrugged. "You want me to help, I need background. Like where did she serve, what happened to her, stuff like that."

"She's a rich girl who wanted adventure."

"So she joined the Army?"

"She believed the advertisements. You seen those, in magazines? They make it look tough and glamorous."

"Is she tough?"

Lamarr nodded. "She's very physical, you know? She loves all that stuff, rock climbing, biking, skiing, hiking, windsurfing. She thought the Army was going to be all rappelling down cliffs with a knife between your teeth."

"And it wasn't?"

"You know damn well it wasn't. Not back then, not

for a woman. They put her in a transport battalion, made her drive a truck."

"Why didn't she quit, if she's rich?"

"Because she's not a quitter. She did great in basic training. She was pushing for something better."

"And?"

"She saw some jerk of a colonel five times, trying to make some progress. He suggested if she was naked throughout the sixth interview, that might help."

"And?"

"She busted him. Whereupon they gave her the transfer she wanted. Infantry close-support unit, about as near the action as a woman was going to get."

"But?"

"You know how it works, right? Rumors? No smoke without fire? The assumption was she *had* screwed the guy, you know, even though she had busted him and he was canned, which made it completely illogical. In the end, she couldn't stand the whispers, and she did finally quit."

"So what's she doing now?"

"Nothing. She's feeling a little sorry for herself."

"You close to her?"

She paused.

"Not very, to be honest," she said. "Not as close as I'd maybe want to be."

"You like her?"

Lamarr made a face. "What's not to like? She's very likable. She's a great person, actually. But I made mistakes, right from the start. Handled it all wrong. I was young, my dad was dead, we were real poor, this rich guy fell in love with my mother and finished up adopting me. I was full of resentment that I was being *rescued*, I guess. So I figured it didn't mean I had to fall in love with *her*. She's only my *stepsister*, I said to myself."

"You never got past it?"

She shook her head. "Not totally. My fault, I admit it. My mother died early, which left me feeling a little isolated and awkward. I didn't handle it well. So now my stepsister is basically just a nice woman I know. Like a close acquaintance. I guess we both feel that way. But we get along OK, what we see of each other."

He nodded. "If they're rich, are you rich too?"

She glanced sideways. Smiled. The crossed teeth flashed, briefly.

"Why?" she said. "You like rich women? Or maybe you think rich women shouldn't hold down jobs? Or *any* women?"

"Just making conversation."

She smiled again. "I'm richer than you'd think. My stepfather has lots of money. And he's very fair with us, even though I'm not really his daughter and she is."

"Lucky you."

She paused.

"And we're going to be a lot richer soon," she said. "Unfortunately. He's real sick. He's been fighting cancer for two years. Tough old guy, but now he's going to die. So there's a big inheritance coming our way."

"I'm sorry he's sick," Reacher said.

She nodded. "Yes, so am I. It's sad."

There was silence. Just the hum of the miles passing under the wheels.

"Did you warn your sister?" Reacher asked.

"My stepsister."

He glanced at her. "Why do you always emphasize she's your stepsister?"

She shrugged at the wheel. "Because Blake will pull me off if he thinks I'm too involved. And I don't want that to happen."

"You don't?"

"Of course I don't. Somebody close to you is in trouble, you want to take care of it yourself, right?"

Reacher looked away.

"You better believe it," he said.

She was quiet for a beat.

"And the family thing is very awkward for me," she said. "All those mistakes came home to haunt me. When my mother died, they could have cut me off, but they just *didn't*. They still both treat me exactly right, all the way, very loving, very generous, very fair and equal, and the more they do, the more I feel really guilty for calling myself a Cinderella at the beginning."

Reacher said nothing.

"You think I'm being irrational again," she said.

He said nothing. She drove on, eyes fixed on the windshield.

"Cinderella," she said. "Although you'd probably call me the ugly sister."

He made no reply to that. Just watched the road.

"Whatever, did you warn her?" he asked again.

She glanced sideways at him and he saw her haul herself back to the present.

"Yes, of course I warned her," she said. "Soon as

Cooke made the pattern clear, I've called her over and over again. She should be safe enough. She spends a lot of time at the hospital with her father, and when she's at home I've told her not to let anybody through the door. Nobody at all, not anybody, no matter who they are."

"She pay attention?"

"I made sure she did."

He nodded. "OK, she's safe enough. Only eighty-seven others to worry about."

AFTER NEW JERSEY came eighty miles of Maryland, which took an hour and twenty minutes to cover. It was raining again, prematurely dark. Then they skirted the District of Columbia and entered Virginia and settled in for the final forty miles of I-95, all the way down to Quantico. The buildings of the city receded behind them and gentle forest built ahead. The rain stopped. The sky lightened. Lamarr cruised fast and then slowed suddenly and turned off the highway onto an unmarked road winding through the trees. The surface was good, but the curves were tight. After a half-mile, there was a neat clearing with parked military vehicles and huts painted dark green.

"Marines," she said. "They gave us sixty acres of land for our place."

He smiled. "That's not how they see it. They figure you stole it."

More curves, another half-mile, and there was another clearing. Same vehicles, same huts, same green paint.

"Camouflage basecoat," Reacher said.

She nodded. "Creepy."

More curves, two more clearings, altogether two miles

deep into the woods. Reacher sat forward and paid attention. He had never been to Quantico before. He was curious. The car rounded a tight bend and came clear of the trees and stopped short at a checkpoint barrier. There was a red-and-white striped pole across the roadway and a sentry's hutch made from bulletproof glass. An armed guard stepped forward. Over his shoulder in the distance was a long, low huddle of honey stone buildings. A couple of squat high-rises standing among them. The buildings crouched alone on undulating lawns. The lawns were immaculate and the way the low buildings spread into them meant their architect hadn't been worried about consuming space. The place looked very peaceful, like a minor college campus or a corporate headquarters, except for the razor-wire perimeter and the armed guard.

Lamarr had the window down and was rooting in her purse for ID. The guy clearly knew who she was, but rules are rules and he needed to see her plastic. He nodded as soon as her hand came clear of the bag. Then he switched his gaze across to Reacher.

"You should have paperwork on him," Lamarr said.

The guy nodded again. "Yeah, Mr. Blake took care of it."

He ducked back to his hutch and came out with a laminated plastic tag on a chain. He handed it through the window and Lamarr passed it on. It had Reacher's name and his old service photograph on it. The whole thing was overprinted with a pale red V.

"V for visitor," Lamarr said. "You wear it at all times."

"Or?" Reacher asked.

"Or you get shot. And I'm not kidding."

The guard was back in his hutch, raising the barrier. Lamarr buzzed her window up and accelerated through. The road climbed the undulations and revealed parking lots in the dips. Reacher could hear gunfire. The flat bark of heavy handguns, maybe two hundred yards away in the trees.

"Target practice," Lamarr said. "Goes on all the time."

She was bright and alert. Like proximity to the mother ship was reviving her. Reacher could see how that could happen. The whole place was impressive. It nestled in a natural bowl, deep in the forest, miles away from anywhere. It felt isolated and secret. Easy to see how it could breed a fierce, loyal spirit in the people fortunate enough to be admitted to it.

Lamarr drove slowly over speed bumps to a parking lot in front of the largest building. She eased nose-first into a slot and shut it down. Checked her watch.

"Six hours ten minutes," she said. "That's real slow. The weather, I guess, plus we stopped too long for lunch."

Silence in the car.

"So now what?" Reacher asked.

"Now we go to work."

The plate-glass doors at the front of the building opened up and Poulton walked out. The sandy-haired little guy with the mustache. He was wearing a fresh suit. Dark blue, with a white button-down and a gray tie. The new color made him less insignificant. More formal. He stood for a second and scanned the lot and then set his course for the car. Lamarr got out to meet him. Reacher sat still and waited. Poulton let Lamarr take her own bag from the trunk. It was a suit carrier in the same black imitation leather as her briefcase.

"Let's go, Reacher," she called.

He ducked his head and slipped the ID chain around his neck. Opened his door and slid out. It was cold and windy. The breeze was carrying the sound of dry leaves tossing, and gunfire.

"Bring your bag," Poulton called.

"I don't have a bag," Reacher said.

Poulton glanced at Lamarr, and she gave him an *I've had this all day* look. Then they turned together and walked toward the building. Reacher glanced at the sky and followed them. The undulating ground gave him a new view with each new step. The land fell away to the left of the buildings, and he saw squads of trainees walking purposefully, or running in groups, or marching away into the woods with shotguns. Standard apparel seemed to be dark blue sweats with *FBI* embroidered in yellow on the front and back, like it was a fashion label or a major-league franchise. To his military eye, it all looked irredeemably civilian. Then he realized with a little chill of shame that that was partly because a healthy percentage of the people doing the walking and running and carrying were women.

Lamarr opened the plate-glass door and walked inside. Poulton waited for Reacher on the threshold.

"I'll show you to your room," he said. "You can stow your stuff."

Up close in daylight, he looked older. There were faint lines in his face, barely visible, like a forty-year-old was wearing a twenty-year-old's skin.

"I don't have any stuff," Reacher said to him. "I just told you that."

Poulton hesitated. There was clearly an itinerary. A timetable to be followed.

"I'll show you anyway," he said.

Lamarr walked away with her bag and Poulton led Reacher to an elevator. They rode together to the third floor and came out on a quiet corridor with thin carpet on the floor and worn fabric on the walls. Poulton walked to a plain door and took a key from his pocket and opened it up. Inside was a standard-issue motel room. Narrow entryway, bathroom on the right, closet on the left, queen bed, table and two chairs, bland decor.

Poulton stayed out in the corridor. "Be ready in ten."

The door sucked shut. There was no handle on the inside. Not quite a standard-issue motel room. There was a view of the woods from the window, but the window didn't open. The frame was welded shut and the handle had been removed. There was a telephone on the nightstand. He picked it up and heard a dial tone. Hit 9 and heard more. He dialed Jodie's private office line. Let it ring eighteen times before trying her apartment. Her machine cut in. He tried her mobile. It was switched off.

He put his coat in the closet and unclipped his toothbrush from his pocket and propped it in a glass on the bathroom vanity. Rinsed his face at the sink and pushed his hair into some kind of shape. Then he sat down on the edge of the bed and waited.

9

EIGHT MINUTES LATER he heard a key in the lock and looked up and expected to see Poulton at the door. But it wasn't Poulton. It was a woman. She looked about sixteen. She had long fair hair in a loose ponytail. White teeth in an open, tanned face. Bright blue eyes. She was wearing a man's suit, extensively tailored to fit. A white shirt and a tie. Small black shoes with low heels. She was over six feet tall, long-limbed, and very slim. And completely spectacular. And she was smiling at him.

"Hi," she said.

Reacher made no reply. Just stared at her. Her face clouded and her smile turned a little embarrassed.

"So you want to do the FAQs right away?"

"The what?"

"The FAQs. Frequently asked questions."

"I'm not sure I have any questions."

"Oh, OK."

She smiled again, relieved. It gave her a frank, guileless look.

"What are the frequently asked questions?" he asked.

"Oh, you know, the stuff most new guys around here ask me. It's really, really tedious."

She meant it. He could see that. But he asked anyway.

"What kind of stuff?" he said.

She made a face, resigned.

"I'm Lisa Harper," she said. "I'm twenty-nine, yes really, I'm from Aspen, Colorado, I'm six feet one, yes really, I've been at Quantico two years, yes I date guys, no I dress like this just because I like it, no I'm not married, no I don't currently have a boyfriend, and no I don't want to have dinner with you tonight."

She finished with another smile and he smiled back.

"Well, how about tomorrow night?" he said.

She shook her head. "All you need to know is I'm an FBI agent, on duty."

"Doing what?"

"Watching you," she said. "Where you go, I go. You're classified SU, status unknown, maybe friendly, maybe hostile. Usually that means an organized-crime plea bargain, you know, some guy ratting out his bosses. Useful to us, but not reliable."

"I'm not organized crime."

"Our file says you might be."

"Then the file is bullshit."

She nodded, and smiled again. "I looked Petrosian up separately. He's a Syrian. Therefore his rivals are Chinese.

And *they* never employ anybody except other Chinese. Implausible they'd use an American WASP like you."

"You point that out to anybody?"

"I'm sure they already know. They're just trying to get you to take the threat seriously."

"Should I take it seriously?"

She nodded. Stopped smiling.

"Yes, you should," she said. "You should think very carefully about Jodie."

"Jodie's in the file?"

She nodded again. "Everything's in the file."

"So why don't I have a handle on my door? My file shows I'm not the guy."

"Because we're very cautious and your profile is very bad. The guy will turn out to be very similar to you."

"You a profiler too?"

She shook her head. The ponytail moved with it. "No, I'm operational. Assigned for the duration. But I listen carefully. Listen and learn, right? So let's go."

She held the door. It closed softly behind him as they walked to a different elevator. This one had buttons for five basement floors in a line beneath 3, 2, and 1. Lisa Harper pressed the bottom button. Reacher stood beside her and tried not to breathe in her scent. The elevator settled with a bump and the door slid back on a gray corridor bright with fluorescent light.

"We call this the Bunker," Harper said. "It used to be our nuclear shelter. Now it's BS."

"That's for damn sure," Reacher said.

"Behavioral Science. And that's a very old joke."

She led him to the right. The corridor was narrow,

and clean, but not public-area clean. It was a working place. It smelled faintly of sweat and old coffee and office chemicals. There were notice boards on the walls and random stacks of stationery cartons in the corners. There was a line of doors in the left-hand wall.

"Here," Harper said.

She stopped him in front of a door with a number on it and reached across him and knocked. Then she used the handle and opened it up for him.

"I'll be right outside," she said.

He went in and saw Nelson Blake behind a crowded desk in a small untidy office. There were maps and photographs taped carefully to the walls. Piles of paper everywhere. No visitor chair. Blake was glowering. His face was red with blood pressure and pale with strain, all at the same time. He was watching a muted television set. It was tuned to a political cable channel. A guy in shirtsleeves was reading something to a committee. The caption read *Director of the FBI*.

"Budget hearings," Blake muttered. "Singing for our damn supper."

Reacher said nothing. Blake kept his eyes on the television.

"Case conference in two minutes," he said. "So listen up for the rules. Consider yourself somewhere between a guest and a prisoner here, OK?"

Reacher nodded. "Harper already explained that."

"Right. She stays with you, all the time. Everything you do, everywhere you go, you're supervised by her. But don't get the wrong idea. You're still Lamarr's boy, only she stays here, because she won't fly. And you'll need to get around some. Whereupon we need to keep an eye on you, so Harper goes too. The only time you're alone is when you're locked in your room. Your duties are what Lamarr tells you they are. You wear your ID at all times."

"OK."

"And don't get ideas about Harper. Thing with her is, she looks nice, but you start messing with her, then she's the bitch from hell, OK?"

"OK."

"Anything else?"

"Is my phone tapped?"

"Of course it is." Blake riffed through papers. Slid a thick finger down a printout. "You just called your girlfriend, private office line, apartment, mobile. No answer."

"Where is she?"

Blake shrugged. "Hell should I know?"

Then he scrabbled in the pile of paper on his desk and came up with a large brown envelope. Held it out.

"With Cozo's compliments," he said.

Reacher took the envelope. It was stiff and heavy. It contained photographs. Eight of them. They were color glossies, eight by ten. Crime scene photographs. They looked like stuff from a cheap skin magazine, except the women were all dead. The corpses were displayed in limp imitations of centerfolds. They were mutilated. Pieces were missing. Things had been inserted into them, here and there.

"Petrosian's handiwork," Blake said. "Wives and sisters and daughters of people who pissed him off."

"So how come he's still running around?"

There was silence for a second.

"There's proof, and then there's *proof*, right?" Blake said.

Reacher nodded. "So where's Jodie?"

"Hell should I know?" Blake said again. "We've got no interest in her as long as you play ball. We're not tailing her. Petrosian can find her himself, if it comes to that. We're not going to deliver her to him. That would be illegal, right?"

"So would breaking your neck."

Blake nodded. "Stop with the threats, OK? You're in no position."

"I know this whole thing was your idea."

Blake shook his head. "I'm not worried about you, Reacher. Deep down, you think you're a good person. You'll help me, and then you'll forget all about me."

Reacher smiled. "I thought you profilers were supposed to be real insightful."

THREE WEEKS IS a nice complicated interval, which is exactly why you chose it. It has no obvious significance. They'll drive themselves mad, trying to understand a three-week interval. They'll have to dig real, real deep before they see what you're doing. Too deep to be feasible. The closer they get to it, the less it will mean. The interval leads nowhere. So the interval makes you safe.

But does it have to be maintained? Maybe. A pattern is a pattern. It ought to be a very strict thing. Very precise. Because that's what they're expecting. Strict adherence to a pattern. It's typical in this sort of case. The pattern protects you. It's important. So it should be maintained. But then again, maybe it shouldn't. Three weeks is a pretty long interval. And pretty boring. So maybe you should speed it up.

But anything less would be very tight, given the work re-
quired. Soon as one was done, the next would have to be
prepared. A treadmill. Difficult work, on a tight schedule.
Not everybody could do it. But you could.

THE CASE CONFERENCE was held in a long low room a
floor above Blake's office. There was light brown fabric
on the walls, worn shiny where people had leaned on it
or brushed against it. One long wall had four recesses let
into it, with blinds and concealed lighting simulating
windows, even though the room was four stories underground. There was a silent television mounted high on
the wall, with the budget hearings playing to nobody.
There was a long table made of expensive wood, surrounded by cheap chairs set at forty-five degree angles so
they faced the head of the table, where there was a large
empty blackboard set against the end wall. The blackboard was modern, like it came from a well-endowed
college. The whole place was airless and quiet and isolated, like a place where serious work was done, like a
postgraduate seminar room.

Harper led Reacher to a seat at the far end from the
blackboard. The back of the class. She sat one place
nearer the action, so he had to look past her shoulder.
Blake took the chair nearest the board. Poulton and Lamarr came in together, carrying files, absorbed in low
conversation. Neither of them glanced anywhere except
at Blake. He waited until the door closed behind them
and then stood up and flipped the blackboard over.

The top right quarter was occupied by a large map of
the United States, dotted with a forest of flags. Ninety-
one of them, Reacher guessed, without trying to count

them all. Most of them were red, but three of them were black. Opposite the map on the left was an eight-by-ten color photograph, cropped and blown up from a casual snapshot taken through a cheap lens onto grainy film. It showed a woman, squinting against the sun and smiling. She was in her twenties, and pretty, a plump happy face framed by curly brown hair.

"Lorraine Stanley, ladies and gentlemen," Blake said. "Recently deceased in San Diego, California."

Underneath the smiling face were more eight-by-tens pinned up in a careful sequence. The crime scene. They were crisper photographs. Professional. There was a long shot of a small Spanish-style bungalow, taken from the street. A close-up of the front door. Wide shots of a hallway, a living room, the master bedroom. The master bathroom. The back wall was all mirror above twin sinks. The photographer was reflected in the mirror, a large person bundled into a white nylon coverall, a shower cap on his head, latex gloves on his hands, a camera at his eye, the bright halo of the strobe caught by the mirror. There was a shower stall on the right, and a tub on the left. The tub was low, with a wide lip. It was full of green paint.

"She was alive three days ago," Blake said. "Neighbor saw her wheeling her garbage to the curb, eight forty-five in the morning, local time. She was discovered yesterday, by her cleaner."

"We got a time of death?" Lamarr asked.

"Approximate," Blake said. "Sometime during the second day."

"Neighbors see anything?"

Blake shook his head. "She took her garbage can back inside, the same day. Nobody saw anything after that."

"MO?"

"Exactly identical to the first two."

"Evidence?"

"Not a damn thing, so far. They're still looking, but I'm not optimistic."

Reacher was focusing on the picture of the hallway. It was a long narrow space leading past the mouth of the living room, back to the bedrooms. On the left was a narrow shelf at waist height, crowded with tiny cactus plants in tiny terra-cotta pots. On the right were more narrow shelves, fixed to the wall at random heights and in random lengths. They were packed with small china ornaments. Most of them looked like dolls, brightly painted to represent national or regional costumes. The sort of things a person buys when she's dreaming of having a home of her own.

"What did the cleaner do?" he asked.

Blake looked all the way down the table. "Screamed a bit, I guess, and then called the cops."

"No, before that. She has her own key?"

"Obviously."

"Did she go straight to the bathroom?"

Blake looked blank and opened a file. Leafed through it and found a faxed copy of an interview report. "Yes, she did. She puts stuff in the toilet bowl, leaves it to work while she does the rest of the house, comes back to it last."

"So she found the body right away, before she did any cleaning?"

Blake nodded.

"OK," Reacher said.

"OK what?"

"How wide is that hallway?"

Blake turned and examined the picture. "Three feet? It's a small house."

Reacher nodded. "OK."

"OK what?"

"Where's the violence? Where's the anger? She answers the door, this guy somehow forces her back through the hallway, through the master bedroom, into the bathroom, and then carries thirty gallons of paint through after her, and he doesn't knock anything off those shelves."

"So?"

Reacher shrugged. "Seems awful quiet to me. I couldn't wrestle somebody down that hallway without touching all that stuff. No way. Neither could you."

Blake shook his head. "He doesn't do any wrestling. Medical reports show the women probably aren't touched at all. It's a quiet scene, because there *is* no violence."

"You happy with that? Profile-wise? An angry soldier looking for retribution and punishment, but there's no uproar?"

"He *kills* them, Reacher. The way I see it, that's retribution enough."

There was silence. Reacher shrugged again. "Whatever."

Blake faced him down the length of the table. "You'd do it differently?"

"Sure I would. Suppose you keep on pissing me off

and I come after you. I don't see myself being especially gentle about it. I'd probably smack you around a little. Maybe a lot. If I was mad with you, I'd have to, right? That's what being mad is all about."

"So?"

"And what about the paint? How does he bring it to the house? We should go to the store and check out what thirty gallons looks like. He must have a car parked outside for twenty, thirty minutes at least. How does nobody see it? A parked car, or a wagon, or a truck?"

"Or a sport-utility, rather like yours."

"Maybe totally identical to mine. But how come nobody sees it?"

"We don't know," Blake said.

"How does he kill them without leaving any marks?"

"We don't know."

"That's a lot you don't know, right?"

Blake nodded. "Yes, it is, smart guy. But we're working on it. We've got eighteen days. And with a genius like you helping us, I'm sure that's all we're going to need."

"You've got eighteen days if he sticks to his interval," Reacher said. "Suppose he doesn't?"

"He will."

"You hope."

Silence again. Blake looked at the table, and then at Lamarr. "Julia?"

"I stand by my profile," she said. "Right now I'm interested in Special Forces. They're stood down one week in three. I'm sending Reacher to poke around."

Blake nodded, reassured. "OK, where?"

Lamarr glanced at Reacher, waiting. He looked at the three black flags on the map.

"Geography is all over the place," he said. "This guy could be stationed anywhere in the United States."

"So?"

"So Fort Dix would be the best place to start. There's a guy I know there."

"Who?"

"A guy called John Trent," Reacher said. "He's a colonel. If anybody's going to help me, he might."

"Fort Dix?" Blake said. "That's in New Jersey, right?"

"It was last time I was there," Reacher said.

"OK, smart guy," Blake said. "We'll call this Colonel Trent, get it set up."

Reacher nodded. "Make sure you mention my name loud and often. He won't be very interested unless you do."

Blake nodded. "That's exactly why we brought you on board. You'll leave with Harper, first thing in the morning."

Reacher nodded, and looked straight at Lorraine Stanley's pretty face.

Yes. Maybe it's time to throw them a curve. Maybe tighten the interval, just a little bit. Maybe tighten it a lot. Maybe cancel it altogether. That would really unsettle them. That would show them how little they know. Keep everything else the same, but alter the interval. Make it all a little unpredictable. How about it? You need to think.

Or maybe let a little of the anger show, too. Because anger is what this is about, right? Anger, and justice. Maybe it's time to make that a little clearer, a little more obvious. Maybe it's time to take the gloves off. A little violence never hurt anybody. And a little violence could make the next one a little more interesting. Maybe a lot more interesting. You need to think about that, too.

So what's it to be? A shorter interval? Or more drama at the scene? Or both? How about both? Think, think, think.

LISA HARPER TOOK Reacher up to ground level and out-side into the chill air just after six in the evening. She led him down an immaculate concrete walkway toward the next building in line. There were knee-high lights set on both sides of the path, a yard apart, already turned on against the gloom of evening. Harper walked with an exaggerated long stride. Reacher wasn't sure if she was trying to match his, or if it was something she'd learned in deportment class. Whatever, it made her look pretty good. He found himself wondering what she'd look like if she was running. Or lying down, with nothing on.

"Cafeteria's in here," she said.

She was ahead of him at another double set of glass doors. She pulled one open and waited until he went inside in front of her.

"To the left," she said.

There was a long corridor with the clattering sound and the vegetable smell of a communal dining room at the end of it. He walked ahead of her. It was warm inside the building. He could sense her at his shoulder.

"OK, help yourself," she said. "Bureau's paying."

The cafeteria was a big double-height room, brightly lit, with molded-plywood chairs at plain tables. There was a service counter along one side. A line of personnel, waiting with trays in their hands. Big groups of trainees in dark blue sweats, separated by senior agents in suits standing in ones and twos. Reacher joined the end of the line, with Harper at his side.

The line shuffled up and he was served a filet mignon the size of a paperback book by a cheerful Spanish guy with ID around his neck. He moved on and got vegetables and fries from the next server in line. He filled a cup with coffee from an urn. He took silverware and a napkin and looked around for a table.

"By the window," Harper said.

She led him to a table for four, standing empty by the glass. The bright light in the room made it full dark outside. She put her tray on the table and took her jacket off. Draped it on the back of her chair. She wasn't thin, but her height made her very slender. Her shirt was fine cotton, and she wore nothing underneath it. That was pretty clear. She undid her cuffs and rolled her sleeves to the elbow, one by one. Her forearms were smooth and brown.

"Nice tan," Reacher said.

She sighed.

"FAQs again?" she said. "Yes, it's all over, and no, I don't especially want to prove it."

He smiled.

"Just making conversation," he said.

She looked straight at him.

"I'll talk about the case," she said. "If you want conversation."

"I don't know much about the case. Do you?"

She nodded. "I know I want this guy caught. Those women were pretty brave, making a stand like that."

"Sounds like the voice of experience."

He cut into his steak and tasted it. It was pretty good. He'd paid forty bucks for worse in city restaurants.

"It's the voice of cowardice," she said. "I haven't made a stand. Not yet anyway."

"You getting harassed?"

She smiled. "Are you kidding?" Then she blushed. "I mean, can I say that without sounding big-headed or anything?"

He smiled back. "Yes, in your case I think you can."

"It's nothing real serious," she said. "Just talk, you know, just comments. Loaded questions, and innuendo. Nobody's said I should sleep with them to get promotion or anything. But it still gets to me. That's why I dress like this now. I'm trying to make the point, you know, I'm just the same as them, really."

He smiled again. "But it's gotten worse, right?"

She nodded, "Right. Much worse."

He made no reply.

"I don't know why," she said.

He looked at her over the rim of his cup. Egyptian cotton button-down, pure white, maybe a thirteen-inch collar, a blue tie knotted neatly in place and rising gently over her small mobile breasts, men's trousers with big darts taken out of them to curve in around her tiny waist. Tanned face, white teeth, great cheekbones, blue eyes, the long blond hair.

"Is there a camera in my room?" he asked.

"A what?"

"A camera," he said again. "You know, video surveillance."

"Why?"

"I'm just wondering if this is a backup plan. In case Petrosian doesn't pan out."

"What do you mean?"

"Why isn't Poulton looking after me? He doesn't seem to have much else to do."

"I don't follow."

"Yes you do. That's why Blake assigned *you*, right? So you could get real close to me? All this vulnerable little-girl-lost stuff? *I don't know why?* So maybe if Blake wants to stop banging on about Petrosian, he's got something else to twist my arm with, like a nice intimate little scene, you and me in my room, on a nice little videocassette he can say he'll send to Jodie."

She blushed. "I wouldn't do a thing like that."

"But he asked you to, right?"

She was quiet for a long time. Reacher looked away and drained his coffee, staring at his own reflection in the glass.

"He practically challenged me to try," he said. "Told me you're the bitch from hell, if anybody puts the moves on."

She was still silent.

"But I wouldn't fall for it, anyway," he said. "Because I'm not stupid. I'm not about to give them any more ammunition."

She was quiet another minute. Then she looked at him and smiled.

"So can we relax?" she said. "Get past it?"

He nodded. "Sure, let's relax. Let's get past it. You can put your jacket back on now. You can stop showing me your breasts."

She blushed again. "I took it off because I was warm. No other reason."

"OK, I'm not complaining."

He turned away again and watched the dark through the window.

"You want dessert?" she asked.

He turned back and nodded. "And more coffee."

"You stay here. I'll get it."

She walked back to the serving counter. The room seemed to fall silent. Every eye was on her. She came back with a tray bearing two ice cream sundaes and two cups of coffee. A hundred people watched her all the way.

"I apologize," Reacher said.

She bent and slid the tray onto the table. "For what?"

He shrugged. "For looking at you the way I've been looking at you, I guess. You must be sick of it. Everybody looking at you all the time."

She smiled. "Look at me as much as you like, and I'll look at you right back, because you aren't the ugliest thing I ever saw either. But that's as far as it's going to go, OK?"

He smiled back. "Deal."

The ice cream was excellent. It had hot fudge sauce all over it. The coffee was strong. If he narrowed his eyes and cut out the rest of the room, he could rate this place about as highly as he had rated Mostro's.

"What do people do here in the evenings?" he asked.

"Mostly they go home," Harper said. "But not you. You go back to your room. Blake's orders."

"We're following Blake's orders now?"

She smiled. "Some of them."

He nodded. "OK, so let's go."

SHE LEFT HIM on the side of the door without the handle. He stood there and heard her footsteps recede across the carpet outside. Then the thump of the elevator door. Then the whine of the car going down. Then the floor fell silent. He walked to the nightstand and dialed Jodie's apartment. The machine cut in. He dialed her office. No answer. He tried her mobile. It was not in service.

He walked to the bathroom. Somebody had supplemented his toothbrush with a tube of toothpaste and a disposable razor and a can of shaving cream. There was a bottle of shampoo on the rim of the tub. There was soap in the dish. Fluffy white towels on the rack. He stripped and hung his clothes on the back of the door. Set the shower to hot and stepped under the water.

He stood there for ten minutes and then shut it off. Toweled himself dry. Walked naked to the window and pulled the drapes. Lay down on the bed and scanned the ceiling. He found the camera. The lens was a black tube the diameter of a nickel, wedged deep in a crack in the molding where the wall met the ceiling. He turned back to the phone. Dialed all the same numbers again. Her apartment. He got the machine. Her office. No reply. Her mobile. Switched off.

10

HE SLEPT BADLY and woke himself up before six in the morning and rolled toward the nightstand. Flicked on the bedside light and checked the exact time on his watch. He was cold. He had been cold all night. The sheets were starched, and the shiny surfaces pulled heat away from his skin.

He reached for the phone and dialed Jodie's apartment. He got the machine. No answer in her office. Her mobile was switched off. He held the phone to his ear for a long time, listening to her cellular company telling him so, over and over again. Then he hung up and rolled out of bed.

He walked to the window and pulled the drapes open. The view faced west and it was still dark night outside. Maybe there was a sunrise behind him on the other side of the building. Maybe it hadn't happened yet. He could hear the distant sound of hard rain on dying leaves. He turned his back on it and walked to the bathroom.

He used the toilet and shaved slowly. Spent fifteen minutes in the shower with the water as hot as he could stand it, getting warm. Then he washed his hair with the FBI's shampoo and toweled it dry. Carried his clothes out of the steam and dressed standing by the bed. Buttoned his shirt and hung his ID around his neck. He figured room service was unlikely, so he just sat down to wait.

He waited forty-five minutes. There was a polite knock at the door, followed by the sound of a key going into the lock. Then the door opened and Lisa Harper was standing there, backlit by the brightness of the corridor. She was smiling, mischievously. He had no idea why.

"Good morning," she said.

He raised his hand in reply. Said nothing. She was in a different suit. This one was charcoal gray, with a white shirt and a dark red tie. An exact parody of the unofficial Bureau uniform, but a whole lot of cloth had been cut out of it to make it fit. Her hair was loose. There was a wave in it, and it hung front and back of her shoulders, very long. It looked golden in the light from the corridor.

"We've got to go," she said. "Breakfast meeting."

He took his coat from the closet as he passed. They rode down to the lobby together and paused at the doors. It was raining hard outside. He pulled his collar up and followed her out. The light had changed from black to gray. The rain was cold. She sprinted down the walkway, and he followed a pace behind, watching her run. She looked pretty good doing it.

Lamarr and Blake and Poulton were waiting for them

in the cafeteria. They were in three of five chairs crowded around a four-place table by the window. They were watching him carefully as he approached. There was a white coffee jug in the center of the table, surrounded by upside-down mugs. A basket of sugar packets and little pots of cream. A pile of spoons. Napkins. A basket of doughnuts. A pile of morning newspapers. Harper took a chair and he squeezed in next to her. Lamarr was watching him, something in her eyes. Poulton looked away. Blake looked amused, in a sardonic kind of a way.

"Ready to go to work?" he asked.

Reacher nodded. "Sure, after I've had some coffee."

Poulton turned the mugs over and Harper poured.

"We called Fort Dix last night," Blake said. "Spoke with Colonel Trent. He said he'll give you all day today."

"That should do it."

"He seems to like you."

"No, he owes me, which is different."

Lamarr nodded. "Good. You need to exploit that. You know what you're looking for, right? Concentrate on the dates. Find somebody whose stand-down weeks match. My guess is he's doing it late in the week. Maybe not exactly the last day, because he's got to get back to base and calm down afterward."

Reacher smiled. "Great deduction, Lamarr. You get paid for this?"

She just looked at him and smiled back, like she knew something he didn't.

"What?" he asked.

"Just keep a civil tongue in your head," Blake said. "You got a problem with what she's suggesting?"

Reacher shrugged. "We do it by dates alone, we're going to come up with maybe a thousand names."

"So narrow it down some. Get Trent to cross-reference against the women. Find somebody who served with one of them."

"Or served with one of the men who got canned," Poulton said.

Reacher smiled again. "Awesome brainpower around this table. It could make a guy feel real intimidated."

"You got better ideas, smart guy?" Blake asked.

"I know what I'm going to do."

"Well, just remember what's riding on it, OK? Lots of women in danger, one of them yours."

"I'll take care of it."

"So get going."

Harper took the cue and stood up. Reacher eased out of his seat and followed her. The three at the table watched him go, something in their eyes. Harper was waiting for him at the cafeteria door, looking back at him, watching him approach, smiling at him. He stopped next to her.

"Why's everybody looking at me?" he asked.

"We checked the tape," she said. "You know, the surveillance camera."

"So?"

She wouldn't answer. He reviewed his time in the room. He'd showered twice, walked around some, pulled the drapes, slept, opened the drapes, walked around some more. That was all.

"I didn't do anything," he said.

She smiled again, wider. "No, you didn't."

"So what's the big deal?"

"Well, you know, you don't seem to have brought any pajamas."

A MOTOR POOL guy brought a car to the doors and left it there with the motor running. Harper watched Reacher get in and then slid into the driver's seat. They drove out through the rain, past the checkpoint, through the Marine perimeter, out to I-95. She blasted north through the spray and a fast forty minutes later turned east across the southern edge of D.C. Cruised hard for ten more minutes and made an abrupt right into the north gate of Andrews Air Force Base.

"They assigned us the company plane," she said.

Two security checks later they were at the foot of an unmarked Learjet's cabin steps. They left the car on the tarmac and climbed inside. It was taxiing before they had their seat belts fastened.

"Should be a half hour to Dix," Harper said.

"McGuire," Reacher corrected. "Dix is a Marine Corps base. We'll land at McGuire Air Force Base."

Harper looked worried. "They told me we're going straight there."

"We are. It's the same place. Different names, is all."

She made a face. "Weird. I guess I don't understand the military."

"Well, don't feel bad about it. We don't understand you either."

They were on approach thirty minutes later with the sharp, abrupt motions a small jet makes in rough air. There was cloud, almost all the way down, then the ground was suddenly in sight. It was raining in Jersey. Dim, and miserable. An Air Force base is a gray place to start with, and the weather wasn't helping any. McGuire's runway was wide enough and long enough to let giant transports struggle into the air, and the Lear touched down and stopped in less than a quarter of its length, like a hummingbird coming to rest on an interstate. It turned and taxied and stopped again on a distant corner of tarmac. A flat-green Chevy was racing through the rain to meet it. By the time the cabin steps were down, the driver was waiting at the bottom. He was a Marine lieutenant, maybe twenty-five, and he was getting wet.

"Major Reacher?" he asked.

Reacher nodded. "And this is Agent Harper, from the FBI."

The lieutenant ignored her completely, like Reacher knew he would.

"The colonel is waiting, sir," he said.

"So let's go. Can't keep the colonel waiting, right?"

Reacher sat in the front of the Chevy with the lieutenant and Harper took the back. They drove out of McGuire into Dix, following narrow roadways with whitewashed curbstones through blocks of warehouses and barracks. They stopped at a huddle of brick offices a mile from McGuire's runway.

"Door on the left, sir," the lieutenant said.

The guy waited in the car, like Reacher knew he would. Reacher got out and Harper followed him, staying close to his shoulder, huddling against the weather. The wind was blowing the rain horizontal. The office building had a group of three unmarked personnel doors in the center of a blank brick wall. Reacher took the left-hand door and led Harper into a spacious anteroom full of metal desks and file cabinets. It was antiseptically clean and obsessively tidy. Brightly lit against the gloom of the morning. Three sergeants worked at separate desks. One of them glanced up and hit a button on his telephone.

"Major Reacher is here, sir," he said into it.

There was a moment's pause and then the inner office door opened and a man stepped out. He was tall, built like a greyhound, short black hair silvering at the temples. He had a lean hand extended, ready to shake.

"Hello, Reacher," John Trent said.

Reacher nodded. Trent owed the second half of his career to a paragraph Reacher had omitted from an official report ten years before. Trent had assumed the paragraph was written and ready to go. He had come to see Reacher, not to plead for its deletion, not to bargain, not to bribe, but just to explain, officer to officer, how he'd made the mistake. Simply because he had needed Reacher to understand it *was* a mistake, not malice or dishonesty. He had left without asking for a thing, and then sat still and waited for the ax. It never came. The report was published and the paragraph wasn't in it. What Trent didn't know was that Reacher had never even written it. Then ten years had passed and the two men hadn't really spoken since. Not until the previous morning, when Reacher had made the first of his urgent calls from Jodie's apartment.

"Hello, Colonel," Reacher said. "This is Agent Harper, from the FBI."

Trent was politer than his lieutenant. His rank meant he had to be. Or maybe he was just more impressed by tall damp blondes dressed like men. Either way, he shook hands. And maybe held on to the shake longer than was necessary. And maybe smiled, just a fraction.

"Pleased to meet you, Colonel," Harper said. "And thanks in advance."

"I haven't done anything yet," Trent said.

"Well, we're always grateful for cooperation anyplace we can get it, sir."

Trent released her hand. "Which is a strictly limited number of places, I expect."

"Fewer than we'd like," she said. "Considering we're all on the same side."

Trent smiled again.

"That's an interesting concept," he said. "I'll do what I can, but the cooperation will be limited. As I'm sure you anticipated. We're going to be examining personnel records and deployment listings that I'm just not prepared to share with you. Reacher and I will do it on our own. There are issues of national and military security at stake. You're going to have to wait out here."

"All day?" she said.

Trent nodded again. "As long as it takes. You comfortable with that?"

It was clear she wasn't. She looked at the floor and said nothing.

"You wouldn't let me see confidential FBI stuff," Trent said. "I mean, you don't really like us any more than we like you, right?"

Harper glanced around the room. "I'm supposed to watch over him."

"I understand that. Your Mr. Blake explained your role to me. But you'll be right here, outside my office. There's only one door. The sergeant will give you a desk."

A sergeant stood up unbidden and showed her to an empty desk with a clear view of the inner office door. She sat down slowly, unsure.

"You'll be OK there," Trent said. "This could take us some time. It's a complicated business. I'm sure you know how paperwork can be."

Then he led Reacher into the inner office and closed the door. It was a large room, windows on two walls, bookcases, cabinets, a big wooden desk, comfortable leather chairs. Reacher sat down in front of the desk and leaned back.

"Give it two minutes, OK?" he said.

Trent nodded. "Read this. Look busy."

He handed over a thick file in a faded green folder from a tall stack. Reacher opened it up and bent to examine it. There was a complicated chart inside, detailing projected aviation-fuel requirements for the coming six-month period. Trent walked back to the door. Opened it wide.

"Ms. Harper?" he called. "Can I get you a cup of coffee?"

Reacher glanced over his shoulder and saw her staring in at him, taking in the chairs, the desk, the stack of files.

"I'm all set, right now," she called back.

"OK," Trent said. "You want anything, just tell the sergeant."

He closed the door again. Walked to the window. Reacher took off his ID tag and laid it on the desk. Stood up. Trent unlatched the window and opened it as wide as it would go.

"You didn't give us much time," he whispered. "But I think we're in business."

"They fell for it right away," Reacher whispered back. "A lot sooner than I thought they would."

"But how did you know you'd have the escort?"

"Hope for the best, plan for the worst. You know how it is."

Trent nodded. Stuck his head out of the window and checked both directions.

"OK, go for it," he said. "And good luck, my friend."

"I need a gun," Reacher whispered.

Trent stared at him and shook his head again, firmly.

"No," he said. "That, I can't do."

"You have to. I need one."

Trent paused. He was agitated. Getting nervous.

"Christ, OK, a gun," he said. "But no ammunition. My ass is already way out on a limb on this thing."

He opened a drawer and took out a Beretta M9. Same weapon as Petrosian's boys had carried, except Reacher could see this one still had its serial number intact. Trent took the clip out and thumbed the bullets back into the drawer, one by one.

"Quiet," Reacher whispered urgently.

Trent nodded and clicked the empty clip back into the grip. Handed the gun to Reacher, butt-first. Reacher took it and put it in his coat pocket. Sat on the window ledge. Turned and swiveled his legs outside.

"Have a nice day," he whispered.

"You too. Take care," Trent whispered back.

Reacher braced himself with his hands and dropped to the ground. He was in a narrow alley. It was still raining. The lieutenant was waiting in the Chevy, ten yards away, motor running. Reacher sprinted for the car and it was rolling before his door was closed. The mile back to

McGuire took little over a minute. The car raced out onto the tarmac and headed straight for a Marine Corps helicopter. Its belly door was standing open and the rotor blade was turning fast. The rain in the air was whipping up into spiral patterns.

"Thanks, kid," Reacher said.

He stepped out of the car and across to the chopper's ramp and ran up into the dark. The door whirred shut behind him and the engine noise built to a roar. He felt the machine come off the ground and two pairs of hands grabbed him and pushed him into his seat. He buckled his harness and a headset was thrust at him. He put it on and the intercom crackle started at the same time as the interior lights came on. He saw he was sitting in a canvas chair between two Marine loadmasters.

"We're going to the Coast Guard heliport in Brooklyn," the pilot called through. "Close as we can get without filing a flight plan, and filing a flight plan ain't exactly on the agenda today, OK?"

Reacher thumbed his mike. "Suits me, guys. And thanks."

"Colonel must owe you big," the pilot said.

"No, he just likes me," Reacher said.

The guy laughed and the helicopter swung in the air and settled to a bellowing cruise.

11

THE COAST GUARD heliport in Brooklyn is situated on the
eastern edge of Floyd Bennett Field, facing an island in
Jamaica Bay called Ruffle Bar, exactly sixty air miles
north and east from McGuire. The Marine pilot kept his
foot on the loud pedal all the way and made the trip in
thirty-seven minutes. He touched down in a circle with
a giant letter H painted inside it and dropped the engines down to idle.

"You've got four hours," he said. "Any longer than
that, we're out of here and you're on your own, OK?"

"OK," Reacher said. He unstrapped himself and
slipped the headset off and followed the ramp down as it
opened. There was a dark blue sedan with Navy mark-
ings waiting on the tarmac with its motor running and
its front passenger door open.

"You Reacher?" the driver yelled.

Reacher nodded and slid in alongside him. The guy stamped on the gas.

"I'm Navy Reserve," he said. "We're helping the colonel out. A little interservice cooperation."

"I appreciate it," Reacher said.

"Don't think twice," the guy said. "So where we headed?"

"Manhattan. Aim for Chinatown. You know where that is?"

"Do I? I eat there three times a week."

He took Flatbush Avenue and the Manhattan Bridge. Traffic was light, but ground transportation still seemed awful slow, after the Lear and the helicopter. It was thirty minutes before Reacher was anywhere near where he wanted to be. A whole eighth of his available time gone. The guy came off the bridge approach and stopped short on a hydrant.

"I'll be waiting right here," he said. "Facing the other direction, exactly three hours from now. So don't be late, OK?"

Reacher nodded.

"I won't," he said.

He slid out of the car and slapped twice on the roof. Crossed the street and headed south. It was cold in New York, and damp, but it wasn't actually raining. There was no sun visible. Just a vague sullen light in the sky where the sun ought to have been. He stopped walking and stood still for a moment. He was twenty minutes from Jodie's office. He started walking again. It was twenty minutes he didn't have. *First things first.* That was his rule. And maybe they'd be watching her place. No way could he be seen in New York today. He shook his head and walked on. Forced himself to concentrate. Glanced at his watch. It was late morning and he started worrying he was too early. On the other hand, he might be timing it just right. There was no way of telling. He had no experience.

After five minutes, he stopped walking again. If any street was going to do it for him, this was the one. It was lined on both sides with Chinese restaurants, crowded together, bright gaudy facades in reds and yellows. There was a forest of signs in Oriental script. Pagoda shapes everywhere. The sidewalks were crowded. Delivery trucks double-parked tight against cars. Crates of vegetables and drums of oil piled on the curbs. He walked the length of the street twice, up and down, carefully inspecting the terrain, learning it. Looking at the alleys. Then he touched the gun in his pocket and set off strolling again, looking for his targets. They would be around somewhere. If he wasn't too early. He leaned on a wall and watched. They would be in a pair. Two of them, together. He watched for a long time. There were plenty of people in pairs, but they weren't the right people. They weren't them. None of them. He was too early.

He glanced at his watch and saw his time ticking away. He pushed off the wall and strolled again. He looked into doorways as he passed. Nothing. He watched the alleys. Nothing. Time ticked on. He walked a block south and a block west and tried another street. Nothing. He waited on a corner. Still nothing. He went another block south, another block west. Nothing. He leaned on a skinny tree and waited, with the watch on his wrist hammering like a machine. Nothing. He walked back to his starting point and leaned on his wall and watched the lunch crowd build to a peak. Then he watched it ebb away. Suddenly more people were coming out of the restaurants than were going in. His time was ebbing away with them. He moved to the end of the street. Checked his watch again. He had been waiting two whole hours. He had one hour left.

Nothing happened. The lunch crowd died away to nothing and the street went quiet. Trucks drove in, stopped, unloaded, drove out again. A light drizzle started, and then it stopped. Low clouds moved across the narrow sky. Time ticked away. He walked east and south. Nothing there. He came back again and walked up one side of the street and down the other. Waited at the corner. Checked his watch, over and over. He had forty minutes left. Then thirty. Then twenty.

Then he saw them. And he suddenly understood why it was now, and not before. They had been waiting for the lunch-hour cash flow to be neatly stashed in the registers. There were two guys. Chinese, of course, young, shiny black hair worn long on their collars. They wore dark pants and light windbreakers, with scarves at their necks, like a uniform.

They were very blatant. One carried a satchel and the other carried a notebook with a pen trapped in the spiral binding. They strolled into each restaurant in turn, slow and casual. Then they strolled out again, with one guy zipping the satchel and the other guy noting something in his book. One restaurant, then two, then three, then four. Fifteen minutes ticked away. Reacher watched. He crossed the street and moved ahead of them. Waited near a restaurant door. Watched them go in. Watched them approach an old guy at the register. They just stood there. Said nothing. The old guy reached into the cash drawer and took out a wad of folded bills. The agreed amount, ready and waiting. The guy with the book took them and handed them to his partner. Wrote something in the book as the money disappeared into the satchel.

Reacher stepped ahead, up to where a narrow alley separated two buildings. He ducked in and waited with his back to the wall, where they wouldn't see him until it was too late. He checked his watch. He had less than five minutes. He timed the two guys in his head. He built a mental picture of their lazy, complacent pace. Followed their rhythm in his mind. Waited. Waited. Then he stepped out of the alley and met them head on. They bumped right into him. He seized a bunch of windbreaker in each hand and leaned backward and swung them through a complete explosive half-circle and smashed them back-first into the alley wall. The guy in his right hand followed the wider arc, and therefore hit harder, and therefore bounced farther. Reacher caught him solidly with his elbow as he came forward off the wall and he went down on the floor. Didn't come back up again. He was the guy with the satchel.

The other guy dropped the book and went for his pocket, but Reacher had Trent's Beretta out first. He stood close and held it angled low, down in the tails of his coat, down toward the guy's kneecap.

"Be smart, OK?" he said.

He reached down with his left and racked the slide. The sound was muffled by the cloth of his coat, but to his practiced ear it sounded horribly empty. No final click of the shell case smacking home. But the Chinese guy didn't notice. Too dizzy. Too shocked. He just pressed himself to the wall like he was trying to back right through it. Put all his weight on one foot, unconsciously preparing for the bullet that would blow his leg away.

"You're making a mistake, pal," he whispered.

Reacher shook his head. "No, we're making a *move*, asshole."

"Who's we?"

"Petrosian," Reacher said.

"Petrosian? You're kidding me."

"No way," Reacher said. "I'm serious. Real serious. This street is Petrosian's now. As of today. As of right now. All of it. The whole street. You clear on that?"

"This street is ours."

"Not anymore. It's Petrosian's. He's taking it over. You want to lose a leg arguing about it?"

"Petrosian?" the guy repeated.

"Believe it," Reacher said, and slammed him left-handed in the stomach. The guy folded forward and Reacher tapped him above the ear with the butt of the gun and dropped him neatly on top of his partner. He clicked the trigger to free the slide and put the gun back in his pocket. Picked up the satchel and tucked it under his arm. Walked out of the alley and turned north.

He was already late. If his watch was a minute slow and the Navy guy's was a minute fast, then the rendezvous was already gone. But he didn't run. Running in the city was too conspicuous. He walked away as fast as he could, stepping one pace to the side for every three paces forward, threading his way along the sidewalks. He turned a corner and saw the blue car, *USNR* painted discreetly on its flank. He saw it moving away from the curb. Saw it lurching out into the traffic stream. Now he ran.

He got to where it had been parked four seconds after it left. Now it was three cars ahead, accelerating to catch the light. He stared after it. The light changed to red. The car accelerated faster. Then the guy chickened out and hit the brakes. The car slammed to a neat stop a foot into the crosswalk. Pedestrians swarmed out in front of it. Reacher breathed again and ran to the intersection and pulled open the passenger door. Dumped himself into the seat, panting. The driver nodded to him. Didn't say a word. Didn't offer any kind of an apology for not waiting. Reacher didn't expect one. When the Navy says three hours, it means three hours. One hundred and eighty minutes, not a second more, not a second less. *Time and tide wait for no man.* The Navy was built on all kinds of bullshit like that.

THE JOURNEY BACK to Trent's office at Dix was the exact reverse of the journey out. Thirty minutes in the car through Brooklyn, the waiting helicopter, the raucous flight back to McGuire, the lieutenant in the staff Chevy waiting on the tarmac. Reacher spent the flight time counting the money in the satchel. There was a total of twelve hundred dollars in there, six folded wads of two hundred each. He gave the money to the load-masters for their next unit party. He tore the satchel along its seams and dropped the pieces through the flare hatch, two thousand feet above Lakewood, New Jersey.

It was still raining at Dix. The lieutenant drove him back to the alley and he walked to Trent's window and rapped softly on the glass. Trent opened it up and he climbed back inside the office.

"We OK?" he asked.

Trent nodded. "She's just been sitting out there, quiet as a mouse, all day. Must be real impressed with our dedication. We worked right through lunch."

Reacher nodded and handed back the empty gun. Took off his jacket. Sat down in his chair. Slipped his ID around his neck again and picked up a file. Trent had moved the stack right to left across the desk, like it had been minutely examined.

"Success?" Trent asked.

"I think so. Time will tell, right?"

Trent nodded and looked out at the weather. He was restless. He had been trapped in his office all day.

"Let her in, if you want," Reacher said. "Show's over now."

"You're all wet," Trent said. "Show's not over until you're dried out."

It took twenty minutes to dry out. He used Trent's phone and called Jodie's numbers. The private office line, the apartment, the mobile. No reply, no reply, out of service. He stared at the wall. Then he read an unclassified file about proposed methods of getting mail to the Marines if they had to go serve in the Indian Ocean. The time he spent on it put him lower in his chair and put a glazed look on his face. When Trent finally opened the door and Harper got her second peek of the day, he was slumped and inert. Exactly like a man looks after an arduous day with paperwork.

"Progress?" she called.

He looked up and sighed at the ceiling. "Maybe."

"Six solid hours, you must have gotten somewhere."

"Maybe," he said again.

There was silence for a moment.

"OK, so let's go," she said.

She stood up behind her desk and stretched. She put her arms way above her head, palms flat, reaching for the ceiling. Some kind of a yoga thing. She arched her face upward and tilted her head and her hair cascaded down her back. Three sergeants and one colonel stared at her.

"So let's go," Reacher said.

"Don't forget your notes," Trent said.

He handed over a sheet of paper. There was a list of maybe thirty names printed on it. Probably Trent's high school football team. Reacher put the list in his pocket and put his coat on and shook Trent's hand. Walked through the anteroom and outside into the rain and stood there breathing for a second like a man who has been sitting down all day. Then Harper nudged him toward the lieutenant's car for the drive back to the Lear.

BLAKE AND POULTON and Lamarr were waiting for them at the same table in the Quantico cafeteria. It was just as dark outside, but now the table was set for dinner, not breakfast. There was a jug of water and five glasses, salt and pepper, bottles of steak sauce. Blake ignored Reacher and glanced at Harper, who nodded back to him, like a reassurance. Blake looked satisfied.

"So, you found our guy yet?" he asked.

"Maybe," Reacher said. "I've got thirty names. He could be one of them."

"So let's see them."

"Not yet. I need more."

Blake stared at him. "Bullshit, you need more. We need to get tails on these guys."

Reacher shook his head. "Can't be done. These guys are in places where you can't go. You even want a warrant on these guys, you're going to have to go to the Secretary of Defense, right after you've been to the judge. And Defense is going to go straight to the Commander-in-Chief, who was the President last time I looked, so you're going to need a damn sight more than I can give you right now."

"So what are you saying?"

"I'm saying let me boil it down some."

"How?"

Reacher shrugged. "I want to go see Lamarr's sister."

"My stepsister," Lamarr said.

"Why?" Blake asked.

Reacher wanted to say *because I'm just killing time, asshole, and I'd rather do it on the road than stuck in here*, but he composed his face into a serious look and shrugged again.

"Because we need to think laterally," he said. "If this guy is killing by category, we need to know why. He can't be mad at a whole *category*, just like that. One of these women must have sparked him off, first time around. Then he must have transferred his rage from the personal to the general, right? So who was it? Lamarr's sister could be a good place to start asking. She got a transfer between units. Two very different units. That doubles her potential contacts, profile-wise."

It sounded professional enough. Blake nodded.

"OK," he said. "We'll set it up. You'll go tomorrow."

"Where does she live?"

"Washington State," Lamarr said. "Someplace outside of Spokane, I think."

"You think? You don't know?"

"I've never been there," she said. "I sure as hell don't get enough vacation time to drive all the way out and drive all the way back."

Reacher nodded. Turned to Blake.

"You should be guarding these women," he said.

Blake sighed heavily. "Do the arithmetic, for God's sake. Eighty-eight women, and we don't know which one is next, seventeen days to go, *if* he sticks to his cycle, three agents every twenty-four hours, that's more than a hundred thousand man-hours, random locations all around the country. We just can't do it. We don't have the agents. We warned the local police departments, of course, but what can *they* do? Like outside of Spokane, Washington, for instance, the local police department is probably one man and a German shepherd. They drive by, time to time, I guess, but that's all we got."

"Have you warned the women, too?"

Blake looked embarrassed and shook his head. "We can't. If we can't guard them, we can't warn them. Because what would we be saying? You're in danger, but sorry girls, you're entirely on your own? Can't be done."

"We need to catch this guy," Poulton said. "That's the only sure way to help these women."

Lamarr nodded. "He's out there, somewhere. We need to bring him in."

Reacher looked at them. Three psychologists. They were trying to push all the right buttons. Trying to make it a challenge. He smiled. "I get the message."

"OK, you go to Spokane tomorrow," Lamarr said.

"Meanwhile I'll work the files some more. You'll review them the day after tomorrow. That gives you the stuff you got from Trent, plus the stuff you get in Spokane, plus what we've already gotten. At which point we'll expect some real progress from you."

Reacher smiled again. "Whatever, Lamarr."

"So eat and get to bed," Blake said. "It's a long way to Spokane. Early start tomorrow. Harper will go with you, of course."

"To bed?"

Blake was embarrassed again. "To Spokane, asshole."

Reacher nodded. "Whatever, Blake."

THE PROBLEM WAS, it *was* a challenge. He was sealed in his room, lying alone on the bed, staring up at the blind eye of the hidden camera. But he wasn't seeing it. His gaze had dissolved just like it used to, into a blur. A *green* blur, like the whole of America had disappeared and returned to grassland and forest, the buildings gone, the roads gone, the noise gone, the population all gone, except for one man, somewhere. Reacher stared into the silent blur, a hundred miles, a thousand miles, three thousand miles, his gaze roving north and south, east and west, looking for the faint shadow, waiting for the sudden movement. *He's out there, somewhere. We need to catch this guy.* He was walking around right now, or sleeping, or planning, or preparing, and he was thinking he was just about the smartest guy on the whole continent.

Well, we'll see about that, Reacher thought. He stirred. He ought to get seriously involved. Or on the other hand, maybe not. It was a big decision, waiting to be made, but it wasn't made yet. He rolled over and closed his eyes. He could think about it later. He could make the decision tomorrow. Or the next day. Whenever.

THE DECISION WAS made. About the interval. The interval was history. Time to speed things up a little. Three weeks was way too long to wait now. This sort of thing, you let the idea creep up on you, you look at it, you consider it, you see its value, you see its appeal, and the decision is really made for you, isn't it? You can't get the genie back in the bottle, not once it's out. And this genie is out. All the way out. Up and running. So you run with it.

12

THERE WAS NO breakfast meeting the next morning. The day started too early. Harper opened the door before Reacher was even dressed. He had his pants on and was smoothing the wrinkles out of his shirt with his palm against the mattress.

"Love those scars," she said.

She took a step closer, looking at his stomach with undisguised curiosity.

"What's that one from?" she asked, pointing to his right side.

He glanced down. The right side of his stomach had a violent tracery of stitches in the shape of a twisted star. They bulged out above the muscle wall, white and angry.

"My mother did it," he said.

"Your *mother*?"

"I was raised by grizzly bears. In Alaska."

She rolled her eyes and moved them up to the left side of his chest. There was a .38-caliber bullet hole there, punched right into the pectoral muscle. The hair was missing from around it. It was a big hole. She could have lost her little finger in it, right up to the first knuckle.

"Exploratory surgery," he said. "Checking if I had a heart."

"You're happy this morning," she said.

He nodded. "I'm always happy."

"Did you get Jodie yet?"

He shook his head. "I haven't tried since yesterday."

"Why not?"

"Waste of time. She's not there."

"Are you worried?"

He shrugged. "She's a big girl."

"I'll tell you if I hear anything."

He nodded. "You better."

"Where are they really from?" she asked. "The scars?"

He buttoned his shirt.

"The gut is from bomb shrapnel," he said. "The chest, somebody shot me."

"Dramatic life."

He took his coat from the closet.

"No, not really. Pretty normal, wouldn't you say? For a soldier? A soldier figuring to avoid physical violence is like a CPA figuring to avoid adding numbers."

"Is that why you don't care about these women?"

He looked at her. "Who says I don't care?"

"I thought you'd be more agitated about it."

"Getting agitated won't achieve anything."

She paused. "So what will?"

"Working the clues, same as always."

"There aren't any clues. He doesn't leave any."

He smiled. "That's a clue in itself, wouldn't you say?"

She used her key from the inside and opened the door.

"That's just talking in riddles," she said.

He shrugged. "Better than talking in *bullshit*, like they do downstairs."

THE SAME MOTOR pool guy brought the same car to the doors. This time he stayed in the driver's seat, sitting square-on like a dutiful chauffeur. He drove them north on I-95 to the National Airport. It was before dawn. There was a halfhearted glow in the sky somewhere three hundred miles to the east, all the way out over the Atlantic Ocean. The only other illumination was from a thousand headlights streaming north toward work. The headlights were mostly on old-model cars. Old, therefore cheap, therefore owned by low-grade people aiming to be at their desks an hour before their bosses, so they would look good and get promotion, whereupon they could drive newer cars to work an hour later in the day. Reacher sat still and watched their shadowed faces as the Bureau driver sped past them, one by one.

Inside the airport terminal, it was reasonably busy. Men and women in dark raincoats walked quickly from one place to another. Harper collected two coach tickets from the United desk and carried them over to the check-in counter.

"We could use some legroom," she said to the guy behind the counter.

She used her FBI pass for photo ID. She snapped it

down like a poker player completing a flush. The guy hit a few keys and came up with an upgrade. Harper smiled, like she was genuinely surprised.

First class was half-empty. Harper took an aisle seat, trapping Reacher against the window like a prisoner. She stretched out. She was in a third different suit, this one a fine check in a muted gray. The jacket fell open and showed a hint of nipple through the shirt, and no shoulder holster.

"Left your gun at home?" Reacher asked.

She nodded. "Not worth the hassle. Airlines want too much paperwork. A Seattle guy is meeting us. Standard practice is he'd bring a spare, should we need one. But we won't, not today."

"You hope."

She nodded. "I hope."

They taxied on time and took off a minute early. Reacher pulled the magazine out and started leafing through. Harper had her tray unfolded, ready for breakfast.

"What did you mean?" she asked. "When you said it's a clue in itself?"

He forced his mind back an hour and tried to remember.

"Just thinking aloud, I guess," he said.

"Thinking about what?"

He shrugged. He had time to kill. "The history of science. Stuff like that."

"Is that relevant?"

"I was thinking about fingerprinting. How old is that?"

She made a face. "Pretty old, I think."

"Turn of the century?"

She nodded. "Probably."

"OK, a hundred years old," he said. "That was the first big forensic test, right? Probably started using microscopes around the same time. And since then, they've invented all kinds of other stuff. DNA, mass spectrometry, fluorescence. Lamarr said you've got tests I wouldn't believe. I bet they can find a rug fiber, tell you where and when somebody bought it, what kind of flea sat on it, what kind of dog the flea came off. Probably tell you what the dog's name is and what brand of dog food it ate for breakfast."

"So?"

"Amazing tests, right?"

She nodded.

"Real science-fiction stuff, right?"

She nodded again.

"OK," he said. "Amazing, science-fiction tests. But this guy killed Amy Callan and beat *all* of those tests, right?"

"Right."

"So what do you call that type of a guy?"

"What?"

"A very, very clever guy, is what."

She made a face. "Among other things."

"Sure, a lot of other things, but whatever else, a very clever guy. Then he did it again, with Cooke. Now what do we call him?"

"What?"

"A very, *very* clever guy. Once might have been luck. Twice, he's damn good."

"So?"

"Then he did it *again*, with Stanley. Now what do we call him?"

"A very, very, very clever guy?"

Reacher nodded. "Exactly."

"So?"

"So that's the clue. We're looking for a very, very, very clever guy."

"I think we *know* that already."

Reacher shook his head. "I don't think you do. You're not factoring it in."

"In what sense?"

"You think about it. I'm only an errand boy. You Bureau people can do all the hard work."

The stewardess came out of the galley with the breakfast trolley. It was first class, so the food was reasonable. Reacher smelled bacon and egg and sausage. Strong coffee. He flipped his tray open. The cabin was half-empty, so he got the girl to give him two breakfasts. Two airline meals made for a pleasant snack. She caught on quick and kept his coffee cup full.

"How aren't we factoring it in?" Harper asked.

"Figure it out for yourself," Reacher said. "I'm not in a helpful mood."

"Is it that he's not a soldier?"

He turned to stare at her. "That's great. We agree he's a really smart guy, and so you say well, then he's obviously not a soldier. Thanks a bunch, Harper."

She looked away, embarrassed. "I'm sorry. I didn't mean it like that. I just can't see how we're not factoring it in."

He said nothing in reply. Just drained his coffee and

climbed over her legs to get to the bathroom. When he got back, she was still looking contrite.

"Tell me," she said.

"No."

"You should, Reacher. Blake's going to ask me about your attitude."

"My attitude? Tell him my attitude is if a hair on Jodie's head gets hurt, I'll tear his legs off and beat him to death with them."

She nodded. "You really mean that, right?"

He nodded back. "You bet your ass I do."

"That's what I don't understand. Why aren't you feeling a little bit of the same way about these women? You liked Amy Callan, right? Not the same way as Jodie, but you liked her."

"I don't understand you, either. Blake wanted to use you like a hooker, and you're acting like he's still your best buddy."

She shrugged. "He was desperate. He gets like that. He's under a lot of stress. He gets a case like this, he's just desperate to crack it."

"And you admire that?"

She nodded. "Sure I do. I admire dedication."

"But you don't share it. Or you wouldn't have said no to him. You'd have seduced me on camera, for the good of the cause. So maybe it's you who doesn't care enough about these women."

She was quiet for a spell. "It was immoral. It annoyed me."

He nodded. "And threatening Jodie was immoral, too. It annoyed *me*."

"But I'm not letting my annoyance get in the way of justice."

"Well, I am. And if you don't like that, tough shit."

THEY DIDN'T SPEAK again, all the way to Seattle. Five hours, without a word. Reacher was comfortable enough with that. He was not a compulsively sociable guy. He was happier *not* talking. He didn't see anything odd about it. There was no strain involved. He just sat there, not talking, like he was making the journey on his own.

Harper was having more trouble with it. He could see she was worried about it. She was like most people. Put her alongside somebody she was acquainted with, she felt she had to be conversing. For her, it was unnatural not to be. But he didn't relent. Five hours, without a single word.

Those five hours were reduced to two by the West Coast clocks. It was still about breakfast time when they landed. The Sea-Tac terminals were filled with people starting out on their day. The arrivals hall had the usual echelon of drivers holding placards up. There was one guy in a dark suit, striped tie, short hair. He had no placard, but he was their guy. He might as well have had *FBI* tattooed across his forehead.

"Lisa Harper?" he said. "I'm from the Seattle Field Office."

They shook hands.

"This is Reacher," she said.

The Seattle agent ignored him completely. Reacher smiled inside. *Touché*, he thought. But then the guy might have ignored him anyway even if they were best buddies, because he was pretty much preoccupied with paying a whole lot of attention to what was under Harper's shirt.

"We're flying to Spokane," he said. "Air taxi company owes us a few favors."

He had a Bureau car parked in the tow lane. He used it to drive a mile around the perimeter road to General Aviation, which was five acres of fenced tarmac filled with parked planes, all of them tiny, one and two engines. There was a cluster of huts with low-budget signs advertising transportation and flying lessons. A guy met them outside one of the huts. He wore a generic pilot's uniform and led them toward a clean white six-seat Cessna. It was a medium-sized walk across the apron. Fall in the Northwest had brighter light than in D.C., but it was just as cold.

The interior of the plane was about the same size Lamarr's Buick had been, and a whole lot more spartan. But it looked clean and well maintained, and the engines started first touch on the button. It taxied out to the runway with the same sensation of tiny size Reacher had felt in the Lear at McGuire. It lined up behind a 747 bound for Tokyo the way a mouse lines up behind an elephant. Then it wound itself up and was off the ground in seconds, wheeling due east, settling to a noisy cruise a thousand feet above the ground.

The airspeed indicator showed more than a hundred and twenty knots, and the plane flew on for two whole hours. The seat was cramped and uncomfortable, and Reacher started wishing he'd thought of a better way to waste his time. He was going to spend fourteen hours in the air, all in one day. Maybe he should have stayed and worked on the files with Lamarr. He imagined a quiet room somewhere, like a library, a stack of papers, a leather chair. Then he pictured Lamarr herself and glanced across at Harper and figured he'd maybe taken the right option after all.

The airfield at Spokane was a modest, modern place, larger than he had expected. There was a Bureau car waiting on the tarmac, identifiable even from a thousand feet up, a clean dark sedan with a man in a suit leaning on the fender.

"From the Spokane satellite office," the Seattle guy said.

The car rolled over to where the plane parked and they were on the road within twenty seconds of the pilot shutting down. The local guy had the destination address written on a pad fixed to his windshield with a rubber suction cup. He seemed to know where the place was. He drove ten miles east toward the Idaho panhandle and turned north on a narrow road into the hills. The terrain was moderate, but there were giant mountains in the middle distance. Snow gleamed on the peaks. The road had a building every mile or so, separated by thick forest and broad meadow. The population density was not encouraging.

The address itself might have been the main house of an old cattle ranch, sold off long ago and refurbished by somebody looking for the rural dream but unwilling to forget the aesthetics of the city. It was boxed into a small lot by new ranch fencing. Beyond the fencing was grazing land, and inside the fencing the same grass had been fed and mowed into a fine lawn. There were trees on the perimeter, contorted by the wind. There was a small barn with garage doors punched into the side and a path veering off from the driveway to the front door. The whole structure stood close to the road and close to its own fencing, like a suburban house standing close to its neighbors, but this one stood close to nothing. The nearest man-made object was at least a mile away north or south, maybe twenty miles away east or west.

The local guys stayed in the car, and Harper and Reacher got out and stood stretching on the shoulder. Then the engine shut down behind them and the stunning silence of the empty country fell on them like a weight. It hummed and hissed and echoed in their ears.

"I'd feel better if she lived in a city apartment," Reacher said.

Harper nodded. "With a doorman."

There was no gate. The ranch fencing just stopped either side of the mouth of the driveway. They walked together toward the house. The driveway was shale. Reassuringly noisy, at least. There was a slight breeze. Reacher could hear it in the power lines. Harper stopped at the front door. There was no bell push. Just a big iron knocker in the shape of a lion's head with a heavy ring held in its teeth. There was a fisheye spyhole above it. The spyhole was new. There were burrs of clean wood where the drill had chipped the paint. Harper grasped the iron ring and knocked twice. The ring thumped on the wood. The sound was loud and dull, and it rolled out over the grassland. Came back seconds later from the hills.

There was no response. Harper knocked again. The sound boomed out. They waited. There was a creak of floorboards inside the house. Footsteps. The sound approached unseen and stopped behind the door.

"Who is it?" a voice called. A woman's voice, apprehensive.

Harper went into her pocket and came out with her badge. It was backed with a slip of leather, the same type of gold-on-gold shield Lamarr had clicked against Reacher's car window. The eagle at the top, head cocked to the left. She held it up, six inches in front of the spyhole.

"FBI, ma'am," she announced. "We called you yesterday, made an appointment."

The door opened with the creak of old hinges and revealed an entrance hall with a woman in it. She was holding the doorknob, smiling with relief.

"Julia's got me so damn nervous," she said.

Harper smiled back in a sympathetic way and introduced herself and Reacher. The woman shook hands with both of them.

"Alison Lamarr," she said. "Really pleased to meet you."

She led the way inside. The hall was square and as large as a room, walled and floored in old pine, which had been stripped and waxed to a fresh color a shade darker than the gold on Harper's badge. There were curtains in yellow checked gingham. Sofas with feather-filled pillows. Old oil lamps converted to take electric bulbs.

"Can I get you guys coffee?" Alison Lamarr asked.

"I'm all set right now," Harper said.

"Yes, please," Reacher said.

She led them through to the kitchen, which was the whole rear quarter of the first floor. It was an attractive space, waxed floor polished to a shine, new cabinets in unostentatious timber, a big country range, a line of gleaming machines for washing clothes and dishes, electric gadgets on the countertops, more yellow gingham at the windows. An expensive renovation, he guessed, but designed to impress only herself.

"Cream and sugar?" she asked.

"Just black," he said.

She was medium height, dark, and she moved with the bounce of a fit, muscular woman. Her face was open and friendly, tanned like she lived outdoors, and her hands were worn, like she maybe installed her own ranch fencing for herself. She smelled of lemon scent and was dressed in clean denim which had been carefully pressed. She wore tooled cowboy boots with clean soles. It looked like she'd made an effort for her visitors.

She poured coffee from a machine into a mug. Handed it to Reacher and smiled. The smile was a mixture of things. Maybe she was lonely. But it proved there was no blood relationship with her stepsister. It was a pleasant smile, interested, friendly, smiled in a way Julia Lamarr had no idea existed. It reached her eyes, which were dark and liquid. Reacher was a connoisseur of eyes, and he rated these two as more than acceptable.

"Can I look around?" he asked.

"Security check?" she said.

He nodded. "I guess."

"Be my guest."

He took his coffee with him. The two women stayed in the kitchen. The house had four rooms on the first floor, entrance, kitchen, parlor, living room. The whole place was solidly built out of good timber. The renovations were excellent quality. All the windows were new storm units in stout wood frames. The weather was cold enough that the screens were out and stored. Each window had a key. The front door was original, old pine two inches thick and aged like steel. Big hinges and a city lock. There was a back hallway with a back door, similar vintage and thickness. Same lock.

Outside there were thick thorny foundation plantings he guessed were chosen for wind resistance, but were as good as anything for stopping people spending time trying to get in the windows. There was a steel cellar door with a big padlock latched through the handles. The garage was a decent barn, less well maintained than the house, but not about to fall down anytime soon. There was a new Jeep Cherokee inside, and a stack of cartons proving the renovations had been recent. There was a new washing machine, still boxed up and sealed. A workbench with power saws and drills stored neatly on a shelf above it.

He went back into the house and up the stairs. Same windows as elsewhere. Four bedrooms. Alison's was clearly the back room on the left, facing west over empty country as far as the eye could see. It would be dark in the mornings, but the sunsets would be spectacular. There was a new master bathroom, stealing space from the next-door bedroom. It held a toilet, and a sink, and a shower. And a tub.

He went back down to the kitchen. Harper was standing by the window, looking out at the view. Alison Lamarr was sitting at the table.

"OK?" she said.

Reacher nodded. "Looks good to me. You keep the doors locked?"

"I do now. Julia made such a fuss about it. I lock the

windows, I lock the doors, I use the spyhole, I put 911 on the speed dial."

"So you should be OK," Reacher said. "This guy isn't into breaking doors down, apparently. Don't open up to anybody, nothing can go wrong."

She nodded. "That's how I figure it. You need to ask me some questions now?"

"That's why they sent me, I guess."

He sat down opposite her. Focused on the gleaming machines on the other side of the room, desperately trying to think of something intelligent to say.

"How's your father doing?" he asked.

"That's what you want to know?"

He shrugged. "Julia mentioned he was sick."

She nodded, surprised. "He's been sick two years. Cancer. Now he's dying. Almost gone, just hanging on day by day. He's in the hospital in Spokane. I go there every afternoon."

"I'm very sorry."

"Julia should come out. But she's awkward with him."

"She doesn't fly."

Alison made a face. "She could get over that, just once in two years. But she's all hung up on this step-family thing, as if it really matters. Far as I'm concerned, she's my sister, pure and simple. And sisters take care of each other, right? She should know that. She's going to be the only relative I've got. She'll be my next of kin, for God's sake."

"Well, I'm sorry about all that, too."

She made another face. "Right now, that's not too important. What can I help you with?"

"You got any feeling for who this guy could be?"

She smiled. "That's rather a basic question."

"It's rather a basic issue. You got any instinct?"

"It's some guy who thinks it's OK to harass women. Or maybe not *OK*, exactly. Could be some guy who just thinks the fallout should be kept behind closed doors."

"Is that an option?" Harper asked. She sat down, next to Reacher.

Alison glanced at her. "I don't really know. I'm not sure there is any middle ground. Either you swallow it, or it goes public in a big way."

"Did you look for the middle ground?"

She shook her head. "I'm the living proof. I just went ballistic. There was no middle ground *there*. At least, I couldn't see any."

"Who was your guy?" Reacher asked.

"A colonel called Gascoigne," she said. "He was always full of shit about coming to him if anything was bothering you. I went to him about getting reassigned. I saw him five times. I wasn't pleading the feminist case or anything. It wasn't a political thing. I just wanted something more interesting to do. And frankly I thought the Army was wasting a good soldier. Because I was good."

Reacher nodded. "So what happened with Gascoigne?"

Alison made a face.

"I didn't see it coming," she said. "At first I thought he was just kidding around."

She paused. Looked away.

"He said I should try next time without my uniform on," she said. "I thought he was asking for a date, you know, meet him in town, some bar, off duty, plain clothes. But then he made it clear, no, he meant right there in his office, stripped off."

Reacher nodded. "Not a very nice suggestion."

She made another face. "Well, he led up to it pretty slow, and he was pretty jokey about it, at first. It was like he was flirting. I almost didn't *notice*, you know? Like he's a man, I'm a woman, it's not a huge surprise, right? But clearly he figured I wasn't getting the message, so then all of a sudden he got *obscene*. He described what I'd have to do, you know? One foot on this corner of his desk, the other foot on the other corner, hands behind my head, motionless for thirty minutes. Then bending over, you know? Like a porno movie. Then it *did* hit me, the rage, all in a split second, and I just went nuclear."

Reacher nodded. "And you busted him?"

"Sure I did."

"How did he react?"

She smiled. "He was puzzled, more than anything. I'm sure he'd done it lots of times before, and gotten away with it. I think he was kind of surprised the rules had changed on him."

"Could he be the guy?"

She shook her head. "No. This guy is *deadly*, right? Gascoigne wasn't like that. He was an old, sad man. Tired, and ineffectual. Julia says this guy is a piece of work. I don't see Gascoigne having that kind of *initiative*, you know?"

Reacher nodded again. "If your sister's profile is correct, this is probably a guy from the background somewhere."

"Right," Alison said. "Maybe not connected with any

specific incident. Maybe some kind of distant observer, turned avenger."

"If Julia's profile is correct," Reacher said again.

There was a short silence.

"Big *if*," Alison said.

"You got doubts?"

"You know I have," she said. "And I know you have, too. Because we both know the same things."

Harper sat forward. "What are you saying?"

Alison made a face. "I just can't see a soldier going to all this *trouble*, not over this issue. It just doesn't work like that. The Army changes the rules *all the time*. Go back fifty years, it's OK to harass blacks, then it's not. It's OK to shoot gook babies, then it's not. A million things like that. Hundreds of men were canned one after the other, for some new invented offense. Truman integrated the Army, nobody started killing the blacks who filed complaints. This is some kind of *new* reaction. I can't understand it."

"Maybe men versus women is more fundamental," Harper said.

Alison nodded. "Maybe it is. I really don't know. But at the end of the day, like Julia says, the target group is so specific, it *has* to be a soldier. Who else could even *identify* us? But it's a very weird soldier, that's for damn sure. Not like any I ever met."

"Really?" Harper said. "Nobody at all? No threats, no comments, while it was all happening?"

"Nothing significant. Nothing more than casual bullshit. Nothing that I recall. I even flew out to Quantico and let Julia hypnotize me, in case there was something buried there, but she said I came up with nothing."

Silence again. Harper swept imaginary crumbs from the table and nodded. "OK. Wasted trip, right?"

"Sorry, guys," Alison said.

"Nothing's ever wasted," Reacher said. "Negatives can be useful too. And the coffee was great."

"You want more?"

"No, he doesn't," Harper said. "We've got to get back."

"OK." She stood up and followed them out of her kitchen. Crossed the hall and opened her front door.

"Don't let anybody in," Reacher said.

Alison smiled. "I don't plan to."

"I mean it," Reacher said. "It looks like there's no force involved. This guy is just walking in. So you might know him. Or he's some kind of a con artist, with some kind of a plausible excuse. Don't fall for it."

"I don't plan to," she said again. "Don't worry about me. And call me if you need anything. I'll be at the hospital afternoons, as long as it takes, but any other time is good. And best of luck."

Reacher followed Harper through the front door, out onto the shale path. They heard the door close behind them, and then the loud sound of the lock turning.

THE LOCAL BUREAU guy saved them two hours' flying time by pointing out that they could hop from Spokane to Chicago and then change there for D.C. Harper did the business with the tickets and found out it was more expensive, which was presumably why the Quantico travel desk hadn't booked it that way in the first place. But she authorized the extra money herself and decided to have the argument later. Reacher admired her for it.

He liked impatience and wasn't keen on another two hours in the Cessna. So they sent the Seattle guy back west alone and boarded a Boeing for Chicago. This time there was no upgrade, because the whole plane was coach. It put them close together, elbows and thighs touching all the way.

"So what do you think?" Harper asked.

"I'm not paid to think," Reacher said. "In fact, so far I'm not getting paid at all. I'm a consultant. So you ask me questions and I'll answer them."

"I did ask you a question. I asked you what you think."

He shrugged. "I think it's a big target group and three of them are dead. You can't guard them, but if the other eighty-eight do what Alison Lamarr is doing, they should be OK."

"You think locked doors are enough to stop this guy?"

"He chooses his own MO. Apparently he doesn't touch anything. If they don't open the door for him, what's he going to do?"

"Maybe change his MO."

"In which case you'll get him, because he'll have to start leaving some hard evidence behind."

He turned to look out of the window.

"That's it?" Harper said. "We should just tell the women to lock their doors?"

He nodded. "I think you should be warning them, yes."

"That doesn't catch the guy."

"You can't catch him."

"Why not?"

"Because of this profiling bullshit. You're not factoring in how smart he is."

She shook her head. "Yes, we are. I've seen the profile. It says he's real smart. And profiling works, Reacher. Those people have had some spectacular successes."

"Among how many failures?"

"What do you mean?"

Reacher turned back to face her. "Suppose I was in Blake's position? He's effectively a nationwide homicide detective, right? Gets to hear about everything. So suppose I was him, getting notified about every single homicide in America. Suppose every single time I said the likely suspect was a white male, age thirty and a half, wooden leg, divorced parents, drives a blue Ferrari. Every single time. Sooner or later, I'd be right. The law of averages would work for me. Then I could shout out hey, I was right. As long as I keep quiet about the ten thousand times I was wrong, I look pretty good, don't I? Amazing deduction."

"That's not what Blake's doing."

"Isn't it? Have you read stuff about his unit?"

She nodded. "Of course I have. That's why I applied for the assignment. There are all kinds of books and articles."

"I've read them too. Chapter one, successful case. Chapter two, successful case. And so on. No chapters about all the times they were wrong. Makes me wonder about how many times that was. My guess is a lot of times. Too many times to want to write about them."

"So what are you saying?"

"I'm saying a scattergun approach will always look good, as long as you put the spotlight on the successes and sweep the failures under the rug."

"That's not what they're doing."

He nodded. "No, it isn't. Not exactly. They're not just guessing. They try to work at it. But it's not an exact science. It's not rigorous. And they're one unit among many, fighting for status and funding and position. You know how organizations work. They've got the budget hearings right now. First, second, and third duty is protecting their own ass against cuts by proclaiming their successes and concealing their failures."

"So you think the profile is worthless?"

He nodded. "I know it is. It's internally flawed. It makes two statements that are incompatible."

"What two statements?"

He shook his head. "No deal, Harper. Not until Blake apologizes for threatening Jodie and pulls Julia Lamarr off the case."

"Why would he do that? She's his best profiler."

"Exactly."

THE MOTOR POOL guy was at the National Airport in D.C. to pick them up. It was late when they arrived back at Quantico. Julia Lamarr met them, alone. Blake was in a budget meeting, and Poulton had signed out and gone home.

"How was she?" Lamarr asked.

"Your sister?"

"My stepsister."

"She was OK," Reacher said.

"What's her house like?"

"Secure," he said. "Locked up tight as Fort Knox."

"But isolated, right?"

"Very isolated," he said.

She nodded. He waited.

"So she's OK?" she said again.

"She wants you to visit," he said.

She shook her head. "I can't. It would take me a week to get there."

"Your father is dying."

"My stepfather."

"Whatever. She thinks you should go out there."

"I can't," she said again. "She still the same?"

Reacher shrugged. "I don't know what she was like before. I only just met her today."

"Dressed like a cowboy, tanned and pretty and sporty?"

He nodded. "You got it."

She nodded again, vaguely. "Different from me."

He looked her over. Her cheap black city suit was dusty and creased, and she was pale and thin and hard. Her mouth was turned down. Her eyes were blank.

"Yes, different from you," he said.

"I told you," she said. "I'm the ugly sister."

She walked away without speaking again. Harper took him to the cafeteria and they ate a late supper together. Then she escorted him up to his room. Locked him inside without a word. He listened to her footsteps fade away in the corridor and undressed and showered. Then he lay down on the bed, thinking, and hoping. And waiting. Above all, waiting. Waiting for the morning.

13

THE MORNING CAME, but it was the wrong morning. He knew it as soon as he reached the cafeteria. He had been awake and waiting thirty minutes before Harper showed up. She unlocked his door and breezed in, looking elegant and refreshed, wearing the same suit as the first day. Clearly she had three suits and wore them in strict rotation. Three suits was about right, he figured, given her likely salary. It was three suits more than he had, because it was a whole salary more than he had.

They rode down in the elevator together and walked between buildings. The whole campus was very quiet. It had a weekend feel. He realized it was Sunday. The weather was better. No warmer, but the sun was out and it wasn't raining. He hoped for a moment it was a sign that this was his day. But it wasn't. He knew that as soon as he walked into the cafeteria.

Blake was at the table by the window, alone. There was a jug of coffee, three upturned mugs, a basket of cream and sugar, a basket of Danish and doughnuts. The bad news was the pile of Sunday newspapers, opened and read and scattered, with the *Washington Post* and *USA Today* and worst of all the *New York Times* just sitting right there in plain view. Which meant there was no news from New York. Which meant it hadn't worked yet, which meant he was going to have to keep on waiting until it did.

With three people at the table instead of five, there was more elbow room. Harper sat down opposite Blake and Reacher sat opposite nobody. Blake looked old and tired and very strained. He looked ill. The guy was a heart attack waiting to happen. But Reacher felt no sympathy for him. Blake had broken the rules.

"Today you work the files," Blake said.

"Whatever," Reacher said.

"They're updated with the Lorraine Stanley material. So you need to spend today reviewing them and you can give us your conclusions at the breakfast meeting tomorrow. Clear?"

Reacher nodded. "Crystal."

"Any preliminaries I should know about?"

"Preliminary what?"

"Conclusions. You got any thoughts yet?"

Reacher glanced at Harper. This was the point where a loyal agent would inform her boss about his objections. But she said nothing. Just looked down and concentrated on stirring her coffee.

"Let me read the files," he said. "Too early to say anything right now."

Blake nodded. "We've got sixteen days. We need to start making some real progress real soon."

Reacher nodded back. "I get the message. Maybe tomorrow we'll get some good news."

Blake and Harper looked at him like it was an odd thing to say. Then they took coffee and Danish and doughnuts and sections of the papers and lingered like they had time to kill. It was Sunday. And the investigation was stalled. That was clear. Reacher recognized the signs. However urgent a thing is, there comes a point where there are no more places to go. The urgency burns out, and you sit there like you've got all the time in the world, while the world rages on around you.

AFTER BREAKFAST HARPER took him to a room pretty much the same as he'd imagined while bucketing along in the Cessna. It was aboveground, quiet, filled with light oak tables and comfortable padded chairs faced with leather. There was a wall of windows, and the sun was shining outside. The only negative was one of the tables held a stack of files about a foot high. They were in dark blue folders, with *FBI* printed on them in yellow letters.

The stack was split into three bundles, each one secured with a thick rubber band. He laid them out on the table, side by side. Amy Callan, Caroline Cooke, Lorraine Stanley. Three victims, three bundles. He checked his watch. Ten twenty-five. A late start. The sun was warming the room. He felt lazy.

"You didn't try Jodie," Harper said.

He shook his head and said nothing.

"Why not?"

"No point. She's obviously not there."

"Maybe she went to your place. Where her father used to live."

"Maybe," he said. "But I doubt it. She doesn't like it there. Too isolated."

"Did you try it?"

He shook his head. "No."

"Worried?"

"I can't worry about something I can't change."

She said nothing. There was silence. He pulled a file toward him.

"You read these?" he asked her.

She nodded. "Every night. I read the files and the summaries."

"Anything in them?"

She looked at the bundles, each one of them four inches thick. "Plenty in them."

"Anything significant?"

"That's your call," she said.

He nodded reluctantly and stretched the rubber band off the Callan file. Opened up the folder. Harper took her jacket off and sat down opposite. Rolled up her shirtsleeves. The sun was directly behind her and it made her shirt transparent. He could see the outside curve of her breast. It swelled gently past the strap of her shoulder holster and fell away to the flatness of her waist. It moved slightly as she breathed.

"Get to work, Reacher," she said.

THIS IS THE tense time. You drive by, not fast, not slow, you look carefully, you keep on going up the road a little, and then you stop and you turn around and you drive back.

You park at the curb, leaving the car facing the right di-rection. You switch the engine off. You take the keys out and put them in your pocket. You put your gloves on. It's cold outside, so the gloves will look OK.

You get out of the car. You stand still for a second, lis-tening hard, and then you turn a complete circle, slowly, looking again. This is the tense time. This is the time when you must decide to abort or proceed. Think, think, think. You keep it dispassionate. It's just an operational judg-ment, after all. Your training helps.

You decide to proceed. You close the car door, quietly. You walk into the driveway. You walk to the door. You knock. You stand there. The door opens. She lets you in. She's glad to see you. Surprised, a little confused at first, then delighted. You talk for a moment. You keep on talk-ing, until the time is right. You'll know the moment, when it comes. You keep on talking.

The moment comes. You stand still for a second, testing it. You make your move. You explain she has to do exactly what you tell her. She agrees, of course, because she has no choice. You tell her you'd like her to look like she's having fun while she's doing it. You explain that'll make the whole thing more agreeable for you. She nods happily, willing to please. She smiles. The smile is forced and artificial, which spoils it somewhat, but it can't be helped. Something is bet-ter than nothing.

You make her show you the master bathroom. She stands there like a real estate agent, showing it off. The tub is fine. It's like a lot of tubs you've seen. You tell her to bring the paint inside. You supervise her all the way. It takes her five trips, in and out of the house, up and down the stairs. There's a lot to carry. She's huffing and puffing. She's start-

ing to sweat, even though the fall weather is cold. You remind her about the smile. She puts it back in place. It looks more like a grimace.

You tell her to find something to lever the lids off with. She nods happily and tells you about a screwdriver in the kitchen drawer. You walk with her. She opens the drawer and finds the screwdriver. You walk with her, back to the bathroom. You tell her to take the lids off, one by one. She's calm. She kneels next to the first can. She works the tip of the screwdriver in under the metal flange of the lid and eases it upward. She works around it in a circle. The lid sucks off. The chemical smell of the paint fills the air.

She moves on to the next can. Then the next. She's working hard. Working quickly. You tell her to be careful. Any mess, she'll be punished. You tell her to smile. She smiles. She works. The last lid comes off.

You pull the folded refuse sack from your pocket. You tell her to place her clothes in it. She's confused. Which clothes? The clothes you're wearing, you tell her. She nods and smiles. Kicks off her shoes. Their weight pulls the folded bag into shape. She's wearing socks. She tugs them off. Drops them in the bag. She unbuttons her jeans. Hops from foot to foot, taking them off. They go in the bag. She unbuttons her shirt. Shrugs it off. Drops it in the bag. She reaches back and fiddles with the catch on her bra. Pulls it off. Her breasts are swinging free. She slips her underpants down and balls them with the bra and drops them in the bag. She's naked. You tell her to smile.

You make her carry the bag down to the front door. You walk behind her. She props the bag against the door. You take her back to the bathroom. You make her empty the cans into the tub, slowly, carefully, one by one. She concentrates hard, tongue between her teeth. The cans are heavy and awkward. The paint is thick. It smells. It runs slowly into the tub. The level creeps up, green and oily.

You tell her she's done well. You tell her you're pleased. The paint is in the tub, and there are no drips anywhere. She smiles, delighted at the praise. Then you tell her the next part is harder. She has to take the empty cans back where she got them. But now she's naked. So she has to make sure nobody can see. And she has to run. She nods. You tell her now the cans are empty they weigh less, so she can carry more each trip. She nods again. She understands. She threads them onto her fingers, five empty cans in each hand. She carries them downstairs. You make her wait. You ease the door open and check. Look and listen. You send her out. She runs all the way there. She replaces the cans. She runs all the way back, breasts bouncing. It's cold outside.

You tell her to stand still and get her breath. You remind her about the smile. She bobs her head apologetically and comes back with the grimace. You take her up to the bathroom again. The screwdriver is still on the floor. You ask her to pick it up. You tell her to make marks on her face with it. She's confused. You explain. Deep scratches will do, you tell her. Three or four of them. Deep enough to draw blood. She smiles and nods. Raises the screwdriver. Scrapes it down the left side of her face, with the blade turned so the point is digging in. A livid red line appears, five inches long. Make the next one harder, you say. She nods. The next line bleeds. Good, you say. Do another. She scratches another. And another. Good, you say. Now make the last one really hard. She nods and smiles. Drags the blade down. The skin tears. Blood flows. Good girl, you say.

She's still holding the screwdriver. You tell her to get into the bath, slowly and carefully. She puts her right foot in. Then her left. She's standing in the paint, up to her calves. You tell her to sit down, slowly. She sits. The paint is up over her waist. Touching the underside of her breasts. You tell her to lie back, slowly and carefully. She slides down into the paint. The level rises, two inches below the lip of the tub. Now you smile. Just right.

You tell her what to do. She doesn't understand at first, because it's a very odd thing to be asked. You explain carefully. She nods. Her hair is thick with paint. She slides down. Now only her face is showing. She tilts her head back. Her hair floats. She uses her fingers to help her. They're slick and dripping with paint. She does exactly what she's been told. She gets it right first time. Her eyes jam open with panic, and then she dies.

You wait five minutes. Just leaning over the tub, not touching anything. Then you do the only thing she can't do for herself. It gets paint on your right glove. Then you press down on her forehead with a fingertip and she slips under the surface. You peel your right glove off inside out. Check the left one. It's OK. You put your right hand in your pocket for safety and you keep it there. This is the only time your prints are exposed.

Your carry the soiled glove in your left hand and walk downstairs in the silence. Slip the glove into the refuse sack with her clothes. Open the door. Listen and watch. Carry the sack outside. Turn around and close the door behind you. Walk down the driveway to the road. Pause behind the car and slip the clean glove in the sack, too. Pop the trunk lid and place the sack inside. Open the door and slide in

behind the wheel. Take the keys from your pocket and start
the engine. Buckle your belt and check the mirror. Drive
away, not fast, not slow.

THE CALLAN FILE started with a summary of her military
career. The career was four years long and the summary
ran to forty-eight lines of type. His own name was mentioned once, in connection with the debacle at the end.
He found he remembered her pretty well. She had been
a small, round woman, cheerful and happy. He guessed
she had joined the Army with no very clear idea of *why*.
There's a definite type of person who takes the same
route. Maybe from a large family, comfortable with shar-
ing, good at team sports in school, academically profi-
cient without being a scholar, they just drift toward it.
They see it as an extension of what they've already
known. Probably they don't see themselves as fighters,
but they know for every person who holds a gun the
Army offers a hundred other niches where there are
trades to be learned and qualifications to be earned.

Callan had passed out of basic training and gone
straight to the ordnance storerooms. She was a sergeant
within twenty months. She shuffled paper and sent consignments around the world pretty much like her con-
temporaries back home, except her consignments were
guns and shells instead of tomatoes or shoes or automobiles. She worked at Fort Withe near Chicago in a warehouse full of the stink of gun oil and the noise of
clattering forklifts. She had been content at first. Then
the rough banter had gotten too much, and her captain
and her major had started stepping over the line and
talking dirty and acting physical. She was no shrinking

violet, but the pawing and the leering eventually brought her to Reacher's office.

Then after she quit she went to Florida, to a beach town on the Atlantic forty miles north of where it stopped being too expensive. She got married there, got separated there, lived there a year, then died there. The file was full of notes and photographs about where and nothing much about how. Her house was a modern one-story crouching under an overhanging roof made of orange tile. The crime scene photographs showed no damage to any doors or windows, no disruption inside, a white-tiled bathroom with a tub full of green paint and a slick indeterminate shape floating in it.

The autopsy showed nothing at all. The paint was designed to be tough and weatherproof and it had a molecular structure designed to cling and penetrate anything it was slapped onto. It covered a hundred percent of the body's external area and it had seeped into the eyes and the nose and the mouth and the throat. Removing it removed the skin. There was no evidence of bruising or trauma. The toxicology was clear. No phenol injection to the heart. No air embolisms. There are many clever ways to kill a person, and the Florida pathologists knew all of them, and they couldn't find any evidence of any of them.

"Well?" Harper said.

Reacher shrugged. "She had freckles. I remember that. A year in the Florida sun, she must have looked pretty good."

"You liked her."

He nodded. "She was OK."

The final third of the file was some of the most

exhaustive crime scene forensics he had ever heard of. The analysis was microscopic, literally. Every particle of dust or fiber in her house had been vacuumed up and analyzed. But there was no evidence of any intruder. Not the slightest sign.

"A very clever guy," Reacher said.

Harper said nothing in reply. He pushed Callan's folder to one side and opened Cooke's. It followed the same format in its condensed narrative structure. She was different from Callan in that she had obviously aimed for the Army right from the start. Her grandfather and her father had been Army men, which creates a kind of military aristocracy, the way certain families see it. She had recognized the clash between her gender and her career intention pretty early, and there were notes about her demands to join her high school ROTC. She had begun her battles early.

She had been an officer candidate, and had started out a second lieutenant. She had gone straight to War Plans, which is where the brainy people waste their time assuming that when push comes to shove your friends stay your friends and your enemies stay your enemies. She had been promoted first lieutenant and posted to NATO in Brussels and started a relationship with her colonel. When she didn't get promoted captain early enough, she complained about him.

Reacher remembered it well. There was no harassment involved, certainly not in the sense that Callan had endured. No strangers had pinched her or squeezed her or made lewd gestures at her with oily gun barrels. But the rules had changed, so that sleeping with somebody you commanded was no longer allowed, so Cooke's colonel went down, and then ate his pistol. She quit and flew home from Belgium to a lakeside cottage in New Hampshire, where she was eventually found dead in a tub full of setting paint.

The New Hampshire pathologists and forensic scientists told the same story their Florida counterparts had, which was absolutely no story at all. The notes and the photographs were the same but different. A gray cedar house crowded by trees, an undamaged door, an undisturbed interior, folksy bathroom decor dominated by the dense green contents of the tub. Reacher skimmed through and closed the folder.

"What do you think?" Harper asked.

"I think the paint is weird," Reacher said.

"Why?"

He shrugged. "It's so *circular*, isn't it? It eliminates evidence on the bodies, which reduces risk, but getting it and transporting it creates risk."

"And it's like a deliberate clue," Harper said. "It underlines the motive. It's definite confirmation it's an Army guy. It's like a taunt."

"Lamarr says it has psychological significance. She says he's reclaiming them for the military."

Harper nodded. "By taking their clothes, too."

"But if he hates them enough to kill them, why would he want to reclaim them?"

"I don't know. A guy like this, who knows how he thinks?"

"Lamarr thinks she knows how he thinks," Reacher said.

Lorraine Stanley's file was the last of the three. Her history was similar to Callan's, but more recent. She was younger. She had been a sergeant, bottom of the totem pole in a giant quartermaster facility in Utah, the only woman in the place. She had been pestered since day one. Her competence had been questioned. One night her barrack was broken into and all her uniform trousers were stolen. She reported for duty the next morning wearing her regulation skirt. The next night, all her underwear was stolen. The next morning she was wearing the skirt and nothing underneath. Her lieutenant called her into his office. Made her stand easy in the middle of the room, one foot either side of a large mirror laid on the floor, while he yelled at her for a paperwork snafu. The whole of the personnel roster filed in and out of the office throughout, getting a good look at the reflection in the mirror. The lieutenant ended up in prison and Stanley ended up serving out another year and then living alone and dying alone in San Diego, in the little bungalow shown in the crime scene photographs, in which the California pathologists and forensics people had found absolutely nothing at all.

"How old are you?" Reacher asked.

"Me?" Harper said. "Twenty-nine. I told you that. It's an FAQ."

"From Colorado, right?"

"Aspen."

"Family?"

"Two sisters, one brother."

"Older or younger?"

"All older. I'm the baby."

"Parents?"

"Dad's a pharmacist, Mom helps him out."

"You take vacations when you were kids?"

She nodded. "Sure. Grand Canyon, Painted Desert, all over. One year we camped in Yellowstone."

"You drove there, right?"

She nodded again. "Sure. Big station wagon full of kids, happy family sort of thing. What's this about?"

"What do you remember about the drives?"

She made a face. "They were endless."

"Exactly."

"Exactly what?"

"This is a real big country."

"So?"

"Caroline Cooke was killed in New Hampshire and Lorraine Stanley was killed three weeks later in San Diego. That's about as far apart as you can get, right? Maybe thirty-five hundred miles by road. Maybe more."

"Is he traveling by road?"

Reacher nodded. "He's got hundreds of gallons of paint to haul around."

"Maybe he's got a stockpile stashed away someplace."

"That just makes it worse. Unless his stash just happened to be on a direct line between where he's based now and New Hampshire *and* southern California, he'd have to detour to get it. It would add distance, maybe a lot of distance."

"So?"

"So he's got a three-, four-thousand-mile road trip, plus surveillance time on Lorraine Stanley. Could he do that in a week?"

Harper made a face. "Call it seventy hours at fifty-five miles an hour."

"Which he couldn't average. He'd pass through towns and road construction. And he wouldn't break the speed limit. A guy this meticulous isn't going to risk some trooper sniffing around his vehicle. Hundreds of gallons of camouflage basecoat is going to arouse some suspicions these days, right?"

"So call it a hundred hours on the road."

"At least. Plus a day or two surveillance when he gets there. That's more than a week, in practical terms. It's ten or eleven days. Maybe twelve."

"So?"

"You tell me."

"This is not some guy working two weeks on, one week off."

Reacher nodded. "No, it's not."

THEY WALKED OUTSIDE and around toward the block with the cafeteria in it. The weather had settled to what fall should be. The air was ten degrees warmer, but still crisp. The lawns were green and the sky was a shattering blue. The dampness had blown away and the leaves on the surrounding trees looked dry and two shades lighter.

"I feel like staying outside," Reacher said.

"You need to work," Harper said.

"I read the damn files. Reading them over again isn't going to help me any. I need to do some thinking."

"You think better outside?"

"Generally."

"OK, come to the range. I need to qualify on handguns."

"You're not qualified already?"

She smiled. "Of course I am. We have to requalify every month. Regulations."

They took sandwiches from the cafeteria and ate as they walked. The outdoor pistol range was Sunday-quiet, a large space the size of a hockey rink, bermed on three sides with high earth walls. There were six separate firing lanes made out of shoulder-high concrete walls running all the way down to six separate targets. The targets were heavy paper, clipped into steel frames. Each paper was printed with a picture of a crouching felon, with target rings radiating out from his heart. Harper signed in with the rangemaster and handed him her gun. He reloaded it with six shells and handed it back, together with two sets of ear defenders.

"Take lane three," he said.

Lane three was in the center. There was a black line painted on the concrete floor.

"Seventy-five feet," Harper said.

She stood square-on and slipped the ear defenders into position. Raised the gun two-handed. Her legs were apart and her knees slightly bent. Her hips were forward and her shoulders back. She loosed off the six shots in a stream, half a second between them. Reacher watched the tendons in her hand. They were tight, rocking the muzzle up and down a fraction each time she pulled.

"Clear," she said.

He looked at her.

"That means you go get the target," she said.

He expected to see the hits arranged on a vertical line maybe a foot long, and when he got down to the other end of the lane, that is exactly what he found. There were two holes in the heart, two in the next ring, and two in the ring connecting the throat with the stomach. He unclipped the paper and carried it back.

"Two fives, two fours, two threes," she said. "Twenty-four points. I pass, just."

"You should use your left arm more," he said.

"How?"

"Take all the weight with your left, and just use your right for pulling the trigger."

She paused.

"Show me," she said.

He stepped close behind her and stretched around with his left arm. She raised the gun in her right and he cupped her hand in his.

"Relax the arm," he said. "Let me take the weight."

His arms were long, but hers were too. She shuffled backward and pressed hard against him. He leaned forward. Rested his chin on the side of her head. Her hair smelled good.

"OK, let it float," he said.

She clicked the trigger on the empty chamber a couple of times. The muzzle was rock steady.

"Feels good," she said.

"Go get some more shells."

She peeled away from in front of him and walked back to the rangemaster's cubicle and got another clip, part loaded with six. He moved into the next lane, where there was a new target. She met him there and nestled back against him and raised her gun hand. He reached around her and cupped it and took the weight. She leaned back against him. Fired twice. He saw the holes appear in the target, maybe an inch apart in the center ring.

"See?" he said. "Let the left do the work."

"Sounds like a political statement."

She stayed where she was, leaning back against him. He could feel the rise and fall of her breathing. He stepped away from behind her and she tried again, by herself. Two shots, fast. The shell cases rang on the concrete. Two more holes appeared in the heart ring. There was a tight cluster of four, in a diamond shape a business card would have covered.

She nodded. "You want the last two?"

She stepped close and handed him the pistol, butt-first. It was a SIG-Sauer, identical to the one Lamarr had held next to his head throughout the car ride into Manhattan. He stood with his back to the target and weighed the gun in his hand. Then he spun abruptly and fired the two bullets, one into each of the target's eyes.

"That's how I'd do it," he said. "If I was real mad with somebody, that's what I'd do. I wouldn't mess around with a damn tub and twenty gallons of paint."

THEY MET BLAKE on the way back to the library room. He looked aimless and agitated all at the same time. There was worry in his face. He had a new problem.

"Lamarr's father died," he said.

"Stepfather," Reacher said.

"Whatever. He died, early this morning. The hospital in Spokane called for her. Now I've got to call her at home."

"Give her our condolences," Harper said.

Blake nodded vaguely and walked away.

"He should take her off the case," Reacher said.

Harper nodded. "Maybe he should, but he won't. And she wouldn't agree, anyway. Her job is all she's got."

Reacher said nothing. Harper pulled the door and ushered him back into the room with the oak tables and the leather chairs and the files. Reacher sat down and checked his watch. Three twenty. Maybe two more hours of daydreaming and then he could eat and escape to the solitude of his room.

IT WAS THREE hours, in the end. And it wasn't daydreaming. He sat and stared into space and thought hard. Harper watched him, anxious. He took the file folders and arranged them on the table, Callan's at the bottom right, Stanley's at the bottom left, Cooke's at the top right, and stared at them, musing about the geography again. He leaned back and closed his eyes.

"Making any progress?" Harper asked.

"I need a list of the ninety-one women," he said.

"OK," she said.

He waited with his eyes closed and heard her leave the room. Enjoyed the warmth and the silence for a long moment, and then she was back. He opened his eyes and saw her leaning over near him and handing him another thick blue file.

"Pencil," he said.

She backed away to a drawer and found a pencil. Rolled it across the table to him. He opened the new file and started reading. First item was a Defense Department printout, four pages stapled together, ninety-one names in alphabetical order. He recognized some of them. Rita Scimeca was there, the woman he'd mentioned to Blake. She was next to Lorraine Stanley. Then there was a matching list with addresses, most of them obtained through the VA's medical insurance operation or mail-forwarding instructions. Scimeca lived in Oregon. Then there was a thick sheaf of background information, Army postdischarge intelligence reports, extensive for some of the women, sketchy for others, but altogether enough for a basic conclusion. Reacher flipped back and forth between pages and went to work with the pencil and twenty minutes later counted up the marks he'd made.

"It was eleven women," he said. "Not ninety-one."

"It was?" Harper said.

He nodded.

"Eleven," he said again. "Eight left, not eighty-eight."

"Why?"

"Lots of reasons. Ninety-one was always absurd. Who would seriously target ninety-one women? Five and a quarter years? It's not credible. A guy this smart would break it down into something manageable, like eleven."

"But how?"

"By limiting himself to what's feasible. A subcategory. What else did Callan and Cooke and Stanley have in common?"

"What?"

"They were alone. Positively and unequivocally alone. Unmarried or separated, single-family houses in the suburbs or the countryside."

"And that's crucial?"

"Of course it is. Think about the MO. He needs somewhere quiet and lonely and isolated. No interruptions. And no witnesses nearby. He has to get all that paint into the house. So look at this list. There are married women, women with new babies, women living with family, parents, women in apartment houses and condos, farms, communes even, women gone back to college. But he wants women who live alone, in houses."

Harper shook her head. "There are more than eleven of those. We did the research. I think it's more than thirty. About a third."

"But you had to check. I'm talking about women who are *obviously* living alone and isolated. At first glance. Because we have to assume the guy hasn't got anybody doing research for him. He's working alone, in secret. All he's got is this list to study."

"But that's *our* list."

"Not exclusively. It's his, too. All this information came straight from the military, right? He had this list before you did."

FORTY-THREE MILES AWAY, slightly east of north, the exact same list was lying open on a polished desk in a small windowless office in the darkness of the Pentagon's interior. It was two Xerox generations newer than Reacher's version, but it was otherwise identical. All the same pages were there. And they had eleven marks on them, against eleven names. Not hasty check marks in pencil, like Reacher had scrawled, but neat underlinings done with a fountain pen and a beveled ruler held away from the paper so the ink wouldn't smudge.

Three of the eleven names had second lines struck through them.

The list was framed on the desk by the uniformed forearms of the office's occupant. They were flat on the wood, and the wrists were cocked upward to keep the hands clear of the surface. The left hand held a ruler. The right hand held a pen. The left hand moved and

placed the ruler exactly horizontal along the inked line
under a fourth name. Then it slid upward a fraction and
rested across the name itself. The right hand moved and
the pen scored a thick line straight through it. Then the
pen lifted off the page.

"So what do we do about it?" Harper asked.

Reacher leaned back and closed his eyes again.

"I think you should gamble," he said. "I think you
should stake out the surviving eight around the clock
and I think the guy will walk into your arms within sixteen days."

She sounded uncertain.

"Hell of a gamble," she said. "It's very tenuous. You're
guessing about what he's guessing about when he looks
at the list."

"I'm supposed to be representative of the guy. So
what I guess should be what he guesses, right?"

"Suppose you're wrong?"

"As opposed to what? The progress you're making?"

She still sounded uncertain. "OK. I guess it's a valid
theory. Worth pursuing. But maybe they thought of it
already."

"Nothing ventured, nothing gained, right?"

She was quiet for a second. "OK, talk to Lamarr, first
thing tomorrow."

He opened his eyes. "You think she'll be here?"

Harper nodded. "She'll be here."

"Won't there be a funeral for her father?"

Harper nodded again. "There'll have to be a funeral,
obviously. But she won't go. She'd miss her *own* funeral,
a case like this."

"OK, but you do the talking, and talk to Blake instead. Keep it away from Lamarr."

"Why?"

"Because her sister clearly lives alone, remember? So her odds just went all the way down to eight to one. Blake will have to pull her off now."

"If he agrees with you."

"He should."

"Maybe he will. But he won't pull her off."

"He should."

"Maybe, but he won't."

Reacher shrugged. "Then don't bother telling him anything. I'm just wasting my time here. The guy's an idiot."

"Don't say that. You need to cooperate. Think about Jodie."

He closed his eyes again and thought about Jodie. She seemed a long way away. He thought about her for a long time.

"Let's go eat," Harper said. "Then I'll go talk to Blake."

FORTY-THREE MILES AWAY, slightly east of north, the uniformed man stared at the paper, motionless. There was a look on his face appropriate to a man making slow progress through a complicated undertaking. Then there was a knock at his door.

"Wait," he called.

He clicked the ruler down onto the wood and capped his pen and clipped it into his pocket. Folded the list and opened a drawer in his desk and slipped the list inside and weighted it down with a book. The book was a Bible, King James Version, black calfskin binding. He placed the ruler flat on top of the Bible and slid the drawer closed. Took keys from his pocket and locked the drawer. Put the keys back in his pocket and moved in his chair and straightened his jacket.

"Come," he called.

The door opened and a corporal stepped inside and saluted.

"Your car is here, Colonel," he said.

"OK, Corporal," the colonel said.

THE SKIES ABOVE Quantico were still clear, but the crispness in the air was plummeting toward a real night chill. Darkness was creeping in from the east, behind the buildings. Reacher and Harper walked quickly and the lights along the path came on in sequence, following their pace, as if their passing was switching the power. They ate alone, at a table for two in a different part of the cafeteria. They walked back to the main building through full darkness. They rode the elevator and she unlocked his door with her key.

"Thanks for your input," she said.

He said nothing.

"And thanks for the handgun tutorial," she said.

He nodded. "My pleasure."

"It's a good technique."

"An old master sergeant taught it to me."

She smiled. "No, not the shooting technique. The tutorial technique."

He nodded again, remembering her back pressed close against his chest, her hips jammed against his, her hair in his face, her feel, her smell.

"Showing is always better than telling. I guess," he said.

"Can't beat it," she replied.

She closed the door on him and he heard her walk away.

14

HE WOKE EARLY, before daybreak. Stood at the window for a spell, wrapped in a towel, staring out into the darkness. It was cold again. He shaved and showered. He was halfway through the Bureau's bottle of shampoo. He dressed standing next to the bed. Took his coat from the closet and put it on. Ducked back into the bathroom and clipped his toothbrush into the inside pocket. Just in case today was the day.

He sat on the bed with the coat wrapped around him against the cold and waited for Harper. But when the key went into the lock and the door opened, it wasn't Harper standing there. It was Poulton. He was keeping his face deliberately blank, and Reacher felt the first stirrings of triumph.

"Where's Harper?" he asked.

"Off the case," Poulton said.

"Did she talk to Blake?"

"Last night."

"And?"

Poulton shrugged. "And nothing."

"You're ignoring my input?"

"You're not here for *input*."

Reacher nodded. "OK. Ready for breakfast?"

Poulton nodded back. "Sure."

The sun was coming up in the east and sending color into the sky. There was no cloud. No damp. No wind. It was a pleasant walk through the early gloom. The place felt busy again. Monday morning, the start of a new week. Blake was at the usual table in the cafeteria, over by the window. Lamarr was sitting with him. She was wearing a black blouse in place of her customary cream. It was slightly faded, like it had been washed many times. There was coffee on the table, and mugs, and milk and sugar, and doughnuts. But no newspapers.

"I was sorry to hear the news from Spokane," Reacher said.

Lamarr nodded, silently.

"I offered her time off," Blake said. "She's entitled to compassionate leave."

Reacher looked at him. "You don't need to explain yourself to me."

"In the midst of life is death," Lamarr said. "That's something you learn pretty quickly around here."

"You're not going to the funeral?"

Lamarr took a teaspoon and balanced it across her forefinger. Stared down at it.

"Alison hasn't called me," she said. "I don't know what the arrangements are going to be."

"You didn't call her?"

She shrugged. "I'd feel like I was intruding."

"I don't think Alison would agree with that."

She looked straight at him. "But I just don't know."

There was silence. Reacher turned a mug over and poured coffee.

"We need to get to work," Blake said.

"You didn't like my theory?" Reacher said.

"It's a guess, not a theory," Blake said back. "We can all guess, as much as we want to. But we can't turn our backs on eighty women just because we enjoy guessing."

"Would they notice the difference?" Reacher asked.

He took a long sip of coffee and looked at the doughnuts. They were wrinkled and hard. Probably Saturday's.

"So you're not going to pay attention?" he asked.

Blake shrugged. "I gave it some consideration."

"Well, give it some more. Because the next woman to die will be one of the eleven I marked, and it'll be on your head."

Blake said nothing and Reacher pushed his chair back.

"I want pancakes," he said. "I don't like the look of those doughnuts."

He stood up before they could object and stepped away toward the center of the room. Stopped at the first table with a *New York Times* on it. It belonged to a guy on his own. He was reading the sports. The front section was discarded to his left. Reacher picked it up. The story he was waiting for was right there, front page, below the fold.

"Can I borrow this?" he asked.

The guy with the interest in sports nodded without looking. Reacher tucked the paper under his arm and walked to the serving counter. Breakfast was set out like a buffet. He helped himself to a stack of pancakes and eight rashers of bacon. Added syrup until the plate was swimming. He was going to need the nutrition. He had a long journey ahead, and he was probably going to be walking the first part of it.

He came back to the table and squatted awkwardly to get the plate down without spilling the syrup or dropping the newspaper. He propped the paper in front of his plate and started to eat. Then he pretended to notice the headline.

"Well, look at that," he said, with his mouth full.

The headline read *Gang Warfare Explodes in Lower Manhattan, Leaves Six Dead*. The story recounted a brief and deadly turf war between two rival protection rackets, one of them allegedly Chinese, the other allegedly Syrian. Automatic firearms and machetes had been used. The body count ran four to two in favor of the Chinese. Among the four dead on the Syrian side was the alleged gang leader, a suspected felon named Almar Petrosian. There were quotes from the NYPD and the FBI, and background reporting about the hundred-year history of protection rackets in New York City, the Chinese tongs, the jockeying between different ethnic groups for their business, which reputedly ran to billions of dollars nationwide.

"Well, look at that," Reacher said again.

They had already looked at it. That was clear. They were all turned away from him. Blake was staring through the window at the streaks of dawn in the sky.

Poulton had his eyes fixed on the back wall. Lamarr was still studying her teaspoon.

"Cozo call you to confirm it?" Reacher asked.

Nobody said a thing, which was the same as a yes. Reacher smiled.

"Life's a bitch, right?" he said. "You get a hook into me, and suddenly the hook isn't there anymore. Fate's a funny thing, isn't it?"

"Fate," Blake repeated.

"So let me get this straight," Reacher said. "Harper wouldn't play ball with the femme fatale thing, and now old Petrosian is dead, so you got no more cards to play. And you're not listening to a word I say anyway, so is there a reason why I shouldn't walk right out of here?"

"Lots of reasons," Blake said.

There was silence.

"None of them good enough," Reacher said.

He stood up and stepped away from the table again. Nobody tried to stop him. He walked out of the cafeteria and out through the glass doors into the chill of dawn. Started walking.

HE WALKED ALL the way out to the guardhouse on the perimeter. Ducked under the barrier and dropped his visitor's pass on the road. Walked on and turned the corner and entered Marine territory. He kept to the middle of the pavement and reached the first clearing after a half-mile. There was a cluster of vehicles and a number of quiet, watchful men. They let him go on. Walking was unusual, but not illegal. He reached the second clearing thirty minutes after leaving the cafeteria. He walked through it and kept on going.

He heard the car behind him five minutes later. He stopped and turned and waited for it. It came near enough for him to see past the dazzle of its running lights. It was Harper, which is what he had expected. She was alone. She drew level with him and buzzed her window down.

"Hello, Reacher," she said.

He nodded. Said nothing.

"Want a ride?" she asked.

"Out or back?"

"Wherever you decide."

"I-95 on-ramp will do it. Going north."

"Hitchhiking?"

He nodded. "I've got no money for a plane."

He slid in next to her and she accelerated gently away, heading out. She was in her second suit and her hair was loose. It spilled all over her shoulders.

"They tell you to bring me back?" he asked.

She shook her head. "They decided you're useless. Nothing to contribute, is what they said."

He smiled. "So now I'm supposed to get all boiled up with indignation and storm back in there and prove them wrong?"

She smiled back. "Something like that. They spent ten minutes discussing the best approach. Lamarr decided they should appeal to your ego."

"That's what happens when you're a psychologist who studied landscape gardening in school."

"I guess so."

They drove on, through the wooded curves, past the last Marine clearing.

"But she's right," he said. "I've got nothing to contribute. Nobody's going to catch this guy. He's too smart. Too smart for me, that's for damn sure."

She smiled again. "A little psychology of your own? Trying to leave with a clear conscience?"

He shook his head. "My conscience is always clear."

"Is it clear about Petrosian?"

"Why shouldn't it be?"

"Hell of a coincidence, don't you think? They threaten you with Petrosian, and he's dead within three days."

"Just dumb luck."

"Yeah, luck. You know I didn't tell them I was *outside* Trent's office all day?"

"Why not?"

"I was covering my ass."

He looked at her. "And what's Trent's office got to do with anything?"

She shrugged. "I don't know. But I don't like coincidences."

"They happen, time to time. Obviously."

"Nobody in the Bureau likes coincidences."

"So?"

She shrugged again. "So they could, you know, dig around. Might make it hard for you, later."

He smiled again. "This is phase two of the approach, right?"

She smiled back, and then the smile exploded into a laugh. "Yeah, phase two. There are about a dozen still to go. Some of them are real good. You want to hear them all?"

"Not really. I'm not going back. They're not listening."

She nodded and drove on. Paused before the junction

with the interstate, and then swooped north up the ramp.

"I'll take you to the next one," she said. "Nobody uses this one except Bureau people. And none of them is going to give you a ride."

He nodded. "Thanks, Harper."

"Jodie's home," she said. "I called Cozo's office. Apparently they had a little surveillance going. She's been away. She got back this morning, in a taxi. Looked like she'd come from the airport. Looks like she's working from home today."

He smiled. "OK, so now I'm definitely out of here."

"We need your input, you know."

"They're not listening."

"You need to make them listen," she said.

"This is phase three?"

"No, this is me. I mean it."

He was silent for a long moment. Then he nodded.

"So why *won't* they listen?"

"Pride, maybe?" she said.

"They need somebody's input," he said. "That's for sure. But not mine. I don't have the resources. And I don't have the authority."

"To do what?"

"To take it out of their hands. They're wasting their time with this profiling shit. It won't get them anywhere. They need to work the clues."

"There aren't any clues."

"Yes, there are. How smart the guy is. And the paint, and the geography, and how quiet the scenes are. They're all clues. They should work them. They've got to mean something. Starting with the motive is starting at the wrong end."

"I'll pass that on."

She pulled off the highway and stopped at the cross street.

"You going to get into trouble?" he asked.

"For failing to bring you back?" she said. "Probably."

He was silent. She smiled.

"That was phase ten," she said. "I'll be perfectly OK."

"I hope so," he said, and got out of the car. He walked north across the street to the ramp and stood all alone and watched her car slide under the bridge and turn back south.

A MALE HITCHHIKER standing six feet five and weighing two hundred and thirty pounds is on the cusp of acceptability for easy rides. Generally, women won't stop for him, because they see a threat. Men can be just as nervous. But Reacher was showered and shaved and clean, and dressed quietly. That shortened the odds, and there were enough trucks on the road with big confident owner-drivers that he was back in New York City within seven hours of starting out.

He was quiet most of the seven hours, partly because the trucks were too noisy for conversation, and partly because he wasn't in the mood for talking. The old hobo demon was whispering to him again. *Where are you going?* Back to Jodie, of course. *OK, smart guy, but what else? What the hell else? Yardwork behind your house? Painting the damn walls?* He sat next to a succession of kindly drivers and felt his brief unsatisfactory excursion into freedom ebb away. He worked on forgetting about it, and felt he succeeded. His final ride was from a New Jersey vegetable truck delivering to Greenwich Village. It rumbled in through the Holland Tunnel. He got out and walked the last mile on Canal and Broadway, all the way down to Jodie's apartment house, concentrating hard on his desire to see her.

He had his own key to her lobby, and he went up in the elevator and knocked on her door. The peephole went dark and light again and the door opened and she was standing there, in jeans and a shirt, tall and slim and vital. She was the most beautiful thing he had ever seen. But she wasn't smiling at him.

"Hey, Jodie," he said.

"There's an FBI agent in my kitchen." she replied.

"Why?"

"Why?" she repeated. "You tell me."

He followed her into the apartment, through to the kitchen. The Bureau guy was a short young man with a wide neck. Blue suit, white shirt, striped tie. He was holding a cell phone up to his face, reporting Reacher's arrival to somebody else.

"What do you want?" Reacher asked him.

"I want you to wait here, sir," the guy said. "About ten minutes, please."

"What's this about?"

"You'll find out, sir. Ten minutes, is all."

Reacher felt like walking out, just to be contrary, but Jodie sat down. There was something in her face. Something halfway between concern and annoyance. The *New York Times* was open on the countertop. Reacher glanced at it.

"OK," he said. "Ten minutes."

He sat down, too. They waited in silence. It was nearer fifteen minutes than ten. Then the buzzer from the street sounded and the Bureau guy went to answer it. He clicked the door release and moved out to the hallway. Jodie sat still and passive, like a guest in her own apartment. Reacher heard the whine of the elevator. He heard it stop. He heard the apartment door open. He heard footsteps on the maple floor.

Alan Deerfield walked into the kitchen. He was in a dark raincoat with the collar turned up. He was moving energetically and he had sidewalk grit on the soles of his shoes and it made him loud and invasive.

"I got six people dead in my city," he said. He saw the *Times* on the counter and walked over and folded it back to reveal the headline. "So I got a couple questions, naturally."

Reacher looked at him. "What questions?"

Deerfield looked back. "Delicate questions."

"So ask them."

Deerfield nodded. "First question is for Ms. Jacob."

Jodie stirred in her chair. Didn't look up.

"What's the question?" she said.

"Where have you been, the last few days?"

"Out of town," she said. "On business."

"Where out of town?"

"London. Client conference."

"London, England?"

"As opposed to what other Londons?"

Deerfield shrugged. "London, Kentucky? London, Ohio? There's a London somewhere in Canada too, I believe. Ontario, maybe."

"London, England," Jodie said.

"You got clients in London, England?"

Jodie was still looking at the floor. "We've got clients everywhere. Especially in London, England."

Deerfield nodded. "You go by the Concorde?"

She looked up. "Yes I did, as a matter of fact."

"Real quick, right?"

Jodie nodded. "Quick enough."

"But expensive."

"I guess."

"But worth it for a partner on important business."

Jodie looked at him. "I'm not a partner."

Deerfield smiled. "Even better, right? They put an associate on the Concorde, got to mean something. Must mean they like you. Must mean you'll be a partner real soon. If nothing comes along and gets in the way."

Jodie said nothing in reply.

"So, London," Deerfield said. "Reacher knew you were there, right?"

She shook her head. "No, I didn't tell him."

There was a pause.

"Scheduled trip?" Deerfield asked.

Jodie shook her head again. "Last-minute."

"And Reacher didn't know?"

"I already told you that."

"OK," Deerfield said. "Information is king, is what I say."

"I don't have to tell him where I go."

Deerfield smiled. "I'm not talking about what information you give Reacher. I'm talking about what information I get out of a situation. Right now I'm getting he didn't know where you were."

"So?"

"That should have worried him. And it did worry him. Right after he got to Quantico, he was trying to get you on the phone. Office, home, mobile. That night, same thing again. Calling, calling, calling, couldn't get you. A worried man."

Jodie glanced up at Reacher. Concern in her face, maybe a little apology.

"I should have told him, I guess."

"Hey, that's up to you. I don't go around telling people how to conduct their relationships. But the interesting thing is, then he stops calling you. Suddenly he's not calling you anymore. Now why is that? Did he find out you were safe over there in London, England?"

She started to reply, and then she stopped.

"I'll take that for a no," Deerfield said. "You were worried about Petrosian, so you told people in your office to clam up about where you were. So as far as Reacher knew, you were still right here in town. But he's suddenly not worried anymore. He doesn't know you're safe and sound in London, England, but maybe he does know you're safe and sound because of some other reason, such as maybe he knows Petrosian isn't going to be around for very much longer."

Jodie's eyes were back on the floor again.

"He's a smart guy," Deerfield said. "My guess is he whistled up some pal of his to set the cat among the pigeons up here in Chinatown, and then he sat back and waited for the tongs to do what they always do when somebody starts messing with them. And he figures he's safe. He knows we'll never find his busy little pal, and he figures those Chinese boys aren't going to tell us diddly, not in a million years, and he knows the exact moment old Petrosian is getting the good news with the machete, he's locked into a room down in Quantico. A smart guy."

Jodie said nothing.

"But a very confident guy," Deerfield said. "He stopped calling you two days before Petrosian finally bought the farm."

There was silence in the kitchen. Deerfield turned to Reacher.

"So am I on the money?" he asked.

Reacher shrugged. "Why should anybody have been worrying about Petrosian?"

Deerfield smiled again. "Oh, sure, we can't talk about that. We'll never admit Blake said a word to you on that subject. But like I told Ms. Jacob, information is king. I just want to be a hundred percent sure what I'm dealing with here. If you stirred it up, just tell me and maybe I'll pat you on the back for a job well done. But if by some chance it was a genuine dispute, we need to know about it."

"I don't know what you're talking about," Reacher said.

"So why did you stop calling Ms. Jacob?"

"That's my business."

"No, it's everybody's business," Deerfield said. "Certainly it's Ms. Jacob's business, right? And it's mine too. So tell me about it. And don't go thinking you're out of the woods yet, Reacher. Petrosian was a piece of shit for sure, but he's still a homicide, and we can crank up a pretty good motive for you anyway, based on what was witnessed by two credible witnesses the other night in

the alley. We could call it a conspiracy with persons unknown. Careful preparation of the case, you could be
inside two years, just waiting for the trial. Jury might let
you go in the end, but then who really knows what a
jury might do?"

Reacher said nothing. Jodie stood up.

"You should leave now, Mr. Deerfield," she said. "I'm
still his lawyer, and this is an inappropriate forum for
this discussion."

Deerfield nodded slowly, and looked around the
kitchen, like he was seeing it for the first time.

"Yes, it sure is, Ms. Jacob," he said. "So maybe we'll
have to continue this discussion someplace more appropriate at some future time. Maybe tomorrow, maybe
next week, maybe next year. Like Mr. Blake pointed out,
we know where you both live."

He turned on the spot, with the grit on his shoes loud
in the silence. They heard him walk through the living
room and they heard the apartment door open and slam
shut.

"So you took Petrosian out," Jodie said.

"I never went near him," Reacher replied.

She shook her head. "Save that stuff for the FBI, OK?
You arranged it or provoked it or engineered it or whatever the correct phrase would be. You took him out, as
surely as if you were standing right next to him with a
gun."

Reacher said nothing.

"And I told you not to do that," she said.

Reacher said nothing.

"Deerfield knows you did it," she said.

"He can't prove it."

"That doesn't matter," she said. "Don't you see that? He can *try* to prove it. And he's not kidding about the two years in jail. A suspicion of gang warfare? A thing like that, the courts will back him up all the way. Denial of bail, continuances, the prosecutors will really go to bat for him. It's not an empty threat. He owns you now. Like I told you he would."

Reacher said nothing.

"Why did you do it?"

He shrugged. "Lots of reasons. It needed doing."

There was a long silence.

"Would my father have agreed with you?" Jodie asked.

"Leon?" Reacher said. He recalled the photographs in Cozo's packet. The photographs of Petrosian's handiwork. The dead women, displayed like centerfolds. Pieces missing, things inserted. "Are you kidding? Leon would have agreed with me in a heartbeat."

"And would he have gone ahead and done what you did?"

"Probably."

She nodded. "Yes, he probably would. But look around you, OK?"

"At what?"

"At everything. What do you see?"

He looked around. "An apartment."

She nodded. "My apartment."

"So?"

"Did I grow up here?"

"Of course not."

"So where did I grow up?"

He shrugged. "All over the place, on Army bases, like I did."

She nodded. "Where did you first meet me?"

"You know where. Manila. On the base."

"Remember that bungalow?"

"Sure I do."

She nodded. "So do I. It was tiny, it stank, and it had cockroaches bigger than my hand. And you know what? That was the best place I ever lived as a kid."

"So?"

She was pointing at her briefcase. It was a leather pilot's case, stuffed with legal paper, parked against the wall just inside the kitchen door. "What's that?"

"Your briefcase."

"Exactly. Not a rifle, not a carbine, not a flame-thrower."

"So?"

"So I live in a Manhattan apartment instead of base quarters, and I carry a briefcase instead of infantry weapons."

He nodded. "I know you do."

"But do you know why?"

"Because you want to, I guess."

"Exactly. *Because I want to*. It was a conscious choice. *My* choice. I grew up in the Army, just like you did, and I could have joined up if I'd wanted to, just like you did. But I didn't want to. I wanted to go to college and law school instead. I wanted to join a big firm and make partner. And why was that?"

"Why?"

"Because I wanted to live in a world with rules."

"Plenty of rules in the Army," he said.

"The wrong rules, Reacher. I wanted civilian rules. *Civilized* rules."

"So what are you saying?"

"I'm saying I left the military all those years ago and I don't want to be back in it now."

"You're not back in it."

"But you make me feel that I am. *Worse* than the military. This thing with Petrosian? I don't want to be in a world with rules like that. You know I don't."

"So what should I have done?"

"You shouldn't have gotten into it in the first place. That night in the restaurant? You should have walked away and called the cops. That's what we do here."

"Here?"

"In the civilized world."

He sat on her kitchen stool and leaned his forearms on her countertop. Spread his fingers wide and placed his palms down flat. The countertop was cold. It was some kind of granite, gray and shiny, milled to reveal tiny quartz speckles throughout its surface. The corners and angles were radiused into perfect quarter-circles. It was an inch thick, and probably very expensive. It was a civilized product. It belonged right there in a world where people agree to labor forty hours, or a hundred, or two hundred, and then exchange the remuneration they get for installations they hope will make their kitchens look nice, inside their expensive remodeled buildings high above Broadway.

"Why did you stop calling me?" she asked.

He looked down at his hands. They lay on the polished granite like the rough exposed roots of small trees.

"I figured you were safe," he said. "I figured you were hiding out someplace."

"You figured," she repeated. "But you didn't know."

"I assumed," he said. "I was taking care of Petrosian, I assumed you were taking care of yourself. I figured we know each other well enough to trust assumptions like that."

"Like we were comrades," she said softly. "In the same unit, a major and a captain maybe, in the middle of some tight dangerous mission, absolutely relying on each other to do our separate jobs properly."

He nodded. "Exactly."

"But I'm not a captain. I'm not in some unit. I'm a lawyer. A lawyer, in New York, all alone and afraid, caught up in something I don't want to be caught up in."

He nodded again. "I'm sorry."

"And you're not a major," she said. "Not anymore. You're a civilian. You need to get that straight."

He nodded. Said nothing.

"And that's the big problem, right?" she said. "We've both got the same problem. You're getting me caught up in something I don't want to be caught up in, and I'm getting you caught up in something you don't want to be caught up in either. The civilized world. The house, the car, living somewhere, doing ordinary things."

He said nothing.

"My fault, probably," she said. "I *wanted* those things. God, did I want them. Makes it kind of hard for me to accept that maybe you *don't* want them."

"I want you," he said.

She nodded. "I know that. And I want *you*. You know that too. But do we want each other's lives?"

The hobo demon erupted in his head, cheering and screaming like a fan watching the winning run soar into the bleachers, bottom of the ninth. *She said it! She said it! Now it's right there, out in the open! So go for it! Jump on it! Just gobble it right up!*

"I don't know," he said.

"We need to talk about it," she said.

But there was no more talking to be done, not then, because the buzzer from the lobby started up an insistent squawk, like somebody was down there on the street leaning on the button. Jodie stood up and hit the door release and moved into the living room to wait. Reacher stayed on his stool at the granite counter, looking at the quartz sparkles showing between his fingers. Then he felt the elevator arrive and heard the apartment door open. He heard urgent conversation and fast light footsteps through the living room and then Jodie was back in the kitchen with Lisa Harper standing at her side.

15

HARPER WAS STILL in her second suit and her hair was still loose on her shoulders, but those were the only similarities with the last time he had seen her. Her long-limbed slowness was all wiped away by some kind of feverish tension, and her eyes were red and strained. He guessed she was as near to distraught as she was ever going to get.

"What?" he asked.

"Everything," she said. "It's all gone crazy."

"Where?"

"Spokane," she said.

"No," he said.

"Yes," she said. "Alison Lamarr."

There was silence.

"Shit," he whispered.

Harper nodded. "Yeah, shit."

"When?"

"Sometime yesterday. He's speeding up. He didn't stick to the interval. The next one should have been two weeks away."

"How?"

"Same as all the others. The hospital was calling her because her father died, and there was no reply, so eventually they called the cops, and the cops went out there and found her. Dead in the tub, in the paint, like all the others."

More silence.

"But how the hell did he get in?"

Harper shook her head. "Just walked right in the door."

"Shit, I don't believe it."

"They've sealed the place off. They're sending a crime scene unit direct from Quantico."

"They won't find anything."

Silence again. Harper glanced around Jodie's kitchen, nervously.

"Blake wants you back on board," she said. "He's signed up for your theory in a big way. He believes you now. Eleven women, not ninety-one."

Reacher stared at her. "So what am I supposed to say to that? Better late than never?"

"He wants you back," Harper said again. "This is getting way out of control. We need to start cutting some corners with the Army. And he figures you've demonstrated a talent for cutting corners."

It was the wrong thing to say. It fell across the kitchen like a weight. Jodie switched her gaze from Harper to the refrigerator door.

"You should go, Reacher," she said.

He made no reply.

"Go cut some corners," she said. "Go do what you're good at."

HE WENT. HARPER had a car waiting at the curb on Broadway. It was a Bureau car, borrowed from the New York office, and the driver was the same guy who had driven him down from Garrison with a gun at his head. But if the guy was confused about Reacher's recent change of status, he didn't show it. Just lit up his red light and took off west toward Newark.

The airport was a mess. They fought through crowds to the Continental counter. The reservation was coming in direct from Quantico as they waited at the desk. Two coach seats. They ran to the gate and were the last passengers to board. The purser was waiting for them at the end of the jetway. She put them in first class. Then she stood near them and used a microphone and welcomed everybody joining her for the trip to Seattle-Tacoma.

"Seattle?" Reacher said. "I thought we were going to Quantico."

Harper felt behind her for the seat-belt buckle and shook her head. "First we're going to the scene. Blake thought it could be useful. We saw the place two days ago. We can give him some direct before-and-after comparisons. He thinks it's worth a try. He's pretty desperate."

Reacher nodded. "How's Lamarr taking it?"

Harper shrugged. "She's not falling apart. But she's real tense. She wants to take complete control of everything. But she won't join us out there. Still won't fly."

The plane was taxiing, swinging wide circles across the tarmac on its way to the takeoff line. The engines were whining up to pitch. There was vibration in the cabin.

"Flying's OK," Reacher said.

Harper nodded. "I know, crashing is the problem."

"Hardly ever happens, statistically."

"Like a Powerball win. But somebody always gets lucky."

"Hell of a thing, not flying. A country this size, it's kind of limiting, isn't it? Especially for a federal agent. I'm surprised they let her get away with it."

She shrugged again. "It's a known quantity. They work around it."

The plane swung onto the runway and stopped hard against the brakes. The engine noise built louder and the plane rolled forward, gently at first, then harder, accelerating all the way. It came up off the ground with no sensation at all and the wheels whined up into their bays and the ground tilted sharply below them.

"Five hours to Seattle," Harper said. "All over again."

"Did you think about the geography?" Reacher asked. "Spokane is the fourth corner, right?"

She nodded. "Eleven potential locations now, all random, and he takes the four farthest away for his first four hits. The extremities of the cluster."

"But why?"

She made a face. "Demonstrating his reach?"

He nodded. "And his speed, I guess. Maybe that's why he abandoned the interval. To demonstrate his efficiency. He was in San Diego, then he's in Spokane a couple of days later, checking out a new target."

"He's a cool customer."

Reacher nodded vaguely. "That's for damn sure. He leaves an immaculate scene in San Diego, then he drives north like a madman and leaves what I bet is another immaculate scene in Spokane. A cool, cool customer. I wonder who the hell he is?"

Harper smiled, briefly and grimly. "We *all* wonder who the hell he is, Reacher. The trick is to find out."

YOU'RE A GENIUS, is who you are. An absolute genius, a prodigy, a superhuman talent. Four down! One, two, three, four down. And the fourth was the best of all. Alison Lamarr herself! You go over and over it, replaying it like a video in your head, checking it, testing it, examining it. But also savoring it. Because it was the best yet. The most fun, the most satisfaction. The most impact. The look on her face as she opened the door! The dawning recognition, the surprise, the welcome!

There were no mistakes. Not a single one. It was an immaculate performance, from the beginning to the end. You replay your actions in minute detail. You touched nothing, left nothing behind. You brought nothing to her house except your still presence and your quiet voice. The terrain helped, of course, isolated in the countryside, nobody for miles around. It made it a real safe operation. Maybe you should have had more fun with her. You could have made her sing. Or dance! You could have spent longer with her. Nobody could have heard anything.

But you didn't, because patterns are important. Patterns protect you. You practice, you rehearse in your mind, you rely on the familiar. You designed the pattern for the worst case, which was probably the Stanley bitch in her awful little subdivision down in San Diego. Neighbors all over the place! Little cardboard houses all crowded on top of each other! Stick to the pattern, that's the key. And keep on thinking. Think, think, think. Plan ahead. Keep on planning. You've done number four, and sure, you're entitled to replay it over and over, to enjoy it for a spell, to savor it, but then you have to just put it away and close the door on it and prepare for number five.

THE FOOD ON the plane was appropriate for a flight that left halfway between lunch and dinner and was crossing all the time zones the continent had to offer. The only sure thing was it wasn't breakfast. Most of it was a sweet pastry envelope with ham and cheese inside. Harper wasn't hungry, so Reacher ate hers along with his own. Then he fueled up on coffee and fell back to thinking. Mostly he thought about Jodie. *But do we want each other's lives?* First, define your life. *Hers* was easy enough to pin down, he guessed. Lawyer, owner, resident, lover, lover of fifties jazz, lover of modern art. A person who wanted to be settled, precisely because she knew what it was like to be rootless. If anybody in the whole world should live on the fourth floor of an old Broadway building with museums and galleries and cellar clubs all around her, it was Jodie.

But what about him? What made him happy? Being with her, obviously. There was no doubt about that. No doubt at all. He recalled the day in June he had walked back into her life. Just recalling it re-created the exact second he laid eyes on her and understood who she was. He had felt a flood of feeling as powerful as an electric shock. It buzzed through him. He was feeling it again, just because he was thinking about it. It was something he had rarely felt before.

Rarely, but not never. He had felt the same thing on random days since he left the Army. He remembered stepping off buses in towns he had never heard of in states he had never visited. He remembered the feel of sun on his back and dust at his feet, long roads stretching out straight and endless in front of him. He remembered peeling crumpled dollar bills off his roll at lonely motel desks, the feel of old brass keys, the musty smell of cheap rooms, the creak of springs as he dropped down on anonymous beds. Cheerful curious waitresses in old diners. Ten-minute conversations with drivers who stopped to pick him up, tiny random slices of contact between two of the planet's teeming billions. The drifter's life. Its charm was a big part of him, and he missed it when he was stuck in Garrison or holed up in the city with Jodie. He missed it bad. Real bad. About as bad as he was missing her right now.

"Making progress?" Harper asked him.

"What?" he said.

"You were thinking hard. Going all misty on me."

"Was I?"

"So what were you thinking about?"

He shrugged. "Rocks and hard places."

She stared at him. "Well, that's not going to get us anywhere. So think about something else, OK?"

"OK," he said.

He looked away and tried to put Jodie out of his mind. Tried to think about something else.

"Surveillance," he said suddenly.

"What about surveillance?"

"We're assuming the guy watches the houses first, aren't we? At least a full day? He might have already been hiding out somewhere, right when we were there."

She shivered. "Creepy. But so what?"

"So you should check motel registers, canvass the neighborhood. Follow up. That's how you're going to do this, by working. Not by trying to do magic five floors underground in Virginia."

"There *was* no neighborhood. You saw the place. We've got nothing to work on. I keep on telling you that."

"And I keep on telling you there's always something to work on."

"Yeah, yeah, he's very smart, the paint, the geography, the quiet scenes."

"Exactly. I'm not kidding. Those four things will lead you to him, sure as anything. Did Blake go to Spokane?"

She nodded. "We're meeting him at the scene."

"So he's going to have to do what I tell him, or I'm not sticking around."

"Don't push it, Reacher. You're Army liaison, not an investigator. And he's pretty desperate. He can make you stick around."

"He's fresh out of threats."

She made a face. "Don't count on it. Deerfield and Cozo are working on getting those Chinese boys to implicate you. They'll ask INS to check for illegals, whereupon they'll find about a thousand in the restaurant kitchens alone. Whereupon they'll start talking about deportations, but they'll also mention that a little cooperation could make the problem go away, whereupon the big guys in the tongs will tell those kids to spill whatever beans we want them to spill. Greatest good for the greatest number, right?"

Reacher made no reply.

"Bureau always gets what it wants," Harper said.

BUT THE PROBLEM with sitting there rerunning it like a video over and over again is that little doubts start to creep in. You go over it and over it and you can't remember if you really did all the things you should have done. You sit there all alone, thinking, thinking, thinking, and it all goes a little blurry and the more you question it, the less sure you get. One tiny little detail. Did you do it? Did you say it? You know you did at the Callan house. You know that for sure. And at Caroline Cooke's place. Yes, definitely. You know that for sure, too. And at Lorraine Stanley's place in San Diego. But what about Alison Lamarr's place? Did you do it? Or did you make her do it? Did you say it? Did you?

You're completely sure you did, but maybe that's just in the rerun. Maybe that's the pattern kicking in and making you assume something happened because it always happened before. Maybe this time you forgot. You become terribly afraid about it. You become sure you forgot. You think hard. And the more you think about it, the more you're sure you didn't do it yourself. Not this time. That's OK, as long as you told her to do it for you. But did you? Did you tell her? Did you say the words? Maybe you didn't. What then?

You shake yourself and tell yourself to calm down. A person of your superhuman talent, unsure and confused? Ridiculous. Absurd! So you put it out of your mind. But it won't go away. It nags at you. It gets bigger and bigger, louder and louder. You end up sitting all alone, cold and sweating, absolutely sure you've made your first small mistake.

THE BUREAU'S OWN Learjet had ferried Blake and his team from Andrews direct to Spokane and he had sent it over to Sea-Tac to collect Harper and Reacher. It was waiting on the apron right next to the Continental gates, and the same guy as before had been hauled out of the Seattle Field Office to meet them at the head of the jetway and point them down the external stairs and outside. It was raining lightly, and cold, so they ran for the Lear's steps and hustled straight inside. Four minutes later, they were back in the air.

Sea-Tac to Spokane was a lot faster in the Lear than it had been in the Cessna. The same local guy in the same car was waiting for them. He still had Alison Lamarr's address written on the pad attached to his windshield. He drove them the ten miles east toward Idaho and then turned north onto the narrow road into the hills. Fifty yards in, there was a roadblock with two parked cars and yellow tape stretched between trees. Above the trees in the far distance were the mountains. It was raining and gray on the western peaks, and the sun was slanting down through the edge of the clouds and gleaming off the tiny threads of snow in the high gullies.

The guy at the roadblock looped the tape off the trees and the car crawled through. It climbed onward, past the isolated houses every mile or so, all the way to the bend before the Lamarr place, where it stopped.

"You need to walk from here," the driver said.

He stayed in the car, and Harper and Reacher stepped out and started walking. The air was damp, full of a kind of suspended drizzle that wasn't really rain but wasn't dry weather either. They rounded the curve and saw the house on the left, crouching low behind its fence and its wind-battered trees, with the road snaking by on the right. The road was blocked by a gaggle of cars. There was a local police black-and-white with its roof lights flashing aimlessly. A pair of plain dark sedans and a black Suburban with black glass. A coroner's wagon, standing with all its doors open. The vehicles were all beaded with raindrops.

They walked closer and the front passenger door on the Suburban opened up and Nelson Blake slid out to meet them. He was in a dark suit with the coat collar turned up against the damp. His face was nearer gray than red, like shock had knocked his blood pressure down. He was all business. No greeting. No apologies, no pleasantries. No I-was-wrong-and-you-were-right.

"Not much more than an hour of daylight left, up here," he said. "I want you to walk me through what you did the day before yesterday, tell me what's different."

Reacher nodded. He suddenly wanted to find something. Something important. Something crucial. Not for Blake. For Alison. He stood and gazed at the fence and the trees and the lawn. They were cared for. They were just trivial rearrangements of an insignificant portion of the planet's surface, but they were motivated by the honest tastes and enthusiasms of a woman now dead. Achieved by her own labors.

"Who's been in there already?" he asked.

"Just the local uniformed guy," Blake said. "The one that found her."

"Nobody else?"

"Nobody."

"Not even you guys or the coroner?"

Blake shook his head. "I wanted your input first."

"So she's still in there?"

"Yes, I'm afraid she is."

The road was quiet. Just a hiss of breeze in the power lines. The red and blue light from the police cruiser's light bar washed over the suit on Blake's back, rhythmically and uselessly.

"OK," Reacher said. "The uniformed guy mess with anything?"

Blake shook his head again. "Opened the door, walked around downstairs, went upstairs, found his way to the bathroom, came right out again and called it in. His dispatcher had the good sense to keep him from going back inside."

"Front door was unlocked?"

"Closed, but unlocked."

"Did he knock?"

"I guess."

"So his prints will be on the knocker, too. And the inside door handles."

Blake shrugged. "Won't matter. Won't have smudged our guy's prints, because our guy doesn't leave prints."

Reacher nodded. "OK."

He walked past the parked vehicles and on past the mouth of the driveway. He walked twenty yards up the road.

"Where does this go?" he called.

Blake was ten yards behind him. "Back of beyond, probably."

"It's narrow, isn't it?"

"I've seen wider," Blake allowed.

Reacher strolled back to join him. "So you should check the mud on the shoulders, maybe up around the next bend."

"What for?"

"Our guy came in from the Spokane road, most likely. Cruised the house, kept on going, turned around, came back. He'd want his car facing the right direction, before he went in and got to work. A guy like this, he'll have been thinking about the getaway."

Blake nodded. "OK. I'll put somebody on it. Meantime, take me through the house."

He called instructions to his team and Reacher joined Harper in the mouth of the driveway. They stood and waited for Blake to catch up with them.

"So walk me through it," he said.

"We paused here for a second," Harper said. "It was awful quiet. Then we walked up to the door, used the knocker."

"Was the weather wet or dry?" Blake asked her.

She glanced at Reacher. "Dry, I guess. A little sunny. Not hot. But not raining."

"The driveway was dry," Reacher said. "Not dusty dry, but the shale had drained."

"So you wouldn't have picked up grit on your shoes?"

"I doubt it."

"OK."

They were at the door.

"Put these on your feet," Blake said. He pulled a roll

of large-sized food bags from his coat pocket. They put a bag over each shoe and tucked the plastic edges down inside the leather.

"She opened up, second knock," Harper said. "I showed her my badge in the spyhole."

"She was pretty uptight," Reacher said. "Told us Julia had been warning her."

Blake nodded sourly and nudged the door with his bagged foot. The door swung back with the same creak of old hinges Reacher remembered from before.

"We all paused here in the hallway," Harper said. "Then she offered us coffee and we all went through to the kitchen to get it."

"Anything different in here?" Blake asked.

Reacher looked around. The pine walls, the pine floors, the yellow gingham curtains, the old sofas, the converted oil lamps.

"Nothing different," he said.

"OK, kitchen," Blake said.

They filed into the kitchen. The floor was still waxed to a shine. The cabinets were the same, the range was cold and empty, the machines under the counter were the same, the gadgets sitting out were undisturbed. There were dishes in the sink and one of the silverware drawers was open an inch.

"The view is different," Harper said. She was standing at the window. "Much grayer today."

"Dishes in the sink," Reacher said. "And that drawer was closed."

They crowded the sink. There was a single plate, a water glass, a mug, a knife and a fork. Smears of egg and toast crumbs on the plate, coffee mud in the mug.

"Breakfast?" Blake said.

"Or dinner," Harper answered. "An egg on toast, that could be dinner for a single woman."

Blake pulled the drawer with the tip of his finger. There was a bunch of cheap flatware in there, and a random assortment of household tools, small screwdrivers, wire strippers, electrical tape, fuse wire.

"OK, then what?" Blake asked.

"I stayed here with her," Harper said. "Reacher looked around."

"Show me," Blake said.

He followed Reacher back to the hallway.

"I checked the parlor and the living room," Reacher said. "Looked at the windows. I figured they were secure."

Blake nodded. "Guy didn't come in the windows."

"Then I went outside, checked the grounds and the barn."

"We'll do the upstairs first," Blake said.

"OK."

Reacher led the way. He was very conscious of where he was going. Very conscious that maybe thirty hours ago the guy had followed the same path.

"I checked the bedrooms. Went into the master suite last."

"Let's do it," Blake said.

They walked the length of the master bedroom. Paused at the bathroom door.

"Let's do it," Blake said again.

They looked inside. The place was immaculate. No sign that anything had ever happened there, except for the tub. It was seven-eighths full of green paint, with the shape of a small muscular woman floating just below the surface, which had skinned over into a slick plastic layer, delineating her body and trapping it there. Every contour was visible. The thighs, the stomach, the breasts. The head, tilted backward. The chin, the forehead. The mouth, held slightly open, the lips drawn back in a tiny grimace.

"Shit," Reacher said.

"Yeah, shit," Blake said back.

Reacher stood there and tried to read the signs. Tried to *find* the signs. But there were none there. The bathroom was exactly the same as it had been before.

"Anything?" Blake asked.

He shook his head. "No."

"OK, we'll do the outside."

They trooped down the stairs, silent. Harper was waiting in the hallway. She looked up at Blake, expectant. Blake just shook his head, like he was saying *nothing there*. Maybe he was saying *don't go up there*. Reacher led him out through the back door into the yard.

"I checked the windows from outside," he said.

"Guy didn't come in the damn window," Blake said for the second time. "He came in the door."

"But how the hell?" Reacher said. "When we were here, you'd called her ahead on the phone, and Harper was flashing her badge and shouting *FBI, FBI*, and she *still* practically hid out in there. And then she was shaking like a leaf when she eventually opened up. So how did this guy get her to do it?"

Blake shrugged. "Like I told you right at the beginning, these women *know* this character. They trust him. He's some kind of an old friend or something. He knocks on the door, they check him out in the spyhole, they get a big smile on their faces, and they open their doors right up."

The cellar door was undisturbed. The big padlock through the handles was intact. The garage door in the side of the barn was closed but not locked. Reacher led Blake inside and stood, in the gloom. The new Jeep was there, and the stacks of cartons. The big washing machine carton was there, flaps slightly open, sealing tape trailing. The workbench was there, with the power tools neatly laid out on it. The shelves were undisturbed.

"Something's different," Reacher said.

"What?"

"Let me think."

He stood there, opening and closing his eyes, comparing the scene in front of him with the memory in his head, like he was checking two photographs side by side.

"The car has moved," he said.

Blake sighed, like he was disappointed. "It would have. She drove to the hospital after you left."

Reacher nodded. "Something else."

"What?"

"Let me think."

Then he saw it.

"Shit," he said.

"What?"

"I missed it. I'm sorry, Blake, but I missed it."

"Missed what?"

"That washing machine carton. She already had a washing machine. Looked brand-new. It's in the kitchen, under the counter."

"So? It must have come right out of that carton. Whenever it was installed."

Reacher shook his head. "No. Two days ago that carton was new and sealed up. Now it's been opened."

"You sure?"

"I'm sure. Same carton, exact same place. But it was sealed up then and it's open now."

Blake stepped toward the carton. Took a pen from his pocket and used the plastic barrel to raise the flap. Stared down at what he saw.

"This carton was here already?"

Reacher nodded. "Sealed up."

"Like it had been shipped?"

"Yes."

"OK," Blake said. "Now we know how he transports the paint. He delivers it ahead of time in washing machine cartons."

You sit there cold and sweating for an hour and at the end of it you know for certain you forgot to reseal the carton. You didn't do it, and you didn't make her do it. That's a fact now, and it can't be denied, and it needs dealing with.

Because resealing the cartons guaranteed a certain amount of delay. You know how investigators work. A just delivered appliance carton in the garage or the basement was going to attract no interest at all. It was going to be way down on the list of priorities. It would be just another part of the normal household clutter they see everywhere. Practically invisible. You're smart. You know how these people work. Your best guess was the primary investigators would never open it at all. That was your prediction, and

*you were proved absolutely right three times in a row.
Down in Florida, up in New Hampshire, down in California, those boxes were items on somebody's inventory, but
they hadn't been opened. Maybe much later when the heirs
came to clear out the houses they'd open them up and find
all the empty cans, whereupon the shit would really hit the
fan, but by then it would be way too late. A guaranteed
delay, weeks or even months.*

*But this time, it would be different. They'd do a walk-
through in the garage, and the flaps on the box would be
up. Cardboard does that, especially in a damp atmosphere
like they have up there. The flaps would be curling back.
They'd glance in, and they wouldn't see Styrofoam packag-
ing and gleaming white enamel, would they?*

THEY BROUGHT IN portable arc lights from the Suburban
and arrayed them around the washing machine carton
like it was a meteor from Mars. They stood there, bent
forward from the waist like the whole thing was radioac-
tive. They stared at it, trying to decode its secrets.

It was a normal-sized appliance carton, built out of
sturdy brown cardboard folded and stapled the way appliance cartons are. The brown board was screen-printed
with black ink. The manufacturer's name dominated each
of the four sides. A famous name, styled and printed like
a trademark. There was the model number of the washing machine below it, and a crude picture representing
the machine itself.

The sealing tape was brown, too. It had been slit
along the top to allow the box to open. Inside the box
was nothing at all except ten three-gallon paint cans.
They were stacked in two layers of five. The lids were

resting on the tops of the cans like they had been laid back into position after use. They were distorted here and there around the circumference where an implement had been used to lever them off. The rims of the cans each had a neat tongue-shaped run of dried color where the paint had been poured out.

The cans themselves were plain metal cylinders. No manufacturer's name. No trademark. No boasts about quality or durability or coverage. Just a small printed label stenciled with a long number and the small words *Camo/Green*.

"These normal?" Blake asked.

Reacher nodded. "Standard-issue field supply."

"Who uses them?"

"Any unit with vehicles. They carry them around for small repairs and touch-ups. Vehicle workshops would use bigger drums and spray guns."

"So they're not rare?"

Reacher shook his head. "The exact opposite of rare."

There was silence in the garage.

"OK, take them out," Blake said.

A crime scene technician wearing latex gloves leaned over and lifted the cans out of the carton, one by one. He lined them up on Alison Lamarr's workbench. Then he folded the flaps of the carton back. Angled a lamp to throw light inside. The bottom of the box had five circular imprints pressed deep into the cardboard.

"The cans were full when they went in there," the tech said.

Blake stepped back, out of the pool of blazing light, into the shadow. He turned his back on the box and stared at the wall.

"So how did it get here?" he asked.

Reacher shrugged. "Like you said, it was delivered, ahead of time."

"Not by the guy."

"No. He wouldn't come twice."

"So by who?"

"By a shipping company. The guy sent it on ahead. FedEx or UPS or somebody."

"But appliances get delivered by the store where you buy them. On a local truck."

"Not this one," Reacher said. "This didn't come from any appliance store."

Blake sighed, like the world had gone mad. Then he turned back and stepped into the light again. Stared at the box. Walked all around it. One side showed damage. There was a shape, roughly square, where the surface of the cardboard had been torn away. The layer underneath showed through, raw and exposed. The angle of the arc lights emphasized its corrugated structure.

"Shipping label," Blake said.

"Maybe one of those little plastic envelopes," Reacher said. "You know, 'Documents enclosed.'"

"So where is it? Who tore it off? Not the shipping company. They don't tear them off."

"The guy tore it off," Reacher said. "Afterward. So we can't trace it back."

He paused. He'd said *we*. Not *you*. *So we can't trace it back*. Not *so you can't trace it back*. Blake noticed it too, and glanced up.

"But how can the delivery happen?" he asked. "In the first place? Say you're Alison Lamarr, just sitting there at home, and UPS or FedEx or somebody shows up with a washing machine you never ordered? You wouldn't accept the delivery, right?"

"Maybe it came when she was out," Reacher said. "Maybe when she was up at the hospital with her dad. Maybe the driver just wheeled it into the garage and left it."

"Wouldn't he need a signature?"

Reacher shrugged again. "I don't know. I've never had a washing machine delivered. I guess sometimes they don't need a signature. The guy who sent it probably specified no signature required."

"But she'd have seen it right there, next time she went in the garage. Soon as she stashed her car, when she got back."

Reacher nodded. "Yes, she must have. It's big enough."

"So what then?"

"She calls UPS or FedEx or whoever. Maybe she tore off the envelope herself. Carried it into the house, to the phone, to give them the details."

"Why didn't she unpack it?"

Reacher made a face. "She figures it's not really hers, why would she unpack it? She'd only have to box it up again."

"She mention anything to you or Harper? Anything about unexplained deliveries?"

"No. But then she might not have connected it. Foul-ups happen, right? Normal part of life."

Blake nodded. "Well, if the details are in the house, we'll find them. Crime scene people are going to spend some time in there, soon as the coroner is through."

"Coroner won't find anything," Reacher said.

Blake looked grim. "This time, he'll have to."

"So you're going to have to do it differently," Reacher said. He concentrated on the *you*. "You should take the whole tub out. Take it over to some big lab in Seattle. Maybe fly it all the way back to Quantico."

"How the hell can we take the whole tub out?"

"Tear the wall out. Tear the roof off, use a crane."

Blake paused and thought about it. "I guess we could. We'd need permission, of course. But this must be Julia's house now, in the circumstances, right? She's next of kin, I guess."

Reacher nodded. "So call her. Ask her. Get permission. And get her to check the field reports from the other three places. This delivery thing might be a one-shot deal, but if it isn't, it changes everything."

"Changes everything how?"

"Because it means it isn't a guy with time to drive a truck all over the place. It means it could be anybody, using the airlines, in and out quick as you like."

BLAKE WENT BACK to the Suburban to make his calls, and Harper found Reacher and walked him fifty yards up the road to where agents from the Spokane office had spotted tire marks in the mud on the shoulders. It had gone dark and they were using flashlights. There were four separate marks in the mud. It was clear what had happened. Somebody had swung nose-in to the left shoulder, wound the power steering around, backed across the road and put the rear tires on the right shoulder, and then swooped away back the way he had come. The front-tire marks were scrubbed into fan shapes by the operation of the steering, but the rear-tire marks opposite were clear enough. They were not wide, not narrow.

"Probably a midsize sedan," the Spokane guy said. "Fairly new radial tires, maybe a 195/70, maybe a fourteen-inch wheel. We'll get the exact tire from the tread pattern. And we'll measure the width between the marks, maybe get the exact model of the car."

"You think it's the guy?" Harper asked.

Reacher nodded. "Got to be, right? Think about it. Anybody else hunting the address sees the house a hundred yards ahead and slows enough to check the mailbox and stop. Even if they don't, they overshoot a couple of yards and just back right up. They don't overshoot fifty yards and wait until they're around the corner to turn. This was a guy cruising the place, watching out, staying cautious. It was him, no doubt about it."

They left the Spokane guys setting up miniature waterproof tents over the marks and walked back toward the house. Blake was standing by the Suburban, waiting, lit from behind by the dome light inside.

"We've got appliance cartons listed at all three scenes," he said. "No information about contents. Nobody thought to look. We're sending local agents back to check. Could be an hour. And Julia says we should go ahead and rip the tub out. I'm going to need some engineers, I guess."

Reacher nodded vaguely and paused, immobilized by a new line of thought.

"You should check on something else," he said. "You should get the list of the eleven women, call the seven he hasn't gotten to yet. You should ask them."

Blake looked at him. "Ask them what? Hi, you still alive?"

"No, ask them if they've had any deliveries they weren't expecting. Any appliances they never ordered. Because if this guy is speeding up, maybe the next one is all ready and set to go."

Blake looked at him some more, and then he nodded and ducked back inside the Suburban and took the car phone out of its cradle.

"Get Poulton to do it," Reacher called. "Too emotional for Lamarr."

Blake just stared at him, but he asked for Poulton anyway. Told him what he wanted and hung up within a minute.

"Now we wait," he said.

"SIR!" THE CORPORAL said.

The list was in the drawer, and the drawer was locked. The colonel was motionless at his desk, staring into the electric gloom of his windowless office, focusing on nothing, thinking hard, trying to recover. The best way to recover would be to talk to somebody. He knew that. *A problem shared is a problem halved.* That's how it works inside a giant institution like the Army. But he couldn't talk to anybody about *this*, of course. He smiled a bitter smile. Stared at the wall, and kept on thinking. *Faith in yourself*, that's what would do it. He was concentrating so hard on recapturing it he must have missed the knock at the door. Afterward he figured it must have been repeated several times, and he was glad he had the list in the drawer, because when the corporal eventually came in he couldn't have hidden it. He couldn't have done anything. He was just motionless, and evidently he was looking blank, because right away the corporal started acting worried.

"Sir?" he said again.

He didn't reply. Didn't move his gaze from the wall.

"Colonel?" the corporal said.

He moved his head like it weighed a ton. Said nothing.

"Your car is here, sir," the corporal said.

THEY WAITED AN hour and a half, crowded inside the Suburban. The evening crept toward night; and it grew very cold. Dense night dew misted the outside of the windshield and the windows. Breathing fogged the inside. Nobody talked. The world around them grew quieter. There was an occasional animal noise in the far distance, howling down at them through the thin mountain air, but there was nothing else at all.

"Hell of a place to live," Blake muttered.

"Or to die," Harper said.

EVENTUALLY YOU RECOVER, and then you relax. You've got a lot of talent. Everything was backed up, double-safe, triple-safe. You put in layer upon layer upon layer of concealment. You know how investigators work. You know they won't find anything beyond the obvious. They won't find where the paint came from. Or who obtained it. Or who delivered it. You know they won't. You know how these people work. And you're too smart for them. Way, way too smart. So you relax.

But you're disappointed. You made a mistake. And the paint was a lot of fun. And now you probably can't use it anymore. But maybe you can think of something even bet-

*ter. Because one thing is for damn sure. You can't stop
now.*

THE PHONE RANG inside the Suburban. It was a loud
electronic blast in the silence. Blake fumbled it out of
the cradle. Reacher heard the indistinct sound of a
voice talking fast. A man's voice, not a woman's. Poulton, not Lamarr. Blake listened hard with his eyes focused nowhere. Then he hung up and stared at the
windshield.

"What?" Harper asked.

"Local guys went back and checked the appliance cartons," Blake said. "They were all sealed up tight, like
new. But they opened them anyway. Ten paint cans in
each of them. Ten empty cans. Used cans, exactly like
we found."

"But the boxes were sealed?" Reacher said.

"Resealed," Blake said. "They could tell, when they
looked closely. The guy resealed the boxes, afterward."

"Smart guy," Harper said. "He knew a sealed carton
wouldn't attract much attention."

Blake nodded to her. "A *very* smart guy. He knows
how we think."

"But not totally smart anymore," Reacher said. "Or
he wouldn't have forgotten to reseal this one, right? His
first mistake."

"He's batting about nine hundred," Blake said. "That
makes him smart enough for me."

"No shipping labels anywhere?" Harper asked.

Blake shook his head. "All torn off."

"Figures," she said.

"Does it?" Reacher asked her. "So here, why should

he remember to tear off the label but forget to reseal the box?"

"Maybe he got interrupted here," she said.

"How? This isn't exactly Times Square."

"So what are you saying? You're downgrading how smart he is? How smart he is seemed awful important to you before. You were going to use how damn smart he is to prove us all wrong."

Reacher looked at her and nodded. "Yes, you are all wrong." Then he turned to Blake. "We really need to talk about this guy's motive."

"Later," Blake said.

"No, now. It's important."

"Later," Blake said again. "You haven't heard the really good news yet."

"Which is what?"

"The other little matter you came up with."

Silence inside the vehicle.

"Shit," Reacher said. "One of the other women got a delivery, right?"

Blake shook his head.

"Wrong," he said. "All *seven* of them got a delivery."

16

"SO YOU'RE GOING to Portland, Oregon," Blake said. "You and Harper."

"Why?" Reacher asked.

"So you can visit with your old friend Rita Scimeca. The lady lieutenant you told us about? Got raped down in Georgia? She lives near Portland. Small village, east of the city. She's one of the eleven on your list. You can get down there and check out her basement. She says there's a brand-new washing machine in there. In a box."

"Did she open it?" Reacher asked.

Blake shook his head. "No, Portland agents checked with her on the telephone. They told her not to touch it. Somebody's on the way over right now."

"If the guy's still in the area, Portland could be his next call. It's close enough."

"Correct," Blake said. "That's why there's somebody on the way over."

Reacher nodded. "So now you're guarding them? What's that thing about barn doors and horses bolting?"

Blake shrugged. "Hey, only seven left alive, makes the manpower much more feasible."

It was a cop's sick humor in a car full of cops of one kind or another, but still it fell a little flat. Blake colored slightly and looked away.

"Losing Alison gets to me, much as anybody," he said. "Like family, right?"

"Especially to her sister, I guess," Reacher said.

"Tell me about it," Blake said. "She was burned as hell when the news came in. Practically hyperventilating. Never seen her so agitated."

"You should take her off the case."

Blake shook his head. "I need her."

"You need something, that's for damn sure."

"Tell me about it."

SPOKANE TO THE small village east of Portland measured about three hundred and sixty miles on the map Blake showed them. They took the car the local agent had used to bring them in from the airport. It still had Alison Lamarr's address handwritten on the top sheet of the pad attached to the windshield. Reacher stared at it for a second. Then he tore it off and balled it up and tossed it into the rear footwell. Found a pen in the glove box and wrote directions on the next sheet: *90W-395S-84W-35S-26W*. He wrote them big enough to see them in the dark when they were tired. Underneath the big figures, he could still see Alison Lamarr's address, printed through by the pressure of the local guy's ball-point.

"Call it six hours," Harper said. "You drive three and I'll drive three."

Reacher nodded. It was completely dark when he started the engine. He turned around in the road, shoulder to shoulder, spinning the wheel, exactly like he was sure the guy had done, but two days later and two hundred yards south. Rolled through the narrow downhill curves to Route 90 and turned right. Once the lights of the city were behind them the traffic density fell away and he settled to a fast cruise west. The car was a new Buick, smaller and plainer than Lamarr's boat, but maybe a little faster because of it. That year must have been the Bureau's GM year. The Army had done the same thing. Staff car purchasing rotated strictly between GM, Ford, and Chrysler, so none of the domestic manufacturers could get pissed at the government.

The road ran straight southwest through hilly terrain. He put the headlights on bright and eased the speed upward. Harper sprawled to his right, her seat reclined, her head tilted toward him. Her hair spilled down and glowed red and gold in the lights from the dash. He kept one hand on the wheel, the other resting down in his lap. He could see lights in his mirror. Halogen headlights, on bright, swinging and bouncing a mile behind him. They were closing, fast. He accelerated to more than seventy.

"The Army teach you to drive this fast?" Harper asked.

He made no reply. They passed a town called Sprague and the road straightened. Blake's map had shown it dead straight all the way to a town called Ritzville, twenty-something miles ahead. Reacher eased up toward eighty miles an hour, but the headlights behind were still closing fast. A long moment later a car blasted past them, a long low sedan, a wide maneuver, turbulent slip-stream, a full quarter-mile in the opposite lane. Then it eased back right and pulled on ahead like the FBI's Buick was crawling through a parking lot.

"*That's* fast," Reacher said.

"Maybe that's the guy," Harper said sleepily. "Maybe he's heading down to Portland too. Maybe we'll get him tonight."

"I've changed my mind," Reacher said. "I don't think he drives. I think he flies."

But he eased the speed a little higher anyway, to keep the distant taillights in sight.

"And then what?" Harper said. "He rents a car at the local airport?"

Reacher nodded in the dark. "That's my guess. Those tire prints they found? Very standard size. Probably some anonymous midsize midrange sedan the rental companies have millions of."

"Risky," Harper said. "Renting cars leaves a paper trail."

Reacher nodded again. "So does buying airplane tickets. But this guy is real organized. I'm sure he's got cast-iron false ID. Following the paper trail won't get anybody anywhere."

"Well, we'll do it anyway, I guess. And it means he's been face-to-face with people at the rental counters."

"Maybe not. Maybe he books ahead and gets express pickup."

Harper nodded. "The return guy would see him, though."

"Briefly."

The road was straight enough to see the fast car a mile ahead. Reacher found himself easing up over ninety, pacing himself behind it.

"How long does it take to kill a person?" Harper asked.

"Depends how you do it," Reacher said.

"And we don't know how he's doing it."

"No, we don't. That's something we need to figure. But whatever way, he's pretty calm and careful about it. No mess anywhere, no spilled paint. My guess is it's got to be twenty, thirty minutes, minimum."

Harper nodded and stretched. Reacher caught a breath of her perfume as she moved.

"So think about Spokane," she said. "He gets off the plane, picks up the car, drives a half hour to Alison's place, spends a half hour there, drives a half hour back, and gets the hell out. He wouldn't hang around, right?"

"Not near the scene, I guess," Reacher said.

"So the rental car could be returned within less than two hours. We should check real short rentals from the airports local to the scenes, see if there's a pattern."

Reacher nodded. "Yes, you should. That's how you'll do this thing, regular hard work."

Harper moved again. Turned sideways in her seat. "Sometimes you say *we* and sometimes you say *you*. You haven't made up your mind, but you're softening a little, you know that?"

"I liked Alison, I guess, what I saw of her."

"And?"

"And I like Rita Scimeca too, what I remember of her. I wouldn't want anything to happen."

Harper craned her head and watched the taillights a mile ahead.

"So keep that guy in sight," she said.

"He flies," Reacher said. "That's not the guy."

IT WASN'T THE guy. At the far limit of Ritzville he stayed on Route 90, swinging west toward Seattle. Reacher peeled off south onto 395, heading straight for Oregon. The road was still empty, but it was narrower and twistier, so he took some of the urgency out of his pace and let the car settle back to its natural cruise.

"Tell me about Rita Scimeca," Harper said.

Reacher shrugged at the wheel. "She was a little like Alison Lamarr, I guess. Didn't look the same, but she had the same feel about her. Tough, sporty, capable. Very unfazed by anything, as I recall. She was a second lieutenant. Great record. She blitzed the officer training."

He fell silent. He was picturing Rita Scimeca in his mind, and imagining her standing shoulder to shoulder with Alison Lamarr. Two fine women, as good as any the Army would ever get.

"So here's another puzzle," he said. "How is the guy controlling them?"

"Controlling?" Harper repeated.

Reacher nodded. "Think about it. He gets into their houses, and thirty minutes later they're dead in the tub, naked, not a mark on them. No disturbance, no mess. How is he doing that?"

"Points a gun, I guess."

Reacher shook his head. "Two things wrong with that. If he's coming in by plane, he doesn't have a gun. You can't bring a gun on a plane. You know that, right? You didn't bring yours."

"*If* he's coming in by plane. That's only a guess right now."

"OK, but I was just thinking about Rita Scimeca. She was a real tough cookie. She was raped, which is how she got on this guy's list, I guess, because three men went to prison and got canned for it. But *five* guys came to get her that night. Only three of them got as far as raping her, because one guy got a broken pelvis and another guy got two broken arms. In other words, she fought like hell."

"So?"

"So wouldn't Alison Lamarr have done the same thing? Even if the guy did have a gun, would Alison Lamarr have been meek and passive for thirty straight minutes?"

"I don't know," Harper said.

"You saw her. She was no kind of a wallflower. She was Army. She had infantry training. Either she'd have gotten mad and started a fight, or she'd have bided her time and tried to nail the guy somewhere along the way. But she didn't, apparently. Why not?"

"I don't know," Harper said again.

"Neither do I," Reacher said back.

"We have to find this guy."

Reacher shook his head. "You're not going to."

"Why not?"

"Because you're all so blinded by this profiling shit you're wrong about the motive, is why not."

Harper turned away and stared out of the window at the blackness speeding past.

"You want to amplify that?" she said.

"Not until I get Blake and Lamarr sitting still and paying attention. I'm only going to say it once."

THEY STOPPED FOR gas just after they crossed the Columbia River outside of Richland. Reacher filled the tank and Harper went inside to the bathroom. Then she came out again and got into the car on the driver's side, ready for her three hours at the wheel. She slid her seat forward while he slid his backward. Raked her hair behind her shoulders and adjusted the mirror. Twisted the key and fired it up. Took off again south and eased her way up to a cruise.

They crossed the Columbia again after it looped away west and then they were in Oregon. I-84 followed the river, right on the state line. It was a fast, empty highway. Up ahead, the vastness of the Cascade Range loomed unseen in the blackness. The stars burned cold and tiny in the sky. Reacher lay back in his seat and watched them through the curve of the side glass, where it met the roof. It was nearly midnight.

"You need to talk to me," Harper said. "Or I'll fall asleep at the wheel."

"You're as bad as Lamarr," Reacher said.

Harper grinned in the dark. "Not quite."

"No, not quite, I guess," Reacher said.

"But talk to me anyway. Why did you leave the Army?"

"That's what you want to talk about?"

"It's a topic, I guess."

"Why does everybody ask me that?"

She shrugged. "People are curious."

"Why? Why shouldn't I leave the Army?"

"Because I think you enjoyed it. Like I enjoy the FBI."

"A lot of it was very irritating."

She nodded. "Sure. The Bureau's very irritating too. Like a husband, I guess. Good points and bad points, but they're *my* points, you know what I mean? You don't get a divorce because of a little irritation."

"They downsized me out of there," he said.

"No, they didn't. We read your record. They downsized *numbers*, but they didn't target you. You volunteered to go."

He was quiet for a mile or two. Then he nodded.

"I got scared," he said.

She glanced at him. "Of what?"

"I liked it the way it was. I didn't want it to change."

"Into what?"

"Something smaller, I guess. It was a huge, huge thing. You've got no idea. It stretched all around the world. They were going to make it smaller. I'd have gotten promotion, so I would have been higher up in a smaller organization."

"What's wrong with that? Big fish in a small pond, right?"

"I didn't want to be a big fish," he said. "I liked being a small fish."

"You weren't a small fish," she said. "A major isn't small."

He nodded. "OK, I liked being a medium-sized fish. It was comfortable. Kind of anonymous."

She shook her head. "That's not enough reason to quit."

He looked up at the stars. They were stationary in the sky, a billion miles above him.

"A big fish in a small pond has no place to swim," he said. "I'd have been in one place, years at a time. Some big desk someplace, then five years on, another bigger desk some other place. Guy like me, no political skills, no social graces, I'd have made full colonel and no farther. I'd have served out my time stuck there. Could have been fifteen or twenty years."

"But?"

"But I wanted to keep moving. All my life, I've been moving, literally. I was scared to stop. I didn't know what being stuck somewhere would feel like, but my guess was I'd hate it."

"And?"

He shrugged. "And now I *am* stuck someplace."

"And?" she said again.

He shrugged again and said nothing. It was warm in the car. Warm, and comfortable.

"Say the words, Reacher," she said. "Get it out. You're stuck someplace, and?"

"And nothing."

"Bullshit, nothing. And?"

He took a deep breath. "And I'm having a problem with it."

The car went quiet. She nodded, like she understood. "Jodie doesn't want to keep moving around, I guess."

"Well, would *you*?"

"I don't know."

He nodded. "Problem is, she *does* know. She and I

grew up the same, always moving, base to base to base, all around the world, a month here, six months there. So she lives the life she lives because she went out there and created it for herself, because it's exactly what she wants. She knows it's exactly what she wants because she knows exactly what the alternative is."

"She could move around a little. She's a lawyer. She could change jobs, time to time."

He shook his head. "Doesn't work that way. It's about career. She'll make partner sometime real soon, the way she's going, and then she'll probably work at the same firm her whole life. And anyway, I'm not talking about a couple of years here, three years there, buy a house, sell a house. I'm talking about if I wake up in Oregon tomorrow and I feel like going to Oklahoma or Texas or somewhere, I just go. With no idea about where I'm going the next day."

"A wanderer."

"It's important to me."

"How important, though?"

He shrugged. "I don't know, exactly."

"How are you going to find out?"

"Problem is, I *am* finding out."

"So what are you going to do?"

He was quiet for another mile.

"I don't know," he said.

"You might get used to it."

"I might," he said. "But I might not. It feels awful deep in my blood. Like right now, middle of the night, heading down the road someplace I've never been, I feel real good. I just can't explain how good I feel."

She smiled. "Maybe it's the company."

He smiled back. "Maybe it is."

"So will you tell me something else?"

"Like what?"

"Why are we wrong about this guy's motive?"

He shook his head. "Wait until we see what we find in Portland."

"What are we going to find in Portland?"

"My guess is a carton full of paint cans, with absolutely no clue as to where they came from or who sent them there."

"So?"

"So then we put two and two together and make four. The way you guys have got it, you ain't making four. You're making some big inexplicable number that's a long, long way from four."

REACHER RACKED HIS seat back a little more and dozed through most of Harper's final hour at the wheel. The second-to-last leg of the trip took them up the northern flank of Mount Hood on Route 35. The Buick changed down to third gear to cope with the gradient, and the jerk from the transmission woke him again. He watched through the windshield as the road looped around behind the peak. Then Harper found Route 26 and swung west for the final approach, down the mountainside, toward the city of Portland.

The nighttime view was spectacular. There was broken cloud high in the sky, and a bright moon, and starlight. There was snow piled in the gullies. The world was like a jagged sculpture in gray steel, glowing below them.

"I can see the attraction of wandering," Harper said. "Sight like this."

Reacher nodded. "It's a big, big planet."

They passed through a sleeping town called Rhododendron and saw a sign pointing ahead to Rita Scimeca's village, five miles farther down the slope. When they got there, it was nearly three in the morning. There was a gas station and a general store on the through road. Both of them were closed up tight. There was a cross street running north into the lower slope of the mountain. Harper nosed up it. The cross street had cross streets of its own. Scimeca's was the third of them. It ran east up the slope.

Her house was easy to spot. It was the only one on the street with lights in the windows. And the only one with a Bureau sedan parked outside. Harper stopped behind the sedan and turned off her lights and the motor died with a little shudder and silence enveloped them. The rear window of the Bureau car was misted with breath and there was a single head silhouetted in it. The head moved and the sedan door opened and a young man in a dark suit stepped out. Reacher and Harper stretched and unclipped their belts and opened their doors. Slid out and stood in the chill air with their breath clouding around them.

"She's in there, safe and sound," the local guy said to them. "I was told to wait out here for you."

Harper nodded. "And then what?"

"Then I stay out here," the guy said. "You do all the talking. I'm security detail until the local cops take over, eight in the morning."

"The cops going to cover twenty-four hours a day?" Reacher asked.

The guy shook his head, miserably.

"Twelve," he said. "I do the nights."

Reacher nodded. *Good enough*, he thought. The house was a big square clapboard structure, built side-on to the street so the front faced the view to the west. There was a generous front porch with gingerbread railings. The slope of the street made room for a garage under the house at the front. The garage door faced sideways, under the end of the porch. There was a short driveway. Then the land sloped upward, so that the rest of the basement would be dug into the hillside. The lot was small, surrounded with tall hurricane fencing marching up the rise. The yard was cultivated, with flowers everywhere, the color taken out of them by the silver moonlight.

"She awake?" Harper asked.

The local guy nodded. "She's in there waiting for you."

17

A WALKWAY CAME off the driveway on the left and looped through the dark around some rockery plantings to a set of wide wooden steps in the center of the front porch. Harper skipped up them but Reacher's weight made them creak in the night silence and before the echo of the sound came back from the hills the front door was open and Rita Scimeca was standing there watching them. She had one hand on the inside doorknob and a blank look on her face.

"Hello, Reacher," she said.

"Scimeca," he said back. "How are you?"

She used her free hand to push her hair off her brow.

"Reasonable," she said. "Considering it's three o'clock in the morning and the FBI has only just gotten around to telling me I'm on some kind of hit list with ten of my sisters, four of whom are already dead."

"Your tax dollars at work," Reacher said.

"So why the hell are you hanging with them?"

He shrugged. "Circumstances didn't leave me a whole lot of choice."

She gazed at him, deciding. It was cold on the porch. The night dew was beading on the painted boards. There was a thin low fog in the air. Behind Scimeca's shoulder the lights inside her house burned warm and yellow. She looked at him a moment longer.

"Circumstances?" she repeated.

He nodded. "Didn't leave me a whole lot of choice."

She nodded back. "Well, whatever, it's kind of good to see you, I guess."

"Good to see you, too."

She was a tall woman. Shorter than Harper, but then most women were. She was muscular, not the compact way Alison Lamarr had been, but the lean, marathon-runner kind of way. She was dressed in clean jeans and a shapeless sweater. Substantial shoes on her feet. She had medium-length brown hair, worn in long bangs above bright brown eyes. She had heavy frown lines all around her mouth. It was nearly four years since he had last seen her, and she looked the whole four years older.

"This is Special Agent Lisa Harper," he said.

Scimeca nodded once, warily. Reacher watched her eyes. A male agent, she'd have thrown him off the porch.

"Hi," Harper said.

"Well, come on in, I guess," Scimeca said.

She still had hold of the doorknob. She was standing on the threshold, leaning forward, unwilling to step out. Harper stepped in and Reacher filed after her. The door closed behind them. They were in the hallway of a decent little house, newly painted, nicely furnished. Very clean, obsessively tidy. It looked like a home. Warm and cozy. A personal space. There were wool rugs on the floor. Polished antique furniture in gleaming mahogany. Paintings on the walls. Vases of flowers everywhere.

"Chrysanthemums," Scimeca said. "I grow them myself. You like them?"

Reacher nodded.

"I like them," he said. "Although I couldn't spell them."

"Gardening's my new hobby," Scimeca said. "I've gotten into it in a big way."

Then she pointed toward a front parlor.

"And music," she said. "Come see."

The room had quiet wallpaper and a polished wood floor. There was a grand piano in the back corner. Shiny black lacquer. A German name inlaid in brass. A big stool was placed in front of it, handsome buttoned leather in black. The lid of the piano was up, and there was music on the stand above the keyboard, a dense mass of black notes on heavy cream paper.

"Want to hear something?" she asked.

"Sure," Reacher said.

She slid between the keyboard and the stool and sat down. Laid her hands on the keys and paused for a second and then a mournful minor-key chord filled the room. It was a warm sound, and low, and she modulated it into the start of a funeral march.

"Got anything more cheerful?" Reacher asked.

"I don't feel cheerful," she said.

But she changed it anyway, into the start of the Moonlight Sonata.

"Beethoven," she said.

The silvery arpeggios filled the air. She had her foot on the damper and the sound was dulled and quiet. Reacher gazed out of the window at the plantings, gray in the moonlight. There was an ocean ninety miles to the west, vast and silent.

"That's better," he said.

She played it through to the end of the first movement, apparently from memory, because the music open on the stand was labeled Chopin. She kept her hands on the keys until the last chord died away to silence.

"Nice," Reacher said. "So, you're doing OK?"

She turned away from the keyboard and looked him in the eye. "You mean have I recovered from being gang-raped by three guys I was supposed to trust with my life?"

Reacher nodded. "Something like that, I guess."

"I thought I'd recovered," she said. "As well as I ever expected to. But now I hear some maniac is fixing to kill me for complaining about it. That's taken the edge off it a little bit, you know?"

"We'll get him," Harper said, in the silence.

Scimeca just looked at her.

"So can we see the new washing machine in the basement?" Reacher asked.

"It's not a washing machine, though, is it?" Scimeca asked. "Not that anybody tells *me* anything."

"It's probably paint," Reacher said. "In cans. Camouflage green, Army issue."

"What for?"

"The guy kills you, dumps you in your bathtub and pours it over you."

"Why?"

Reacher shrugged. "Good question. There's a whole bunch of pointy heads working on that right now."

Scimeca nodded and turned to Harper. "You a pointy head?"

"No, ma'am, I'm just an agent," Harper said.

"You ever been raped?"

Harper shook her head. "No, ma'am, I haven't."

Scimeca nodded again.

"Well, don't be," she said. "That's my advice."

There was silence.

"It changes your life," Scimeca said. "It changed mine, that's for damn sure. Gardening and music, that's all I've got now."

"Good hobbies," Harper said.

"Stay-at-home hobbies," Scimeca said back. "I'm either in this room or within sight of my front door. I don't get out much and I don't like meeting people. So take my advice, don't let it happen to you."

Harper nodded. "I'll try not to."

"Basement," Scimeca said.

She led the way out of the parlor to a door tucked under the stairs. It was an old door, made up of pine planks painted many times. There was a narrow staircase behind it, leading down toward cold air smelling faintly of gasoline and tire rubber.

"We have to go through the garage," Scimeca said.

There was a new car filling the space, a long low Chrysler sedan, painted gold. They walked single file along its flank and Scimeca opened a door in the garage wall. The musty smell of a basement bloomed out at them. Scimeca pulled a cord and a hot yellow light came on.

"There you are," she said.

The basement was warm from a furnace. It was a large square space with wide storage racks built on every wall. Fiberglass insulation showed between the ceiling joists. There were heating pipes snaking up through the floorboards. There was a carton standing alone in the middle of the floor. It was at an angle to the walls, untidy against the neat shelving surrounding it. It was the same carton. Same size, same brown board, same black printing, same picture, same manufacturer's name. It was taped shut with shiny brown tape and it looked brand-new.

"Got a knife?" Reacher asked.

Scimeca nodded toward a work area. There was pegboard screwed to the wall, and it was filled with tools hanging in neat rows. Reacher took a linoleum knife off a peg, carefully, because in his experience the peg usually came out with the tool. But not this one. He saw that each peg was secured to the board with a neat little plastic device.

He came back to the box and slit the tape. Reversed the knife and used the handle to ease the flaps upward. He saw five metal circles, glowing yellow. Five paint can lids, reflecting the overhead light. He poked the knife handle under one of the wire hoops and lifted one of the cans up to eye level. Rotated it in the light. It was a plain metal can, unadorned except for a small white label printed with a long number and the words *Camo/Green*.

"We've seen a few of those in our time," Scimeca said. "Right, Reacher?"

He nodded. "A few."

He lowered the can back into the box. Pushed the

flaps down and walked over and hung the knife back where it had been. Glanced across at Scimeca.

"When did this come?" he asked.

"I don't remember," she said.

"Roughly?"

"I don't know," she said. "Maybe a couple months ago."

"A couple of *months*?" Harper said.

Scimeca nodded. "I guess. I don't really remember."

"You didn't order it, right?" Reacher said.

Scimeca shook her head. "I already have one. It's over there."

She pointed. There was a laundry area in the corner. Washer, dryer, sink. A vacuumed rug in the angle of the corner. White plastic baskets and detergent bottles lined up precisely on a countertop.

"Thing like this, you'd remember," Reacher said. "Wouldn't you?"

"I assumed it's for my roommate, I guess," she said.

"You have a roommate?"

"Had. She moved out, couple of weeks ago."

"And you figured this is hers?"

"Made sense to me," Scimeca said. "She's setting up housekeeping on her own, she needs a washing machine, right?"

"But you didn't ask her?"

"Why should I? I figured it's not for me, who else could it be for?"

"So why did she leave it here?"

"Because it's heavy. Maybe she's getting help to move it. It's only been a couple of weeks."

"She leave anything else behind?"

Scimeca shook her head. "This is the last thing."

Reacher circled the carton. Saw the square shape where the packing documents had been torn away.

"She took the paperwork off," he said.

Scimeca nodded again. "She would, I guess. She'd need to keep her affairs straight."

They stood in silence, three people surrounding a tall cardboard carton, vivid yellow light, jagged dark shadows.

"I'm tired," Scimeca said. "Are we through? I want you guys out of here."

"One last thing," Reacher said.

"What?"

"Tell Agent Harper what you did in the service."

"Why? What's that got to do with anything?"

"I just want her to know."

Scimeca shrugged, puzzled. "I was in armaments proving."

"Tell her what that was."

"We tested new weapons incoming from the manufacturer."

"And?"

"If they were up to spec, we passed them to the quartermasters."

Silence. Harper glanced at Reacher, equally puzzled.

"OK," he said. "Now we're out of here."

Scimeca led the way through the door to the garage. Pulled the cord and killed the light. Led them past her car and up the narrow staircase. Out into the foyer. She crossed the floor and checked the spyhole in the front door. Opened it up. The air outside was cold and damp.

"Good-bye, Reacher," she said. "It was nice to see you again."

Then she turned to Harper.

"You should trust him," she said. "I still do, you know. Which is one hell of a recommendation, believe me."

The front door closed behind them as they walked down the path. They heard the sound of the lock turning from twenty feet away. The local agent watched them get into their car. It was still warm inside. Harper started the motor and put the blower on high to keep it that way.

"She had a roommate," she said.

Reacher nodded.

"So your theory is wrong. Looked like she lived alone, but she didn't. We're back to square one."

"Square two, maybe. It's still a subcategory. Has to be. Nobody targets ninety-one women. It's insane."

"As opposed to what?" Harper said. "Putting dead women in a tub full of paint?"

Reacher nodded again.

"So now what?" he said.

"Back to Quantico," she said.

It took nearly nine hours. They drove to Portland, took a turboprop to Sea-Tac, Continental to Newark, United to D.C., and a Bureau driver met them and drove them south into Virginia. Reacher slept most of the way, and the parts when he was awake were just a blur of fatigue. He struggled into alertness as they wound through Marine territory. The FBI guard on the gate reissued his visitor's tag. The driver parked at the main doors. Harper led the way inside and they took the elevator four floors underground to the seminar room with the shiny walls and the fake windows and the photographs of Lorraine Stanley pinned to the blackboard. The television was playing silently, reruns of the day on the Hill. Blake and Poulton and Lamarr were at the table with drifts of paper in front of them. Blake and Poulton looked busy and harassed. Lamarr was as white as the paper in front of her, her eyes deep in her head and jumping with strain.

"Let me guess," Blake said. "Scimeca's box came a couple of months ago and she was kind of vague about why. And there was no paperwork on it."

"She figured it was for her roommate," Harper said. "She didn't live alone. So the list of eleven doesn't mean anything."

But Blake shook his head.

"No, it means what it always meant," he said. "Eleven women who *look* like they live alone to somebody studying the paperwork. We checked with all the others on the phone. Eighty calls. Told them we were customer services people with a parcel company. Took us hours. But none of them knew anything about unexpected cartons. So there are eighty women out of the loop, and eleven in it. So Reacher's theory still holds. The roommates surprised him, they'll surprise the guy."

Reacher glanced at him, gratified. And a little surprised.

"Hey, credit where it's due?" Blake said.

Lamarr nodded and moved and wrote a note on the end of a lengthy list.

"I'm sorry for your loss," Reacher said to her.

"Maybe it could have been avoided," she said. "You know, if you'd cooperated like this from the start."

There was silence.

"So we've got seven out of seven," Blake said. "No paperwork, vague women."

"We've got one other roommate situation," Poulton said. "Then three of them have been getting regular mis-deliveries and they've gotten slow about sorting them out. The other two were just plain vague."

"Scimeca was pretty vague, for sure," Harper said.

"She was traumatized," Reacher said. "She's doing well to function at all."

Lamarr nodded. A small, sympathetic motion of her head.

"Whatever, she's not leading us anywhere, right?" she said.

"What about the delivery companies?" Reacher asked. "You chasing them?"

"We don't know who they were," Poulton said. "The paperwork is missing, seven cartons out of seven."

"There aren't too many possibilities," Reacher said.

"Aren't there?" Poulton said back. "UPS, FedEx, DHL, Airborne Express, the damn United States Postal Service, whoever, plus any number of local subcontractors."

"Try them all," Reacher said.

Poulton shrugged. "And ask them what? Out of all the ten zillion packages you delivered in the last two months, can you remember the one we're interested in?"

"You have to try," Reacher said. "Start with Spokane. Remote address like that, middle of nowhere, the driver might recall it."

Blake leaned forward and nodded. "OK, we'll try it up there. But only there. Gets impossible, otherwise."

"Why are the women so vague?" Harper asked.

"Complex reasons," Lamarr answered. "Like Reacher said, they're traumatized, all of them, at least to some extent. A large package, coming into their private territory unasked, it's an invasion of sorts. The mind blocks it out. It's what I would expect to see in cases like these."

Her voice was low and strained. Her bony hands were laid on the table in front of her.

"I think it's weird," Harper said.

Lamarr shook her head, patiently, like a teacher.

"No, it's what I would expect," she said again. "Don't look at it from your own perspective. These women were assaulted, figuratively, literally, both. That does things to a person."

"And they're all worried now," Reacher said. "Guarding them meant telling them. Certainly Scimeca looked pretty shaken. And she should be. She's pretty isolated out there. If I was the guy, I'd be looking at her next. I'm sure she's capable of arriving at the same conclusion."

"We need to catch this guy," Lamarr said.

Blake nodded. "Not going to be easy, now. Obviously we'll keep round-the-clock security on the seven who got the packages, but he'll spot that from a mile away, so we won't catch him at a scene."

"He'll disappear for a while," Lamarr said. "Until we take the security off again."

"How long are we keeping the security on?" Harper asked.

There was silence.

"Three weeks," Blake said. "Any longer than that, it gets crazy."

Harper stared at him.

"Has to be a limit," he said. "What do you want here? Round-the-clock guards, the rest of their damn lives?"

Silence again. Poulton butted his papers into a pile.

"So we've got three weeks to find the guy," he said.

Blake nodded and laid his hands on the table. "Plan is we spell each other twenty-four hours a day, three weeks, starting now. One of us sleeps while the others work. Julia, you get the first rest period, twelve hours, starting now."

"I don't want it."

Blake looked awkward. "Well, want it or not, you got it."

She shook her head. "No, I need to stay on top of this. Let Poulton go first."

"No arguments, Julia. We need to get organized."

"But I'm fine. I need to work. And I couldn't sleep now, anyway."

"Twelve hours, Julia," Blake said. "You're entitled to time off anyway. Compassionate leave of absence, twice over."

"I won't go," she said back.

"You will."

"I can't," she said. "I need to be involved right now."

She sat there, implacable. Resolution in her face. Blake sighed and looked away.

"Right now, you can't be involved," he said.

"Why not?"

Blake looked straight at her. "Because they just flew

your sister's body in for the autopsy. And you can't be involved in that. I can't let you."

She tried to answer. Her mouth opened and closed twice, but no sound came out. Then she blinked once and looked away.

"So, twelve hours," Blake said.

She stared down at the table.

"Will I get the data?" she asked quietly.

Blake nodded.

"Yes, I'm afraid you'll have to," he answered.

18

THE LOCAL BUREAU team in Spokane had worked hard through the night and gotten good cooperation from a construction business and a crane-hire operation and a trucking crew and an air cargo operator. The construction workers tore Alison Lamarr's bathroom apart and disconnected the plumbing. Bureau crime scene specialists wrapped the whole tub in heavy plastic while the builders took out the window and removed the end wall down to floor level. The crane crew fixed canvas slings under the wrapped tub and brought their hook in through the hole in the end of the building and eased the heavy load out into the night. It swung through the chill air and dropped slowly down to a wooden crate lashed to a flatbed truck idling on the road. The truckers pumped expanding foam into the crate to cushion the cargo and nailed the lid down tight and drove straight to the airport in Spokane. The crate was loaded into a waiting plane and flown direct to Andrews Air Force Base, where a helicopter collected it and took it on down to Quantico. Then it was off-loaded by a forklift and set down gently in a laboratory loading bay and left waiting there for an hour while the Bureau's forensic experts figured out exactly how to proceed.

"At this point, the cause of death is all I want," Blake said.

He was sitting on one side of a long table in the pathology conference room, three buildings and five floors away from the Behavioral Science facility. Harper was sitting next to him, and then Poulton next to her, and then Reacher at the end of the row. Opposite them was Quantico's senior pathologist, a doctor called Stavely, which was a name Reacher thought he recognized from somewhere. Clearly the guy had some kind of a famous reputation. Everybody was treating him with deference. He was a large red-faced man, oddly cheerful. His hands were big and red and looked clumsy, although presumably they weren't. Next to him was his chief technician, a quiet thin man who looked preoccupied.

"We read the stuff from your other cases," Stavely said, and stopped.

"Meaning?" Blake asked.

"Meaning I'm not exactly filled with optimism," Stavely said. "New Hampshire is a little remote from the action, I agree, but they see plenty down in Florida and California. I suspect if there was anything to find, you'd know about it by now. Good people, down there."

"Better people up here," Blake said.

Stavely smiled. "Flattery will get you anywhere, right?"

"It's not flattery."

Stavely was still smiling. "If there's nothing to find, what can we do?"

"Got to be something," Blake said. "He made a mistake this time, with the box."

"So?"

"So maybe he made more than one mistake, left something you'll find."

Stavely thought about it. "Well, don't hold your breath, is all I'm saying."

Then he stood up abruptly and knitted his thick fingers together and flexed his hands. Turned to his technician. "So are we ready?"

The thin guy nodded. "We're assuming the paint will be dried hard on the top surface, maybe an inch, inch and a half. If we cut it away from the tub enamel all around we should be able to slide a body bag in and scoop her out."

"Good," Stavely said. "Keep as much paint around her as you can. I don't want her disturbed."

The technician hurried out and Stavely followed him, evidently assuming the other four would file out behind him, which they did, with Reacher last in line.

THE PATHOLOGY LAB was no different from the others Reacher had seen. It was a large low space, brightly lit by an illuminated ceiling. The walls and the floor were white tile. In the middle of the room was a large examination table sculpted from gleaming steel. The table had

a drain canal pressed into the center. The drain was
plumbed straight into a steel pipe running down through
the floor. The table was surrounded by a cluster of
wheeled carts loaded with tools. Hoses hung from the
ceiling. There were cameras on stands, and scales, and
extractor hoods. There was a low hum of ventilation and
a strong smell of disinfectant. The air was still and cold.

"Gowns, and gloves," Stavely said.

He pointed to a steel cupboard filled with folded nylon gowns and boxes of disposable latex gloves. Harper
handed them out.

"Probably won't need masks," Stavely said. "My guess
is the paint will be the worst thing we smell."

They smelled it as soon as the gurney came in through
the door. The technician was pushing it and the body
bag lay on it, bloated and slick and smeared with green.
Paint seeped from the closure and ran down the steel
legs to the wheels and left parallel tracks across the white
tile. The technician walked between the tracks. The
gurney rattled and the bag rolled and wobbled like a giant balloon filled with oil. The technician's arms were
smeared with paint to his shoulders.

"Take her to X ray first," Stavely said.

The guy steered the gurney in a new direction and
headed for a closed room off the side of the lab. Reacher
stepped ahead and pulled the door for him. It felt like it
weighed a ton.

"Lined with lead," Stavely said. "We really zap them
in there. Big, big doses, so we can see everything we
want to see. Not like we have to worry about their long-
term health, is it?"

The technician was gone for a moment and then he

stepped back into the lab and eased the heavy door closed behind him. There was a distant powerful hum which lasted a second and then stopped. He went back and came out pushing the gurney again. It was still making tracks across the tile. He stopped it alongside the examination table.

"Roll her off," Stavely said. "I want her facedown."

The technician stepped beside him and leaned across the table and grasped the nearer edge of the bag with both hands and lifted it half off the gurney, half onto the table. Then he walked around to the other side and took the other edge and flipped it up and over. The bag flopped zipper-side down and the mass inside it sucked and rolled and wobbled and settled. Paint oozed out onto the polished steel. Stavely looked at it and beyond it to the floor, which was all crisscrossed with green tracks.

"Overshoes, people," he said. "It'll get everywhere."

They stepped away and Harper found pairs of plastic footwear in a locker and handed them out. Reacher slipped his on and stepped back and watched the paint. It seeped out through the zipper like a thick slow tide.

"Get the film," Stavely said.

The technician ducked back to the X-ray room and came out with large gray squares of film which mapped Alison Lamarr's body. He handed them to Stavely. Stavely fanned through them and held them up against the light from the ceiling.

"Instant," he said. "Like Polaroid. The benefits of scientific progress."

He shuffled them like a dealer and separated one of them and held it up. Ducked away to a light box on the wall and hit the switch and held the film against the light with his big fingers splayed.

"Look at that," he said.

It was a photograph of the midsection from just below the sternum to just above the pubic area. Reacher saw the outlines of ghostly gray bones, ribs, spine, pelvis, with a forearm and a hand lying across them at an angle. And another shape, dense and so bright it shone pure white. Metal. Slim and pointed, about as long as the hand.

"A tool of some sort," Stavely said.

"The others didn't have anything like that," Poulton said.

"Doc, we need to see it right away," Blake said. "It's important."

Stavely shook his head. "It's underneath her body right now, because she's upside down. We'll get there, but it won't be real soon."

"How long?"

"Long as it takes," Stavely said. "This is going to be messy as hell."

He clipped the gray photographs in sequence on the light box. Then he walked the length of the ghostly display and studied them.

"Her skeleton is relatively undamaged," he said. He pointed to the second panel. "Left wrist was cracked and healed, probably ten years ago."

"She was into sports," Reacher said. "Her sister told us."

Stavely nodded. "So we'll check the collarbone."

He moved left and studied the first panel. It showed

the skull and the neck and the shoulders. The collar-bones gleamed and swooped down toward the sternum.

"Small crack," Stavely said, pointing. "It's what I'd expect. An athlete with a cracked wrist will usually have a cracked collarbone too. They fall off their bike or their Rollerblades or whatever, throw out their arm to break their fall, end up breaking their bones instead."

"But no fresh injuries?" Blake asked.

Stavely shook his head. "These are ten years old, maybe more. She wasn't killed by blunt trauma, if that's what you mean."

He hit the switch and the light behind the X rays went out. He turned back to the examination table and knitted his fingers again and his knuckles clicked in the silence.

"OK," he said. "Let's go to work."

He pulled a hose from a reel mounted on the ceiling and turned a small faucet built into its nozzle. There was a hissing sound and a stream of clear liquid started running. A heavy, slow liquid with a sharp, strong smell.

"Acetone," Stavely said. "Got to clear this damn paint."

He used the acetone sluice on the body bag and on the steel table. The technician used handfuls of kitchen towel, wiping the bag and pushing the thick liquid into the drain. The chemical stink was overpowering.

"Ventilator," Stavely said.

The technician ducked away and twisted a switch behind him and the fans in the ceiling changed up from a hum to a louder roar. Stavely held the nozzle closer and the bag began to turn from wet green to wet black. Then he held the hose low down on the table and set up a swirling rinse under the bag straight into the drain.

"OK, scissors," he said.

The technician took scissors from a cart and snipped a corner of the bag. Green paint flooded out. The acetone swirl caught it and it eddied sluggishly to the drain. It kept on coming, two minutes, three, five. The bag settled and drooped as it emptied. The room went quieter under the roar of the fan and the hiss of the hose.

"OK, the fun starts here," Stavely said.

He handed the hose to the technician and used a scalpel from the cart to slit the bag lengthwise from end to end. He made sideways cuts top and bottom and peeled the rubber back slowly. It lifted and sucked away from skin. He folded it back in two long flaps. Alison Lamarr's body was revealed, lying facedown, slimy and slick with paint.

Stavely used the scalpel and slit the rubber around the feet, up alongside the legs, around the contours of the hips, up her flanks, close to her elbows, around her shoulders and head. He pulled away the strips of rubber until the bag was gone, all except for the front surface, which was trapped between the crust of paint and the steel of the table.

The crust of paint was top down to the table, because she was upside down. Its underside was bubbled and jellified. It looked like the surface of a distant alien planet. Stavely started rinsing its edges, where it was stuck to her skin.

"Won't that damage her?" Blake asked.

Stavely shook his head. "It's the same stuff as nail polish remover."

The skin turned greenish white where the paint washed off. Stavely used his gloved fingertips to peel the crust away. The strength in his hands moved the body. It lifted and fell, slackly. He pushed the hose underneath her, probing for stubborn adhesions. The technician stood next to him and lifted her legs. Stavely reached under them and cut the crust and the rubber together, peeling it away up to her thighs. The acetone ran continuously, rinsing the green stream into the drain.

Stavely moved up to the head. Placed the hose against the nape of her neck and watched as the chemical flooded her hair. Her hair was a nightmare. It was matted and crusted with paint. It had floated up around her face like a stiff tangled cage.

"I'm going to have to cut it," he said.

Blake nodded, somber.

"I guess so," he said.

"She had nice hair," Harper said. Her voice was quiet under the noise from the fan. She half turned and backed off a step. Her shoulder touched Reacher's chest. She left it there a second longer than she needed to.

Stavely took a fresh scalpel from the cart and traced through the hair, as close to the paint crust as he could get. He slid a powerful arm under the shoulders and lifted. The head came free, leaving hair matted into the crust like mangrove roots tangled into a swamp. He cut through the crust and the rubber and pulled another section free.

"I hope you catch this guy," he said.

"That's the plan," Blake said back, still somber.

"Roll her over," Stavely said.

She moved easily. The acetone mixed with the slick

paint was like a lubricant against the dished steel of the table. She slid face up and lay there, ghastly under the lights. Her skin was greenish white and puckered, stained and blotched with paint. Her eyes were open, the lids rimmed with green. She wore the last remaining square of the body bag stuck to her skin from her breasts to her thighs, like an old-fashioned bathing suit protecting her modesty.

Stavely probed with his hand and found the metal implement under the rubber. He cut through the bag and wormed his fingers inside and pulled the object out in a grotesque parody of surgery.

"A screwdriver," he said.

The technician washed it in an acetone bath and held it up. It was a quality tool with a heavy plastic handle and a handsome chromed-steel shaft with a crisp blade.

"Matches the others," Reacher said. "From her kitchen drawer, remember?"

"She's got scratches on her face," Stavely said suddenly.

He was using the hose, washing her face. Her left cheek had four parallel incisions running down from the eye to the jaw.

"Did she have these before?" Blake asked.

"No," Harper and Reacher said together.

"So what's that about?" Blake said.

"Was she right-handed?" Stavely asked.

"I don't know," Poulton said.

Harper nodded. "I think so."

Reacher closed his eyes and trawled back to her kitchen, watched her pouring coffee from the jug.

"Right-handed," he said.

"I agree," Stavely said. He was examining her arms and hands. "Her right hand is larger than the left. The arm is heavier."

Blake was leaning over, looking at the damaged face. "So?"

"I think they're self-inflicted," Stavely said.

"Are you sure?"

Stavely was circling the head of the table, looking for the best light. The wounds were swelled by the paint, raw and open. Green, where they should have been red.

"I can't be sure," he said. "You know that. But probability suggests it. If the guy did them, what are the chances he would have put them in the only place she could have put them herself?"

"He made her do it," Reacher said.

"How?" Blake asked.

"I don't know how. But he makes them do a hell of a lot. I think he makes them put the paint in the tub themselves."

"Why?"

"The screwdriver. It's to get the lids off with. The scratches were an afterthought. If he'd been thinking about the scratches, he'd have made her get a knife from the kitchen instead of the screwdriver. Or as well as the screwdriver."

Blake stared at the wall. "Where are the cans right now?"

"Materials Analysis," Poulton said. "Right here. They're examining them."

"So take the screwdriver over there. See if there are any marks that match."

The technician put the screwdriver in a clear plastic

evidence bag and Poulton shrugged off his gown and kicked off his overshoes and hurried out of the room.

"But why?" Blake said. "Why make her scratch herself like that?"

"Anger?" Reacher said. "Punishment? Humiliation? I always wondered why he wasn't more violent."

"These wounds are very shallow," Stavely said. "I guess they bled a little, but they didn't hurt much. The depth is absolutely consistent, all the way down each of them. So she wasn't flinching."

"Maybe ritual," Blake said. "Symbolic, somehow. Four parallel lines mean anything?"

Reacher shook his head. "Not to me."

"How did he kill her?" Blake asked. "That's what we need to know."

"Maybe he stabbed her with the screwdriver," Harper said.

"No sign of it," Stavely said. "No puncture wounds visible anyplace that would kill a person."

He had the final section of the body bag peeled back and was washing paint away from her midsection, probing with his gloved fingers under the acetone jet. The technician lifted the rubber square away and then she lay naked under the lights, collapsed and limp and utterly lifeless. Reacher stared at her and remembered the bright vivacious woman who had smiled with her eyes and radiated energy like a tiny sun.

"Is it possible you can kill somebody and a pathologist can't tell how?" he asked.

Stavely shook his head.

"Not this pathologist," he said.

He shut off the acetone stream and let the hose retract

into its reel on the ceiling. Stepped back and turned the ventilation fan back to normal. The room turned quiet again. The body lay on the table, as clean as it was ever going to get. The pores and folds of skin were stained green and the skin itself was lumpy and white like something that lives at the bottom of the sea. The hair was spiky with residue, roughly hacked around the scalp, framing the dead face.

"Fundamentally two ways to kill a person," Stavely said. "Either you stop the heart, or you stop the flow of oxygen to the brain. But to do either thing without leaving a mark is a hell of a trick."

"How would you stop the heart?" Blake asked.

"Short of firing a bullet through it?" Stavely said. "Air embolism would be the best way. A big bubble of air, injected straight into the bloodstream. Blood circulates surprisingly fast, and an air bubble hits the inside of the heart like a stone, like a tiny internal bullet. The shock is usually fatal. That's why nurses hold up the hypodermic and squirt a little liquid out and flick it with their nail. To be sure there's no air in the mix."

"You'd see the hypodermic hole, right?"

"Maybe, maybe not. And definitely not on a corpse like this. The skin is ruined by the paint. But you'd see the internal damage to the heart. I'll check, of course, when I open her up, but I'm not optimistic. They didn't find anything like that on the other three. And we're assuming a consistent MO here, right?"

Blake nodded. "What about oxygen to the brain?"

"Suffocation, in layman's terms," Stavely said. "It can be done without leaving much evidence. Classic thing would be an old person, wasted and weak, gets a pillow held over the face. Pretty much impossible to prove. But this isn't an old person. She's young and strong."

Reacher nodded. He had suffocated a man once, way back in his long and checkered career. He had needed all of his considerable strength to hold the guy's face down on a mattress, while he bucked and thrashed and died.

"She'd have fought like crazy," he said.

"Yes, I think she would," Stavely said. "And look at her. Look at her musculature. She wouldn't have been a pushover."

Reacher looked away instead. The room was silent and cold. The awful green paint was everywhere.

"I think she was alive," he said. "When she went in the tub."

"Reasoning?" Stavely asked.

"There was no mess," Reacher said. "None at all. The bathroom was immaculate. What was she, one twenty? One twenty-five? Hell of a dead weight to heave into the tub without making some kind of a mess."

"Maybe he put the paint in afterward," Blake said. "On top of her."

Reacher shook his head. "It would have floated her up, surely. It looks like she slipped right in there, like you get into a bath. You know, you point your toe, you get under the water."

"We'd need to experiment," Stavely said. "But I think I agree she died in the tub. The first three, there was no evidence they were touched at all. No bruising, no abrasions, no nothing. No postmortem damage either. Moving a corpse usually damages the ligaments in the joints, because there's no muscle tension there to protect them.

At this point, my guess is they did whatever they did strictly under their own power."

"Except kill themselves," Harper said.

Stavely nodded. "Suicide in bathtubs is pretty much limited to drowning while drunk or drugged, or opening your veins into warm water. Obviously, this isn't suicide."

"And they weren't drowned," Blake said.

Stavely nodded again. "The first three weren't. No fluid of any kind in the lungs. We'll know about this one soon as she's opened up, but I would bet against it."

"So how the hell did he do it?" Blake said.

Stavely stared down at the body, something like compassion in his face.

"Right now, I have no idea," he said. "Give me a couple of hours, maybe three, I might find something."

"No idea at all?"

"Well, I had a theory," Stavely said. "Based on what I read about the other three. Problem is, now I think the theory is absurd."

"What theory?"

Stavely shook his head. "Later, OK? And you need to leave now. I'm going to cut her up, and I don't want you here for that. She needs privacy, time like this."

19

THEY LEFT THEIR gowns and overshoes in a tangle by the door and turned left and right through walkways and corridors to the pathology building's front exit. They took the long way around through the parking lots to the main building, as if brisk motion through chill fall air would rid them of the stink of paint and death. They rode the elevator four floors underground in silence. Walked through the narrow corridor and spilled into the seminar room and found Julia Lamarr sitting alone at the table, looking up at the silent television screen.

"You're supposed to be out of here," Blake said to her.

"Any conclusions?" she asked quietly. "From Stavely?"

Blake shook his head. "Later. You should have gone home."

She shrugged. "I told you. I can't go home. I need to be on top of this."

"But you're exhausted."

"You saying I'm not effective?"

Blake sighed. "Julia, give me a break. I've got to organize. You collapse with exhaustion, you're no good to me."

"Not going to happen."

"It was an order, you realize that?"

Lamarr waved a hand, like a gesture of refusal. Harper stared at her.

"It was an order," Blake said again.

"And I ignored it," Lamarr said. "So what are you going to do? We need to work. We've got three weeks to catch this guy. That's not a lot of time."

Reacher shook his head. "That's plenty of time."

Harper turned her stare on him.

"If we talk about his motive, right now," he said.

There was silence. Lamarr stiffened in her seat.

"I think his motive is clear," she said.

There was ice in her voice. Reacher turned to face her, softening his expression, trying to defer to the fact that her family had been wiped out in the space of two days.

"It isn't to me," he said.

Lamarr turned to Blake, appealing.

"We can't start arguing this all over again," she said. "Not now."

"We have to," Reacher said.

"We've done this work already," she snapped.

"Relax, people," Blake called. "Just relax. We've got three weeks, and we're not going to waste any of it arguing."

"You're going to waste all of it, if you keep on like this," Reacher said.

There was suddenly tension in the air. Lamarr stared down at the table. Blake was silent. Then he nodded.

"You've got three minutes, Reacher," he said. "Tell us what's on your mind."

"You're wrong about his motive," Reacher said. "That's what's on my mind. It's keeping you away from looking in the right places."

"We've done this work already," Lamarr said again.

"Well, we need to do it over," Reacher said, gently. "Because we won't find the guy if we're looking in the wrong places. That stands to reason, right?"

"Do we need this?" Lamarr said.

"Two minutes and thirty seconds," Blake said. "Give us what you've got, Reacher."

Reacher took a breath. "This is a very smart guy, right? Very, very smart. Smart in a very particular way. He's committed four homicides, bizarre, elaborate scenarios, and he hasn't left the slightest shred of evidence behind. He's only made one mistake, by leaving one box open. And that was a fairly trivial mistake, because it's not getting us anywhere. So we've got a guy who's successfully handled a thousand decisions, a thousand details, under urgent and stressful conditions. He's killed four women and so far we don't even know *how*."

"So?" Blake said. "What's your point?"

"His intelligence," Reacher said. "It's a specific type. It's practical, efficient, real-world. He's got his feet on the ground. He's a planner, and he's pragmatic. He's a problem solver. He's intensely rational. He deals with *reality*."

"So?" Blake said again.

"So let me ask you a question. You got a problem with black people?"

"What?"

"Just answer the question."

"No, I don't."

"Good or bad as anybody, right?"

"Sure. Good or bad."

"What about women? Good or bad as anybody, right?"

Blake nodded. "Sure."

"So what if some guy is saying to you that black people are no good, or women are no good?"

"I'd say he's wrong."

"You'd *say* he's wrong, and you'd *know* he's wrong, because deep down you know what the truth of the matter is."

Blake nodded again. "Sure. So?"

"So that's my experience, too. Racists are fundamentally wrong. Sexists, too. No room for argument about it. Fundamentally, it's a completely irrational position to hold. So think about it. Any guy who gets in a big tantrum about this harassment issue is a guy who's *wrong*. Any guy who blames the victims is *very* wrong. And any guy who goes around looking for revenge against the victims is *very* wrong. He's got a screw loose. His brain doesn't function right. He's not rational. He's not dealing with reality. He's can't be. Deep down, he's some kind of an idiot."

"So?"

"But our guy isn't an idiot. We just agreed he's very smart. Not eccentric smart, not lunatic smart, but real-world smart, rational and pragmatic and practical. He's dealing with reality. We just agreed on that."

"So?"

"So he's not motivated by anger at these women. He can't be. It's not possible. You can't be real-world smart and real-world dumb, all at the same time. You can't be rational *and* irrational. You can't deal with reality and simultaneously *not* deal with it."

There was silence again.

"We *know* what his motive is," Lamarr said. "What else could it be? The target group is too exact for it to be anything else."

Reacher shook his head. "Like it or not, the way you're describing his motive, you're calling him deranged. But a deranged guy couldn't commit these crimes."

Lamarr clamped her teeth. Reacher heard them click and grind. He watched her. She shook her head. Her thin hair moved with it, stiff, like it was full of lacquer.

"So what's his real motive, smart guy?" she asked, her voice low and quiet.

"I don't know," Reacher said.

"You don't know? You better be kidding. You question my expertise and you don't *know*?"

"It'll be something simple. It always is, right? Ninety-nine times out of a hundred, the simple thing is the correct thing. Maybe doesn't work like that for you guys down here, but that's how it works out there in the real world."

Nobody said a word. Then the door opened, and Poulton walked into the silence, small and sandy with a faint smile hanging there under his mustache. The smile disappeared as soon as the atmosphere hit him. He sat down quietly next to Lamarr and pulled a stack of paper in front of him, defensively.

"What's going on?" he asked.

Blake nodded toward Reacher. "Smart guy here is challenging Julia's reading of the motive."

"So what's wrong about the motive?"

"Smart guy is about to tell us. You're just in time for the expert seminar."

"What about the screwdriver?" Reacher asked. "Any conclusions?"

Poulton's smile came back. "Either that screwdriver or an identical one was used to lever the lids off. The marks match perfectly. But what's all this about the motive?"

Reacher took a breath and looked around at the faces opposite him. Blake, hostile. Lamarr, white and tense. Harper, curious. Poulton, blank.

"OK, smart guy, we're listening," Blake said.

"It'll be something simple," Reacher said again. "Something simple and obvious. And common. And lucrative enough to be worth protecting."

"He's protecting something?"

Reacher nodded. "That's my guess. I think maybe he's eliminating witnesses to something."

"Witnesses to what?"

"Some kind of a racket, I suppose."

"What kind of a racket?"

Reacher shrugged. "Something big, something systematic, I guess."

There was silence.

"Inside the Army?" Lamarr asked.

"Obviously," Reacher said.

Blake nodded.

"OK," he said. "A big systematic racket, inside the Army. What is it?"

"I don't know." Reacher said.

There was silence again. Then Lamarr buried her face in her hands. Her shoulders started moving. She started rocking back and forward in her chair. Reacher stared at her. She was sobbing, like her heart was breaking. He realized it a moment later than he should have, because she was doing it absolutely silently.

"Julia?" Blake called. "You OK?"

She took her hands away from her face. Gestured helplessly with her hands, *yes, no, wait*. Her face was white and contorted and anguished. Her eyes were closed. The room was silent. Just the rasp of her breathing.

"I'm sorry," she gasped.

"Don't be sorry," Blake said. "It's the stress."

She shook her head, wildly. "No, I made a terrible mistake. Because I think Reacher's right. He's got to be. So I was wrong, all along. I screwed up. I missed it. I should have seen it before."

"Don't worry about it now," Blake said.

She lifted her head and stared at him. "Don't *worry* about it? Don't you see? All the time we wasted?"

"Doesn't matter," Blake said, limply.

She stared on at him. "Of course it *matters*. Don't you see? My sister died because I wasted all this time. It's my fault. *I killed her*. Because I was wrong."

Silence again. Blake stared at her, helplessly.

"You need to take time out," he said.

She shook her head. Wiped her eyes. "No, no, I need to work. I already wasted too much time. So now I need to think. I need to play catch-up."

"You should go home. Take a couple of days."

Reacher watched her. She was collapsed in her chair like she had taken a savage beating. Her face was blotched red and white. Her breathing was shallow, and her eyes were blank and vacant.

"You need rest," Blake said.

She stirred and shook her head.

"Maybe later," she said.

There was silence again. Then she hauled herself upright in her chair and fought to breathe.

"Maybe later I'll rest," she said. "But first I *work*. First, we *all* work. We've got to think. We've got to think about the Army. What's the racket?"

"I don't know," Reacher said again.

"Well think, for God's sake," she snapped. "What racket is he protecting?"

"Give us what you've got, Reacher," Blake said. "You didn't go this far without something on your mind."

Reacher shrugged.

"Well, I had half an idea," he said.

"Give us what you've got," Blake said again.

"OK, what was Amy Callan's job?"

Blake looked blank and glanced at Poulton.

"Ordnance clerk," Poulton said.

"Lorraine Stanley's?" Reacher asked.

"Quartermaster sergeant."

Reacher paused.

"Alison's?" he asked.

"Infantry close-support," Lamarr said, neutrally.

"No, before that."

"Transport battalion," she said.

Reacher nodded. "Rita Scimeca's job?"

Harper nodded. "Weapons proving. Now I see why you made her tell me."

"Why?" Blake asked.

"Because what's the potential link?" Reacher asked. "Between an ordnance clerk, a quartermaster sergeant, a transport driver, a weapons prover?"

"You tell me."

"What did I take from those guys at the restaurant?"

Blake shrugged. "I don't know. That's James Cozo's business, in New York. I know you stole their money."

"They had handguns," Reacher said. "M9 Berettas, with the serial numbers filed off. What does that mean?"

"They were illegally obtained." Reacher nodded. "From the Army. M9 Berettas are military-issue."

Blake looked blank. "So what?"

"So if this is some Army guy protecting a racket, the racket most likely involves theft, and if the stakes are high enough for killing people, the theft most likely involves weapons, because that's where the money is. And these women were all in a position where they could have witnessed weapons theft. They were right there in the chain, transporting and testing and warehousing weapons, all day long."

There was silence. Then Blake shook his head.

"You're crazy," he said. "It's too coincidental. The overlap is ridiculous. What are the chances all these witnesses would also be harassment victims?"

"It's only an idea," Reacher said. "But the chances are actually pretty good, the way I see it. The only *real* harassment victim was Julia's sister. Caroline Cooke doesn't count, because that was a technicality."

"What about Callan and Stanley?" Poulton asked. "You don't call that harassment?"

Reacher shook his head. But Lamarr beat him to the punch. She was leaning forward, fingers drumming on the table, life back in her eyes, completely on the ball.

"No, think about it, people," she said. "Think about it *laterally*. They weren't harassment victims *and* witnesses. They were harassment victims *because* they were witnesses. If you're some Army racketeer and you've got a woman in your unit who's not turning a blind eye to what you need her to be turning a blind eye to, what do you do about it? You get rid of her, is what. And what's the quickest way to do that? You make her uncomfortable, sexually."

There was silence. Then Blake shook his head again.

"No, Julia," he said. "Reacher's seeing ghosts, is all. It's still way too coincidental. Because what are the chances he'd just happen to be in a restaurant alley one night and stumble across the back end of the same racket that's killing our women? A million to one, minimum."

"A billion to one," Poulton said.

Lamarr stared at them.

"*Think*, for God's sake," she said. "Surely he's not saying he saw the *same* racket that's killing our women. Probably he saw a completely different racket. Because there must be hundreds of rackets in the Army. Right, Reacher?"

Reacher nodded.

"Right," he said. "The restaurant thing set me thinking along those lines, is all, in general terms."

There was silence again. Blake colored red.

"There are hundreds of rackets?" he said. "So how does that help us? Hundreds of rackets, hundreds of Army people involved, how are we going to find the right one? Needle in a damn haystack. It'll take three years. We've got three weeks."

"And what about the paint?" Poulton asked. "If he's eliminating witnesses, he'd walk up and shoot them in the head, silenced .22. He wouldn't mess with all this other stuff. All this ritual is classic serial homicide."

Reacher looked at him.

"Exactly," he said. "Your perception of the motive is defined by the *manner* of the killings. Think about it. If they *had* all got a silenced .22 in the head, what would you have thought?"

Poulton said nothing. But there was doubt in his eyes. Blake sat forward and put his hands on the table.

"We'd have called them executions," he said. "Wouldn't have altered our assessment of the motive."

"No, be honest with me," Reacher said. "I think you'd have been a little more open-minded. You'd have cast your net a little wider. Sure, you'd have considered the harassment angle, but you'd have considered other things too. More ordinary things. Bullets to the head, I think you'd have considered more routine reasons."

Blake sat there, hesitant and silent. Which was the same thing as a confession.

"Bullets to the head are kind of *normal*, right?" Reacher said. "In your line of work? So you'd have looked at *normal* reasons too. Like eliminating witnesses to a crime. Bullets to the head, I think right now you'd be all over the Army scams, looking for some efficient enforcer. But the guy deflected you by dressing it up with all this bizarre bullshit. He hid his true motive. He smoke-screened it. He camouflaged it. He pushed you into this weird psychological arena. He manipulated you, because he's very smart."

Blake was still silent.

"Not that you needed much manipulation," Reacher said.

"This is just speculation," Blake said.

Reacher nodded. "Of course it is. I told you, it's only half an idea. But that's what you do down here, right? You sit here all day long wearing the seat out of your pants, speculating about half-ideas."

Silence in the room.

"It's bullshit," Blake said.

Reacher nodded again. "Yes, maybe it is. But maybe it isn't. Maybe it's some Army guy making big bucks out of some scam these women knew about. And he's hiding behind this harassment issue, by dressing it up like a psychodrama. He knew you'd jump right on it. He knew he could make you look in the wrong place. Because he's very smart."

Silence.

"Your call," Reacher said.

There was silence.

"Julia?" Blake said.

The silence continued. Then Lamarr nodded, slowly. "It's a viable scenario. Maybe more than viable. It's possible he could be exactly right. Possible enough that I think we should check it out, maximum effort, immediately."

The silence came back.

"I think we shouldn't waste any more time," Lamarr whispered.

"But he's wrong," Poulton said.

He was riffing through paper, and his voice was loud and joyful.

"Caroline Cooke makes him wrong," he said. "She was in War Plans at NATO. High-level office work. She was never anywhere near weapons or warehouses or quartermasters."

Reacher said nothing. Then the silence was broken by the door. It opened up and Stavely hurried into the room, big and busy and intrusive. He was dressed in a white lab coat, and his wrists were smeared green where the paint had lapped up above his gloves. Lamarr stared at the marks and went whiter than his coat. She stared for a long moment and then closed her eyes and swayed like she was about to faint. She gripped the tabletop in front of her, thumbs underneath, pale fingers above, spread outward with the thin tendons standing out like quivering wires.

"I want to go home now," she said, quietly.

She reached down and gathered up her bag. Threaded the strap onto her shoulder and pushed back her chair and stood up. Walked slowly and unsteadily to the door, her eyes fixed on the remnants of her sister's last moments of life daubed across Stavely's stained wrists. Her head turned as she walked to keep them in view. Then she wrenched her gaze away and opened the door. Passed through it and let it close silently behind her.

"What?" Blake said.

"I know how he kills them," Stavely said. "Except there's a problem."

"What problem?" Blake asked.

"It's impossible."

20

"I CUT A FEW corners," Stavely said. "You need to understand that, OK? You guys are in a big hurry, and we think we're dealing with a consistent MO, so all I did was look at the questions that the first three left behind. I mean, we all know what it *isn't*, right?"

"It isn't everything, far as we know," Blake said.

"Right. No blunt trauma, no gunshots, no stab wounds, no poison, no strangulation."

"So what is it?"

Stavely moved a complete circle around the table and sat down at an empty chair, on his own, three seats from Poulton and two from Reacher.

"Did she drown?" Poulton asked.

Stavely shook his head. "No, just like the first three didn't. I took a look at her lungs, and they were completely clear."

"So what is it?" Blake asked again.

"Like I told you," Stavely said. "You stop the heart, or you deny oxygen to the brain. So first, I looked at her heart. And her heart was perfect. Completely undamaged. Same as the other three. And these were fit women. Great hearts. It's easier to spot the damage on a good heart. An older person might have a bad heart, with preexisting damage, you know, furring or scarring from previous cardiac trouble, and that can hide new damage. But these were perfect hearts, like athletes. Any trauma, it would have stuck out a mile. But there wasn't any. So he didn't stop their hearts."

"So?" Blake asked.

"So he denied them oxygen," Stavely said. "It's the only remaining possibility."

"How?"

"Well, that's the big question, isn't it? Theoretically he could have sealed off the bathroom and pumped the oxygen out and replaced it with some inert gas."

Blake shook his head. "That's absurd."

"Of course it is," Stavely said. "He'd have needed equipment, pumps, tanks of gas. And we'd have found residue in the tissues. Certainly in the lungs. There aren't any gases we wouldn't have detected."

"So?"

"So he choked off their airways. It's the only possibility."

"You said there are no signs of strangulation."

Stavely nodded. "There aren't. That's what got me interested. Strangulation normally leaves massive trauma to the neck. All kinds of bruising, internal bleeding. It sticks out a mile. Same for garroting."

"But?"

"There's something called gentle strangulation."

"Gentle?" Harper said. "Awful phrase."

"What is it?" Poulton asked.

"A guy with a big arm," Stavely said. "Or a padded coat sleeve. Gentle consistent pressure, that will do it."

"So is that it?" Blake asked.

Stavely shook his head. "No, it isn't. No external marks, but to get far enough to kill them, you leave internal damage. The hyoid bone would be broken, for instance. Certainly cracked, at least. Other ligament damage too. It's a very fragile area. The voice box is there."

"And you're going to tell me there was no damage, I guess," Blake said.

"Nothing gross," Stavely said. "Did she have a cold when you met with her?"

He looked at Harper, but Reacher answered.

"No," he said.

"Sore throat?"

"No."

"Husky voice?"

"She seemed pretty healthy to me."

Stavely nodded. Looked pleased. "There was some very, very slight swelling inside the throat. It's what you'd get recovering from a head cold. Mucus drip might do it, or a very mild strep virus. Ninety-nine times in a hundred, I'd ignore it completely. But the other three had it too. That's a little coincidental for me."

"So what does it mean?" Blake asked.

"It means he pushed something down their throats," Stavely said.

Silence in the room.

"Down their throats?" Blake repeated.

Stavely nodded. "That was my guess. Something soft, something which would slip down and then expand a little. Maybe a sponge. Were there sponges in the bathrooms?"

"I didn't see one in Spokane," Reacher said.

Poulton was back in the piles of paper. "Nothing on the inventories."

"Maybe he removed them," Harper said. "He took their clothes."

"Bathrooms without sponges," Blake said slowly. "Like the dog that didn't bark."

"No," Reacher said. "There wasn't a sponge *before*, is what I meant."

"You sure?" Blake asked.

Reacher nodded. "Totally."

"Maybe he brings one with him," Harper said. "The type he prefers."

Blake looked away, back to Stavely. "So that's how he's doing it? Sponges down their throats?"

Stavely stared at his big red hands, resting on the tabletop.

"It has to be," he said. "Sponges, or something similar. Like Sherlock Holmes, right? First you eliminate the impossible, and whatever you're left with, however improbable, has *got* to be the answer. So the guy is choking them to death by pushing something soft down their throats. Something soft enough not to cause blunt trauma internally, but something dense enough to block the air."

Blake nodded, slowly. "OK, so now we know." Stavely shook his head. "Well, no, we don't. Because it's impossible."

"Why?"

Stavely just shrugged miserably.

"Come here, Harper," Reacher said.

She looked at him, surprised. Then she smiled briefly and stood up and scraped her chair back and walked toward him.

"Show, don't tell, right?" she said.

"Lie on the table, OK?" he asked.

She smiled again and sat on the edge of the table and swiveled into position. Reacher pulled Poulton's pile of paper over and pushed it under her head.

"Comfortable?" he asked.

She nodded and fanned her hair and lay back like she was at the dentist. Pulled her jacket closed over her shirt.

"OK," Reacher said. "She's Alison Lamarr in the tub."

He pulled the top sheet of paper out from under her head and glanced at it. It was the inventory from Caroline Cooke's bathroom. He crumpled it into a ball.

"This is a sponge," he said. Then he glanced at Blake. "Not that there was one in the room."

"He brought it with him," Blake said.

"Waste of time if he did," Reacher said. "Because watch."

He put the crumpled paper to Harper's lips. She clamped them tight.

"How do I get her to open her mouth?" he asked. "In

the full and certain knowledge that what I'm doing is going to kill her?"

He leaned close and used his left hand under her chin, his fingers and thumb up on her cheeks. "I could squeeze, I guess. Or I could clamp her nose until she had to breathe. But what would *she* do?"

"This," Harper said, and threw a playful roundhouse right which caught Reacher high on the temple.

"Exactly," he said. "Two seconds from now, we're fighting, and there's a gallon of paint on the floor. Another gallon all over me. To get anywhere with this, I'd have to get right in the tub with her, behind her or on top of her."

"He's right," Stavely said. "It's just impossible. They'd be fighting for their lives. No way to force something into somebody's mouth against their will, without leaving bruises on their cheeks, their jaws, all over them. Flesh would tear against their teeth, their lips would be bruised and cut, maybe the teeth themselves would loosen. And they'd be biting and scratching and kicking. Traces under their nails. Bruised knuckles. Defensive injuries. It would be a fight to the death, right? And there's no evidence of fighting. None at all."

"Maybe he drugged them," Blake said. "Made them passive, you know, like that date-rape thing." Stavely shook his head.

"Nobody was drugged," he said. "Toxicology is absolutely clear, all four cases."

The room went silent again and Reacher pulled Harper upright by the hands. She slid off the table and dusted herself down. Walked back to her seat.

"So you've got no conclusions?" Blake asked.

Stavely shrugged. "Like I said, I've got a great conclusion. But it's an impossible conclusion."

Silence.

"I told you, this is a very smart guy," Reacher said. "Too smart for you. Way too smart. Four homicides, and you *still* don't know how he's doing it."

"So what's the answer, smart guy?" Blake said. "You going to tell us something four of the nation's best pathologists can't tell us?"

Reacher said nothing.

"What's the answer?" Blake asked again.

"I don't know," Reacher said.

"Great. You don't know."

"But I'll find out."

"Yeah, like how?"

"Easy. I'll go find the guy, and I'll ask him."

FORTY-ONE MILES AWAY, slightly east of north, the colonel was two miles from his office, after a ten-mile journey. He had taken the shuttle bus from the Pentagon's parking lot and gotten off near the Capitol. Then he had hailed a cab and headed back over the river to the National Airport's main terminal. His uniform was in a leather one-suiter slung on his shoulder, and he was cruising the ticket counters at the busiest time of day, completely anonymous in a teeming crush of people.

"I want Portland, Oregon," he said. "Open round-trip, coach."

A clerk entered the code for Portland and his computer told him he had plenty of availability on the next nonstop.

"Leaves in two hours," he said.

"OK," the colonel said.

"YOU THINK YOU'LL find the guy?" Blake repeated.

Reacher nodded. "I'll have to, won't I? It's the only way."

There was silence in the conference room for a moment. Then Stavely stood up.

"Well, good luck to you, sir," he said.

He walked out of the room and closed the door softly behind him.

"You *won't* find the guy," Poulton said. "Because you're wrong about Caroline Cooke. She never served in ordnance warehousing or weapons testing. She proves your theory is shit."

Reacher smiled. "Do I know all about FBI procedures?"

"No, you don't."

"So don't talk to me about the Army. Cooke was an officer candidate. Fast-track type. Had to be, to finish up in War Plans. People like that, they send them all over the place first, getting an overview. That summary you've got in your file is incomplete."

"It is?"

Reacher nodded. "Has to be. If they listed everywhere she was posted, you'd have ten pages before she made first lieutenant. You check back with Defense, get the details, you'll find she was someplace that could tie her in."

The silence came back. There was a faint rush from the forced-air heating and a buzz from a failing fluorescent tube. A high-pitched whistle from the silent television. That was all. Nothing else. Poulton stared at Blake. Harper stared at Reacher. Blake looked down at his fingers, which were tapping on the table with silent fleshy impacts.

"Can you find him?" he asked.

"Somebody's got to," Reacher said. "You guys aren't getting anywhere."

"You'll need resources."

Reacher nodded. "A little help would be nice."

"So I'm gambling here."

"Better than putting all your chips behind a loser."

"I'm gambling big-time. With a lot at stake."

"Like your career?"

"Seven women, not my career."

"Seven women *and* your career."

Blake nodded, vaguely. "What are the odds?"

Reacher shrugged. "With three weeks to do it in? It's a certainty."

"You're an arrogant bastard, you know that?"

"No, I'm realistic, is all."

"So what do you need?"

"Remuneration," Reacher said.

"You want to get paid?"

"Sure I do. You're getting paid, right? I do all the work, only fair I get something out of it too."

Blake nodded. "You find the guy, I'll speak to Deerfield up in New York, get the Petrosian thing forgotten about."

"Plus a fee."

"How much?"

"Whatever you think is appropriate."

Blake nodded again. "I'll think about it. And Harper

goes with you, because right now the Petrosian thing ain't forgotten about."

"OK. I can live with that. If she can."

"She doesn't get a choice," Blake said. "What else?"

"Set me up with Cozo. I'll start in New York. I'll need information from him."

Blake nodded. "I'll call him. You can see him tonight."

Reacher shook his head. "Tomorrow morning. Tonight, I'm going to see Jodie."

21

THE MEETING BROKE up in a sudden burst of energy. Blake took the elevator one floor down, back to his office to place the call to James Cozo in New York. Poulton had calls of his own to make to the Bureau office in Spokane, where the local guys were checking with parcel carriers and car rental operations. Harper went up to the travel desk to organize airline tickets. Reacher was left alone in the seminar room, sitting at the big table, ignoring the television, staring at a fake window like he was looking out at a view.

He sat like that for nearly twenty minutes, just waiting. Then Harper came back in. She was carrying a thick sheaf of new paperwork.

"More bureaucracy," she said. "If we pay you, we've got to insure you. Travel desk regulations."

She sat down opposite him and took a pen from her inside pocket.

"Ready for this?" she said.

He nodded.

"Full name?" she asked.

"Jack Reacher," he said.

"That the whole thing?"

He nodded. "That's it."

"Not a very long name, is it?"

He shrugged. Said nothing. She wrote it down. Two words, eleven letters, in a space which ran the whole width of the form.

"Date of birth?"

He told her. Saw her calculating his age. Saw surprise in her face.

"Older or younger?" he asked.

"Than what?"

"Than you thought."

She smiled. "Oh, older. You don't look it."

"Bullshit," he said. "I look about a hundred. Certainly I feel about a hundred."

She smiled again. "You probably clean up pretty good. Social Security number?"

His generation of servicemen, it was the same as his military ID. He rattled through it in the military manner, random monotone sounds representing whole numbers between zero and nine.

"Full address?"

"No fixed abode," he said.

"You sure?"

"Why wouldn't I be?"

"What about Garrison?"

"What about it?"

"Your house," she said. "That would be your address, right?"

He stared at her. "I guess so. Sort of. I never really thought about it."

She stared back. "You own a house, you've got an address, wouldn't you say?"

"OK, put Garrison."

"Street name and number?"

He dredged it up from his memory and told her.

"Zip?"

He shrugged. "I don't know."

"You don't know your own zip code?"

He was quiet for a second. She looked at him.

"You've got it real bad, haven't you?" she said.

"Got what?"

"Whatever. Call it denial, I guess."

He nodded, slowly. "Yes, I guess I've got it real bad."

"So what are you going to do about it?"

"I don't know. Maybe I'll get used to it."

"Maybe you won't."

"What would *you* do?"

"People should do what they really want," she said. "I think that's important."

"Is that what you do?"

She nodded. "My folks wanted me to stay in Aspen. They wanted me to be a teacher or something. I wanted to be in law enforcement. It was a big battle."

"It's not my parents doing this to me. They're dead."

"I know. It's Jodie."

He shook his head. "No, it's not Jodie. It's me. I'm doing this to myself."

She nodded again. "OK."

The room went quiet.

"So what should I do?" he asked.

She shrugged, warily. "I'm not the person to ask."

"Why not?"

"I might not give the answer you want."

"Which is?"

"You want me to say you should stay with Jodie. Settle down and be happy."

"I do?"

"I think so."

"But you can't say that?"

She shook her head.

"No, I can't," she said. "I had a boyfriend. It was pretty serious. He was a cop in Aspen. There's always tension, you know, between cops and the Bureau. Rivalry. Silly, really, no reason for it, but it's there. It spread into personal things. He wanted me to quit. Begged me. I was torn, but I said no."

"Was that the right choice?"

She nodded. "For me, yes, it was. You have to do what you really want."

"Would it be the right choice for me?"

She shrugged. "I can't say. But probably."

"First I need to figure out what I really want."

"You know what you really want," she said. "Everybody always does, instinctively. Any doubt you're feeling is just noise, trying to bury the truth, because you don't want to face it."

He looked away, back to the fake window.

"Occupation?" she asked.

"Silly question," he said.

"I'll put consultant."

He nodded. "That dignifies it, somewhat."

Then there were footsteps in the corridor and the door opened again and Blake and Poulton hurried inside. More paper in their hands, and the glow of progress in their faces.

"We're maybe halfway to starting to get somewhere," Blake said. "News in from Spokane."

"The local UPS driver quit three weeks ago," Poulton said. "Moved to Missoula, Montana, works in a warehouse. But they spoke to him by phone and he thinks maybe he remembers the delivery."

"So doesn't the UPS office have paperwork?" Harper asked.

Blake shook his head. "They archive it after eleven days. And we're looking at two months ago. If the driver can pinpoint the day, we might get it."

"Anybody know anything about baseball?" Poulton asked.

Reacher shrugged. "Couple of guys worked out an overall all-time top ten and only two players had the letter *u* in their names."

"Why baseball?" Harper asked.

"Day in question, some Seattle guy hit a grand slam," Blake said. "The driver heard it on his radio, remembers it."

"Seattle, he would remember it," Reacher said. "Rare occurrence."

"Babe Ruth," Poulton said. "Who's the other one?"

"Honus Wagner," Reacher said.

Poulton looked blank. "Never heard of him."

"And Hertz came through," Blake said. "They think they remember a real short rental, Spokane airport, the exact day Alison died, in and out inside about two hours."

"They got a name?" Harper asked.

Blake shook his head. "Their computer's down. They're working on it."

"Don't the desk people remember?"

"Are you kidding? Lucky if those people remember their *own* names."

"So when will we get it?"

"Tomorrow, I guess. Morning, with a bit of luck. Otherwise the afternoon."

"Three-hour time difference. It'll be the afternoon for us."

"Probably."

"So does Reacher still go?"

Blake paused and Reacher nodded.

"I still go," he said. "The name will be phony, for sure. And the UPS thing will lead nowhere. This guy's way too smart for basic paper-trail errors."

Everybody waited. Then Blake nodded.

"I guess I agree," he said. "So Reacher still goes."

THEY GOT A ride in a plain Bureau Chevrolet and were at the airport in D.C. before dark. They lined up for the United shuttle with the lawyers and the lobbyists. Reacher was the only person on the line not wearing a business suit, male or female. The cabin crew seemed to know most of the passengers and greeted them at the airplane door like regulars. Harper walked all the way down the aisle and chose seats right at the back.

"No rush to get off," she said. "You're not seeing Cozo until tomorrow."

Reacher said nothing.

"And Jodie won't be home yet," she said. "Lawyers work hard, right? Especially the ones fixing to be partner."

He nodded. He'd just gotten around to figuring the same thing.

"So we'll sit here," she said. "It's quieter."

"The engines are right back here," he said.

"But the guys in the suits aren't."

He smiled and took the window seat and buckled up.

"And we can talk back here," she said. "I don't like people listening."

"We should sleep," he said. "We're going to be busy."

"I know, but talk first. Five minutes, OK?"

"Talk about what?"

"The scratches on her face," she said. "I need to understand what that's about."

He glanced across at her. "Why? You figuring to crack this all on your own?"

She nodded. "I wouldn't turn down the opportunity to make the arrest."

"Ambitious?"

She made a face. "Competitive, I guess."

He smiled again. "Lisa Harper against the pointy-heads."

"Damn right," she said. "Plain-vanilla agents, they treat us like shit."

The engines wound up to a scream and the plane rolled backward from the gate. Swung its nose around and lumbered toward the runway.

"So what about the marks on her face?" Harper asked.

"I think it proves my point," Reacher said. "I think it's the single most valuable piece of evidence we've gotten so far."

"Why?"

He shrugged. "It was so halfhearted, wasn't it? So tentative? I think it proves the guy is hiding behind appearances. It proves he's pretending. Like there's me, looking at the cases, and I'm thinking where's the violence? Where's the anger? And simultaneously somewhere the guy is reviewing his progress, and he's thinking *oh my God, I'm not showing any anger*, and so on the next one he tries to show some, but he's not really feeling any, so it comes across as really nothing much at all."

Harper nodded. "Not even enough to make her flinch, according to Stavely."

"Bloodless," Reacher said. "Almost literally. Like a technical exercise, which it was, because this whole thing is a technical exercise, some cast-iron down-to-earth motive hiding behind a psycho masquerade."

"He made her do it to herself."

"I think so."

"But why would he?"

"Worried about fingerprints? About revealing if he's left-handed or right-handed? Demonstrating his control?"

"It's a lot of control, don't you think? But it explains why it was so halfhearted. She wouldn't really hurt herself."

"I guess not," he said, sleepily.

"Why Alison, though? Why did he wait until number four?"

"Ceaseless quest for perfection, I suppose. A guy like this, he's thinking and refining all the time."

"Does it make her special in some way? Significant?"

Reacher shrugged. "That's pointy-head stuff. If they thought so, I'm sure they'd have said."

"Maybe he knew her better than the others. Worked with her more closely."

"Maybe. But don't stray into their territory. Keep your feet on the ground. You're plain-vanilla, remember?"

Harper nodded. "And the plain-vanilla motive is money."

"Has to be," Reacher said. "Always love or money. And it can't be love, because love makes you crazy, and this guy isn't crazy."

The plane turned and stopped hard against its brakes at the head of the runway. Paused for a second and jumped forward and accelerated. Unstuck itself and lifted heavily into the air. The lights of D.C. spun past the window.

"Why did he change the interval?" Harper asked over the noise of the climb.

Reacher shrugged. "Maybe he just wanted to."

"Wanted to?"

"Maybe he just did it for fun. Nothing more disruptive for you guys than a pattern that changes."

"Will it change again?"

The plane rocked and tilted and leveled, and the engine noise fell away to a cruise.

"It's over," Reacher said. "The women are guarded, and you'll be making the arrest pretty soon."

"You're that confident?"

Reacher shrugged again. "No point going in expecting to lose."

He yawned and jammed his head between the seatback and the plastic bulkhead. Closed his eyes.

"Wake me when we get there," he said.

BUT THE THUMP and whine of the wheels coming down woke him, three thousand feet above and three miles east of La Guardia in New York. He looked at his watch and saw he'd slept fifty minutes. His mouth tasted tired.

"You want to get some dinner?" Harper asked him.

He blinked and checked his watch again. He had at least an hour to kill before Jodie's earliest possible ETA. Probably two hours. Maybe three.

"You got somewhere in mind?" he asked back.

"I don't know New York too well," she said. "I'm an Aspen girl."

"I know a good Italian," he said.

"They put me in a hotel on Park and Thirty-sixth," she said. "I assume you're staying at Jodie's."

He nodded. "I assume I am, too."

"So is the restaurant near Park and Thirty-sixth?"

He shook his head. "Cab ride. This is a big town."

She shook her head in turn. "No cabs. They'll send a car. Ours for the duration."

The driver was waiting at the gate. Same guy who had driven them before. His car was parked in the tow lane outside Arrivals, with a large card with the Bureau shield printed on it propped behind the windshield. Congestion was bad, all the way into Manhattan. It was the second half of rush hour. But the guy drove like he had nothing to fear from the traffic cops and they were out-side Mostro's within forty minutes of the plane touching down.

The street was dark, and the restaurant glowed like a promise. Four tables were occupied and Puccini was playing. The owner saw Reacher on the sidewalk and hurried to the door, beaming. Showed them to a table and brought the menus himself.

"This is the place Petrosian was leaning on?" Harper asked.

Reacher nodded toward the owner. "Look at the little guy. Did he deserve that?"

"You should have left it to the cops."

"That's what Jodie said."

"She's clearly a smart woman."

It was warm inside the huge room, and Harper slipped her jacket off and twisted to hang it over the back of her chair. Her shirt twisted with her, tightening and loosen-ing. First time since he'd met her, she was wearing a bra. She followed his gaze and blushed.

"I wasn't sure who we'd be meeting," she said.

He nodded.

"We'll be meeting somebody," he said. "That's for damn sure. Sooner or later."

The way he said it made her glance up at him.

"Now you really want this guy, right?" she said.

"Yes, now I do."

"For Amy Callan? You liked her, didn't you?"

"She was OK. I liked Alison Lamarr better, what I saw of her. But I want this guy for Rita Scimeca."

"She likes you too," she said. "I could tell."

He nodded again.

"Did you have a relationship with her?"

He shrugged. "That's a very vague word."

"An affair?"

He shook his head. "I only met her after she was raped. *Because* she was raped. She wasn't in any kind of a state to be having affairs. Still isn't, by the look of it. I was a little older than she was, maybe five or six years. We got very friendly, but it was like a paternalistic thing, you know, which I guess she needed, but she hated it at the same time. I had to work hard to make it feel at least brotherly, as I recall. We went out a few times, but like big brother and little sister, always completely platonic. She was like a wounded soldier, recuperating."

"That's how she saw it?"

"Exactly like that," he said. "Like a guy who has his leg shot off. It can't be denied, but it can be dealt with. And she was dealing with it."

"And now this guy is setting her back."

Reacher nodded. "That's the problem. Hiding behind this harassment thing, he's pounding on an open wound. If he was up-front about it, it would be OK. Rita could accept that as a separate problem, I think. Like a one-legged guy could deal with getting the flu. But it's coming across like a taunt, about her past."

"And that makes you mad."

"I feel responsible for Rita, he's messing with her, so he's messing with me."

"And people shouldn't mess with you."

"No, they shouldn't."

"Or?"

"Or they're deep in the shit."

She nodded, slowly.

"You've convinced me," she said.

He said nothing.

"You convinced Petrosian too, I guess," she said.

"I never went near Petrosian," he said. "Never laid eyes on him."

"But you *are* kind of arrogant, you know?" she said. "Prosecutor, judge, jury, executioner, all in one? What about the rules?"

He smiled.

"Those *are* the rules," he said. "People mess with me, they find that out pretty damn quick."

Harper shook her head. "We arrest this guy, remember? We find him and we arrest him. We're going to do this properly. According to *my* rules, OK?"

He nodded. "I already agreed to that."

Then the waiter came over and stood near, pen poised. They ordered two courses each and sat in silence until the food came. Then they ate in silence. There wasn't much of it. But it was as good as always. Maybe even better. And it was on the house.

AFTER COFFEE THE FBI driver took Harper to her hotel uptown and Reacher walked down to Jodie's place, alone and enjoying it. He let himself into her lobby and rode up in the elevator. Let himself into her apartment. The air was still and silent. The rooms were dark. Nobody home. He switched on lamps and closed blinds. Sat down on the living room sofa to wait.

22

THIS TIME THERE will be guards. You know that for sure. So this time will be difficult. You smile to yourself and correct your phraseology. Actually, this time will be very difficult. Very, very difficult. But not impossible. Not for you. It will be a challenge, is all. Putting guards into the equation will elevate the whole thing up a little nearer to interesting. A little nearer the point where your talent can really flex and stretch like it needs to. It will be a challenge to relish. A challenge to beat.

But you don't beat anything without thinking. You don't beat anything without careful observation and planning. The guards are a new factor, so they need analysis. But that's your strength, isn't it? Accurate, dispassionate analysis. Nobody does it better than you. You've proved that, over and over again, haven't you? Four whole times.

So what do the guards mean to you? Initial question,

who are the guards? Out here in the sticks a million miles from nowhere, first impression is you're dealing with dumb-ass local cops. No immediate problem. No immediate threat. But the downside is, out here in the sticks a million miles from nowhere, there aren't enough dumb-ass local cops to go around. Some tiny Oregon township outside of the Portland city limits won't have enough cops to keep up a twenty-four-hour watch. So they'll be looking for help, and you know that help will come from the FBI. You know that for sure. The way you predict it, the locals will take the day, and the Bureau will take the night.

Given the choice, obviously you aren't going to tangle with the Bureau. So you're going to avoid the night. You're going to take the day, when all that stands between you and her is some local fat boy in a Crown Vic full of cheeseburger wrappers and cold coffee. And you're going to take the day because the day is a more elegant solution. Broad daylight. You love the phrase. They use it all the time, don't they?

"The crime was committed in broad daylight," you whisper to yourself.

Getting past the locals in broad daylight won't be too hard. But even so, it's not something you're going to undertake lightly. You're not going to rush in. You're going to watch carefully, from a distance, until you see how it goes. You're going to invest some time in careful, patient observation. Fortunately, you've got a little time. And it won't be hard to do. The place is mountainous. Mountainous places have two characteristics. Two advantages. First of all, they're already full of idiots hanging out in sweaters with field glasses around their necks. And second of all, mountainous terrain makes it easy to see point A from

point B. You just get yourself concealed high up on some
peak or knoll or whatever the hell they call them. Then you
settle in, and you gaze downward, and you watch. And
you wait.

REACHER WAITED A long time in the stillness of Jodie's
living room. His posture on the sofa changed from sitting to sprawling. After an hour he swiveled around and
lay down. Closed his eyes. Opened them again and
struggled to stay awake. Closed them again. Kept them
closed. Figured he'd catch ten minutes. Figured he'd
hear the elevator. Or the door. But when it came to it, he
heard neither. He woke up and found her bending over
him, kissing his cheek.

"Hey, Reacher," she said softly.

He pulled her to him and held her in a tight silent
embrace. She hugged back, one-handed because she was
still carrying her briefcase, but hard.

"How was your day?" he asked.

"Later," she whispered.

She dropped the briefcase and he pulled her down on
top of him. She struggled out of her coat and let it fall.
The silk lining whispered and sighed. She was in a wool
dress with a zipper all the way down the back to the base
of her spine. He unzipped it slowly and felt the warmth
of her body underneath. She pushed up with her elbows
sharp points in his stomach. Her hands scrabbled at his
shirt. He pushed the dress off her shoulders. She pulled
his shirt out of his waistband. Tore at his belt.

She stood up and her dress fell to the floor. She held
out her hand and he took it and she led him to the bedroom. They stumbled out of their clothes as they walked.

Made it to the bed. It was white and cool. Neon glow from the city outside lit it in random patterns.

She pushed him down, with her hands on his shoulders. She was strong, like a gymnast. Urgent and energetic and lithe on top of him. He was lost. They finished filmed in sweat in a tangle of sheets. She was pressed against him. He could feel her heart hammering on his chest. Her hair was in his mouth. He was breathing hard. She was smiling. Her face was tucked into his shoulder and he could feel the smile against his skin. The shape of her mouth, the cool of her teeth. The impatient curve in the muscles of her cheek.

She was beautiful in a way he couldn't describe. She was tall and lean and graceful, and blond and faintly tanned and she had spectacular hair and eyes. But she was more than that. She was shot through with energy and will and passion. Crackling with restless intelligence, like electricity. He traced his hand down the smooth curve of her back. She stretched her foot all the way down his leg and tried to lace her toes into his. The secret smile was still there, against his neck.

"Now you can ask me about my day," she said.

Her words were muffled by his shoulder.

"How was your day?" he asked.

She put her hand flat on his chest and pushed herself up onto her elbow. Made a shape with her mouth and blew her hair off her face. Then the smile came back.

"It was great," she said.

He smiled in turn.

"Great how?" he asked.

"Secretary gossip," she said. "Mine talked to one from upstairs over lunch."

"And?"

"There's a partners' meeting in a few days."

"And?"

"The upstairs secretary had just typed the agenda. They're going to make a partnership offer."

He smiled. "Who to?"

She smiled back. "To one of the associates."

"Which one?"

"Guess."

He pretended to think about it. "They'd go for somebody special, right? The best they got? The smartest, hardest-working, most charming and all that?"

"That's usually what they do."

He nodded. "Congratulations, babe. You deserve it. You really do."

She smiled happily and threaded her arms around his neck. Pressed herself down in a full-body hug, head to toe.

"Partner," she said. "What I always wanted."

"You deserve it," he said again. "You really do."

"A partner at thirty," she said. "Can you believe it?"

He stared up at the ceiling and smiled. "Yes, I can believe it. If you'd gone into politics, you'd be president by now."

"I can't believe it," she said. "I never can, when I get what I want."

Then she was quiet for a second.

"But it hasn't happened yet," she said. "Maybe I should wait until it has."

"It'll happen," he said.

"It's only an agenda. Maybe they'll all vote no."

"They won't," he said.

"There'll be a party," she said. "Will you come?"

"If you want me to. If I won't ruin your image."

"You could buy a suit. Wear your medals. You'd blow them away."

He was quiet for a spell, thinking about buying a suit. If he did, it would be the first suit he'd ever worn.

"Have *you* got what you want?" she asked.

He wrapped his arms around her. "Right now?"

"Overall?"

"I want to sell the house," he said.

She lay still for a moment.

"OK," she said. "Not that you need my permission."

"It burdens me down," he said. "I can't handle it."

"You don't need to explain to me."

"I could live the rest of my life on the money I get for it."

"You'd have to pay taxes."

He nodded. "Whatever. What's left would buy me plenty of motel rooms."

"You should think carefully. It's the only asset you've got."

"Not to me. Money for motels is an asset. The house is a burden."

She was silent.

"I'm going to sell my car, too," he said.

"I thought you liked it," she said.

He nodded. "It's OK. For a car. I just don't like owning things."

"Owning a car isn't exactly the end of the world."

"It is to me. Too much hassle. It needs insurance, all that kind of stuff."

"You don't have insurance?"

"I thought about it," he said. "They need all kinds of paperwork first."

She paused.

"How will you get around?"

"Same as I always did, hitch rides, take the bus."

She paused again.

"OK, sell the car if you want to," she said. "But maybe keep the house. It's useful."

He shook his head, next to hers. "It drives me crazy."

He felt her smile.

"You're the only person I know who *wants* to be homeless," she said. "Most people try real hard to avoid it."

"There's nothing I want more," he said. "Like you want to make partner, I want to be free."

"Free of me too?" she asked, quietly.

"Free of the house," he said. "It's a burden. Like an anchor. You're not."

She unwrapped her arms from his neck and propped herself on an elbow.

"I don't believe you," she said. "The house anchors you and you don't like it, but I anchor you too, don't I?"

"The house makes me feel bad," he said. "You make me feel good. I only know how I feel."

"So you'd sell the house but you'd stick around New York?"

He was quiet for a beat.

"I'd maybe move around a little," he said. "You travel. You're busy a lot of the time. We could make it work."

"We'd drift apart."

"I don't think so."

"You'd stay away longer and longer."

He shook his head. "It'll be the same as it's been all year. Except I won't have the house to worry about."

"You've made up your mind, right?"

He nodded. "It's driving me crazy. I don't even know the zip code. Presumably because I don't *want* to know, deep down."

"You don't need my permission," she said again.

Then she was silent.

"You upset?" he asked, uselessly.

"Worried," she said.

"It won't change anything," he said.

"So why do it?"

"Because I have to."

She didn't reply.

THEY FELL ASLEEP like that, in each other's arms, with a strand of melancholy laced through the afterglow. Morning came and there was no time for more talk. Jodie showered and left with no breakfast and without asking him what he was doing or when he'd be back. He showered and dressed and locked up the apartment and rode down to the street and found Lisa Harper waiting for him. She was dressed in her third suit and she was leaning on the fender of the Bureau car. The day was bright with cold sun and the light was on her hair. The car was stopped at the curb with angry traffic swarming around it. The Bureau driver was motionless behind the wheel, staring straight ahead. The air was full of noise.

"You OK?" she asked.

He shrugged. "I guess."

"So let's go."

The driver fought traffic twenty blocks uptown and went underground into the same crowded garage Lamarr had brought him to. They used the same elevator in the corner. Rode up to the twenty-first floor. Stepped out into the same quiet gray corridor. The driver preceded them like a host and pointed to his left.

"Third door," he said.

James Cozo was behind his desk and looked as though he might have been there for an hour. He was in shirtsleeves. His jacket was on a hanger on a bentwood hat stand. He was watching television, political cable, an earnest reporter in front of the Capitol, rapid cutaways to the Hoover Building. The budget hearings.

"The return of the vigilante," he said.

He nodded to Harper and closed a file. Muted the television sound and pushed back from his desk and rubbed his hands over his narrow face, like he was washing without water.

"So what do you want?" he asked.

"Addresses," Reacher said. "For Petrosian's boys."

"The two you put in the hospital? They won't be pleased to see you."

"They'll be pleased to see me leave."

"You going to hurt them again?"

"Probably."

Cozo nodded. "Suits me, pal."

He pulled a file from a stack and rooted through it. Copied an address onto a slip of paper.

"They live together," he said. "They're brothers."

Then he thought again and tore the paper into shreds. Reversed the open file on the desk and took a new sheet of paper. Tossed a pencil on top of it.

"You copy it," he said. "Don't want my handwriting anywhere near this, literally or metaphorically."

The address was near Fifth, on Sixty-sixth Street.

"Nice neighborhood," Reacher said. "Expensive."

Cozo nodded again. "Lucrative operation."

Then he smiled.

"Well, it was," he said. "Until you got busy down in Chinatown."

Reacher said nothing.

"Take a taxi," Cozo said to Harper. "And you stay out of the way. No overt Bureau involvement here, OK?"

She nodded, reluctantly.

"Have fun," Cozo said.

THEY WALKED OVER to Madison with Harper craning like a tourist. Caught a cab uptown and got out on the corner of Sixtieth Street.

"We'll walk the rest of the way," Reacher said.

"We?" Harper said. "Good. I want to stay involved."

"You have to stay involved," Reacher said. "Because I won't get in without you."

The address led them six blocks north to a plain, medium-height apartment building faced with gray brick. Metal window frames, no balconies. Air conditioners built through the walls under the windows. No awning over the sidewalk, no doorman. But it was clean and well kept.

"Expensive place?" Harper asked.

Reacher shrugged. "I don't know. Not the most expensive, I guess. But they won't be giving them away."

The street door was open. The lobby was narrow, with hard stucco walls carefully streaked with paint so they looked a little like marble. There was a single elevator at the back of the lobby, with a narrow brown door.

The apartment they wanted was on the eighth floor. Reacher touched the elevator button and the door rolled back. The car was lined with bronze mirror on all four sides. Harper stepped in and Reacher crowded after her. Pressed 8. An infinite number of reflections rode up with them.

"You knock on their door," Reacher said. "Get them to open up. They won't if they see me in the spyhole."

She nodded and the elevator stopped on 8. The door rolled back. They stepped out on a dull landing the same shape as the lobby. The apartment they were looking for was in the back of the building on the right.

Reacher stood flat against the wall and Harper stood in front of the door. She bent forward and then back to flip her hair off her face. Took a breath and raised her hand and knocked on the door. Nothing happened for a moment. Then Harper stiffened like she was under scrutiny. There was a rattle of chain from the inside and the door opened a crack.

"Building management," Harper said. "I need to check the air conditioners."

Wrong season, Reacher thought. But Harper was more than six feet tall and had blond hair more than a yard long and her hands in her pockets so the front of her shirt was pulled tight. The door pushed shut for a second and the chain rattled again and the door swung back. Harper stepped inside like she was accepting a gracious invitation.

Reacher peeled off the wall and followed her in before the door closed again. It was a small dark apartment with a view of the light well. Everything was brown, rugs, furniture, drapes. There was a small foyer opening to a small living room. The living room held a sofa and two armchairs, and Harper. And both of the guys Reacher had last seen leaving the alley behind Mostro's.

"Hey, guys," he said.

"We're brothers," the first guy said, irrelevantly.

They both had broad strips of hospital gauze taped to their foreheads, stark white, a little longer and broader than the labels Reacher had stuck there. One of them had bandages on his hands. They were dressed identically in sweaters and golf pants. Without their bulky overcoats, they looked smaller. One guy was wearing boat shoes. The other was wearing moccasin slippers that looked like he'd made them himself from a mail-order kit. Reacher stared at them and felt his aggression drain away.

"Shit," he said.

They stared back at him.

"Sit down," he said.

They sat, side by side on the sofa. They watched him, with fearful eyes hooded under the ludicrous gauze.

"Are these the right guys?" Harper asked. Reacher nodded.

"Things change, I guess," he said.

"Petrosian's dead," the first guy said.

"We know that already," Reacher said back.

"We don't know nothing else," the second guy said. Reacher shook his head. "Don't say that. You know plenty of things."

"Like what?"

"Like where Bellevue is."

The first guy looked nervous. "Bellevue?"

Reacher nodded. "The hospital they took you to."

Both brothers looked at the wall.

"You liked it there?" Reacher asked.

Neither one of them replied.

"You want to go back there?"

No reply.

"Big emergency room there, right?" Reacher said. "Good for fixing all kinds of things. Broken arms, broken legs, all kinds of injuries."

The brother with the bandaged hands was older. The spokesman.

"What do you want?" he said.

"A trade."

"What for what?"

"Information," Reacher said. "In exchange for not sending you back to Bellevue."

"OK," the guy said.

Harper smiled. "That was easy."

"Easier than I thought it would be," Reacher said.

"Things change," the guy said. "Petrosian's dead."

"Those guns you had," Reacher said. "Where did you get them?"

The guy was wary.

"The guns?" he said.

"The guns," Reacher repeated. "Where did you get them?"

"Petrosian gave them to us," the guy said.

"Where did he get them from?"

"We don't know."

Reacher smiled and shook his head. "You can't say that. You can't just say *we* don't know. It's not convincing. You could say *I* don't know, but you can't answer for your brother. You can't know for sure what he knows, can you?"

"We don't know," the guy said again.

"They came from the Army," Reacher said.

"Petrosian bought them," the guy said.

"He *paid* for them," Reacher said.

"He bought them."

"He arranged their purchase, I accept that."

"He gave them to us," the younger brother said.

"Did they come in the mail?"

The older brother nodded. "Yes, in the mail."

Reacher shook his head. "No, they didn't. He sent you to pick them up someplace. Probably a whole consignment."

"He picked them up himself."

"No, he didn't. He sent you. Petrosian wouldn't go himself. He sent you, in that Mercedes you were using."

The brothers stared at the wall, thinking, like there was a decision to be made.

"Who are you?" the older one asked.

"I'm nobody," Reacher said.

"Nobody?"

"Not a cop, not FBI, not ATF, not anybody."

No reply.

"So there's an upside and a downside here," Reacher said. "You tell me stuff, it stays with me. Doesn't have to go any farther. I'm interested in the Army, not you. The downside is, you *don't* tell me, I'm not concerned with sending you off to court with all kinds of civil rights. I'm concerned with sending you back to Bellevue with all kinds of broken arms and legs."

"You INS?" the guy asked.

Reacher smiled. "Mislaid your green cards?"

The brothers said nothing.

"I'm not INS," Reacher said. "I told you, I'm not anything. I'm nobody. Just a guy who wants an answer. You tell me the answer, you can stay here as long as you want, enjoy the benefits of American civilization. But I'm getting impatient. Those shoes aren't going to do it forever."

"Shoes?"

"I don't want to hit a guy wearing slippers like that."

There was silence.

"New Jersey," the older brother said. "Through the Lincoln Tunnel, there's a roadhouse set back where Route 3 meets the turnpike."

"What's it called?"

"I don't know," the guy said. "Somebody's Bar, is all I know. Mac something, like Irish."

"Who did you see in there?"

"Guy called Bob."

"Bob what?"

"Bob, I don't know. We didn't exchange business cards or anything. Petrosian just told us Bob."

"A soldier?"

"I guess. I mean, he wasn't in uniform or nothing. But he had real short hair."

"How does it go down?"

"You go in the bar, you find him, you give him the cash, he takes you in the parking lot and gives you the stuff out of the trunk of his car."

"A Cadillac," the other guy said. "An old DeVille, some dark color."

"How many times?"

"Three."

"What stuff?"

"Berettas. Twelve each trip."

"What time of day?"

"Evening time, around eight o'clock."

"You have to call him ahead?"

The younger brother shook his head.

"He's always in there by eight o'clock," he said. "That's what Petrosian told us."

Reacher nodded.

"So what does Bob look like?" he asked.

"Like you," the older brother said. "Big and mean."

23

THE LAW PROVIDES that a narcotics conviction can be accompanied by confiscation of assets, which means that the DEA in New York City ends up with more automobiles than it can possibly ever need, so it loans out the surplus to other law enforcement agencies, including the FBI. The FBI uses those vehicles when it needs some anonymous transport that doesn't look like government-issue. Or when it needs to preserve some respectable distance between itself and some unspecified activity taking place. Therefore James Cozo withdrew the Bureau's sedan and the services of its driver and tossed Harper the keys to a black one-year-old Nissan Maxima currently parked in the back row of the underground lot.

"Have fun," he said again.

Harper drove. It was the first time she had driven in New York City, and she was nervous about it. She threaded around a couple of blocks and headed south on Fifth and motored slowly, with the taxis plunging and darting and honking around her.

"OK, what now?" she said.

Now we waste some time, Reacher thought.

"Bob's not around until eight," he said. "We've got the whole afternoon to kill."

"I feel like we should be doing something."

"No rush," Reacher said. "We've got three weeks."

"So what do we do?"

"First we eat," Reacher said. "I missed breakfast."

YOU'RE HAPPY TO miss breakfast because you need to be sure. The way you predict it, it's going to be a straight twelve-hour/twelve-hour split between the local police department and the Bureau, with changeovers at eight in the evening and eight in the morning. You saw it happen at eight in the evening yesterday, so now you're back bright and early to see it happen again at eight this morning. Missing a crummy help-yourself-in-the-lobby motel breakfast is a small price to pay for that kind of certainty. So is the long, long drive into position. You're not dumb enough to rent a room anywhere close by.

And you're not dumb enough to take a direct route, either. You wind your way through the mountains and leave your car on a gravel turnout a half-mile from your spot. The car is safe enough there. The only reason they built the turnout in the first place is that assholes are always leaving their cars there while they go watching eagles or scrambling over rocks or hiking up and down. A rental car parked neatly on the gravel is as invisible as the ski bags on the airport carousel. Just part of the scenery.

You climb away from the road up a small hill maybe a hundred feet high. There are scrawny trees all over the place, a little more than shoulder high. They have no leaves, but the terrain keeps you concealed. You're in a kind of wide trench. You step left and right to pass tumbled boulders. At the top of the hill you follow the ridge to the left. You duck low as the ground starts to fall away on the other side. You drop to your knees and shuffle forward to where two giant rocks rest on each other, giving a wonderful random view of the valley through the triangle they make between them. You lean your right shoulder on the right-hand rock and Lieutenant Rita Scimeca's house slides into the exact center of your field of view, just a little more than two hundred yards away.

The house is slightly north and west of your position, so you're getting a full-frontal of the street side. It's maybe three hundred feet down the mountain, so the whole thing is laid out like a plan. The Bureau car is right there, parked outside. A clean Buick, dark blue. One agent in it. You use your field glasses. The guy is still awake. His head is upright. He's not looking around much. Just staring forward, bored out of his skull. You can't blame him. Twelve hours through the night, in a place where the last big excitement was somebody's Christmas bake sale.

It's cold in the hills. The rock is sucking heat out of your shoulder. There's no sun. Just sullen clouds stacked up over the giant peaks. You turn away for a moment and pull on your gloves. Pull your muffler up over the lower half of your face. Partly for the warmth, partly to break up the clouds of steam your breathing is creating in the air. You turn back. Move your feet and squirm around. Get comfortable. You raise the glasses again.

The house has a wire fence all the way around the perimeter of the yard. There's an opening onto a driveway. The driveway is short. A single garage door stands at the end of it, under the end of the front porch. There's a path off the driveway that loops around through some neat rockery planting to the front door. The Bureau car is parked at the sidewalk right across the driveway opening, just slightly up the hill from dead center. Facing down the rise. That puts the driver's line of vision directly in line with the mouth of the path. Intelligent positioning. If you walk up the hill to the house, he sees you coming all the way. You come on him from behind, he maybe spots you in his mirror, and he sees you for certain as soon as you pass him by. Then he gets a clear back view all the way as you walk up the looping path. Intelligent positioning, but that's the Bureau for you.

You see movement a half-mile to the west and two hundred feet farther down the mountain. A black-and-white Crown Victoria, nosing through a right-angle turn. Prowling, slow. It snuffles through the turns and enters her road. A cloud of white vapor trails from the tailpipe. The engine is cold. The car has been parked up all night behind a quiet station house. It comes up the street and slows and stops flank to flank with the Buick. The cars are a foot apart. You don't see it for sure but you know the windows are buzzing down. Greetings are being exchanged. Information is being passed on. It's all quiet, the Bureau guy is saying. Have a nice day, he's adding. The local cop is grunting. Pretending to be bored, while secretly he's thrilled to have an important mission. Maybe the first he's ever had. See you later, the Bureau guy is saying.

The black-and-white moves up the hill and turns in the road. The Buick's engine starts and the car lurches as the

agent slams it into drive. The black-and-white noses in be-
hind it. The Buick moves away down the hill. The black-
and-white rolls forward and stops. Exactly where the Buick
was, inch for inch. It bounces twice on its springs and set-
tles. The motor stops. The white vapor drifts and disap-
pears. The cop turns his head to the right and gets exactly
the same view of the path the Bureau guy had gotten.
Maybe not such a dumb-ass, after all.

HARPER DROVE THE Maxima into a commercial parking
garage on West Ninth Street, right after Reacher told
her the grid pattern was about to finish and the street
layout was about to get messy. They walked back east
and south and found a bistro with a view of Washington
Square Park. The waitress had a copy of a digest-sized
philosophy journal to lean her order pad on. A student
from NYU, making ends meet. The air was cold, but the
sun was out. The sky was blue.

"I like it here," Harper said. "Great city."

"I told Jodie I'm selling the house," Reacher said.

She looked across at him. "She OK with that?"

He shrugged. "She's worried. I don't see why. It
makes me a happier person, how can that worry her?"

"Because it makes you a footloose person."

"It won't change anything."

"So why do it?"

"That's what she said."

Harper nodded. "She would. People do things for a
reason, right? So she's thinking, what's the reason
here?"

"Reason is I don't want to own a house."

"But reasons have layers. That's only the top layer. She's asking herself, OK, *why* doesn't he want to own a house?"

"Because I don't want the hassle. She knows that. I told her."

"Bureaucratic type of hassle?"

He nodded. "It's a big pain in the ass."

"Yes, it is. A real big pain in the ass. But she's thinking bureaucratic hassle is just a kind of symbol for something else."

"Like what?"

"Like wanting to be footloose."

"You're just going around in a circle."

"I'm just telling you how she's thinking."

The philosophy student brought coffee and Danish. Left a check written out in a neat, academic hand. Harper picked it up.

"I'll take care of it," she said.

"OK," Reacher said.

"You need to convince her," Harper said. "You know, make her believe you're going to stick around, even though you're selling the house."

"I told her I'm selling my car too," he said.

She nodded. "That might help. Sounds like a stick-around thing to do."

He paused for a beat.

"I told her I might travel a little," he said.

She stared at him. "Christ, Reacher, that's not very reassuring, is it?"

"She travels. She's been to London twice this year. I didn't make a big fuss about it."

"How much do you plan to travel?"

He shrugged again. "I don't know. A little, I guess. I like getting around. I really do. I told you that."

Harper was quiet for a second.

"You know what?" she said. "Before you convince *her* you're going to stick around, maybe you should convince yourself."

"I am convinced."

"Are you? Or do you figure you'll be in and out, as and when?"

"In and out a little, I guess."

"You'll drift apart."

"That's what she said."

Harper nodded. "Well, I'm not surprised."

He said nothing. Just drank his coffee and ate his Danish.

"It's make-your-mind-up time," Harper said. "On the road or off the road, you can't do both together."

His lunch break will be the first big test. That's your preliminary conclusion. At first you wondered about bathroom arrangements, but he just went inside and used hers. He got out of the car after about ninety minutes, after his morning coffee had worked its way through. He stood stretching on the sidewalk. Then he walked up the looping path and rang the doorbell. You adjusted the focus on the field glasses and got a pretty good side view. You didn't see her. She stayed in the house. You saw his body language, a little awkward, a little embarrassed. He didn't speak. He didn't ask. Just presented himself at the door. So the arrangement had been set up ahead of time. Tough on Sci-

meca, you think to yourself, psychologically speaking. A
raped woman, random intrusion of a large male person
for some explicit penis-based activity. But it happened
smoothly enough. He went in, and the door closed, a min-
ute passed, the door opened again, and he came back out.
He walked back to the car, looking around some, paying
attention. He opened the car door, slid inside, and the
scene went back to normal.

So, no opportunity with the bathroom breaks. His lunch
break would be the next chance. No way the guy is going
twelve hours without eating. Cops are always eating. That's
your experience. Doughnuts, pastries, coffee, steak and
eggs. Always eating.

HARPER WANTED A view of the city. She was like a tourist.
Reacher walked her south through Washington Square
Park and all the way down West Broadway to the World
Trade Center. It was about a mile and three quarters.
They sauntered slowly and spent fifty minutes doing
it. The sky was bright and cold and the city was teem-
ing. Harper was enjoying it.

"We could go up to the restaurant," Reacher said.
"Bureau could buy me lunch."

"I just bought you lunch," Harper said.

"No, that was a late breakfast."

"You're always eating," she said.

"I'm a big guy," he said. "I need nutrition."

They checked their coats in the lobby and rode up to
the top of the building. Waited in line at the restaurant
desk, with Harper pressed up against the wall of windows, gazing out at the view. She showed her badge and

they got a table for two, right at a window facing directly back up West Broadway and Fifth Avenue beyond, from a quarter-mile high.

"Awesome," she said.

It was awesome. The air was crisp and clear and the view extended a hundred miles. The city was khaki far below them in the fall light. Packed, intricate, infinitely busy. The rivers were green and gray. The outer boroughs faded into Westchester and Connecticut and Long Island. In the other direction, New Jersey crowded the bank and curved away in the far distance.

"Bob's over there," she said.

"Someplace," Reacher agreed.

"Who is Bob?"

"He's an asshole."

She smiled. "Not a very exact description, criminologically speaking."

"He's a storeman," Reacher said. "A nine-to-five guy, if he's in the bar every night."

"He's not our guy, right?"

He's nobody's guy, Reacher thought.

"He's small-time," he said. "Selling out of the trunk of his car in the parking lot? No ambition. Not enough at stake to make it worth killing people."

"So how can he help us?"

"He can name names. He's got suppliers, and he knows who the other players are. One of the other players will name more names, and then another and another."

"They all know each other?"

Reacher nodded. "They carve it up. They have specialties and territories, same as anybody else."

"Could take us a long time."

"I like the geography here," Reacher said.

"The geography? Why?"

"It makes sense. You're in the Army, you want to steal weapons, where do you steal them from? You don't creep around the barracks at night and pull them out from every footlocker you see. That way, you get yourself about eight hours' grace until the guys wake up and say hey, where's my damn Beretta?"

"So where do you steal them from?"

"Someplace they won't be missed, which means storage. Find a stockpile facility where they're laid up ready for the next war."

"And where are those?"

"Look at an interstate map."

"Why interstate?"

"Why do you think the interstates were built? Not so the Harper family could drive from Aspen to Yellowstone Park on vacation. So the Army could move troops and weapons around, fast and easy."

"They were?"

Reacher nodded. "Sure they were. Eisenhower built them in the fifties, height of the Cold War thing, and Eisenhower was a West Pointer, first and last."

"So?"

"So you look where the interstates all meet. That's where they put the storage, so the stuff can go any which way, moment's notice. Mostly just behind the coasts, because old Ike wasn't too worried about parachutists dropping into Kansas. He was thinking of ships coming in from the sea."

"And Jersey is good for that?"

Reacher nodded again. "Great strategic location. Therefore lots of storage, therefore lots of theft."

"Therefore Bob might know something?"

"He'll point us in a new direction. That's about all we can count on from Bob."

HIS LUNCH BREAK is no good. No good at all. You keep the field glasses tight to your eyes and watch the whole thing happen. A second black-and-white prowl car noses around the corner and moves slowly up the hill. It stops flank to flank against the first one and stays there, motor running. Two of the damn things, side by side. Probably the whole of the police department's fleet, right there in front of you.

You get a partial view. The driver's window is down on both cars. There's a brown paper sack and a closed cup of coffee. The new guy lifts them across the gap, elbow high to keep them upright. You adjust the focus on the field glasses. You see the waiting cop reach out. The scene is flat and two-dimensional and grainy, like the optics are at their limit. The cop takes the coffee first. His head turns as he finds the cup holder inside. Then he takes the bag. He props it on the ledge of his door and unrolls the top. Glances down. Smiles. He has a big, meaty face. He's looking at a cheeseburger or something. Maybe two of them, and a wedge of pie.

He rolls the top of the sack again and swings it inside. Almost certainly dumps it on his passenger seat. Then his head is moving. They're chatting. The cop is animated. He's a young guy. The flesh of his face is tight with youth. He's full of himself. Enchanted with his important mission. You watch him for a long moment. Watch the happy ex-

*pression on his face. Wonder what that face will look like
when he walks to her door for a bathroom break and gets no
reply to his knock. Because right there and then you decide
two things. You're going in there, to do the job. And you're
going to work it without killing the cop first, just because
you want to see that expression change.*

THE NISSAN MAXIMA was briefly a drug dealers' favorite
ride, so Reacher felt OK about using it to get out to the
Jersey bar. It would look innocent enough parked in the
lot. It would look *real*. Unmarked government cars never
did. A normal person spends twenty grand on a sedan,
he goes ahead and orders the chrome wheels and the
pearl coat along with it. But the government never did,
so their cars looked obvious, artificially plain, like they
had big signs painted on the side saying *this is a police
unmarked*. And if Bob saw such a thing in the lot, he'd
break the habit of a lifetime and spend his evening someplace else.

Reacher drove. Harper preferred not to, not in the
dark and the rush hour. And rush hour was bad. Traffic
was slow up the spine of Manhattan and jammed at the
entrance to the tunnel. Reacher played with the radio
and found a station where a woman was telling him how
long he was going to have to wait. Forty, forty-five minutes. That was about twice as slow as walking, which was
exactly how it felt.

They inched forward, deep under the Hudson River.
His backyard was sixty miles upstream. He sat there and
traced its contours in his mind, testing his decision. It
was a nice enough yard, as yards go. Certainly it was
fertile. You turned your head, the grass was a foot high

when you turned it back. It had a lot of trees. Maples, which had been cute in the early fall. Cedars, which Leon must have planted himself, because they were placed in artful groups. Leaves came off the maples and little purple berries came off the cedars. When the leaves were down, there was a wide view of the opposite bank of the river. West Point was right there, and West Point had been an important part of Reacher's life.

But he was not a nostalgic guy. Part of being a drifter means you look forward, not backward. You concentrate on what's ahead. And he felt in his gut that a big part of looking ahead was looking for *newness*. Looking for places you hadn't been and things you hadn't seen. And the irony of his life was that although he had covered most of the earth's surface, one time or another, he felt he hadn't seen much. A lifetime in the service was like rushing down a narrow corridor, eyes fixed firmly to the front. There was all kinds of enticing stuff off to the sides, which you rushed past and ignored. Now he wanted to take the side trips. He wanted a crazy zigzag, any direction he felt like, any old time he wanted.

And returning to the same place every night wouldn't do it. So his decision was the right one. He said the words to himself. *Sell the house. The house is on the market. The house is for sale. The house is sold.* He said the words and a weight came up off of him. It wasn't just the *practical* weight, although that was important. No more fretting about leaks in the pipes and bills in the mail and oil deliveries and insurance coverage. It was the *release*. Like he was back in the world, unburdened. He was free and ready to go. It was like a door opening and sunlight flooding in. He smiled to himself in the thrumming darkness of the tunnel, Harper at his side.

"You actually enjoying this?" she said.

"Best mile of my life," he answered.

You wait and and you watch, hour after hour. Perfectionism like that, you don't find everywhere. But you are perfect, and you have to stay perfect. You have to stay sure. And by now you're sure the cop is a permanent fixture. He eats in his car, he uses her bathroom from time to time, and that's it. So you think about hijacking the cop, maybe tomorrow morning, just before eight o'clock, and impersonating him. Replacing him on duty. You think about sitting in his car for a spell and then walking up to Scimeca's door and knocking, like you were ready to relieve yourself. You think about that for around a second and a half, and then you reject it, of course. His uniform wouldn't fit. And you'd be expected to chat with the Bureau guy at the eight o'clock handover. He'd know you were a fake, straight off the bat. It's not like he's dealing with a big anonymous police department like he'd get in New York or L.A.

So either the cop has to be moved, or you have to go in right past him. At first you toy with the idea of a diversion. What would it take to get him out of there? A major automobile accident at the crossroads, maybe. A fire in the school, perhaps. But as far as you know the village doesn't have a school. You've seen yellow buses on the road, heading in and out toward Portland. The school is probably in another jurisdiction. And an automobile accident would be hard to stage. Certainly you're not about to involve yourself in one. And how do you induce two other drivers to get in a crash?

Maybe a bomb threat. But where? At the station house? That would be no good. The cop would be told to stay where he was, safely out of the way, until it was checked out. So where else? Some spot where people are gathered, maybe. Somewhere the whole police department would be needed to handle the evacuation. But this is a tiny place. Where do people gather? The church, maybe. You can see a spire, down near the through road. But you can't wait until next Sunday. The library? Probably nobody in there. Two old dears at most, sitting there doing their needlepoint, ignoring the books. Evacuation could be handled by the other cop on his own in about three and a half seconds.

And a bomb threat would mean a phone call. You start to think about that. Where from? Calls can be traced. You could head back to the airport in Portland and call from there. Tracing a call to an airport pay phone is the same thing as not tracing it at all. But then you're miles out of position at the critical time. A safe call, but a useless call. Catch-22. And there are no pay phones within a million miles of where you're crouched, not in the middle of the damn Rocky Mountains or whatever the hell they call them. And you can't use your mobile, because eventually the call would appear on your bill, which ultimately is the same thing as a confession in open court. And who can you call? You can't allow anybody to hear your voice. It's too distinctive. Too dangerous.

But the more you think about it, the more your strategy centers around the phone. There's one person you can safely let hear your voice. But it's a geometric problem. Four dimensional. Time and space. You have to call from right

*here, in the open, within sight of the house, but you can't
use your mobile. Impasse.*

THEY DROVE OUT of the tunnel and streamed west with
the traffic. Route 3 angled slightly north toward the
Turnpike. It was a shiny night in New Jersey, damp asphalt everywhere, sodium lights with evening fog haloes
strung like necklaces. There were lit billboards and neon
signs left and right. Establishments of every nature behind lumpy blacktop yards.

The roadhouse they were looking for was in the back
of a leftover lot where three roads met. It was labeled
with a beer company's neon sign which said *Mac-
Stiophan's*, which as far as Reacher understood Gaelic
meant *Stevenson's*. It was a low building with a flat roof.
Its walls were faced with brown boards and there was a
green neon shamrock in every window. Its parking lot
was badly lit and three-quarters empty. Reacher put the
Maxima at a casual angle across two spaces near the
door. Slid out and looked around. The air was cold. He
turned a full circle in the dark, scanning the lot against
the lights from the street.

"No Cadillac DeVille," he said. "He's not here yet."

Harper looked at the door, cautiously.

"We're a little early," she said. "I guess we'll wait."

"You can wait out here," he said. "If you prefer."

She shook her head.

"I've been in worse places," she said.

It was hard for Reacher to imagine where and when.
The outer door led to a six-by-six lobby with a cigarette
machine and a sisal mat worn smooth and greasy with
use. The inner door led to a low dark space full of the

stink of beer fumes and smoke. There was no ventilation running. The green shamrocks in the windows shone inward as well as outward and gave the place a pale ghostly glare. The walls were dark boards, dulled and sticky with fifty years of cigarettes. The bar was a long wooden structure with halved barrels stuck to the front. There were tall barstools with red vinyl seats and lower versions of the same thing scattered around the room near tables built of lacquered barrels with plywood circles nailed to their tops. The plywood was rubbed smooth and dirty from thousands of wrists and hands.

There was a bartender behind the bar and eight customers in the body of the room. All of them had glasses of beer set on the plywood in front of them. All of them were men. All of them were staring at the newcomers. None of them was a soldier. They were all wrong for the military. Some were too old, some were too soft, some had long dirty hair. Just ordinary workingmen. Or maybe unemployed. But they were all hostile. They were silent, like they had just stopped talking in the middle of low muttered sentences. They were staring, like they were trying to intimidate.

Reacher swept his gaze over all of them, pausing on each face, long enough to let them know he wasn't impressed, and short enough to stop them thinking he was in any way interested. Then he stepped to the bar and rolled a stool out for Harper.

"What's on draft?" he asked the bartender.

The guy was wearing an unwashed dress shirt with no collar. Pleats all the way down the front. He had a dish towel squared over his shoulder. He was maybe fifty, gray-faced, paunchy. He didn't answer.

"What have you got?" Reacher asked again.

No reply.

"Hey, are you deaf?" Harper called to the guy.

She was half on and half off the stool, one foot on the floor, the other on the rung. Her jacket was draped open and she was twisting around from the waist. Her hair was loose down her back.

"Let's make a deal," she said. "You give us beer, we give you money, take it from there. Maybe you could turn it into a business, you know, call it running a saloon."

The guy turned to her.

"Haven't seen you in here before," he said.

Harper smiled. "No, we're new customers. That's what it's all about, expanding your customer base, right? Do it well enough, and you'll be the barroom king of the Garden State, no time at all."

"What do you want?" the guy said.

"Two beers," Reacher said.

"Apart from that?"

"Well, we're already enjoying the ambiance and the friendly welcome."

"People like you don't come in a place like mine without wanting something."

"We're waiting for Bob," Harper said.

"Bob who?"

"Bob with real short hair and an old Cadillac De-Ville," Reacher said. "Bob from the Army, comes in here eight o'clock every night."

"You're waiting for him?"

"Yes, we're waiting for him," Harper said.

The guy smiled. Yellow teeth, some of them missing.

"Well, you've got a long wait, then," he said.

"Why?"

"Buy a drink, and I'll tell you."

"We've been trying to buy a drink for the last five minutes," Reacher said.

"What do you want?"

"Two beers," Reacher said. "Whatever's on tap."

"Bud or Bud Light."

"One of each, OK?"

The guy took two glasses down from an overhead rack and filled them. The room was still silent. Reacher could feel eight pairs of eyes on his back. The guy placed the beers on the bar. There was an inch of soapy foam on the top of each of them. The guy peeled two cocktail napkins from a stack and dealt them out like cards. Harper pulled a wallet from her pocket and dropped a ten between the glasses.

"Keep the change," she said. "So why have we got a long wait for Bob?"

The guy smiled again and slid the ten backward. Folded it into his hand and put his hand in his pocket.

"Because Bob's in jail, far as I know," he said.

"What for?"

"Some Army thing," the guy said. "I don't know the details, and I don't *want* to know the details. That's how you do business in this part of the Garden State, miss, begging your damn pardon, your fancy ideas notwithstanding."

"What happened?" Reacher asked.

"Military policemen came in and grabbed him up right here, right in this room."

"When?" Reacher asked.

"Took six of them to get him. They smashed a table. I just got a check from the Army. All the way from Washington, D.C. The Pentagon. In the mail."

"When was this?" Reacher asked.

"When the check came? Couple days ago."

"No, when did they arrest him?"

"I'm not sure," the guy said. "They were still playing baseball, I remember that. Regular season, too. Couple months ago, I guess."

24

THEY LEFT THE beer untouched on the bar and headed back to the parking lot. Unlocked the Nissan and slid inside.

"Couple months is no good," Harper said. "Puts him right outside the picture."

"He was never *in* the picture," Reacher said. "But we'll go talk to him anyway."

"How can we do that? He's in the Army system some-where."

He looked at her. "Harper, I was a military policeman for thirteen years. If I can't find him, who can?"

"He could be anywhere."

"No, he couldn't. If this dump is his local bar, it means he was posted somewhere near here. Low-grade guy like that, a regional MP office will be handling him. Two-month time span, he's not court-martialed yet, so he's in a holding pattern at a regional MP HQ, which for this region is Fort Armstrong outside of Trenton, which is less than two hours away."

"You sure?"

He shrugged. "Unless things have changed a hell of a lot in three years."

"Some way you can check?" she asked.

"I don't need to check."

"We don't want to waste time here," she said.

He said nothing back and she smiled and opened her bag. Came out with a folded cellular phone the size of a cigarette packet.

"Use my mobile," she said.

EVERYBODY USES MOBILES. They use them all the time, just constantly. It's a phenomenon of the modern age. Everybody's talk, talk, talking, all the time, little black telephones pressed up to their faces. Where does all that conversation come from? What happened to all that conversation before mobiles were invented? Was it all bottled up? Burning ulcers in people's guts? Or did it just develop spontaneously because technology made it possible?

It's a subject you're interested in. Human impulses. Your guess is a small percentage of calls made represents useful exchange of information. But the vast majority must fall into one of two categories, either the fun aspect, the sheer delight of doing something simply because you can, or else the ego-building self-important bullshit aspect. And your observation is that it splits pretty much along gender lines. It's not an opinion you'd care to voice in public, but privately you're sure women talk because they enjoy it, and men talk because it builds them up. Hi, honey, I'm just getting off the plane, they say. So what? Like, who cares?

But you're confident that men's use of mobiles is more closely connected to their ego needs, so it's necessarily a stronger attachment, and therefore a more frequent urge. So if you steal a phone from a man, it will be discovered earlier, and reacted to with a greater degree of upset. That's your judgment. Therefore you're sitting in the airport food court watching the women.

The other major advantage of women is that they have smaller pockets. Sometimes, no pockets at all. Therefore they carry bags, into which goes all their stuff. Their wallets, their keys, their makeup. And their mobile phones. They take them out to use them, maybe rest them on the table for a spell, and then put them right back in their bags. If they get up for a coffee refill, of course, they take their bags with them. That's ingrained. Always keep your pocketbook with you. But some of them have other bags too. There are laptop cases, which these days are made with all kinds of extra compartments for the disks and the CD-ROM thing and the cables. And some of them have pockets for mobiles, little external leather rectangles the same shape as the cigarettes-and-lighter cases women carried back when people smoked. Those other cases, they don't always take them with them. If they're just stepping away to the beverage counter, they often leave them at the table, partly to keep their place claimed, partly because who can carry a pocketbook and a laptop case and a hot cup of coffee?

But you're ignoring the women with the laptop cases. Because those expensive leather articles imply some kind of *serious purpose. Their owners might get home in an hour and want to check their e-mail or finalize a pie chart or something, whereupon they open their laptop case and find their phone is gone. Police notified, account canceled, calls traced, all within an hour. No good at all.*

So the women you're watching are the nonbusiness travelers. The ones with the little nylon backpacks carried as cabin baggage. And you're specifically watching the ones heading out of town, not in toward home. They're going to make a last couple of calls from the airport and then stuff their phones into their backpacks and forget all about them, because they're flying out of the local coverage area and they don't want to pay roaming charges. Maybe they're vacationing overseas, in which case their phones are as useless to them as their house keys. Something they have to take along, but not something they ever think about.

The one particular target you're watching most closely is a woman of about twenty-three or -four, maybe forty feet away. She's dressed comfortably like she's got a long flight ahead, and she's leaning back in her chair with her head tilted left and her phone trapped in her shoulder. She's smiling vacantly as she talks, and playing with her nails. Picking at them and turning her hands in the light to look at them. This is a lazy say-nothing chat with a girlfriend. No intensity in her face. She's just talking for the sake of talking.

Her carry-on bag is on the floor near her feet. It's a small designer backpack, all covered in little loops and catches and zippers. It's clearly so complicated to close that she's left it gaping open. She picks up her coffee cup and puts it down again. It's empty. She talks and checks her watch and cranes to look at the beverage counter. She wraps up the chat. Flips her phone closed and drops it in her backpack Picks up a matching pocketbook and stands up and wheels away to get more coffee.

You're on your feet instantly. Car keys in your hand. You hustle straight across the court, ten feet, twenty, thirty. You're swinging the keys. Looking busy. She's in line. About to be served. You drop your keys and they skid across the tiles. You bend to retrieve them. Your hand skims her bag. You come back up with the keys and the phone together. You walk on. The keys go back in your pocket. The phone stays in your hand. Nothing more ordinary than somebody walking through an airport lounge holding a mobile.

You walk at normal pace. Stop and lean on a pillar. You flip the phone open and hold it at your face, pretending to make a call. Now you're invisible. You're a person leaning on a pillar making a call. There are a dozen of you within a twenty-foot radius. You look back. She's back at her table, drinking her coffee. You wait, whispering nothing into the phone. She drinks. Three minutes. Four. Five. You press random buttons and start talking again. You're on a new call. You're busy. You're one of the guys. She stands up. Yanks on the cords of her backpack to close it up. Picks it up by the cords and bounces it against its own weight to make them tight. She buckles the catches. Swings the pack onto one shoulder and picks up her pocketbook. Opens it to check her ticket is accessible. Closes it again. She looks around once and strides purposefully out of the food court. Straight toward you. She passes within five feet and disappears toward the departure gates. You flip the phone closed and slip it into the pocket of your suit and you walk

out the other way. You smile to yourself as you go. Now the
crucial call is going to end up on someone else's bill.

THE PHONE CALL to the Fort Armstrong duty officer revealed nothing at all on the surface, but the guy's eva-
sions were voiced in such a way that a thirteen-year
Army cop like Reacher took them to be confirmation as
good as he'd get if they were written in an affidavit
sworn before a notary public.

"He's there," he said.

Harper had been eavesdropping, and she didn't look
convinced.

"They tell you that for sure?" she asked.

"More or less," he said.

"So is it worth going?"

He nodded. "He's there, I guarantee it."

The Nissan had no maps in it, and Harper had no idea
of where she was. Reacher had only anecdotal knowledge of New Jersey geography. He knew how to get
from A to B, and then from B to C, and then from C to
D, but whether that was the most efficient direct route
all the way from A to D, he had no idea. So he came out
of the lot and headed for the turnpike on-ramp. He figured driving south for an hour would be a good start.
He realized within a minute he was using the same road
Lamarr had driven him on, just a few days before. It was
raining lightly and the Nissan rode harder and lower
than her big Buick. It was right down there in the tunnel of spray. The windshield was filmed with city grease
and the wipers were blurring the view out with every
alternate stroke. *Smear, clear, smear, clear.* The needle
on the gas gauge was heading below a quarter.

"We should stop," Harper said. "Get gas, clean the window."

"And buy a map," Reacher said.

He pulled off into the next service area. It was pretty much identical to the place Lamarr had used for lunch. Same layout, same buildings. He rolled through the rain to the gas pumps and left the car at the full-service island. The tank was full and the guy was cleaning the windshield when he got back, wet, carrying a colored map which unfolded awkwardly into a yard-square sheet.

"We're on the wrong road," he said. "Route 1 would be better."

"OK, next exit," Harper said, craning over. "Use 95 to jump across."

She used her finger to trace south down Route 1. Found Fort Armstrong on the edge of the yellow shape that represented Trenton.

"Close to Fort Dix," she said. "Where we were before."

Reacher said nothing. The guy finished with the windshield and Harper paid him through her window. Reacher wiped rain off his face with his sleeve and started the motor. Threaded his way back to the highway and watched for the turn onto 95.

I-95 was a mess, with heavy traffic. Route 1 was better. It curved through Highland Park and then ran dead straight for nearly twenty miles, all the way into Trenton. Reacher remembered Fort Armstrong as a left-hand turn coming north out of Trenton, so coming south it was a right-hand turn, onto another dead straight approach road, which took them all the way to a vehicle barrier outside a two-story brick guardhouse. Beyond the guardhouse were more roads and buildings. The roads were flat with whitewashed curbs and the buildings were all brick with radiused corners and external stairways made of welded tubular steel painted green. Window frames were metal. Classic Army architecture of the fifties, built with unlimited budgets and unlimited scope. Unlimited optimism.

"The U.S. military," Reacher said. "We were kings of the world, back then."

There was dimmed light in the guardhouse window next to the vehicle barrier. A sentry was visible, silhouetted against the light, bulky in a rain cape and helmet. He peered through the window and stepped to the door. Opened it up and came out to the car. Reacher buzzed his window down.

"You the guy who called the captain?" the sentry asked.

He was a heavy black guy. Low voice, slow accent from the Deep South. Far from home on a rainy night. Reacher nodded. The sentry grinned.

"He figured you might show up in person," he said. "Go ahead in."

He stepped back into the guardhouse and the barrier came up. Reacher drove carefully over the tire spikes and turned left.

"That was easy," Harper said.

"You ever met a retired FBI agent?" Reacher asked.

"Sure, once or twice. Couple of the old guys."

"How did you treat them?"

She nodded. "Like that guy treated you, I guess."

"All organizations are the same," he said. "Military

police more so than the others, maybe. The rest of the Army hates you, so you stick together more."

He turned right, then right again, then left.

"You been here before?" Harper asked.

"These places are all the same," he said. "Look for the biggest flower bed, that's where the general office is."

She pointed. "That looks promising."

He nodded. "You got the idea."

The headlight beams played over a rose bed the size of an Olympic pool. The roses were just dormant stalks, sticking up out of a surface lumpy with horse manure and shredded bark. Behind them was a low symmetrical building with whitewashed steps leading up to double doors in the center. A light burned in a window in the middle of the left-hand wing.

"Duty office," Reacher said. "The sentry called the captain soon as we were through the gate, so right now he's walking down the corridor to the doors. Watch for the light."

The fanlights above the doors lit up with a yellow glow.

"Now the outside lights," Reacher said.

Two carriage lamps mounted on the door pillars lit up. Reacher stopped the car at the bottom of the steps.

"Now the doors open," he said.

The doors opened inward and a man in uniform stepped through the gap.

"That was me, about a million years ago," Reacher said.

The captain waited at the top of the steps, far enough out to be in the light from the carriage lamps, far enough in to be sheltered from the drizzle. He was a head shorter than Reacher had ever been, but he was broad and he looked fit. Dark hair neatly combed, plain steel eyeglasses. His uniform jacket was buttoned, but his face looked open enough. Reacher slid out of the Nissan and walked around the hood. Harper joined him at the foot of the whitewashed steps.

"Come in out of the rain," the captain called.

His accent was East Coast urban. Bright and alert. He had an amiable smile. Looked like a decent guy. Reacher went up the steps first. Harper saw his shoes leaving wet stains on the whitewash. Glanced down and saw her own were doing the same thing.

"Sorry," she said.

The captain smiled again.

"Don't worry," he said. "The prisoners paint them every morning."

"This is Lisa Harper," Reacher said. "She's with the FBI."

"Pleased to meet you," the captain said. "I'm John Leighton."

The three of them shook hands all around at the doors and Leighton led them inside. He turned off the carriage lamps with a switch inside the doors and then killed the hallway light.

"Budgets," he said. "Can't waste money."

Light from his office was spilling out into the corridor, and he led them toward it. Stood at his door and ushered them inside. The office was original fifties, updated only where strictly necessary. Old desk, new computer, old file cabinet, new phone. There were crammed bookcases and every surface was overloaded with paper.

"They're keeping you busy," Reacher said.

Leighton nodded. "Tell me about it."

"So we'll try not to take up too much of your time."

"Don't worry. I called around, after you called me, naturally. Friend of a friend said I should push the boat out. Word is you were a solid guy, for a major."

Reacher smiled, briefly.

"Well, I always tried to be," he said. "For a major. Who was the friend of the friend?"

"Some guy worked for you when you worked for old Leon Garber. He said you were a stand-up guy and old Garber always swore by you, which makes you pretty much OK as long as this generation is still in harness."

"People still remember Garber?"

"Do Yankees fans still remember Joe DiMaggio?"

"I'm seeing Garber's daughter," Reacher said.

"I know," Leighton said. "Word gets around. You're a lucky guy. Jodie Garber's a nice lady, from what I recall."

"You know her?"

Leighton nodded. "I met her on the bases, when I was coming up."

"I'll remember you to her."

Then he lapsed into silence, thinking about Jodie, and Leon. He was going to sell the house Leon had left him, and Jodie was worrying about it.

"Sit down," Leighton said. "Please."

There were two upright chairs in front of the desk, tubular metal and canvas, like the things storefront churches threw away a generation ago.

"So how can I help you?" Leighton said, aiming the question at Reacher, looking at Harper.

"She'll explain," Reacher said.

She ran through it all from the beginning, summarizing. It took seven or eight minutes. Leighton listened attentively, interrupting her here and there.

"I know about the women," he said. "We heard."

She finished with Reacher's smoke screen theory, the possible Army thefts, and the trail which led from Petrosian's boys in New York to Bob in New Jersey.

"His name is Bob McGuire," Leighton said. "Quartermaster sergeant. But he's not your guy. We've had him two months, and he's too dumb, anyway."

"We figured that," Harper said. "Feeling was he could name names, maybe lead us to somebody more likely."

"A bigger fish?"

Harper nodded. "Somebody doing enough business to make it worth killing witnesses."

Leighton nodded back.

"Theoretically, there might be such a person," he said, cautiously.

"You got a name?"

Leighton looked at her and shook his head. Leaned back in his chair and rubbed the heels of his hands over his eyes. Suddenly looked very tired.

"Problem?" Reacher asked.

"How long have you been out?" Leighton asked back, eyes closed.

"About three years, I guess," Reacher said.

Leighton yawned and stretched and returned to an upright position.

"Things have changed," he said. "Time marches on, right?"

"What's changed?"

"Everything," Leighton said. "Well, this, mainly." He

leaned over and tapped his computer monitor with his nail. It made a glassy ringing *thunk*, like a bottle. "Smaller Army, easier to organize, more time on our hands. So they computerized us, completely. Makes communication a whole lot easier. Makes it so we all know each other's business. Makes inventories easier to manage. You want to know how many Willys Jeep tires we got in store, even though we don't use Willys Jeeps anymore? Give me ten minutes, I can tell you."

"So?"

"So we keep track of everything, much better than we used to. For instance, we know how many M9 Berettas have ever been delivered, we know how many have ever been legitimately issued, and we know how many we got in store. And if those numbers didn't add up, we'd be worrying about it, believe me."

"So do the numbers add up?"

Leighton grinned, briefly. "They do now. That's for damn sure. Nobody's stolen an M9 Beretta from the U.S. Army in the last year and a half."

"So what was Bob McGuire doing two months ago?" Reacher asked.

"Selling out the last of his stockpile. He'd been thieving ten years, at least. A little computer analysis made it obvious. Him, and a couple dozen others in a couple dozen different locations. We put procedures in place to dry up the stealing and we rounded up all the bad guys selling whatever they still had left."

"All of them?"

"Computer says so. We were leaking weapons like crazy, all kinds of descriptions, couple of dozen locations, so we arrest a couple dozen guys, and the leakage has stopped. McGuire was about the last, maybe second-to-last, I'm not sure."

"No more weapons theft?"

"Yesterday's news," Leighton said. "You're behind the times."

There was silence.

"Good job," Reacher said. "Congratulations."

"Smaller Army," Leighton said. "More time on our hands."

"You got them *all*?" Harper asked.

Leighton just nodded. "All of them. Big push, world-wide. There weren't that many. Computers did the trick."

Silence in the office.

"Well, shit, there goes that theory," she said.

She stared at the floor. Leighton shook his head, cautiously.

"Maybe not," he said. "We've got a theory of our own."

She looked up again. "The big fish?"

Leighton nodded. "Right."

"Who is he?"

"He's only theoretical, as of now."

"Theoretical?"

"He's not active," Leighton said. "He's not stealing anything. Like I told you, we identified all the leaks and we plugged them all. Couple dozen guys waiting for trial, all the leak locations accounted for. But the way we picked them up was we sent undercover guys in, to buy the stuff. Entrapment. Bob McGuire, for instance, he sold a couple of Berettas to a couple of lieutenants in a bar."

"We were just there," Harper said. "MacStiophan's, near the New Jersey Turnpike."

"Right," Leighton said. "Our guys bought two M9s out of the trunk of his car, two hundred bucks apiece, which is about a third of what the Army pays for them, by the by. So then we haul McGuire in and we start ripping him apart. We know more or less exactly how many pieces he's stolen over the years, because of the inventory analysis on the computer, and we figure an average price, and we start looking for where the money has gone. And we find about a half of it, either in bank accounts or in the form of stuff he's bought."

"So?" Reacher said.

"So nothing, not right then. But we're pooling information and the story is pretty much the same everywhere. They've all got about a half of their money missing. More or less the exact same proportion everywhere. And these guys are not the smartest guys you've ever met, right? They couldn't hide their money from us. And even if they could, why would they all hide exactly half of it? Why wouldn't some of them hide all of it, or two thirds, or three quarters? You know, whatever, a different proportion in each case?"

"Enter the theoretical big fish," Reacher said.

Leighton nodded. "Exactly. How else to explain it? It was like a puzzle with a missing piece. We started to figure some kind of a godfather figure, you know, some big guy in the shadows, maybe organizing everything, maybe offering protection in exchange for half the profit."

"Or half the guns," Reacher said.

"Right," Leighton said.

"Somebody running a protection racket," Harper said. "Like a scam inside a scam."

"Right," Leighton said again.

There was a long pause.

"Looks good from our point of view," Harper said. "Guy like that, he's smart and capable, and he has to run around taking care of problems in various random locations. Could explain why he's interested in so many different women. Not because all the women knew *him*, but because maybe each one of them knew one of his clients."

"Timing is good for you too," Leighton said. "If our guy is your guy, he started planning two, three months ago, when he heard his clients were starting to go down."

Harper sat forward. "What was the volume of business like two, three years ago?"

"Pretty heavy," Leighton said. "You're really asking how much these women could have seen, right?"

"Right."

"They could have seen plenty," Leighton said.

"So how good is your case?" she asked. "Against Bob McGuire, for instance?"

Leighton shrugged. "Not brilliant. We've got him for the two pieces he sold to our guys, of course, but that's only two pieces. The rest of it is basically circumstantial, and the fact the money doesn't tie up properly weakens the hell out of it."

"So eliminating the witnesses before the trials makes sense."

Leighton nodded. "Makes a hell of a lot of sense, I guess."

"So who is this guy?"

Leighton rubbed his eyes again. "We have no idea. We don't even know for sure there *is* a guy. He's just a guess right now. Just our theory."

"Nobody's saying anything?"

"Not a damn word. We've been asking, two months solid. We've got two dozen guys, all of them with their mouths shut tight. We figure the big guy's really put the frighteners on."

"He's scary, that's for sure," Harper said. "From what we know about him."

There was silence in Leighton's office. Just the brittle patter of rain on the windows.

"If he exists," Leighton said.

"He exists," Harper said.

Leighton nodded. "We think so too."

"Well, we need his name, I guess," Reacher said.

No reply.

"I should go talk to McGuire for you," Reacher said.

Leighton smiled. "I figured you'd be saying that before long. I was all set to say no, it's improper. But you know what? I just changed my mind. I just decided to say yes, go ahead. Be my guest."

THE CELL BLOCK was underground, like it always is in a regional HQ, below a squat brick building with an iron door, standing alone on the other side of the rose bed. Leighton led them over there through the rain, their collars turned up against the damp and their chins ducked down to their chests. Leighton used an old-fashioned bellpull outside the iron door and it opened after a second to reveal a bright hallway with a huge master sergeant standing in it. The sergeant stepped aside and Leighton led them in.

Inside, the walls were made of brick faced with white porcelain glaze. The floors and the ceilings were smooth troweled concrete painted shiny green. Lights were fluorescent tubes behind thick metal grilles. Doors were iron, with square barred openings at the top. There was a cubbyhole office on the right, with a wooden rack of keys on four-inch metal hoops. There was a big desk, piled high with video recorders taping milky-gray flickering images from twelve small monitor screens. The screens showed twelve cells, eleven of them empty and one of them with a humped shape under a blanket on the bed.

"Quiet night at the Hilton," Reacher said.

Leighton nodded. "Gets worse Saturday nights. But right now McGuire's our only guest."

"The video recording is a problem," Reacher said.

"Always breaking down, though," Leighton said.

He bent to examine the pictures on the monitors. Braced his hands on the desk. Bent closer. Rolled his right hand until his knuckle touched a switch. The recorders stopped humming and the *REC* legends disappeared from the corners of the screens.

"See?" he said. "Very unreliable system."

"It'll take a couple hours to fix," the sergeant said. "At least."

The sergeant was a giant, shiny skin the color of coffee. His uniform jacket was the size of a field tent. Reacher and Harper would have fitted into it together. Maybe Leighton, too. The guy was the exact ideal-issue MP noncom.

"McGuire's got a visitor, Sergeant," Leighton said. An off-the-record voice. "Doesn't need to go in the log."

Reacher took off his coat and his jacket. Folded them and left them on the sergeant's chair. The sergeant took a hoop of keys off the wooden board and moved to the inside door. Unlocked it and swung it back. Reacher stepped through and the sergeant closed the door and locked it again behind him. Pointed to the head of a staircase.

"After you," he said.

The staircase was built of bricks, rounded at the nose of each stair. The walls either side were the same white glaze. There was a metal handrail, bolted through to the wall every twelve inches. Another locked door at the bottom. Then a corridor, then another locked door. Then a lobby, with three locked doors to three blocks of cells. The sergeant unlocked the middle door. Flipped a switch and fluorescent light stuttered and flooded a bright white area forty feet by twenty. There was an access zone the length of the block and about a third of its depth. The rest of the space was divided into four cells delineated by heavy iron bars. The bars were thickly covered in shiny white enamel paint. The cells were about ten feet wide, maybe twelve deep. Each cell had a video camera opposite, mounted high on the wall. Three of the cells were empty, with their gates folded back. The fourth was locked closed. It held McGuire. He was struggling awake, sitting up, surprised by the light.

"Visitor for you," the sergeant called.

There were two tall wooden stools in the corner of the access zone nearest the exit door. The sergeant carried the nearer one over and placed it in front of McGuire's cell. Walked back and sat on the other. Reacher ignored the stool and stood with his hands behind his back, gazing silently through the bars. McGuire was pushing his blanket aside and swinging his feet to the floor. He was wearing an olive undershirt and olive shorts. He was a big guy. More than six feet tall, more than two hundred pounds, more than thirty-five years old. Heavily muscled, a thick neck, big arms, big legs. Thinning hair cropped close, small eyes, a couple of tattoos. Reacher stood absolutely still, watching him, saying nothing.

"Hell are you?" McGuire said. His voice matched his bulk. It was deep, and the words were half swallowed by a heavy chest. Reacher made no reply. It was a technique he had perfected half a lifetime ago. Just stand absolutely still, don't blink, say nothing. Wait for them to run through the possibilities. *Not a buddy. Not a lawyer. Who, then?* Wait for them to start worrying.

"Hell are you?" McGuire said again.

Reacher walked away. He stepped over to where the master sergeant was sitting and bent to whisper in his ear. The giant's eyebrows came up. *You sure?* Reacher whispered again. The guy nodded and stood up and handed Reacher the hoop of keys. Went out through the door and closed it behind him. Reacher hung the keys on the knob and walked back to McGuire's cell. McGuire was staring through the bars at him.

"What do you want?" he said.

"I want you to look at me," Reacher replied.

"What?"

"What do you see?"

"Nothing," McGuire said.

"You blind?"

"No, I ain't blind."

"Then you're a liar," Reacher said. "You don't see nothing."

"I see some guy," McGuire said.

"You see some guy bigger than you who had all kinds of special training while you spent your time shuffling paper in some piece-of-shit quartermaster's stores."

"So?"

"So nothing. Just something to bear in mind for later, is all."

"What's later?"

"You'll find out," Reacher said.

"What do you want?"

"I want proof."

"Of what?"

"Of exactly how dumb a piece of shit like you really is."

McGuire paused. His eyes narrowed, pushed into deep furrows by his brow.

"Easy for you to talk like that," he said. "Standing six feet away from these bars."

Reacher took an exaggerated pace forward.

"Now I'm two feet from the bars," he said. "And you're still a dumb piece of shit."

McGuire took a step forward, too. He was a foot inside the cell, holding a bar in each fist. A level gaze in his eyes. Reacher stepped forward again.

"Now I'm a foot from the bars, same as you," he said. "And you're *still* a dumb piece of shit."

McGuire's right hand came off the bar and closed into a fist and his whole arm rammed straight out like a pis-

ton. It was headed for Reacher's throat. Reacher caught
the wrist and swayed and whipped the fist past his head
and rocked his weight back and hauled McGuire tight
up against the inside of the bars. Twisted the wrist palm-
out and walked left and bent the arm back against the
elbow joint.

"See how dumb you are?" he said. "I keep on walking, I break your arm."

McGuire was gasping against the pressure. Reacher
smiled briefly and dropped the wrist. McGuire stared at
him and hauled his arm back inside, rolling the shoulder, testing the damage.

"What do you want?" he said again.

"Want me to open the cell gate?"

"What?"

"Keys are right over there. You want the gate open,
even things up a little?"

McGuire's eyes narrowed a little more. He nodded.
"Yeah, open the damn gate."

Reacher stepped away and lifted the hoop of keys off
the knob of the exit door. Shuffled through them and
found the right one. He'd handled plenty of cell keys.
He could pick one out blindfolded. He stepped back and
unlocked the gate. Swung it open. McGuire stood still.
Reacher walked away and put the hoop of keys back on
the doorknob. Stood facing the door, his back to the
cell.

"Sit down," he called. "I left the stool there for
you."

He sensed McGuire coming out of the cell. Heard his
bare feet on the concrete floor. Heard them stop.

"What do you want?" McGuire said again.

Reacher kept his back turned. Straining to sense McGuire's approach. It wasn't happening.

"It's complicated," he said. "You're going to have to juggle a number of factors."

"What factors?" McGuire asked, blankly.

"First factor is I'm unofficial, OK?" Reacher said.

"What does that mean?"

"You tell me."

"I don't know," McGuire said.

Reacher turned around. "It means I'm not an Army cop, I'm not a civilian cop, in fact I'm not anything at all."

"So?"

"So there's no comeback on me. No disciplinary procedures, no pension to lose, no nothing."

"So?"

"So if I leave you walking on crutches and drinking through a straw the rest of your life, there's nothing anybody can do to me. And we got no witnesses in here."

"What do you want?"

"Second factor is whatever the big guy says he'll do to you, I can do worse."

"What big guy?"

Reacher smiled. McGuire's hands bunched into fists. Heavy biceps, big shoulders.

"Now it gets sophisticated," Reacher said. "You need to concentrate real hard on this part. Third factor is, if you give me the guy's name, he goes away somewhere else, forever. You give me his name, he can't get to you. Not ever, you understand?"

"What name? What guy?"

"The guy you were paying off with half your take."

"No such guy."

Reacher shook his head. "We're past that stage now, OK? We know there's such a guy. So don't make me smack you around before we even get to the important part."

McGuire tensed up. Breathed hard. Then he quieted down. His body slackened slightly and his eyes narrowed again.

"So concentrate," Reacher said. "You think that to rat him out puts you in the shit. But you're wrong. What you need to understand is, you rat him out and actually it makes you safe, the whole rest of your life, because people are looking at him for a bunch of things a whole lot worse than ripping off the Army."

"What's he done?" McGuire asked.

Reacher smiled. He wished the video cameras had sound. *The guy exists.* Leighton would be dancing around the office.

"The FBI thinks he killed four women. You give me his name, they'll put him away forever. Nobody's even going to ask him about anything else."

McGuire was silent. Thinking about it. It wasn't the speediest process Reacher had ever seen.

"Two more factors," he said. "You tell me right now, I'll put in a good word for you. They'll listen to me, because I used to be one of them. Cops stick together, right? I can get you easy time."

McGuire said nothing.

"Last factor," Reacher said gently. "You need to understand, sooner or later you'll tell me anyway. It's just a question of timing. Your choice. You can tell me right now, or you can tell me in a half hour, right after I've broken your arms and legs and I'm about to snap your spine."

"He's a bad guy," McGuire said.

Reacher nodded. "I'm sure he's real bad. But you need to prioritize. Whatever he says he's going to do, that's theoretical, way off in the future, and like I told you, it isn't going to happen anyway. But what I'm going to do, it's going to happen right now. Right here."

"You ain't going to do nothing," McGuire said.

Reacher turned and picked up the wooden stool. Flipped it upside down and held it chest high with his hands around two of the legs. Took a firm backhand grip and bunched his shoulders and pulled steadily. Then he breathed hard and snapped his elbows back and the legs tore away from the rungs. The rungs clattered to the floor. He reversed the stool and held the seat in his left hand and splintered a leg free with his right. Dropped the wreckage and retained the leg. It was about a yard long, the size and weight of a ball bat.

"Now you do the same," he said.

McGuire tried hard. He turned over his own stool and grasped the legs. His muscles bunched and the tattoos swelled, but he got nowhere with it. He just stood there, holding the stool upside down.

"Too bad," Reacher said. "I tried to make it fair."

"He was Special Forces," McGuire said. "He was in Desert Storm. He's real tough."

"Doesn't matter," Reacher said. "He resists, the FBI will shoot him down. End of problem."

McGuire said nothing.

"He won't know it came from you," Reacher said.

"They'll make it look like he left some evidence behind."

McGuire said nothing. Reacher swung the leg of the
stool.

"Left or right?" he asked.

"What?" McGuire said.

"Which arm you want me to break first?"

"LaSalle Kruger," McGuire said. "Supply battalion
CO. He's a colonel."

25

STEALING THE PHONE was candy from a baby, but the re-
connaissance is a bitch. Timing it right was the first prior-
ity. You needed to wait for complete darkness, and you
wanted to wait for the daytime cop's final hour. Because
the cop is dumber than the Bureau guy, and because somebody's last hour is always better than somebody else's first
hour. Attention will have waned. Boredom will have set
in. His eyes will have glazed and he'll be thinking ahead to
a beer with his buddies or a night in front of the television
with his wife. Or however the hell he spends his downtime.

So your window extends to about forty minutes, say seven
to seven-forty. You plan it in two halves. First the house,
then the surrounding area. You drive back from the airport and you approach on the through road. You drive
straight through the junction three streets from her house.
You stop at a hikers' parking area two hundred yards far-

ther north. There's a wide gravel trail leading east up the slope of Mount Hood. You get out of your car and you turn your back on the trail and you work your way west and north through lightly wooded terrain. You're about level with your first position, but on the other side of her house, behind it, not in front of it.

The terrain means the houses don't have big yards. There are slim cultivated strips behind the buildings, then fences, then steep hillside covered in wild brush. You ease through the brush and come out at her fence. Stand motionless in the dark and observe. Drapes are drawn. It's quiet. You can hear a piano playing, very faintly. The house is built into the hillside, and it's at right angles to the street. The side is really the front. The porch runs all the way along it. Facing you is a wall dotted with windows. No doors. You ease along the fence and check the other side, which is really the back of the house. No doors there either. So the only ways in are the front door on the porch, and the garage door facing the street. Not ideal, but it's what you expected. You've planned for it. You've planned for every contingency.

"OK, COLONEL KRUGER," Leighton said. "We're on your ass now."

They were back in the duty office, damp from the jog through the nighttime rain, high with elation, flushed with cold air and success. Handshakes had been exchanged, high fives had been smacked, Harper had laughed and hugged Reacher. Now Leighton was scrolling through a menu on his computer screen, and Reacher and Harper were sitting side by side in front of his desk on the old upright chairs, breathing hard. Harper was still smiling, basking in relief and triumph.

"Loved that business with the stool," she said. "We watched the whole thing on the video screen."

Reacher shrugged.

"I cheated," he said. "I chose the right stool, is all. I figured visiting time, that sergeant sits on the one by the door, wriggles around a little because he's bored. Guy that size, the joints were sure to be cracked. The thing practically fell apart."

"But it looked real good."

"That was the plan. First rule is to look real good."

"OK, he's in the personnel listings," Leighton said. "LaSalle Kruger, bird colonel, right there."

He tapped the screen with his nail. It made the same glassy *thunk* they'd heard before. Like a bottle.

"Has he been in trouble?" Reacher asked.

"Can't tell, yet," Leighton said. "You think he'll have an MP record?"

"Something happened," Reacher said. "Special Forces in Desert Storm, and now he's working supply? What's that about?"

Leighton nodded. "It needs explaining. Could be disciplinary, I guess."

He exited the personnel listings and clicked on another menu. Then he paused.

"This will take all night," he said.

Reacher smiled. "You mean you don't want us to see anything."

Leighton smiled back. "Right first time, pal. You can smack the prisoners around as much as you want, but you can't look at the computer stuff. You know how it is."

"I sure do," Reacher said.

Leighton waited.

"That inventory thing about the jeep tires?" Harper said suddenly. "Could you trace some missing camouflage paint in there?"

"Maybe," Leighton said. "Theoretically, I guess."

"Eleven women on his list, look for about three hundred gallons," she said. "If you could put Kruger together with the paint, that would do it for me."

Leighton nodded.

"And dates," she said. "Find out if he was off duty when the women were killed. And match the locations, I guess. Confirm there were thefts where the women served. Prove they saw something."

Leighton looked across at her. "The Army is going to just love me, right? Kruger's our guy, and I'm busting my ass all night so we can give him away to the Bureau."

"I'm sorry," she said. "But the jurisdiction issue is clear, isn't it? Homicide beats theft."

Leighton nodded, suddenly somber.

"Like scissors beats paper," he said.

You've seen enough of the house. Standing there in the dark staring at it and listening to her play the damn piano isn't going to change anything. So you step away from the fence and duck into the brush and work your way east and south, back toward the car. You get there and dust yourself off and slide in and start it up and head back down through the crossroads. Part two of your task ahead, and you've got about twenty minutes to complete it in. You drive on. There's a small shopping center two miles west of the junction, left-hand side of the road. An old-fashioned

*one-story mall, shaped like a squared-off letter C. A super-
market in the middle like a keystone, small single-unit
stores spreading either side of it. Some of them are boarded
up and empty. You pull into the parking lot at the far end
and you nose along the fire lane, looking. You find exactly
what you want, three stores past the supermarket. It's nothing you didn't expect to find, but still you clench your fist
and bang it on the rim of the steering wheel. You smile to
yourself.*

*Then you turn the car around and idle back through the
lot, checking it out, and your smile dies. You don't like it.
You don't like it at all. It's completely overlooked. Every
storefront has a direct view. It's badly lit now, but you're
thinking about daylight. So you drive around behind the
arm of the C, and your smile comes back again. There's a
single row of overspill parking back there, facing plain
painted delivery doors in the back walls of the stores. No
windows. You stop the car and look around. A complete
circle. This is your place. No doubt about it. It's perfect.*

*Then you drive back into the main lot and you park up
alongside a small group of other vehicles. You kill the motor and wait. You watch the through road. You wait and
watch ten minutes, and then you see the Bureau Buick
heading by, not fast, not slow, reporting for duty.*

"Have a nice night," you whisper.

*Then you start your car again and wind around the
parking lot and drive off in the opposite direction.*

LEIGHTON RECOMMENDED A motel a mile down Route 1
toward Trenton. He said it was where the prisoners' visitors stayed, it was cheap, it was clean, it was the only
place for miles around and he knew the phone number.

Harper drove, and they found it easily enough. It looked fine from the outside, and it had plenty of vacancies.

"Number twelve is a nice double," the desk clerk said.

Harper nodded.

"OK, we'll take it," she said.

"We will?" Reacher said. "A double?"

"Talk about it later," she said.

She paid cash and the desk guy handed over a key.

"Number twelve," he said again. "Down the row a piece."

Reacher walked through the rain, and Harper brought the car. She parked it in front of the cabin and found Reacher waiting at the door.

"What?" she said. "It's not like we're going to sleep, is it? We're just waiting for Leighton to call. May as well do that in here as in the car."

He just shrugged and waited for her to unlock the door. She opened up and went inside. He followed.

"I'm too excited to sleep, anyway," she said.

It was a standard motel room, familiar and comforting. It was overheated and the rain was loud on the roof. There were two chairs and a table at the far end of the room by a window. Reacher walked through and sat in the right-hand chair. Put his elbows on the table and his head in his hands. Kept very still. Harper moved around, restlessly.

"We've got him, you know that?" she said.

Reacher said nothing.

"I should call Blake, give him the good news," Harper said.

Reacher shook his head. "Not yet."

"Why not?"

"Let Leighton finish up. Quantico gets involved at this point, they'll pull him off. He's only a captain. They'll haul in some two-star asshole, and he'll never get near the facts for the bullshit. Leave it with Leighton, let him get the glory."

She was in the bathroom, looking at the rack of towels and the bottles of shampoo and the packets of soap. She came out and took her jacket off. Reacher looked away.

"It's perfectly safe," she said. "I'm wearing a bra."

Reacher said nothing.

"What?" she asked. "Something's on your mind."

"It is?"

She nodded. "Sure it is. I can tell. I'm a woman. I'm intuitive."

He looked straight at her. "Truth is I don't especially want to be alone in a room with you and a bed."

She smiled, happily, mischievously. "Tempted?"

"I'm only human."

"So am I," she said. "If I can control myself, I'm sure you can."

He said nothing.

"I'm going to take a shower," she said.

"Christ," he muttered.

IT'S A STANDARD *motel room, like a thousand you've seen coast to coast. Doorway, bathroom on the right, closet on the left, queen bed, dresser, table and two chairs. Old television, ice bucket, awful pictures on the wall. You hang your coat in the closet, but you keep your gloves on. No need* to leave fingerprints all over the place. No real possibility of them ever finding the room, but you've built your whole life on being careful. The only time you take your gloves off is when you're washing, and motel bathrooms are safe enough. You check out at eleven, and by twelve a maid is spraying cleaner all over every surface and wiping everything with a wet cloth. Nobody ever found a meaningful fingerprint in a motel bathroom.

You walk through the room and you sit in the left-hand chair. You lean back, you close your eyes, and you start to think. Tomorrow. It has to be tomorrow. You plan the timing by working backward. You need dark before you can get out. That's the fundamental consideration. That drives everything else. But you want the daytime cop to find her. You accept that's just a whim on your part, but hey, if you can't brighten things up with a little whimsy, what kind of life is that? So you need to be out after dark, but before the cop's last bathroom break. That specifies a pretty exact time, somewhere between six and six-thirty. Call it five-forty, for a margin. No, call it five-thirty, because you really need to be back in position to see the cop's face.

OK, five-thirty. Twilight, not really dark, but it's acceptable. The longest time you spent in any of the previous places was twenty-two minutes. In principle this one won't be any longer, but you're going to allow a full half hour. So you need to be inside and started by five. Then you think it through from her point of view, and it's pretty clear you need to be making the phone call at about two o'clock.

So, check out of this dump before eleven, you're over there before twelve, you wait and watch, you make the call at two. It's decided. You open your eyes and stand up. Undress

and use the bathroom. Pull back the covers and slide into
bed, wearing nothing but your gloves.

HARPER CAME OUT of the bathroom wearing nothing
but a towel. Her face was scrubbed and her hair was wet.
Under the weight of the water, it hung down past her
waist. Without makeup, her face looked vulnerable.
Cornflower-blue eyes, white teeth, cheekbones, skin.
She looked about fourteen, except she was more than six
feet tall. And that kind of height made a standard-issue
motel towel seriously deficient in terms of length.

"I think I better call Blake," she said. "I should really
check in."

"Don't tell him anything," Reacher said. "I mean it,
things will spin out of control."

She nodded. "I'll just tell him we're close."

He shook his head. "Vaguer than that, OK? Just say
we're seeing some guy tomorrow who might have something connected."

"I'll be careful," she said. She sat down at the mirror.
The towel rode up. She started looking at her hair.

"Can you get my phone out of my pocketbook for
me?" she called.

He walked to the bed and slipped his hand into her
bag. Things in there released faint fragrance as they
moved. He found the phone and slipped it out and carried it over to her.

"Be real vague, OK?" he said again.

She nodded and opened the phone.

"Don't worry," she said.

"I guess I'll shower too."

She smiled. "Enjoy. I won't come in, I promise."

He went into the bathroom and closed the door. Harper's clothes were hanging from the hook on the back. All of them. The underwear was white and lacy. He thought about setting the shower icy cold, but decided to rely on willpower alone. So he set it hot and stripped off his clothes. Dumped them in a pile on the floor. Took the folding toothbrush from his jacket pocket and cleaned his teeth with plain water. Then he stood under the shower and washed with the same soap and shampoo Harper had used. He stood for a long time, trying to relax. Then he gave it up and turned the handle to cold. He held it there, gasping. One minute. Two. Then he shut it off and groped for a towel.

She knocked on the door.

"Are you done?" she called. "I need my clothes."

He unfolded the towel and wrapped it around his waist.

"OK, come in," he called.

"Just pass them out," she called back.

He bunched them into his hand and lifted them off the hook. Cracked the door and passed them through. She took them and walked away. He toweled himself almost dry and dressed, awkward in the narrow space. Combed his hair with his fingers. He stood still for a minute. Then he rattled the door handle and came out. She was standing by the bed, wearing some of her clothes. The rest of them were folded over the back of the dresser chair. Her hair was combed back. Her phone was closed, lying next to the ice bucket.

"What did you tell him?" he asked.

"Just what you said. We're meeting some guy in the morning, nothing specific."

She was wearing the shirt, but the tie was draped over the chair. So was the bra. And the suit trousers.

"He have anything to say?" he asked.

"Poulton's in Spokane," she said. "The Hertz thing came to nothing, just some woman on business. But the UPS guy is coming through with stuff. They're talking tonight, but they're three hours behind, so we won't hear anything until morning, probably. But they identified the date from the baseball thing and UPS is pulling the records."

"Won't say LaSalle Kruger on the paperwork, that's for sure."

"Probably not, but that doesn't matter anymore, does it? We found him."

She sat down on the edge of the bed, her back to him.

"Thanks to you," she said. "You were absolutely right, a smart guy with a good solid plain-vanilla motive."

She stood up again, restless. Paced the small area between the bed and the table. She was wearing the underpants. He could see that, through the shirttails. Her ass was wonderful. Her legs were lean. And long. Her feet were small and delicate, for her height.

"We should celebrate," she said.

Reacher propped the pillows on the far side of the bed and leaned back against them. Looked up at the ceiling and concentrated on the sound of the rain battering on the roof.

"No room service in a place like this," he said.

She turned to face him. The first two buttons on her shirt were undone. Thing like that, the effect depends on how far apart the buttons are. If they're close together, it doesn't mean much. But these were well spaced out, maybe three or four inches between each of them.

"It's Jodie, isn't it?" she said.

He nodded. "Of course it is."

"Wasn't for her, you'd want to, right?"

"I do want to," he said.

Then he paused.

"But I won't," he said. "Because of her."

She looked at him, and then she smiled.

"I like that in a guy, I guess," she said.

He said nothing.

"Steadfastness," she said.

He said nothing. There was silence. Just the sound of the rain on the roof, relentless and insistent.

"It's an attractive characteristic," she said.

He looked at the ceiling.

"Not that you're short of attractive characteristics," she said.

He listened to the rain. She sighed, just a tiny sound. She moved away, just an inch. But enough to ease the crisis.

"So you're going to stick around New York," she said.

He nodded again. "That's the plan."

"She'll be pissed about the house. Her father willed it to you."

"She might be," he said. "But she'll have to deal with it. The way I see it, he left me a choice, more than anything. The house, or the money I'd get for it. My choice. He knew what I was like. He wouldn't be surprised. Or upset either."

"But it's an emotional issue."

"I don't see why," he said. "It wasn't her childhood home or anything. They never really lived there. She didn't grow up there. It's just a wooden building."

"It's an anchor. That's how she sees it."

"That's why I'm selling it."

"Therefore naturally she'll worry."

He shrugged. "She'll learn. I'll stick around, house or no house."

The room went quiet again. The rain was easing. She sat down on the bed, opposite him. Tucked her bare knees up under her.

"I still feel like celebrating," she said.

She put her hand palm down in the space between them and leaned over.

"Celebration kiss," she whispered. "Nothing more, I promise."

He looked at her and reached around with his left arm and pulled her close. Kissed her on the lips. She put her hand behind his head and pushed her fingers into his hair. Tilted her head and opened her mouth. He felt her tongue on his teeth. In his mouth. He closed his eyes. Her tongue was urgent. Deep in his mouth. It felt good. He opened his eyes and saw hers, too close to focus on. They were shut tight. He let her go and pulled away, full of guilt.

"Something I need to tell you," he said.

She was breathless, and her hair was a mess.

"What?"

"I'm not being straight with you," he said.

"How not?"

"I don't think Kruger's our guy."

"*What?*"

There was silence. They were inches apart, on the bed. Her hand was still laced behind his head, in his hair.

"He's Leighton's guy," Reacher said. "I don't think he's ours. I never really did."

"*What?* You always did. This was *your* theory, Reacher. Why back away from it now?"

"Because I didn't really mean it, Harper. I was just thinking aloud. Bullshitting, basically. I'm very surprised there even *is* such a guy."

She pulled her hand away, astonished.

"But this was *your* theory," she said again.

He shrugged. "I just made it up. I didn't mean any of it. I just wanted some kind of a plausible excuse to get me out of Quantico for a spell."

She stared at him. "You *made it up*? You didn't *mean* it?"

He shrugged. "It was halfway convincing, I guess. But I didn't believe in it."

"So why the hell say it?"

"I told you. I just wanted to get out of there. To give myself time to think. And it was an experiment. I wanted to see who would support it and who would oppose it. I wanted to see who really wants this thing solved."

"I don't believe this," she said. "Why?"

"Why not?"

"We *all* want it solved," she said.

"Poulton opposed it," Reacher said.

She stared at him, from a foot away.

"What *is* this to you? A *game*?" she said.

He said nothing. She was silent, a minute, two, three.

"What the hell are you *doing*?" she said. "There are lives at stake here."

Then there was pounding at the door. Loud, insistent knocking. She pulled away from him. He let her go and put his feet on the floor and stood up. Ran his hand through his hair and walked toward the door. A new barrage started up. A heavy hand, knocking hard.

"OK," he called. "I'm coming."

The pounding stopped. He opened the door. There was an Army Chevrolet parked at an angle outside the room. Leighton was standing on the stoop, his hand raised, his jacket open, raindrops on the shoulders.

"Kruger's our guy," he said.

He pushed past, inside the room. Saw Harper buttoning her shirt.

"Excuse me," he said.

"It's hot in here," she said, looking away.

Leighton looked down at the bed, like he was surprised.

"He's our guy, for sure," he said. "Everything fits like a glove."

Harper's mobile started ringing. It was over by the ice bucket, on the dresser, squawking like an alarm clock. Leighton paused. Gestured *I can wait*. Harper scrambled over the bed and flipped the phone open. Reacher heard a voice, feathery and distorted and faraway. Harper listened to it and Reacher watched the color drain out of her face. Watched her close the phone and put it down like it was fragile as crystal.

"We're recalled to Quantico," she said. "Effective immediately. Because they got Caroline Cooke's full record. You were right, she was all over the place. But she was never anywhere near weapons. Not ever. Not within a million miles, not for a minute."

"That's what I'm here to tell you," Leighton said. "Kruger's our guy, but he isn't yours."

Reacher just nodded.

26

LEIGHTON WALKED THE length of the room and sat down at the table, in the right-hand chair. Same chair as Reacher had used. He put his elbows on the table and his head in his hands. Same gesture.

"First thing, there was no list," he said. He looked up at Harper. "You asked me to check thefts where the women worked, so I needed a list of the women to do that, obviously, so I tried to find one, but I couldn't, OK? So I made some calls, and what happened was when your people came to us a month ago, we had to generate a list from scratch. It was a pain in the ass, trawling through all the records. So some guy had a bright idea, took a shortcut, called one of the women herself, some bullshit pretext. We think it was actually Alison Lamarr, and *she* supplied the list. Seems they'd set up a big support group among themselves, couple of years ago."

"Scimeca called them her sisters," Reacher said. "Remember that? She said four of my sisters are dead."

"It was their own list?" Harper said.

"We didn't have one," Leighton said again. "And then Kruger's records started coming in, and the dates and places didn't match. Not even close."

"Could he have falsified them?"

Leighton shrugged. "He *could* have. He was an ace at falsifying his inventories, that's for damn sure. But you haven't heard the kicker yet."

"Which is?"

"Like Reacher said, Special Forces to supply battalion needs some explaining. So I checked it out. He was a top boy in the Gulf. Big star, a major. They were out in the desert, behind the lines, looking for mobile SCUD launchers, small unit, bad radio. Nobody else had any real clear idea of where they were, hour to hour. So they start the artillery barrage and Kruger's unit gets all chewed up under it. Friendly fire. Bad casualties. Kruger himself was seriously hurt. But the Army was his life, so he wanted to stay in, so they gave him the promotion all the way up to bird colonel and stuck him somewhere his injuries wouldn't disqualify him, hence the desk job in supply. My guess is we'll find he got all bitter and twisted afterward and started running the rackets as a kind of revenge or something. You know, against the Army, against life itself."

"But what's the kicker?" Harper asked.

Leighton paused.

"The friendly fire," he said. "The guy lost both his legs."

Silence.

"He's in a wheelchair."

"Shit," she said.

"Yeah, shit. No way he's running up and down any stairs to any bathrooms. Last time he did that was ten years ago."

She stared at the wall.

"OK," she said slowly. "Bad idea."

"I'm afraid so, ma'am. And they're right about Cooke. I checked her too, and she never held anything heavier than a pen, her whole short career. That was something else I was going to have to tell you."

"OK," she said again.

She examined the wall.

"But thanks anyway," she said. "And now we're out of here. Back to Quantico, face the music."

"Wait," Leighton said. "You need to hear about the paint."

"More bad news?"

"Weird news," Leighton said. "I started a search for reports about missing camo green, like you asked me to. Only definitive thing was hidden in a buried file, closed-access. A theft of a hundred and ten three-gallon cans."

"That's it," Harper said. "Three hundred thirty gallons. Eleven women, thirty gallons each."

"Evidence was clear," Leighton said, "They fingered a supply sergeant in Utah."

"Who was he?"

"She," Leighton said. "She was Sergeant Lorraine Stanley."

Total silence.

"But that's impossible," Harper said. "She was one of the victims."

Leighton shook his head. "I called Utah. Got hold of the investigating officer. I got him out of bed. He says it was Stanley, no doubt about it. Means and opportunity. She'd tried to cover her tracks, but she wasn't smart enough about it. It was clear-cut. They didn't proceed against her because it was politically impossible right then. She'd just come off of the harassment thing, not long before. No way were they going to start in on her at that point. So they just watched her, until she quit. But it was her."

"One victim stole the paint?" Reacher said. "And another provided the list of names?"

Leighton nodded, somber. "That's how it was, I promise you. And you know I wouldn't bullshit one of Garber's boys."

Reacher just nodded.

THERE WAS NO more conversation. No more talk. The room went silent. Leighton sat at the table. Harper dressed mechanically. Reacher put his coat on and found the Nissan keys in Harper's jacket. Went outside and stood in the rain for a long moment. Then he unlocked the car and slid inside. Started the motor and waited. Harper and Leighton came out together. She crossed to the car and he walked back to his. He waved, just a brief motion of his hand. Reacher put the Nissan in drive and pulled slowly out of the lot.

"Check the map for me," he said.

"I-295 and then the Turnpike," she said.

He nodded. "I know it after that. Lamarr showed me."

"Why the hell would Lorraine Stanley steal the paint?"

"I don't know," he said.

"And you want to tell me *why*?" she asked. "You *knew* this Army thing was nothing, but you made us spend thirty-six hours on it. Why?"

"I already told you," he said. "It was an experiment, and I needed time to think."

"About what?"

He didn't answer. She went quiet for a spell.

"Good job we didn't go all the way celebrating," she said.

He didn't reply to that either. Didn't speak again, the whole way. He just found the right roads and drove on through the rain. He had new questions in his head, and he tried to think of some answers, but nothing would come. The only thing in his mind was the feel of her tongue in his mouth. It felt different from Jodie's. Tasted different. He guessed everybody's was different.

He DROVE FAST and it took a fraction under three hours from the outskirts of Trenton all the way back to Quantico. He turned in at the unmarked road off 95 and drove through the Marine checkpoints in the dark and waited at the vehicle barrier. The FBI sentry shone a flashlight on their badges and their faces and raised the striped pole and waved them through. They eased over the speed bumps and wound slowly through the empty parking lots and pulled up opposite the glass doors. It had stopped raining back in Maryland. Virginia was dry.

"OK," Harper said. "Let's go get our asses chewed."

Reacher nodded. Killed the motor and the lights and sat in the silence for a beat. Then they looked at each other and slid out of the car and stepped to the doors.

Took a deep breath. But the atmosphere inside the building was very calm. It was quiet. Nobody was around. Nobody was waiting for them. They went down in the elevator to Blake's underground office. Found him sitting in there at his desk with one hand resting on the telephone and the other holding a curled sheet of fax paper. The television was playing silently, political cable, men in suits at an impressive table. Blake was ignoring it. He was staring at a spot on his desk equidistant from the fax paper and the phone and his face was totally blank. Harper nodded to him, and Reacher said nothing.

"Fax in from UPS," Blake said. His voice was gentle. Amiable, even benign. He looked crestfallen, adrift, confused. He looked beaten.

"Guess who sent the paint to Alison Lamarr?" he said.

"Lorraine Stanley," Reacher said.

Blake nodded.

"Correct," he said. "From an address in a little town in Utah, that turned out to be a self-storage facility. And guess what else?"

"She sent all of it."

Blake nodded again. "UPS has got eleven consecutive consignment numbers showing eleven identical cartons going to eleven separate addresses, including Stanley's own place in San Diego. And guess what else?"

"What?"

"She didn't even *have* her own place when she first put the paint in the storage facility. She waited the best part of a year until she was settled, then she went back up to Utah and dispatched it all. So what do you make of that?"

"I don't know," Reacher said.

"Neither do I," Blake said.

Then he picked up the phone. Stared at it. Put it down again.

"And Poulton just called," he said. "From Spokane. Guess what he had to say?"

"What?"

"He just got through interviewing the UPS driver. The guy remembers pretty well. Isolated place, big heavy box, I guess he would."

"And?"

"Alison was there when he called. She was listening to the ball game too, radio on in the kitchen. She asked him inside, gave him coffee, they heard the grand slam together. A little hollering, a little dancing around, another coffee, he tells her he's got a big heavy box for her."

"And?"

"And she says oh, good. He goes back out and wheels it off the tail lift on a hand truck, she clears a space for it in the garage, he brings it in, he dumps it, and she's all smiles about it."

"Like she was expecting it?"

Blake nodded. "That was the guy's impression. And then what does she do?"

"What?"

"She tears off the 'Documents enclosed' thing and carries it back to the kitchen with her. He follows, to finish up his mug of coffee. She pulls the delivery note out of the plastic, and she shreds it up into small pieces, and she dumps them in the trash, along with the plastic."

"Why?"

Blake shrugged. "Who the hell knows? But this guy worked UPS four years, and six times out of ten people were home for him, and he never saw such a thing before."

"Is he reliable?"

"Poulton thinks so. Says he's a solid guy, clear, articulate, ready to swear the whole damn thing on a stack of Bibles."

"So what's your take?"

Blake shook his head. "I had any idea, you'd be the first to know."

Nighttime silence in the office.

"I apologize," Reacher said. "My theory led us nowhere."

Blake made a face. "Don't think twice. It was our call. It was worth a try. We wouldn't have let you go, otherwise."

"Is Lamarr around?"

"Why?"

"I should apologize to her, too."

Blake shook his head. "She's at home. She hasn't been back. Says she's a wreck, and she's right. Can't blame her."

Reacher nodded. "A lot of stress. She should get away."

Blake shrugged. "Where to? She won't get on a damn plane. And I don't want her driving anyplace, the state she's in."

Then his eyes hardened. He seemed to come back down to earth.

"I'm going to look for another consultant," he said. "When I find one, you're out of here. You're getting nowhere. You'll have to take your chances with the New York people."

Reacher nodded.

"OK," he said.

Blake looked away and Harper took her cue and led Reacher out of the office. Into the elevator, up to ground level, up to the third floor. They walked together through the corridor to the familiar door.

"Why was she expecting it?" Harper said. "Why was Alison expecting the box of paint, when all the others weren't?"

He shrugged. "I don't know."

Harper opened his door.

"OK, good night," she said.

"You mad at me?"

"You wasted thirty-six hours."

"No, I invested thirty-six hours."

"In what?"

"I don't know, yet."

She shrugged. "You're a weird guy."

He nodded. "So people say."

Then he kissed her chastely on the cheek, before she could duck away. He stepped into his room. She waited until the door swung shut before she walked back to the elevator.

THE SHEETS AND the towels had been changed. There was new soap and shampoo. A new razor and a fresh can of shaving cream. He upended a glass and put his tooth-brush in it. Walked to the bed and lay down, fully dressed, still in his coat. Stared up at the ceiling. Then he rolled up onto one elbow and picked up the phone.

Dialed Jodie's number. It rang four times, and he heard her voice, slow and sleepy.

"Who is it?" she said.

"Me," he said back.

"It's three o'clock in the morning."

"Nearly."

"You woke me up."

"I'm sorry."

"Where are you?"

"Locked up in Quantico."

She paused, and he heard the hum of the line and the faraway night sounds of New York. Faint isolated car horns, the whoop of a distant siren.

"How's it going?" she asked.

"It's not," he said. "They're going to replace me. I'll be home soon."

"Home?"

"New York," he said.

She was silent. He heard a quiet, urgent siren. Probably right there on Broadway, he thought. Under her window. A lonely sound.

"The house won't change anything," he said. "I told you that."

"It's the partnership meeting tomorrow," she said.

"So we'll celebrate," he said. "When I get back. As long as I'm not in jail. I'm still not out of the woods with Deerfield and Cozo yet."

"I thought they were going to forget about it."

"If I delivered," he said. "And I haven't delivered."

She paused again.

"You shouldn't have gotten involved in the first place."

"I know that."

"But I love you," she said.

"Me too," he said. "Good luck for tomorrow."

"You too."

He hung up and lay back down and resumed his survey of the ceiling. Tried to see her up there, but all he saw instead were Lisa Harper and Rita Scimeca, who were the last two women he'd wanted to take to bed but couldn't, for force of circumstance. Scimeca, it would have been totally inappropriate. Harper, it would have been an infidelity. Perfectly sound reasons, but reasons not to do something don't kill the original impulse. He thought about Harper's body, the way she moved, the guileless smile, her frank engaging stare. He thought about Scimeca's face, the invisible bruises, the hurt in her eyes. Her rebuilt life out there in Oregon, the flowers, the piano, the shine of her furniture wax, the buttoned-up defensive domesticity. He closed his eyes and then opened them and stared hard at the white paint above him. Rolled onto his elbow again and picked up the phone. Dialed 0, hoping to get a switchboard.

"Yes?" said a voice he had never heard before.

"This is Reacher," he said. "Up on the third floor."

"I know who you are and where you are."

"Is Lisa Harper still in the building?"

"Agent Harper?" the voice said. "Hold, please."

The line went quiet. No music. No recorded advertisements. No *your call is very important to us.* Just nothing. Then the voice came back.

"Agent Harper is still here," it said.

"Tell her I want to see her," Reacher said. "Right away."

"I'll pass that message on," the voice said.

Then the line went dead. Reacher swung his feet to the floor and sat on the edge of the bed, facing the door, waiting.

THREE O'CLOCK IN the morning in Virginia was midnight on the Pacific coast, and midnight was Rita Scimeca's habitual bedtime. She followed the same routine every night, partly because she was naturally an organized person, and partly because that aspect of her nature had been rigorously reinforced by her military training, and anyway when you've always lived alone and always will, how many ways *are* there of getting yourself to bed?

She started in the garage. Turned off the power to the door opener, slid the bolts into place, checked the car was locked, turned off the light. Locked and bolted the door through to the basement, checked the furnace. Walked upstairs, turned off the basement light, locked the door out to the hallway. Checked the front door was locked, did the bolts, put the chain on.

Then she checked the windows. There were fourteen windows in the house, and all of them had locks. Late fall and cold, they were all closed and locked anyway, but still she checked each one of them. It was her routine. Then she returned to the front parlor with a rag for the piano. She had played four hours, mostly Bach, mostly half speed, but she was getting there. Now she had to wipe down the keyboard. It was important to remove the acid from the skin of her fingers. She knew the keys were actually some kind of sophisticated plastic and were probably impervious, but it was a devotional thing. If she treated the piano right, it would reward her.

She wiped the keyboard vigorously, rumbling down at the bass end, tinkling all the way up to the top of the eighty-eight keys. She closed the lid and turned out the light and returned the rag to the kitchen. Turned out the kitchen light and felt her way in the dark up to her bedroom. Used the bathroom, washed her hands, her teeth, her face, all in her usual strict order. She stood at an angle to the sink, so she didn't have to look at the tub. She hadn't looked at the tub since Reacher had told her about the paint.

Then she stepped through to her bedroom and slid under the covers. Pulled her knees up and hugged them. She was thinking about Reacher. She liked him. She really did. It had been good to see him. But then she rolled the other way and put him out of her mind, because she didn't expect ever to see him again.

He waited twenty minutes before the door opened and Harper came back. She didn't knock, just used her key and walked right in. She was in shirtsleeves, rolled up to the elbows. Her forearms were slim and tanned. Her hair was loose. She wasn't wearing a bra. Maybe it was still in the motel room in Trenton.

"You wanted me?" she asked.

"You still on the case?" he asked.

She stepped into the room and glanced at herself in the mirror. Stood next to the dresser and turned to face him.

"Sure," she said. "Advantage of being a plain-vanilla agent, you don't get the blame for other people's crazy ideas."

He was silent. She looked at him.

"What did you want?" she said.

"I wanted to ask you a question," he said. "What would have happened if we'd already known about the paint delivery and we'd asked Alison Lamarr about it instead of the UPS guy? What would she have said?"

"The same as he said, presumably. Poulton told us the guy is solid."

"No," Reacher said. "He's solid, but she would have lied to us."

"She would? Why?"

"Because they're all lying to us, Harper. We've spoken to seven women, and they all lied to us. Vague stories about roommates and mistakes? All bullshit. If we'd gotten to Alison before, she'd have given us the same kind of a story."

"How do you know?"

"Because Rita Scimeca was lying to us. That's for damn sure. I just figured that out. She didn't have any roommate. Never. It just doesn't fit."

"Why not?"

"Everything's wrong about it. You saw her place. You saw how she lives. All buttoned up and prissy? Everything was so neat and clean and polished. Obsessive. Living like that, she couldn't stand anybody else in her house. She even threw *us* out pretty damn quick, and I was her friend. And she didn't need a roommate for money. You saw her car, some big new sedan. And that piano. You know how much a grand piano costs? More than the car, probably. And did you see the tools on her pegboard? The pegs were all held in with little plastic loops."

"You're basing this on loops in her pegboard?"

"On everything. It's all indicative."

"So what are you saying?"

"I'm saying she was expecting the delivery, just like Alison was. Just like they *all* were. The cartons came, they all said *oh good*, just like Alison did, they all made space, they all stored their cartons."

"It's not possible. Why would they?"

"Because the guy has got some kind of a hold over them," Reacher said. "He's forcing them to *participate*. He forced Alison to give him their own list of names, he forced Lorraine Stanley to steal the paint, he forced her to hide it in Utah, he forced her to send it out at the right time, he forced each one of them to accept the delivery and then store it until he was ready. He forced each one of them to destroy the delivery notes immediately and he had each of them ready to lie about it afterward if anything unraveled before he got to them."

Harper stared at him. "But how? How the hell? How would he *do* all that?"

"I don't know," Reacher said.

"Blackmail?" she said. "Threats? Fear? Is he saying, play along and the others die but you live? Like he's conning them all separately?"

"I just don't know. Nothing fits. They weren't an especially fearful bunch, were they? Certainly Alison didn't look it. And I *know* Rita Scimeca isn't afraid of much."

She was still staring at him.

"But it's not just participation, is it?" she said. "It's more than that. He's forcing them to be *happy* about it too. Alison said *oh good* when her carton came."

Silence in the room.

"Was she *relieved* or something?" she said. "Did he promise her, you get your carton by UPS instead of FedEx or in the afternoon instead of the morning or on some particular day of the week it means you're definitely going to be OK?"

"I don't know," he said again.

Silence.

"So what do you want me to do?" Harper asked.

He shrugged. "Just keep on thinking, I guess. You're the only one can do anything about it now. The others won't get anywhere, not if they keep on heading the direction they've been going."

"You've got to tell Blake."

He shook his head. "Blake won't listen to me. I've exhausted my credibility with him. It's up to you now."

"Maybe you've exhausted your credibility with me, too."

She sat down on the bed next to him, like she was suddenly unsteady on her feet. He was looking at her, something in his eyes.

"What?" she said.

"Is the camera on?"

She shook her head. "They gave up on that. Why?"

"Because I want to kiss you again."

"Why?"

"I liked it, before."

"Why should I want to kiss *you* again?"

"Because you liked it before too."

She blushed. "Just a kiss?"

He nodded.

"Well, OK, I guess," she said.

She turned to him and he took her in his arms and

kissed her. She moved her head like she had before. Pressed harder and put her tongue against his lips and his teeth. Into his mouth. He moved his hand down to her waist. She laced her fingers into his hair. Kissed harder. Her tongue was urgent. Then she put her hand on his chest and pushed herself away. Breathed hard.

"We should stop now," she said.

"I guess," he said.

She stood up, unsteady. Bent forward and back and tossed her hair behind her shoulders.

"I'm out of here," she said. "I'll see you tomorrow."

She opened the door. Stepped outside. He heard her wait in the corridor until the door swung shut again. Then he heard her walk away to the elevator. He lay back on the bed. Didn't sleep. Just thought about obedience and acquiescence, and means and motives and opportunities. And truth and lies. He spent five solid hours thinking about all of those things.

SHE CAME BACK at eight in the morning. She was showered and glowing and wearing a different suit and tie. She looked full of energy. He was tired, and crumpled and sweaty and hot and cold all at the same time. But he was standing just inside the door with his coat buttoned, waiting for her, his heart hammering with urgency.

"Let's go," he said. "Right now."

Blake was in his office, at his desk, same as he had been before. Maybe he'd been there all night. The UPS fax was still at his elbow. The television was still playing silently. Same channel. Some Washington reporter was standing on Pennsylvania Avenue, the White House behind his shoulder. The weather looked good. Bright blue sky, clear cold air. It would be an OK day for travel.

"Today you work the files again," Blake said.

"No, I need to get to Portland," Reacher said. "Will you lend me the plane?"

"The plane?" Blake repeated. "What are you, crazy? Not in a million years."

"OK," Reacher said.

He moved to the door. Took a last look at the office and stepped into the corridor. Stood still and quiet in the center of the narrow space. Harper crowded past him.

"Why Portland?" she asked.

He looked at her. "Truth, and lies."

"What does that mean?"

"Come with me and find out."

27

"What the hell's going on?" she asked.

He shook his head.

"I can't say it out loud," he said. "You'd think I was completely crazy. You'd just walk away from me."

"What's crazy? Tell me."

"No, I can't. Right now, it's just a house of cards. You'd blow it down. Anybody would blow it down. So you need to see it for yourself. Hell, I need to see it for *myself*. But I want you there, for the arrest."

"What arrest? Just tell me."

He shook his head again. "Where's your car?"

"In the lot."

"So let's go."

Reveille had been 0600 the whole of Rita Scimeca's service career, and she stuck to the habit in her new civilian life. She slept six hours out of twenty-four, midnight until six in the morning, a quarter of her life. Then she got up to face the other three quarters.

An endless procession of empty days. Late fall, there was nothing to be done in the yard. The winter temperatures were too savage for any young vegetation to make it through. So planting was restricted to the spring, and pruning and cleanup was finished by the end of the summer. Late fall and winter, the doors stayed locked and she stayed inside.

Today, she was scheduled to work on Bach. She was trying to perfect the three-part inventions. She loved them. She loved the way they moved forward, on and on, inescapably logical, until they ended up back where they started. Like Maurits Escher's drawings of staircases, which went up and up and up all the way back to the bottom. Wonderful. But they were very difficult pieces to play. She played them very slowly. Her idea was to get the notes right, then the articulation, then the meaning, and then last of all to get the speed right. Nothing worse than playing Bach fast and badly.

She showered in the bathroom and dressed in the bedroom. She did it quickly, because she kept the house cold. Fall in the Northwest was a chilly season. But today there was brightness in the sky. She looked out of her window and saw streaks of dawn spearing east to west like rods of polished steel. It would be cloudy, she guessed, but with a halo of sun visible. It would be like a lot of her days. Not good, not bad. But livable.

HARPER PAUSED FOR a second in the underground corridor and then led Reacher to the elevator and up into the daylight. Outside into the chill air and across the landscaping to her car. It was a tiny yellow two-seater. He realized he had never seen it before. She unlocked it and he ducked his head and folded himself into the passenger seat. She glanced hard at him once and dumped her bag in his lap and climbed down into the driver's seat. Shoulder room was tight. It was a stick shift, and her elbow hit his when she put it in gear.

"So how do we get there?"

"We'll have to go commercial," he said. "Head for National, I guess. You got credit cards?"

She was shaking her head.

"They're all maxed out," she said. "They'll get refused."

"All of them?"

She nodded. "I'm broke right now."

He said nothing.

"What about you?" she asked.

"I'm always broke," he said.

THE FIFTH OF Bach's three-part inventions was labeled BWV 791 by scholars and was one of the hardest in the canon, but it was Rita Scimeca's favorite piece in all the world. It depended entirely on tone, which came from the mind, down through the shoulders and the arms and the hands and the fingers. The tone had to be whimsical, but confident. The whole piece was a confection of nonsense, and the tone had to confess to that, but simultaneously it had to sound utterly serious for the effect to develop properly. It had to sound polished, but insane. Secretly, she was sure Bach was crazy.

Her piano helped. Its sound was big enough to be

sonorous, but delicate enough to be nimble. She played the piece all the way through twice, half speed, and she was reasonably pleased with what she heard. She decided to play for three hours, then stop and have some lunch, and then get ahead with the housework. She wasn't sure about the afternoon. Maybe she would play some more.

YOU TAKE UP your position early. Early enough to be settled before the eight o'clock changeover. You watch it happen. It's the same deal as yesterday. The Bureau guy, still awake, but no longer very attentive. The arrival of the Crown Vic. The flank-to-flank pleasantries. The Buick starts up, the Crown Vic turns in the road, the Buick rolls away down the hill, the Crown Vic crawls forward and settles into its space. The engine dies, and the guy's head turns. He sinks low in his seat, and his last shift as a cop begins. After today, they won't trust him to direct traffic around the Arctic Circle.

"SO HOW DO we get there?" Harper asked again.

Reacher paused.

"Like this," he said.

He opened her pocketbook and took out her phone and nipped it open. Closed his eyes and tried to recall sitting in Jodie's kitchen, dialing the number. Tried to remember the precious sequence of digits. He entered them slowly. Hopefully. He pressed send. Heard ring tone for a long moment. Then the call was answered. A deep voice, slightly out of breath.

"Colonel John Trent," it said.

"Trent, this is Reacher. You still love me?"

"What?"

"I need a ride, two people, Andrews to Portland, Oregon."

"Like when?"

"Like right now, immediately."

"You're kidding, right?"

"No, we're on our way there. We're a half hour out." Silence for a second.

"Andrews to Portland, Oregon, right?" Trent said.

"Right."

"How fast do you need to get there?"

"Fastest you got."

Silence again.

"OK," Trent said.

Then the line went dead. Reacher folded the phone.

"So is he doing it?" Harper asked.

Reacher nodded.

"He owes me," he said. "So let's go."

She let in the clutch and drove out of the lot, into the approach road. The tiny car rode hard over the speed bumps. She passed by the FBI guard and accelerated into the curve and blasted through the first Marine checkpoint. Reacher saw heads turning in the corner of his eye, startled faces under green helmets.

"So what is it?" she asked again.

"Truth, and lies," he said. "And means, motive, opportunity. The holy trinity of law enforcement. Three out of three is the real deal, right?"

"I can't even get one out of three," she said. "What's the key?"

They cleared the second Marine checkpoint, traveling fast. More swiveling helmeted heads watched them go.

"Bits and pieces," he said. "We know everything we

need to know. Some of it, we've known for days. But we screwed up everywhere, Harper. Big mistakes and wrong assumptions."

She made the blind left, north onto 95. Traffic was heavy. They were in the far outer echoes of D.C.'s morning rush hour. She changed lanes and was balked by the cars ahead and braked hard.

"Shit," he said.

"Don't worry," she said. "Scimeca's guarded out there. They all are."

"Not well enough. Not until we get there. This is a cool, cool customer."

She nodded and dodged left and right, looking for the fastest lane. They were all slow. Her speed dropped from forty to thirty. Then all the way down to twenty.

You use your field glasses and you watch his first bathroom break. He's been in the car an hour, swilling the coffee he brought with him. Now he needs to unload it. The driver's door opens and he pivots in his seat and puts his big feet down on the ground and hauls himself out. He's stiff from sitting. He stretches, steadying himself with a hand on the roof of the car. He closes the door and walks around the hood, into the driveway. Up the path. You see him step up onto the porch. You see his hand move to the bell push. You see him step back and wait.

You don't see her at the door. The angle is wrong. But he nods and smiles at something and steps inside. You keep the field glasses focused and three or four minutes later he's back on the porch, moving away, looking over his shoulder, talking. Then he turns ahead and walks back down the path. Down the driveway. Around the hood of his car. He gets back in. The suspension eases downward on his side and his door closes. He sinks down in his seat. His head turns. He watches.

SHE FLICKED THE tiny car right and put it on the shoulder. Eased the speed up to thirty, thirty-five, and hauled past the stalled traffic on the inside. The shoulder was rough and littered with gravel and debris. On their left, the tires on the stationary eighteen-wheelers were taller than the car.

"What mistakes?" she said. "What wrong assumptions?"

"Very, very ironic ones, in the circumstances," he said. "But it's not entirely our fault. I think we swallowed a few big lies, too."

"What lies?"

"Big, beautiful, breathtaking lies," he said. "So big and so obvious, nobody even saw them for what they were."

SHE BREATHED HARD and tried to relax again after the cop went back out. He was in and out, in and out, all day long. It ruined her concentration. To play this thing properly, you needed to be in some kind of trance. And the damn silly cop kept on interrupting it.

She sat down and played it through again, a dozen times, fifteen, twenty, all the way from the first measure to the last. She was note-perfect, but that was nothing. Was the meaning there? Was there emotion in the sound? Thought? On the whole, she reckoned there was. She played it again, once, then twice. She smiled to herself. Saw her face reflected back from the glossy black of the keyboard lid and smiled again. She was making progress. Now all she had to do was bring the speed up. But not too much. She preferred Bach played slowly. Too much speed trivialized it. Although it *was* fundamentally trivial music. But that was all part of Bach's mind game, she thought. He deliberately wrote trivial music that just begged to be played with great ceremony.

She stood up and stretched. Closed the keyboard lid and walked out to the hallway. Lunch was the next problem. She had to force herself to eat. Maybe everybody who lived alone had the same problem. Solo mealtimes weren't much fun.

There were footprints on the hallway parquet. Big muddy feet. The damn cop, ruining everything. Spoiling her musical concentration, spoiling the shine of her floors. She stared at the mess, and while she was staring, the doorbell rang. The idiot was here *again*. What the hell was the matter with him? Where was his bladder control? She stepped around the footprints and opened the door.

"No," she said.

"What?"

"No, you can't use the bathroom. I'm sick of it."

"Lady, I need to," he said. "That was the arrangement."

"Well, the arrangement has changed," she said. "I don't want you coming in here anymore. It's ridiculous. You're driving me crazy."

"I have to be here."

"It's ridiculous," she said again. "I don't need your protection. Just go away, will you?"

She closed the door, firmly. Locked it tight and walked away to the kitchen, breathing hard.

HE DOESN'T GO in. You watch very carefully. He just stands there on the porch, at first surprised. Then a little disgruntled. You can see it right there in his body language. He says three things, leaning fractionally backward in self-defense, and then the door must be closing in his face, because he steps back suddenly. He looks wounded. He stands still and stares and then turns around and walks back down the path, twenty seconds after walking up it. So what's that about?

He walks around the hood of his car and opens the door. Doesn't get all the way in. He sits sideways with his feet still out on the road. He leans over and picks up his radio mike. Holds it in his hand for thirty seconds, looking at it, thinking. Then he puts it back. Obviously he's not going to call it in. He's not going to tell his sergeant, Sir, she won't let me pee anymore. So what's he going to do? Is this going to change anything?

THEY GOT TO Andrews by driving most of the way on the shoulder and pushing in and out of the inside lane when necessary. The base itself was an oasis of calm. Nothing much was happening. There was a helicopter in the air, but it was far enough away to be noiseless. Trent had left Reacher's name at the gate. That was clear, because the guard was expecting them. He raised the barrier and told them to park at the Marine transport office and inquire within.

Harper put the yellow car in line with four dull olive Chevrolets and killed the motor. Joined Reacher on the blacktop and followed him to the office door. A corporal stared at her and passed them to a sergeant who stared at her and passed them to a captain. The captain stared at her and told them a new transport Boeing's flight test was being rerouted to Portland instead of San Diego. He said they could hitch a ride on it. He said they would be the only passengers. Then he said takeoff was scheduled in three hours.

"Three hours?" Reacher repeated.

"Portland's a civilian airport," the captain said. "It's a flight plan problem."

Reacher was silent. The guy just shrugged.

"Best the colonel could do," he said.

28

THE CAPTAIN SHOWED them to a preflight waiting room on the second floor. It was a utilitarian space, lit by fluorescent tubes, linoleum on the floor, plastic stacking chairs in untidy formation around low tables. Old coffee rings on the tables, a trash can in the corner full of discarded cups.

"It's not much," the captain said. "But then it's all we got. All kinds of top brass wait in here."

Reacher thought *do they wait three hours?* But he said nothing. Just thanked the guy and stood at the window and stared out at the runways. Nothing much was happening down there. Harper joined him for a second and then turned back and sat down in a chair.

"Talk to me," she said. "What is it?"

"Start with the motive," he said. "Who's got a motive?"

"I don't know."

"Go back to Amy Callan. Suppose she'd been the only victim? Who would you be looking at for a motive?"

"Her husband."

"Why her husband?"

"Dead wife, you always look at the husband," she said. "Because motives are often personal. And the closest connection to a wife is a husband."

"And *how* would you be looking at him?"

"How? Same as always. We'd sweat him, sweat his alibi, keep on going until something busted open."

"And he wouldn't hold up, right?"

"Sooner or later, he'd crack."

Reacher nodded. "OK, so suppose it *is* Amy Callan's husband. How does he avoid getting sweated like that?"

"He can't avoid it."

"Yes, he can. He can avoid it by going out and finding a bunch of women with some kind of a similarity with his wife and killing them too. Doing it in some bizarre fashion that he knows is going to get everybody rushing off on some flight of fancy. In other words he can camouflage his chosen target behind a farrago of bullshit. He can take the spotlight off of himself by burying the personal connection in a crowd. Like where's the best place to hide a grain of sand?"

She nodded. "On the beach."

"Right," he said.

"So is it Callan's husband?"

"No, it isn't," he said. "But?"

"But we only need a motive against one of the women," she said. "Not all of them together. All but one are just decoys. Sand on the beach."

"Camouflage," he said. "Background noise."

"So which one? Which one is the real target?"

Reacher said nothing. Moved away from the window and sat down to wait.

You wait. It's cold up there in the hills. Cold, and uncomfortable, crouched next to the rocks. The wind is blowing in from the west, and it's damp. But you just wait. Surveillance is important. Certainty is everything. You know that if you stay focused, you can do anything. Anything at all. So you wait.

You watch the cop in his car and amuse yourself thinking about his plight. He's a few hundred feet away, but he's in a different world. You can step away from your rock and you've got a million acres of mountainside to use as a bathroom. He's down there in civilization. Streets, sidewalks, people's yards. He can't use them. He'd be arrested. He'd have to arrest himself. And he's not running the motor. So the car must be cold. Does that make it better or worse?

You watch him, and you wait.

THE CAPTAIN CAME back a little before the three hours were up. He led them downstairs and out through the same door they had used on the way in. A staff car was waiting there.

"Have a pleasant flight," he said.

The car drove them a mile around the perimeter track and then cut across toward a Boeing airliner standing alone on the apron. Fuel bowsers were disconnecting and ground crew were swarming. The plane was brand-new and stark white.

"We don't paint them until we know they work right," the driver said.

There was a wheeled ladder at the forward cabin door. Flight crew in uniform clustered at the top, with fat briefcases and clipboards thick with paper.

"Welcome aboard," the copilot said. "You should be able to find an empty seat."

There were two hundred and sixty of them. It was a regular passenger plane with the fripperies stripped out. No televisions, no in-flight magazines, no stewardess call buttons. No blankets, no pillows, no headsets. The seats were all the same color, khaki. The fabric was crisp and it smelled new. Reacher took three seats for himself and sat sideways, propped up against the window.

"We've done a lot of flying, the last few days," he said.

Harper sat down behind him. Buckled her belt.

"That's for sure," she said.

"Listen up, guys," the copilot called to them down the aisle. "This is a military flight, not FAA, so you get the military preflight announcement, OK? Which is, don't worry, because we ain't going to crash. And if we do, you're mashed into ground beef and burned to a cinder anyway, so what's to worry about?"

Reacher smiled. Harper ignored the guy.

"So which one is the real target?" she asked again.

"You can figure it out," Reacher said.

The plane moved back and turned. Headed out for the runway. A minute later it was in the air, smooth, quiet, and powerful. Then it was over the sprawl of D.C., climbing hard. Then it was high in the clouds, settling to a westward cruise.

• • •

THE GUY'S STILL holding it in. He hasn't moved out of his car, and his car has stayed right there in front of her house. You watched his partner bring his lunch bag. There was a twenty-ounce cup of coffee with it. Poor bastard is going to be real miserable real soon. But it doesn't affect your plan. How could it? It's two o'clock, and time for the call.

You open the stolen mobile. Dial her number. Press on the little green telephone pictogram. You hear the connection go through. You hear ring tone. You crouch low in the lee of your rock, ready to speak. It's warmer down there. You're out of the wind. The ring tone continues. Is she going to answer? Maybe she won't. The type of contrary bitch who won't let her bodyguard use her bathroom might not be above ignoring her phone. You feel a momentary thrill of panic. What are you going to do? What if she doesn't pick up?

She picks up.

"Hello?" she says.

She's wary, annoyed, defensive. She thinks it's the police sergeant, about to complain. Or the Bureau coordinator, about to persuade her back into line.

"Hello, Rita," you say.

She hears your voice. You feel her relax.

"Yes?" she says.

You tell her what you want her to do.

"NOT THE FIRST one," Harper said. "The first one would be random. Leading us away from the scent. Probably not the second either. The second establishes the pattern."

"I agree," Reacher said. "Callan and Cooke were background noise. They started the smoke screen."

Harper nodded. Went quiet. She had moved out from behind him. Now she was sprawled across the opposite row in the empty plane. It was a weird feeling. Familiar, but strange. Nothing around them but neat uniform rows of vacant seats.

"But he wouldn't leave it too late," Harper said. "He's got a target, he'd want to hit it before anything unraveled, right?"

"I agree," Reacher said again.

"So it's the third or the fourth."

Reacher nodded. Said nothing.

"But which one?" Harper asked. "What's the key?"

"Everything," Reacher said. "Same as it always was. The clues. The geography, the paint, the lack of violence."

Lunch was a cold wrinkled apple and a square of Swiss cheese, which was about all her refrigerator had to offer. She served it to herself on a plate, to preserve some semblance of order. Then she washed the plate and put it back in the cupboard and walked through the hallway and unlocked the front door. Stood in the cold for a second and walked down her path to the driveway. The police car was still parked right across the opening. The cop saw her coming and buzzed his passenger window down.

"I came to apologize," she said. She kept it as sweet as she could. "I shouldn't have said what I said. It's just getting to me a little, is all. Of course you should come in, anytime you need to."

The guy was staring at her, half puzzled, like he was thinking *women!* to himself. She kept her smile going and lifted her eyebrows and tilted her head like she was reinforcing her invitation.

"Well, I'll come in right now," the guy said. "If you're sure it's OK."

She nodded and waited for him to get out. She noticed he left the passenger window down. The car would be cold when he got back. She led him back up the path. He was hurrying behind her. Poor guy must be desperate, she thought.

"You know where it is," she said.

She waited in the hallway. He came back out of the powder room with a relieved expression on his face. She held the front door for him.

"Anytime," she said. "Just ring the bell."

"OK, ma'am," he said. "If you're sure."

"I'm sure," she said. "I appreciate what you're doing for me."

"What we're here for," the guy said, proud and shy.

She watched him all the way back to the car. Locked the door again and stepped into the parlor. Stood and looked at the piano and decided to give it another forty-five minutes. Maybe an hour.

THAT'S BETTER. AND the timing might be about right. You can't be sure. You're an expert in a lot of things, but you're not a urologist. You watch him on the way back to the car, and you figure he's too young to be into prostate trouble, so all that's going to count is the fullness of his bladder balanced against his natural reluctance to bother her again. Two-thirty now, he's bound to want to go at least twice

*more before eight. Probably once before and once after she's
dead.*

THE CLOUD CLEARED over North Dakota. The ground
was visible seven miles below them. The copilot wandered back into the cabin and pointed down to where he
was born. A little town south of Bismarck. The Missouri
River ran through it, a tiny silver thread. Then the guy
wandered back again and left Reacher puzzling over
navigation. He knew nothing about it. Virginia to Oregon, he'd have flown across Kentucky, Illinois, Iowa,
Nebraska, Wyoming, Idaho. He wouldn't have gone up
to North Dakota. But something called great circle
routes made it shorter to go way out of your way. He
knew that. But he didn't understand it. How could it be
quicker to go way out of your way?

"Lorraine Stanley stole the paint," Harper said. "The
lack of violence proves the guy is faking it. But what
does the geography prove?"

"We talked about that," Reacher said.

"It demonstrates scope."

He nodded. "And speed."

She nodded in turn.

"And mobility," he added. "Don't forget mobility."

IN THE END, she played for an hour and a half. The cop
stayed away and she relaxed and her touch improved,
better than it had ever been. Her mind locked on to the
notes and she brought the speed higher and higher,
right to the point where the forward motion got a little
ragged. Then she backed it off and settled at a point just
a little slower than the tempo was marked. But what the

hell, it sounded magnificent. Maybe even better than it would played at exactly the right speed. It was involving, logical, stately. She was pleased with it.

She pushed back on the stool and knitted her fingers and flexed them above her head. Then she closed the keyboard lid and stood up. Stepped out to the hallway and skipped up the stairs to her bathroom. Stood at the mirror and brushed her hair. Then she went back down to the coat closet and took out her jacket. It was short enough to be comfortable in the car and warm enough for the weather. She changed her shoes for her heavier pair. Unlocked the door to the basement stairs and went down. Unlocked the door to the garage and used the key-chain remote to open her car. The light came on inside. She switched the power on for the opener and slid into the car and started the engine while the garage door rumbled upward.

She backed onto the driveway and hit the button to close the door again. Twisted in her seat and saw the police cruiser parked in her way. She left the motor running and got out and walked down toward it. The cop was watching her. He buzzed the window open.

"I'm going to the store," she said.

The guy looked at her for a second, like this was outside the range of permissible scenarios.

"How long you going to be gone?" he asked.

She shrugged.

"Half hour, an hour," she said.

"The store?" he said.

She nodded. "I need some things."

He stared some more, and arrived at a decision.

"OK, but I wait here," he said. "We're watching the

house, not you personally. Domicile-based crimes, that's what we do."

She nodded again. "That's fine. Nobody's going to grab me at the store."

The cop nodded back. Said nothing. He started his engine and backed up the slope far enough that she could maneuver out past him. He watched her roll away down the hill, and then he eased back into position.

You see the garage door open, you see the car come out, you see the door close again. You see her stop on her driveway, and you see her get out. You watch the conversation through the Crown Vic's window. You see the cop back up, you see her reverse out onto the roadway. The cop moves back into position, she takes off down the hill. You smile to yourself and ease backward under the cover of the rocks. You stand up. You go to work.

She made the left at the bottom of her hill, and then the right onto the through road toward the city of Portland. It was cold. Another week of falling temperatures, and it would be snowing. Then her choice of automobile would start to look a little silly. Everybody else had big four-wheel-drives, either jeeps or pickup trucks. She had gone for a swoopy low-slung sedan, about four times longer than it was high. Gold paint, chrome wheels, butter-soft tan leather inside. It looked like a million dollars, but it was front-wheel-drive only, no traction control. Ground clearance was enough for a decent-sized snowball and not much more. The rest of the winter, she'd be walking or begging rides from her neighbors.

But it was smooth and quiet and it rode like a dream.

She drove the two miles west and slowed for the left into the shopping center. Waited for an oncoming truck to labor past and swooped into the parking lot. Turned tight and drove around behind the right-hand arm of stores and parked up alone in the overspill lane. Pulled the key and dropped it in her bag. Got out and walked through the cold toward the supermarket.

It was warmer inside. She took a cart and walked every aisle, using time. There was no system in her shopping. She just looked at everything and took what she figured she was out of. Which was not very much, because the market didn't sell the things she was really interested in. No music books, no garden plants. She ended up with little enough in the cart to get her into the express line at the checkout.

The girl put it all into one paper sack and she paid cash for it and walked out with the sack cradled in her arms. Turned right on the narrow sidewalk and window-shopped her way along the row. Her breath hung in the air. She stopped outside the hardware store. It was an old-fashioned place. It carried a little bit of everything. She had shopped there before, for sacks of bonemeal and ericaceous fertilizer to help her azaleas.

She juggled the grocery sack into one arm and pulled the door. A bell rang. There was an old guy in a brown coat at the register. He nodded a greeting. She moved forward into the crowded aisles. Walked past the tools and the nails and found the decorating section. There were rolls of cheap wallpaper and packets of paste. Paint-brushes and paint rollers. And cans of paint. A display as tall as she was. Color charts were held in racks clipped to the shelves. She put her groceries on the floor and took a chart from a rack and opened it up. It was banded into colors like a huge rainbow. A big variety of shades.

"Help you, miss?" a voice said.

It was the old guy. He'd crept up behind her, helpful and anxious for a sale.

"Does this stuff mix with water?" she asked.

The old guy nodded.

"They call it latex," he said. "But that just means water-based. You can thin it with water, clean the roller with water."

"I want a dark green," she said.

She pointed at the chart.

"Maybe like this olive," she said.

"The avocado is attractive," the old guy said.

"Too light," she said.

"You going to thin it with water?" he asked.

She nodded. "I guess."

"That'll make it lighter still."

"I think I'll take the olive," she said. "I want it to look kind of military."

"OK," the old guy said. "How much?"

"One can," she said. "A gallon."

"Won't go far," he said. "Although if you thin it, that'll help."

He carried it back to the register for her and rang up the sale. She paid cash and he put it in a bag with a free wooden stirring stick. The store's name was printed off-center on the stick.

"Thank you," she said.

She carried the grocery sack in one hand and the hardware bag in the other. Walked along the row of stores. It was cold. She looked up and checked the sky. It was blackening with clouds. They were scurrying in from the west. She looped around behind the last store. Hurried to her car. Dumped her bags on the backseat and climbed in and slammed her door and started the engine.

THE COP WAS cold, which kept his attention focused. Summertime, sitting and doing nothing could make him sleepy, but there was no chance of that with the temperature as low as it was now. So he saw the approaching figure when it was still about a hundred yards away down the hill. The crest of the slope meant he saw the head first, then the shoulders, then the chest. The figure was walking purposefully toward him, rising up over the foreshortened horizon, revealing more and more of itself, getting bigger. The head was gray, thick hair neatly trimmed and brushed. The shoulders were dressed in Army uniform. Eagles on the shoulder boards, eagles through the lapels, a colonel. A clerical collar where the shirt and tie should be. A padre. A military chaplain, approaching fast up the sidewalk. His face bobbed up and down with every stride. The white band of the collar moved below it. The guy was walking quickly. Practically marching.

He stopped suddenly a yard from the cop's right headlight. Just stood on the sidewalk with his neck craned, looking up at Scimeca's house. The cop buzzed the passenger window down. He didn't know what to say. Some local citizen, he'd call, *Sir, step this way*, with enough tone in there to cancel out the *sir*. But this was a padre and a bird colonel. Practically a gentleman.

"Excuse me?" he called.

The colonel looked around and stepped the length of the fender. Bent down. He was tall. He put one hand on the Crown Vic's roof and the other on the door. Ducked his head and looked straight in through the open window.

"Officer," he said.

"Help you?" the cop asked.

"I'm here to visit with the lady of the house," the padre said.

"She's not home, temporarily," the cop said. "And we've got a situation here."

"A situation?"

"She's under guard. Can't tell you why. But I'm going to have to ask you to step inside the car and show me some ID."

The colonel hesitated for a second, like he was confused. Then he straightened up and opened the passenger door. Folded himself into the seat and put his hand inside his jacket. Came out with a wallet. Flipped it open and pulled a worn military ID. Passed it across to the cop. The cop read it over and checked the photograph against the face next to him. Handed it back and nodded.

"OK, Colonel," he said. "You can wait in here with me, if you like. I guess it's cold out there."

"It sure is," the colonel said, although the cop noticed he was sweating lightly. Probably from the fast walk up the hill, he figured.

"I'M NOT GETTING anyplace," Harper said.

The plane was on descent. Reacher could feel it in his ears. And he could feel abrupt turns. The pilot was military, so he was using the rudder. Civilian pilots avoid using the rudder. Using the rudder makes the plane slew, like a car skids. Passengers don't like the feeling. So civilian pilots turn by juicing the engines on one side and backing off on the others. Then the plane comes around smoothly. But military pilots don't care about their passengers' comfort. It's not like they've bought tickets.

"Remember Poulton's report from Spokane?" he said.

"What about it?"

"That's the key. Something big and obvious."

SHE MADE THE left off the main road and the right into her street. The cop was back in the way again. Somebody was in the front seat next to him. She stopped on the crown of the road, ready to turn in, hoping he'd take the hint and move, but he just opened his door and got out, like he needed to talk to her. He walked across, stiff from sitting, and placed his hand on the roof of her car and bent down. She opened her window and he peered in and glanced at the shopping bags on the backseat.

"Get what you need?" he asked.

She nodded.

"No problems?"

She shook her head.

"There's a guy here to see you," he said. "A padre, from the Army."

"The guy in your car?" she said, like she had to say something, although it was pretty obvious. She could see the collar.

"Colonel somebody," the cop said. "His ID is OK."

"Get rid of him," she said.

The cop was startled.

"He's all the way from D.C.," he said. "His ID says he's based there."

"I don't care where he's based. I don't want to see him."

The cop said nothing. Just glanced back over his shoulder. The colonel was getting out of the car. Easing up to his full height on the sidewalk. Walking over. Scimeca left her motor running and opened her door. Slid out and stood up and watched him coming, pulling her jacket tight around her in the cold.

"Rita Scimeca?" the padre asked, when he was close enough.

"What do you want?"

"I'm here to see if you're OK."

"OK?" she repeated.

"With your recovery," he said. "After your problems."

"My *problems*?"

"After the assault."

"And if I'm not OK?"

"Then maybe I can help you."

His voice was warm and low and rich. Infinitely believable. A church voice.

"The Army send you?" she asked. "Is this official?"

He shook his head.

"I'm afraid not," he said. "I've argued it with them many times."

She nodded. "If they offer counseling, they're admitting liability."

"That's their view," the colonel said. "Regrettably. So this is a private mission. I'm acting against strict orders, in secret. But it's a matter of conscience, isn't it?"

Scimeca glanced away.

"Why me in particular?" she asked. "There were a lot of us."

"You're my fifth," he said. "I started with the ones who are obviously living alone. I thought that's where my help might be needed most. I've been all over the place. Some fruitful trips, some wasted trips. I try not to force myself on people. But I feel I have to try."

She was silent for a moment. Very cold.

"Well, you've wasted another trip, I'm afraid," she said. "I decline your offer. I don't want your help."

The colonel was not surprised, not unsurprised. "Are you sure?"

She nodded.

"Totally sure," she said.

"Really? Please think about it. I came a long way."

She didn't answer. Just glanced at the cop, impatiently. He shuffled his feet, calling the colonel's attention his way.

"Asked and answered," he said, like a lawyer.

There was silence in the street. Just the beat of Scimeca's motor idling, the drift of exhaust, a sharp chemical tang in the fall air.

"I'm going to have to ask you to leave now, sir," the cop said. "We've got a situation here."

The colonel was still for a long moment. Then he nodded.

"The offer is always open," he said. "I could come back, anytime."

He turned abruptly and walked back down the hill, moving fast. The slope swallowed him up, legs, back, head. Scimeca watched him below the horizon and slid back into her car. The cop nodded to himself and tapped twice on the roof.

"Nice car," he said, irrelevantly.

She said nothing.

"Right," the cop said.

He walked back to his cruiser. Reversed it up the hill with his door hanging open. She turned into her driveway. Pushed the button on the remote and the garage door rumbled upward. She drove inside and pushed the button again. Saw the cop moving back into position before the door came down and left her in darkness.

She opened her door and the dome light clicked on. She pulled the little lever at her side and popped the trunk. Got out of the car and took her bags from the backseat and carried them through to the basement. Carried them up the stairs to the hallway and through to the kitchen. Placed them side by side on the counter-top and sat down on a stool to wait.

It's a low-slung car, so although the trunk is long enough and wide enough, it's not very tall. So you're lying on your side, cramped. Your legs are drawn up, like a fetal position. Getting in was no problem. She left the car unlocked, just like you told her to. You watched her walk away to the store, and then you just stepped over and opened the driver's door and found the lever and popped the trunk. Closed the door again and walked around and lifted the lid. Nothing to it. Nobody was watching. You sort of rolled inside and pulled the lid closed on top of you. It was easy.

There were reinforcing members on the underside. Easy to grasp.

It's a long wait in there. But then you feel her get back in and you hear the engine start. You feel a growing patch of heat under your thigh where the exhaust runs under the trunk floor. It's not a comfortable ride. You bounce around a little. You follow the turns in your mind and you know when she arrives back at her place. You hear the cop talking. There's a problem. Then you hear some idiot padre, pleading. You tense up in there. You start to panic. What the hell is going on? What if she asks him in? But she gets rid of him. You hear the ice in her voice. You smile in the dark and open and close your hands in triumph. You hear it when she drives into the garage. The acoustics change. The engine goes louder. You hear the exhaust beating against the walls and the floor. Then she shuts it down and it goes very quiet.

She remembers to pop the trunk. You knew she would, because you told her not to forget. Then you hear her footsteps moving away and you hear the basement door open and close. You ease the trunk lid upward and you climb out. You stand and stretch in the dark. Rub your thigh where the heat has hurt it. Then you move around to the front of the car. You pull your gloves on tighter and you sit down on the fender and you wait.

29

THE PLANE LANDED at Portland International like any
other Boeing, but it stopped rolling some way short of
the terminal and waited on a distant apron. A pickup
with a staircase bolted to the load bed came slowly out
to meet it. The pickup was followed by a minivan. Both
vehicles were shiny clean and painted in Boeing's corporate colors. The flight crew stayed on board to analyze
computer data. The minivan took Reacher and Harper
around to the arrivals lane, where the taxis waited. Head
of the line was a battered Caprice with a checkerboard
stripe down the side. The driver wasn't local. He needed
to check his map to find the road east toward the tiny
village on the slopes of Mount Hood.

SHE WAS IN the house all of five minutes, and then the
doorbell went. The cop was back. She came out of the

kitchen and walked the length of the hallway and unlocked the door. Opened it up. He was standing there on the porch, not saying anything, trying to communicate his request with the rueful expression on his face

"Hi," she said.

Then she just looked at him. Didn't smile or anything.

"Hi," he said back.

She waited. She was going to make him say it anyway. It was nothing to be embarrassed about.

"Guess what?" he said.

"What?"

"Can I use the powder room?"

Cold air was swirling in around her legs. She could feel it striking through her jeans.

"Of course," she said.

She closed the door behind him, to keep some warmth in. Waited next to it, while he disappeared and then came back again.

"Nice and warm in here," he said.

She nodded, although it wasn't really true. She kept the house as cold as she could stand it. For the piano tone. So the wood didn't dry out.

"Cold out there in the car," he said.

She nodded again.

"Run the motor," she said. "Get the heater going."

He shook his head. "Not allowed. Can't idle the engine. Some pollution thing."

"So take off for a spell," she said. "Drive around, get warm. I'll be OK here."

Clearly it wasn't the invitation he was looking for, but he thought about it. Then he shook his head again.

"They'd take my badge," he said. "I've got to stay here."

She said nothing.

"Sorry to bother you with that padre," he said, making the point he'd intervened, and gotten rid of him.

She nodded.

"I'll bring you some hot coffee," she said. "Five minutes, OK?"

He looked pleased. A shy smile.

"Then I'll need the powder room again," he said. "Goes right through me."

"Whenever," she said.

She closed the door on him and went back to the kitchen and set her coffee machine going. Waited on the stool next to the shopping bags until it was done. She found the biggest mug she owned and poured the coffee. Added cream from the refrigerator and sugar from the cupboard. He looked like a cream-and-sugar guy, young, a little fat. She carried the mug outside and walked down the path. Steam swirled off the coffee and hung in a thin horizontal band all the way to the sidewalk. She tapped on his window and he turned and smiled and buzzed the glass down. He took the cup, awkwardly, two-handed.

"Thanks," he said.

He touched it to his lips like an extra gesture of politeness and she walked away, into the driveway, up the path, in through the door. She closed it behind her and locked it and turned around to find the visitor she was expecting standing quietly at the head of the stairs from the garage.

"Hello, Rita," the visitor said.

"Hello," she said back.

THE TAXI DROVE south on 205 and found the left turn east on 26. It rode like its next trip should be to the scrap heap. The colors inside the door seams didn't match the outside. It had probably already done three years in New York, and maybe three more in the suburbs of Chicago. But it moved along steadily enough, and its meter clicked a lot slower than it would have in New York or Chicago. And that was important, because Reacher had just realized he had almost no money in his pockets.

"Why is a demonstration of mobility important?" Harper asked.

"That's one of the big lies," Reacher said. "We just swallowed it whole."

SCIMECA STOOD THERE inside her front door, calmly. The visitor gazed back at her from the other end of the hallway, eyes inquiring.

"Did you buy the paint?"

She nodded.

"Yes, I did," she said.

"So, are you ready?"

"I'm not sure."

The visitor watched her a moment longer, just gazing, very calm, eyes steady.

"Are you ready now?"

"I don't know," she said.

The visitor smiled.

"I think you're ready. I really do. What do you think? Are you ready?"

She nodded, slowly.

"Yes, I'm ready," she said.

"Did you apologize to the cop?"

She nodded again. "Yes, I told him I was sorry."

"He has to be allowed in, right?"

"I told him, whenever he needs it."

"He has to find you. He has to be the one. That's the way I want it."

"OK," Scimeca said.

The visitor was silent for a long moment, just standing there, saying nothing, watching carefully. Scimeca waited, awkward.

"Yes, he should be the one to find me," she said. "If that's the way you want it."

"You did good with the padre," the visitor said.

"He wanted to help me."

"Nobody can help you."

"I guess not," Scimeca said.

"Let's go into the kitchen," the visitor said.

Scimeca moved away from the door. Squeezed past the visitor in the narrow hallway and led the way into her kitchen.

"The paint is right here," she said.

"Show me."

Scimeca took the can out of the bag and held it up by the wire handle.

"It's olive green," she said. "Closest they had."

The visitor nodded. "Good. You did very well."

Scimeca blushed with pleasure. A tiny pink flush under the white of her skin.

"Now you need to concentrate," the visitor said. "Because I'm going to give you a lot of information."

"What about?"

"About what I want you to do."

Scimeca nodded.

"OK," she said.

"First thing, you have to smile for me," the visitor said. "That's very important. It means a lot to me."

"OK," Scimeca said.

"So can you smile for me?"

"I don't know."

"Try it, OK?"

"I don't smile much anymore."

The visitor nodded, sympathetic. "I know, but just try now, OK?"

Scimeca ducked her head and concentrated and came back up with a shy, weak smile. Just a faint new angle to her lips, but it was something. She held it, desperately.

"That's nice," the visitor said. "Now remember, I want you smiling all the time."

"OK."

"Got to be happy in our work, right?"

"Right."

"We need something to open the can."

"My tools are downstairs," Scimeca said.

"Have you got a screwdriver?"

"Of course," Scimeca said. "I've got eight or nine."

"Go get a big one for me, would you?"

"Sure."

"And don't forget the smile, OK?"

"Sorry."

THE MUG WAS too big for the Crown Vic's cup holder, so he drank all the coffee straight off because he couldn't put it down between sips. That always happened. At a party, if he was standing up holding a bottle, he drank it much faster than if he was sitting at a bar where he could sometimes rest it on the napkin. Like smoking. If there was an ashtray to rest the butt in, the cigarette lasted much longer than if he was walking around with it, whereupon he demolished it in about a minute and a half.

So he was sitting there with the empty mug resting on his thigh, thinking about carrying it back up to the house. *Here's your mug back*, he could say. *Thanks very much*. It would give him another chance to drop a hint about how cold he was. Maybe he could get her to put a chair in the hallway, and he could finish his shift inside. Nobody could complain about that. Better protection that way.

But he was nervous about ringing the bell again. She was an uptight character, that was for damn sure. Who knows how she might react, even though he was being real polite, just returning her mug? Even though he'd gotten rid of the chaplain for her? He bounced the mug up and down on his knee and tried to balance out between how cold he was and how offended she might get.

THE TAXI DROVE on, through Gresham, through Kelso, through Sandy. Route 26 picked up a name, Mount Hood Highway. The grade steepened. The old V-8 dug deep and rumbled upward.

"Who is it?" Harper asked.

"The key is in Poulton's report from Spokane."

"It is?"

He nodded. "Big and obvious. But it took me some time to spot it."

"The UPS thing? We went through all of that."

He shook his head. "No, before that. The Hertz thing. The rental car."

Sᴄɪᴍᴇᴄᴀ ᴄᴀᴍᴇ ʙᴀᴄᴋ up the basement stairs with a screwdriver in her hand. It was the third-largest she had, about eight inches long, with a blade fine enough to slip between the can and the lid, but broad enough to make an effective lever.

"I think this is the best one," she said. "You know, for the purpose."

The visitor looked at it from a distance. "I'm sure it's fine. As long as you're comfortable with it. You'll be using it, not me."

Scimeca nodded.

"I think it's good," she said.

"So where's your bathroom?"

"Upstairs."

"Want to show me?"

"Sure."

"Bring the paint," the visitor said. "And the screwdriver."

Scimeca went back to the kitchen and picked up the can.

"Do we need the stirring stick too?" she called.

The visitor hesitated. *New procedure, needs a new technique.*

"Yes, bring the stirring stick."

The stick was about twelve inches long, and Scimeca

clasped it together with the screwdriver in her left hand. Picked up the can by the handle with her right.

"This way," she said.

She led the way out of the kitchen and up the stairs. Across the upstairs hallway and into her bedroom. Across the bedroom and into the bathroom.

"This is it," she said.

The visitor looked it over, and felt like an expert on bathrooms. This one was the fifth, after all. It was medium-budget, probably. A little old-fashioned. But it suited the age of the house. A fancy marble confection would have looked wrong.

"Put the stuff down on the floor, OK?"

Scimeca bent and put the can down. The metal made a faint liquid *clonk* as it hit the tile. She folded the wire handle down and balanced the screwdriver and the stick across the lid. The visitor came out with a folded garbage sack, black plastic, from a coat pocket. Shook it out and held it open.

"I need you to put your clothes in here."

HE GOT OUT of the car, with the mug in his hand. Walked around the hood and into the driveway. Up the looping path. Up the porch steps. He juggled the mug into the other hand, ready to ring the bell. Then he paused. It was very quiet inside. No piano music. Was that good or bad? She was kind of obsessive, always playing the same thing over and over again. Probably didn't like being interrupted in the middle of it. But the fact that she wasn't playing might mean she was doing something else important. Maybe taking a nap. The Bureau guy said she got up at six. Maybe she took a siesta in the afternoon. Maybe she was reading a book. Whatever she was doing, she probably wasn't just sitting there hoping he'd come to her door. She hadn't shown any inclinations along those lines before.

He stood there, indecisive, his hand held out a foot away from her bell. Then he dropped it to his side and turned around and went back down the steps to the path. Back down the path to the driveway. Back around the hood of his car. He got in and leaned over and stood the mug upright in the passenger footwell.

SCIMECA LOOKED CONFUSED.

"What clothes?" she asked.

"The clothes you're wearing," the visitor said.

Scimeca nodded, vaguely.

"OK," she said.

"I'm not happy with the smile, Rita," the visitor said. "It's slipping a little."

"Sorry."

"Check it out in the mirror, tell me if that's a happy face."

Scimeca turned to the mirror. Gazed for a second and started working on the muscles in her face, one by one. The visitor watched her reflection.

"Make it a big one. Real cheerful, OK?"

Scimeca turned back.

"How's this?" she said, smiling as wide as she could.

"Very good," the visitor said. "You want to make me happy, right?"

"Yes, I do."

"So put your clothes in the bag."

Scimeca took off her sweater. It was a heavy knit item with a tight neck. She hauled the hem up and stretched it over her head. Shook it right side out and leaned over and dropped it in the bag. Second layer was a flannel blouse, washed so many times it was soft and shapeless. She unbuttoned it all the way down and pulled the tails out of the waistband of her jeans. Shrugged it off and dropped it in the bag.

"Now I'm cold," she said.

She unbuttoned the jeans and undid the zip and pushed them down her legs. Kicked off her shoes and stepped out of the jeans. Rolled the shoes and the jeans together and put them in the bag. Peeled off her socks and shook them out and threw them in, one at a time.

"Hurry up, Rita," the visitor said.

Scimeca nodded and put her hands behind her back and unhooked her bra. Pulled it off and tossed it in the bag. Slipped her panties down and stepped out of them. Crushed them into a ball and threw them into the bag. The visitor closed the neck of the bag and dropped it on the floor. Scimeca stood there, naked, waiting.

"Run the bath," the visitor said. "Make it warm, since you're cold."

Scimeca bent down and put the stopper in the drain. It was a simple rubber item, secured by a chain. She opened the faucets, three-quarters hot and one-quarter cold.

"Open the paint," the visitor said.

Scimeca squatted down and picked up the screwdriver. Worked the tip into the crack and levered. Rotated the can under the screwdriver, once, twice, until the lid sucked free.

"Be careful. I don't want any mess."

Scimeca laid the lid gently on the tile. Looked up, expectant.

"Pour the paint in the tub."

She picked up the can, both hands. It was wide, not easy to hold. She clamped it between her palms and carried it to the tub. Twisted from the waist and tipped it over. The paint was thick. It smelled of ammonia. It ran slowly over the lip of the can and poured into the water. The swirl from the faucets caught it. It eddied into a spiral pattern and sank like a weight. The water started dissolving the edges of the spiral and thin green color drifted through the tub like clouds. She held the can upside down until the thick stream thinned, and then stopped.

"Careful," the visitor said. "Now put the can down. And don't make a mess."

She turned the can the right way up and squatted again and placed it gently on the tile next to the lid. It made a hollow, empty sound, damped slightly by the residue coating the metal.

"Now get the stirring stick. Mix it up."

She picked up the stick and knelt at the edge of the tub. Worked the stick into the thick sunken mass and stirred.

"It's mixing," she said.

The visitor nodded. "That's why you bought latex."

The color changed as the paint dissolved. It went from dark olive to the color of grass growing in a damp grove. It thinned, all the way down to the consistency of milk. The visitor watched carefully. It was OK. Not as dramatic as the real thing, but it was dramatic enough to be using paint at all, in the circumstances.

"OK, that'll do. Put the stick in the can. No mess."

Scimeca pulled the stick out of the green water and shook it carefully. Reached back and stood it upright in the empty can.

"And the screwdriver."

She stood the screwdriver next to the stick.

"Put the lid back on."

She picked the lid up by the edge and laid it across the top of the can. It canted up at a shallow angle, because the stirring stick was too tall to let it go all the way down.

"You can turn the faucets off now."

She turned back to the tub and shut off the water. The level was up to within six inches of the rim.

"Where did you store your carton?"

"In the basement," she said. "But they took it away."

The visitor nodded. "I know. But can you remember exactly where it was?"

Scimeca nodded in turn.

"It was there for a long time," she said.

"I want you to put the can down there," the visitor said. "Right where the carton was. Can you do that?"

Scimeca nodded.

"Yes, I can do that," she said.

She raised the metal hoop. Eased it up alongside the unsteady lid. Carried the can out in front of her, one hand on the handle, the other palm down against the lid, securing it. She went down the stairs and through the hallway and down to the garage and through to the basement. Stood for a second with her feet on the cold concrete floor, trying to get it exactly right. Then she stepped to her left and placed the can on the floor, in the center of the space the carton had occupied.

THE TAXI WAS struggling on a long hill past a small shopping center. There was a supermarket, with rows of stores flanking it. A parking lot, mostly empty.

"Why are we here?" Harper asked.

"Because Scimeca is next," Reacher said.

The taxi labored onward. Harper shook her head.

"Tell me who."

"Think about *how*," Reacher said. "That's the absolute final proof."

SCIMECA MOVED THE empty can an inch to the right. Checked carefully. Nodded to herself and turned and ran back upstairs. She felt she ought to hurry.

"Out of breath?" the visitor asked.

Scimeca gulped and nodded.

"I ran," she said. "All the way back."

"OK, take a minute."

She breathed deeply and pushed her hair off her face.

"I'm OK," she said.

"So now you have to get into the tub."

Scimeca smiled.

"I'll get all green," she said.

"Yes," the visitor said. "You'll get all green."

Scimeca stepped to the side of the tub and raised her foot. Pointed her toe and put it in the water.

"It's warm," she said.

The visitor nodded. "That's good."

Scimeca took her weight on the foot in the water and brought the other in after it. Stood there in the tub up to her calves.

"Now sit down. Carefully."

She put her hands on the rim and lowered herself down.

"Legs straight."

She straightened her legs and her knees disappeared under the green.

"Arms in."

She let go of the rim and put her hands down beside her thighs.

"Good," the visitor said. "Now slide down, slowly and carefully."

She shuffled forward in the water. Her knees came up. They were stained green, dark and then pale where little rivulets of paint flowed over her skin. She lay back and felt the warmth moving up her body. She felt it lap over her shoulders.

"Head back."

She tilted her head and looked up at the ceiling. She felt her hair floating.

"Have you ever eaten oysters?" the visitor asked.

She nodded. She felt her hair swirl in the water as she moved her head.

"Once or twice," she said.

"You remember how it feels? They're in your mouth, and you just suddenly swallow them whole? Just gulp them down?"

She nodded again.

"I liked them," she said.

"Pretend your tongue is an oyster," the visitor said.

She glanced sideways, puzzled.

"I don't understand," she said.

"I want you to swallow your tongue. I want you to just gulp it down, real sudden, like it was an oyster."

"I don't know if I can do that."

"Can you try?"

"Sure, I can try."

"OK, give it a go, right now."

She concentrated hard, and tried. Gulped it back, suddenly. But nothing happened. Just a noise in her throat.

"Doesn't work," she said.

"Use your finger to help," the visitor said. "The others all had to do that."

"My finger?"

The visitor nodded. "Push it back in there with your finger. It worked for the others."

"OK."

She raised her hand. Thin paint ran off her arm, with thicker globules where the mixing wasn't perfect.

"Which finger?" she asked.

"Try the middle," the visitor said. "It's the longest."

She extended her middle finger and folded the others. Opened her mouth.

"Put it right under your tongue," the visitor said. "And push back hard."

She opened her mouth wider and pushed back hard.

"Now swallow."

She swallowed. Then her eyes jammed open in panic.

30

THE CAB PULLED up nose to nose with the police cruiser. Reacher was the first one out, partly because he was tense, and partly because he needed Harper to pay the driver. He stood on the sidewalk and glanced around. Stepped back into the street and headed for the cop's window.

"Everything OK?" he asked.

"Who are you?" the cop said.

"FBI," Reacher said. "Is everything OK here?"

"Can I see a badge?"

"Harper, show this guy your badge," Reacher called.

The taxi backed off and pulled a wide curb-to-curb turn in the road. Harper put her purse back in her pocketbook and came out with her badge, gold on gold, the eagle on top with its head cocked to the left. The cop glanced across at it and relaxed. Harper put it back in her bag and stood on the sidewalk, looking up at the house.

"It's all quiet here," the cop said, through his window.

"She in there?" Reacher asked him.

The cop pointed at the garage door.

"Just got back from the store," he said.

"She went out?"

"I can't stop her from going out," the cop said.

"You check her car?"

"Just her and two shopping bags. There was a padre came calling for her. From the Army, some counseling thing. She sent him away."

Reacher nodded. "She would. She's not religious."

"Tell me about it," the cop said.

"OK," Reacher said. "We're going inside."

"Just don't ask for the powder room," the cop said.

"Why not?"

"She's kind of touchy about being disturbed."

"I'll take the risk," Reacher said.

"Well, can you give her this for me?" the cop asked.

He ducked down in his car and came back with an empty mug from the passenger footwell. Handed it out through the window.

"She brought me coffee," he said. "Nice lady when you get to know her."

"Yes, she is," Reacher said.

He took the mug and followed Harper into the driveway. Up the looping path, up the porch steps, to the door. Harper pressed the bell. He listened to the sound echoing to silence off the polished wood inside. Harper waited ten seconds and pressed again. A burst of purring metallic noise, then echoes, then silence.

"Where is she?" she said.

She hit the bell for the third time. Noise, echoes, silence. She looked at him, worried. He looked at the lock on the door. It was a big heavy item. Probably new. Probably carried all kinds of lifetime warranties and insurance discounts. Probably had a thick casehardened latch fitted snugly into a steel receptacle chiseled neatly into the doorframe. The doorframe was probably Oregon pine felled a hundred years ago. The best construction timber in history, dried like iron over a century.

"Shit," he said.

He stepped back to the edge of the porch and balanced the cop's empty mug on the rail. Danced forward and smashed the sole of his foot against the lock.

"Hell are you doing?" Harper said.

He whirled back and hit the door again, once, twice, three times. Felt the timbers yield. He grasped the porch railings like a ski jumper and bounced twice and hurled himself forward. Straightened his leg and smashed his whole two hundred and thirty pounds into an area the size of his heel directly over the lock. The frame splintered and part of it followed the door into the hallway.

"Upstairs," he gasped.

He raced up, with Harper crowding his back. He ducked into a bedroom. Wrong bedroom. Inferior linens, a cold musty smell. A guest room. He ducked into the next door. The right bedroom. A made bed, dimpled pillows, the smell of sleep, a telephone and a water glass on the nightstand. A connecting door, ajar. He stepped across the room and shoved it open. He saw a bathroom.

Mirrors, a sink, a shower stall.

A tub full of hideous green water.

Scimeca in the water.

And Julia Lamarr.

Julia Lamarr, turning and rising and twisting off her perch on the rim of the tub, whirling around to face him. She was wearing a sweater and pants and black leather gloves. Her face was white with hate and fear. Her mouth was half-open. Her crossed teeth were bared in panic. He seized her by the front of the sweater and spun her around and hit her once in the head, a savage, abrupt blow from a huge fist powered by blind anger and crushing physical momentum. It caught her solidly on the side of the jaw and her head snapped back and she bounced off the opposite wall and went down like she was hit by a truck. He didn't see her make it to the floor because he was already turning back to the tub. Scimeca was arched up out of the slime, naked, rigid, eyes bulging, head back, mouth open in agony.

Not moving.

Not breathing.

He put a hand under her neck and held her head up and straightened the fingers on his other hand and stabbed them into her mouth. Couldn't reach her tongue. He balled his hand and punched and forced his knuckles all the way inside. Her mouth made a giant ghastly O around his wrist and the skin of his hand tore against her teeth and he scrabbled in her throat and hooked a finger around her tongue and hauled it back. It was slippery, like a live thing. It was long and heavy and muscular. It curled tight against itself and eased up out of her throat and flopped back into her mouth. He pulled his hand free and tore more skin. Bent down to blow air into her lungs but as his face got near hers he felt a convulsive exhalation from her and a desperate cough and then her chest started heaving. Giant ragged breaths sucked in and out. He cradled her head. She was wheezing. Tortured cracked sounds in her throat.

"Set the shower running," he screamed.

Harper ran to the stall and turned on the water. He slid his hand under Scimeca's back and pulled the stopper out of the drain. The thick green water eddied away around her body. He lifted her under the shoulders and the knees. Stood up and stepped back and held her in the middle of the bathroom, dripping green slime everywhere.

"Got to get this stuff off of her," he said, helplessly.

"I'll take her," Harper said gently.

She caught her under the arms and backed herself into the shower, fully dressed. Jammed herself into a corner of the stall and held the limp body upright like a drunk. The shower turned the paint light green, and then reddened skin showed through as it rinsed away. Harper held her tight, two minutes, three, four. She was soaked to the skin and her clothes were smeared with green. She moved around in a bizarre halting dance, so the shower could catch every part of Scimeca's body. Then she maneuvered carefully backward until the water was rinsing the sticky green out of her hair. It kept on coming, endlessly. Harper was tiring. The paint was slick. Scimeca was sliding out of her grasp.

"Get towels," she gasped. "Find a bathrobe."

They were on a row of hooks, directly above where Lamarr was lying inert. Reacher took two towels and

Harper staggered forward out of the stall. Reacher held a towel in front of him and Harper passed Scimeca to him. He caught her through the thickness of the towel and wrapped her in it. Harper turned off the hissing water and took the other towel. Stood there in the sudden silence, breathing hard, wiping her face. Reacher lifted Scimeca off her feet and carried her out of the bathroom, into the bedroom. Laid her down gently on the bed. Leaned over her and wiped the wet hair off her face. She was still wheezing hard. Her eyes were open, but they were blank.

"Is she OK?" Harper called.

"I don't know," Reacher said.

He watched her breathing. Her chest rose and fell, rose and fell, urgently, like she had just run a mile.

"I think so," he said. "She's breathing."

He caught her wrist and felt for the pulse. It was there, strong and fast.

"She's OK," he said. "Pulse is good."

"We should get her to the hospital," Harper called.

"She'll be better here," Reacher said.

"But she'll need sedation. This will have blown her mind."

He shook his head. "She'll wake up, and she won't remember a thing."

Harper stared at him. "Are you kidding?"

He looked up at her. She was standing there, holding a bathrobe, soaked to the skin and smeared with paint. Her shirt was olive green and transparent.

"She was hypnotized," he said.

He nodded toward the bathroom.

"That's how she did it all," he said. "Everything, every

damn step of the way. She was the Bureau's biggest expert."

"Hypnosis?" Harper said.

He took the bathrobe from her and laid it over Scimeca's passive form. Tucked it tight around her. Bent his
head and listened to her breathing. It was still strong,
and it was slowing down. She looked like a person in a
deep sleep, except her eyes were wide open and staring at
nothing.

"I don't believe it," Harper said.

Reacher used the corner of the towel and dried Scimeca's face.

"That's how she did it all," he said again.

He used his thumbs and closed Scimeca's eyes. It
seemed like the right thing to do. She breathed lower
and turned her head an inch. Her wet hair dragged on
the pillow. She turned her head the other way, scrubbing
her face into the pillow, restlessly, like a sleeping woman
confused by her dreams. Harper stared at her, immobile.
Then she turned around and stared and spoke to the
bathroom door.

"When did you know?" she asked.

"For sure?" he said. "Last night."

"But how?" she said.

Reacher used the towel again, where thin green fluid
was leaking down out of Scimeca's hair.

"I just went around and around," he said. "Right
from the beginning, for days and days, thinking, thinking, thinking, driving myself crazy. It was a real *what if*
thing. And then it turned into a *so what else* thing."

Harper stared at him. He pulled the bathrobe higher
on Scimeca's shoulder.

"I knew they were wrong about the motive," he said. "I knew it all along. But I couldn't understand it. They're smart people, right? But they were so *wrong*. I was asking myself why? *Why?* Had they gotten dumb all of a sudden? Were they blinded by their professional specialty? That's what I thought it was, at first. Small units inside big organizations are so defensive, aren't they? Innately? I figured a bunch of psychologists paid to unravel very complex things wouldn't be too willing to give it up and say no, this is something very ordinary. I thought it might be subconscious. But eventually I passed on that. It's just too irresponsible. So I went around and around. And in the end the only answer left was they were wrong because they *wanted* to be wrong."

"And you knew Lamarr was driving the motive," Harper said. "Because it was her case, really. So you suspected her."

He nodded.

"Exactly," he said. "Soon as Alison died, I had to think about Lamarr doing it, because there was a close connection, and like you said, close family connections are always significant. So then I asked myself what if she did them all? What if she's camouflaging a personal motive behind the randomness of the first three? But I couldn't see how. Or why. There was no personal motive. They weren't best buddies, but they got along OK. There were no family issues. No unfairness about the inheritance, for instance. It was going to be equal. No jealousy there. And she couldn't fly, so how could it be her?"

"But?"

"But then the dam broke. Something Alison said. I remembered it much later. She said her father was dying but *sisters take care of each other, right?* I thought she was talking about emotional support or something. But then I thought what if she meant it another way? Like some people use the phrase? Like you did, when we had coffee in New York and the check came and you said you'd take care of it? Meaning you'd pay for me, you'd treat me? I thought what if Alison meant that she'd take care of Julia financially? Share with her? Like she knew the inheritance was all coming her way and Julia was getting nothing and was all uptight about it? But Julia had told me everything was equal, and she was already rich, anyway, because the old man was generous and fair. So I suddenly asked myself what if she's lying about that? What if the old guy *wasn't* generous and fair? What if she's *not* rich?"

"She was *lying* about that?"

Reacher nodded. "Had to be. Suddenly it made a lot of sense. I realized she doesn't *look* rich. She dresses very cheap. She has cheap luggage."

"You based it on her *luggage?*"

He shrugged. "I told you it was a house of cards. But in my experience if somebody's got money outside of their salary, it shows up somewhere. It might be subtle and tasteful, but it's there. And with Julia Lamarr, it wasn't there. So she was poor. So she was lying. And Jodie told me her firm has this *so what else* thing. If they find a guy lying about something, they ask themselves *so what else?* What else is he lying about? So I thought what if she's lying about the relationship with her sister too? What if she still hates her and resents her, like when she was a little kid? And what if she's lying about the equal inheritance? What if there's no inheritance for her at all?"

"Did you check it out?"

"How could I? But check it out yourself and you'll see. It's the only thing that fits. So then I thought what the hell else? What if *everything* is a lie? What if she's lying about not flying? What if that's a big beautiful lie too, just sitting there, so big and obvious nobody thinks twice about it? I even asked you how she gets away with it. You said everybody just works around it, like a law of nature. Well, we all did. We just worked around it. Like she intended. Because it made it absolutely impossible it was her. But it was a lie. It had to be. Fear of flying is way too irrational for her."

"But it's an impossible lie to tell. I mean, either a person flies, or she doesn't."

"She used to, years ago," Reacher said. "She told me that. Then presumably she grew to hate it, so she stopped. So it was convincing. Nobody who knows her now ever saw her fly. So everybody believed her. But when it came to it, she could put herself on a plane. If it was worth it to her. And this was worth it to her. Biggest motive you ever saw. Alison was going to get everything, and she wanted it for herself. She was Cinderella, all burning up with jealousy and resentment and hatred."

"Well, she fooled me," Harper said. "That's for sure."

Reacher stroked Scimeca's hair.

"She fooled everybody," he said. "That's why she did the far corners first. To make everybody think about the geography, the range, the reach, the distance. To move herself right outside the picture, subconsciously."

Harper was quiet for a beat. "But she was so upset. She *cried*, remember? In front of us all?"

Reacher shook his head. "She wasn't upset. She was

frightened. It was her time of maximum danger. Remember just before that? She refused to take her rest period. Because she knew she needed to be around, to control any fallout from the postmortem. And then I started questioning the motive, and she got tense as hell because I might be heading in the right direction. But then I said it was weapons theft in the Army, and she cried, but not because she was upset. She cried with *relief*, because she was still safe. I hadn't smoked her out. And you remember what she did next?"

Harper nodded. "She started backing you up on the weapons theft thing."

"Exactly," Reacher said. "She started making my case for me. Putting words in my mouth. She said we should think laterally, go for it, maximum effort. She jumped on the bandwagon, because she saw the bandwagon was heading in the wrong direction. She was thinking hard, improvising like crazy, sending us all down another blind alley. But she wasn't thinking hard *enough*, because that bandwagon was always bullshit. There was a flaw in it, a mile wide."

"What flaw?"

"It was an impossible coincidence that the eleven witnesses could be the only eleven women obviously living alone afterward. I told you it was partly an experiment. I wanted to see who *wouldn't* support it. Only Poulton wouldn't. Blake was out of it, upset because Lamarr was upset. But Lamarr backed it all the way. She backed it big-time, because it made her safe. And then she went home, with everybody's sympathy. But she didn't go home. At least not for more than the time it takes to pack a bag. She came straight here and went to work."

Harper went pale.

"She actually confessed," she said. "Right then and there, before she left. Remember that? She said *I killed my sister*. Because of wasting time, she said. But it was really true. It was a sick joke."

Reacher nodded. "She's sick as hell. She killed four women for her stepfather's money. And this paint thing? It was always so bizarre. So bizarre, it was overwhelming. But it was difficult, too. Can you imagine the practicalities? Why would a person use a trick like that?"

"To confuse us."

"And?"

"Because she enjoyed it," Harper said, slowly. "Because she's really sick."

"Sick as hell," Reacher said again. "But very smart, too. Can you imagine the planning? She must have started two whole years ago. Her stepfather fell ill about the same time her sister came out of the Army. She started putting it all together right then. Very, very meticulous. She got the support group list direct from her sister, picked out the ones who obviously lived alone, like I did, then she visited all eleven of them, secretly, probably weekends, by plane. Walked in everywhere she needed to because she was a woman with an FBI shield, just like you walked into Alison's place the other day and you walked past that cop just now. Nothing more reassuring than a woman with an FBI shield, right? Then she maybe gave them some story about how the Bureau was trying to finally nail the military, which must have gratified them. Said she was starting a big investigation. Sat them down in their own living rooms and asked if she could hypnotize them for background information on the issue."

"Including her own sister? But how could she do that without Alison knowing she flew there?"

"She made Alison come to Quantico for it. Remember that? Alison said she'd flown out to Quantico so Julia could hypnotize her for deep background. But there were no questions about deep background. No questions at all, in fact, just instructions for the future. She told her what to do, just like she told all of them what to do. Lorraine Stanley was still serving then, so she told her to steal the paint and hide it. The others, she told them to expect a carton sometime in the future and store it. She told all of them to expect another visit from her, and in the meantime to deny everything if they were ever asked about anything. She even scripted the bullshit stories for them, bogus roommates and random delivery mistakes."

Harper nodded and stared at the bathroom door.

"So then she told Stanley to activate the deliveries," she said. "And then she went back to Florida and killed Amy Callan. Then Caroline Cooke. And she knew as soon as she killed Cooke, a serial pattern would be established and the whole thing would fall into Blake's lap at Quantico, whereupon she was right there to start misdirecting the investigation. God, I should have spotted it. She insisted on working the case. And she insisted on staying with it. It was perfect, wasn't it? Who did the profile? She did. Who insisted on the military motive? She did. Who said we're looking for a soldier? She did. She even hauled you in as an *example* of what we were looking for."

Reacher said nothing. Harper stared at the door.

"But Alison was the only real target," she said. "And

that's why she dropped the interval, I guess. Because she was all hyped up and excited and couldn't wait."

"She made us do her surveillance," Reacher said. "She asked us about Alison's place, remember? She was abandoning the interval, so she didn't have time for surveillance, so she got us to do it for her. Remember that? Is it isolated? Is the door locked? We did her scouting for her."

Harper closed her eyes. "She was off duty the day Alison died. It was Sunday. Quantico was quiet. I never even thought about it. She knew nobody would think about it, on a Sunday. She knows nobody's there."

"She's very smart," Reacher said.

Harper nodded. Opened her eyes. "And I guess it explains the lack of evidence everywhere. She knows what we look for at the scene."

"And she's a woman," Reacher said. "The investigators were looking for a man, because she told them to. Same with the rental cars. She knew if anybody checked they would come back with a woman's name, which would be ignored. Which is exactly what happened."

"But what name?" Harper asked. "She'd need ID for the rental."

"For the airlines, too," Reacher said. "But I'm sure she's got a drawerful of ID. From women the Bureau has sent to prison. You'll be able to match them up, relevant dates and places. Innocent feminine names, meaning nothing."

Harper looked rueful. "I passed that message on, remember? From Hertz? *It was nothing,* I said, *just some woman on business.*"

Reacher nodded. "She's very smart. I think she even

dressed the same as the victims, while she was in their houses. She watched them, and if they wore a cotton dress, she wore a cotton dress. If they wore pants, she wore pants. Like she's in here now wearing an old sweater like Scimeca's. So any fibers she leaves behind will be discounted. She asked us what Alison was wearing, remember? No time for surveillance, so she asked us, all innocent and roundabout. Is she still all sporty and tanned and dressed like a cowboy? We said yes, she is, so no doubt she went in there wearing denim jeans and boots."

"And she scratched her face because she hated her."

Reacher shook his head.

"No, I'm afraid that was my fault," he said. "I kept questioning the lack of violence, right in front of her. So she supplied some, the very next time around. I should have kept my big mouth shut."

Harper said nothing.

"And that's how I knew she'd be here," Reacher said. "Because she was trying to imitate a guy like me, all along. And I said I would go for Scimeca next. So I knew she'd be here, sooner or later. But she was a little quicker than I thought. And we were a little slower. She didn't waste any time, did she?"

Harper glanced at the bathroom door. Shuddered. Glanced away.

"How did you figure the hypnotism thing?" she asked.

"Like everything else," Reacher said. "I thought I knew who, and why, but the *how* part looked absolutely impossible, so I just went around and around. That's why I wanted to get out of Quantico. I wanted space to think. It took me a real long time. But eventually, it was the only possibility. It explained everything. The passivity, the obedience, the acquiescence. And why the scenes looked the way they did. Looked like the guy never laid a finger on them, because she never *did* lay a finger on them. She just reestablished the spell and told them what to do, step by step. They did everything themselves. Right down to filling their own tubs, swallowing their own tongues. The only thing she did herself was what I did, pull their tongues back up afterward, so the pathologists wouldn't catch on."

"But how did you know about the tongues?"

He was quiet for a beat.

"From kissing you," he said.

"Kissing me?"

He smiled. "You've got a great tongue, Harper. It set me thinking. Tongues were the only things which fitted Stavely's autopsy findings. But I figured there was no way to *make* somebody swallow their own tongue, until I realized it was Lamarr, and she was a hypnotist, and then the whole thing fell together."

Harper was silent.

"And you know what?" Reacher said.

"What?"

"The very first night I met her, she wanted to hypnotize me. For deep background, she said, but obviously she was going to tell me to look convincing and get absolutely nowhere. Blake pestered me to do it, and I said no, because she'll make me run naked down Fifth Avenue. Like a joke. But it was awful near the truth."

Harper shivered. "Where would she have stopped?"

"Maybe one more," Reacher said. "Six would be enough. Six would have done it. Sand on the beach."

She stepped over and sat down next to him on the bed. Stared down at Scimeca, inert beneath the bathrobe.

"Will she be OK?" she asked.

"Probably," Reacher said. "She's tough as hell."

Harper glanced at him. His shirt and pants were wet and smeared. His arms were green, right up to the shoulders.

"You're all wet," she said, absently.

"So are you," he said. "Wetter than me."

She nodded. Went quiet.

"We're both wet," she said. "But at least now it's over."

He said nothing.

"Here's to success," she said.

She leaned over and threaded her damp arms around his neck. Pulled him close and kissed him, hard on the mouth. He felt her tongue on his lips. Then it stopped moving. She pulled away.

"Feels weird," she said. "I won't be able to do this ever again without thinking bad things about tongues."

He said nothing.

"Horrible way to die," she said.

He looked at her and smiled.

"You fall off a horse, you've got to get right back on," he said.

He leaned toward her and cupped a hand behind her head and pulled her close. Kissed her on the mouth. She was completely still for a beat. Then she got back into it. She held the kiss for a long moment. Then she pulled away, smiling shyly.

"Go wake her up," Reacher said. "Make the arrest,

start the questioning. You've got a big case ahead of you."

"She won't talk to me."

He looked down at Scimeca's sleeping face.

"She will," he said. "Tell her the first time she clams up, I'll break her arm. The second time, I'll grind the bones together."

Harper shivered again and turned away. Stood up and stepped out to the bathroom. The bedroom went quiet. No sound anywhere, just Scimeca's breathing, steady but noisy, like a machine. Then Harper came back in, a long moment later, white in the face.

"She won't talk to me," she said.

"How do you know? You didn't ask her anything."

"Because she's dead."

Silence.

"You killed her."

Silence.

"When you hit her."

Silence.

"You broke her neck."

Then there were loud footsteps in the hallway below them. Then they were on the stairs. Then they were in the corridor outside the bedroom. The cop stepped into the room. He was holding his mug. He had retrieved it from the porch railing. He stared.

"Hell's going on?" he said.

31

SEVEN HOURS LATER it was well past midnight. Reacher was locked up alone in a holding pen inside the FBI's Portland Field Office. He knew the cop had called his sergeant and the sergeant had called his Bureau contact. He knew Portland called Quantico and Quantico called the Hoover Building and the Hoover Building called New York. The cop relayed all that information, breathless with excitement. Then his sergeant arrived in person and he clammed up. Harper disappeared somewhere and an ambulance arrived to take Scimeca to the hospital. He heard the police department cede jurisdiction to the FBI without any kind of a struggle. Then two Portland agents arrived to make the arrest. They cuffed him and drove him to the city and dumped him in the holding pen and left him there.

It was hot in the cell. His clothes dried within an

hour, stiff as boards and stained olive with paint. Apart from that, nothing happened. He guessed it was taking time for people to assemble. He wondered if they would come to Portland, or if they'd fly him back to Quantico. Nobody told him anything. Nobody came near him. He was left alone. He spent the time worrying about Scimeca. He imagined harassed strangers in the emergency room, probing and fussing over her.

It stayed quiet until after midnight. Then things started happening. He heard sounds in the building. Arrivals, urgent conversations. First person he saw was Nelson Blake. *They're coming here*, he thought. *They must have discussed a position and fired up the Lear. Timing was about right.* The inner door opened and Blake walked past the bars and glanced into the cell, something in his face. *You really screwed up now*, he was saying. He looked tired and strained. Red and pale, all at the same time.

It went quiet again for an hour. Past one o'clock in the morning, Alan Deerfield arrived, all the way from New York. The inner door opened and he walked in, silent and morose, red eyes behind the thick glasses. He paused. Glanced through the bars. The same contemplative look he'd used all those nights ago. *So you're the guy, huh?*

He walked back out and it went quiet again, another hour. Past two o'clock, a local agent came in with a bunch of keys. He unlocked the door.

"Time to talk," he said.

He led him out of the cell block into a corridor. Down the corridor to a conference room. Smaller than the New York facility, but just as cheap. Same lighting, same big table. Deerfield and Blake were sitting together on one side. There was a chair positioned opposite. He walked around and sat down in it. There was silence for a long moment. Nobody spoke, nobody moved. Then Blake sat forward.

"I've got a dead agent," he said. "And I don't like that."

Reacher looked at him.

"You've got four dead women," he said. "Could have been five."

Blake shook his head. "Never was going to be five. We had the situation under control. Julia Lamarr was right there rescuing the fifth when you killed her."

The room went silent again. Reacher nodded, slowly.

"That's your position?" he asked.

Deerfield looked up.

"It's a viable proposition," he said. "Don't you think? She makes some kind of breakthrough in her own time, she overcomes her fear of flying, she gets herself out here right on the heels of the perpetrator, she arrives in the nick of time, she's about to start emergency medical procedures when you burst in and hit her. She's a hero, and you go to trial for the murder of a federal agent."

Silence again.

"Can you make the chronology work?" Reacher asked.

Blake nodded. "Sure we can. She's at home, say, nine o'clock in the morning East Coast, she gets herself outside Portland by five, Pacific. That's eleven hours. Plenty of time to get a brainstorm and get herself to National and get on a plane."

"The cop see the bad guy get in the house?"

Deerfield shrugged. "We figure the cop fell asleep. You know what these country boys are like."

"He saw a padre come calling. He was awake then."

Deerfield shook his head. "Army will say they never sent a padre. He must have dreamed it."

"Did he see *her* get in the house?"

"Still asleep."

"How did she get in?"

"Knocked on the door, interrupted the guy. He bolted out past her, she didn't chase him because she wanted to check on Scimeca, because she's a humanitarian."

"The cop see the guy running out?"

"Still asleep."

"And she took the time to lock the door behind her, even though she was rushing upstairs because she's such a humanitarian?"

"Evidently."

The room went quiet.

"Scimeca come around yet?" Reacher asked.

Deerfield nodded. "We called the hospital. She remembers nothing about anything. We assume she must be blanking it out. We'll get a boatload of shrinks to say that's perfectly normal."

"Is she OK?"

"She's fine."

Blake smiled. "But we won't pursue her for a description of her attacker. Our shrinks will say that would be grossly insensitive, given her circumstances."

The room went quiet again.

"Where's Harper?" Reacher said.

"On suspension," Blake said.

"For not following the party line?"

"She's unduly affected by a romantic illusion," Blake said. "She told us some fantastic bullshit story."

"You see your problem, right?" Deerfield said. "You hated Lamarr from the start. So you killed her for personal reasons of your own and invented a story to cover yourself. But it's not a very good story, is it? There's no support for it. You can't put Lamarr anywhere near any of the scenes."

"She never left any evidence," Reacher said.

Blake smiled. "Ironic, isn't it? That's exactly what you said to us, right at the outset. You said all we had was we *thought* a person like you did it. Well, now all you got is you *think* Lamarr did it."

"Where's her car?" Reacher asked. "She drove up to Scimeca's place from the airport, where's her car?"

"The perp stole it," Blake said. "He must have snuck around the back on foot, originally, not knowing the cop was asleep. She surprised him, he took off in her car."

"You going to find a rental in her real name?"

Blake nodded. "Probably. We can usually find what we need to."

"What about the flight in from D.C.? You going to find her real name in the airline computer?"

Blake nodded again. "If we need to."

"You see your problem, right?" Deerfield said again. "It's just not acceptable to have a dead agent, without somebody being responsible."

Reacher nodded. "And it's not acceptable to admit an agent was a killer."

"Don't even think about it," Blake said.

"Even though she *was* a killer?"

"She wasn't a killer," Deerfield said. "She was a loyal agent, doing a fine job."

Reacher nodded.

"Well, I guess this means I'm not going to get paid," he said.

Deerfield made a face, like there was a bad smell in the room.

"This is not a joke, Reacher," he said. "Let's be real clear about that. You're in big trouble. You can say whatever the hell you want. You can say you had suspicions. But you'll look like an idiot. Nobody will listen to you. And it won't matter anyway. Because if you had suspicions, you should have let Harper arrest her, right?"

"No time."

Deerfield shook his head. "Bullshit."

"Was she visibly in the act of harming Scimeca?" Blake asked.

"I needed her out of my way."

"Our counsel will say even *if* you had mistaken but sincere prior suspicions, you should have gone straight for Scimeca in the tub and let Harper deal with Lamarr behind you. It was two against one. It would have *saved* you time, right? If you were so concerned with your old buddy?"

"It might have saved me half a second."

"Half a second could have been critical," Deerfield said. "Life-or-death medical situation like that? Our counsel will make a big point out of it. He'll say spending precious time hitting somebody proves something, like personal animosity."

The room went quiet. Reacher looked down at the table.

"Law buff like you knows all about it," Blake said. "Honest mistakes occur but even so, actions in defense of a victim need to happen right at the exact time the victim is getting assaulted. Not afterward. Afterward is revenge, pure and simple."

Reacher said nothing.

"And you can't claim it was mistaken *and* accidental," Blake said. "You once told me you know all about how to break someone's skull, and no way would it happen by accident. That guy in the alley, remember? Petrosian's boy? And what goes for skulls goes for necks, right? So it wasn't an accident. It was deliberate homicide."

There was silence.

"OK," Reacher said. "What's the deal?"

"You're going to jail," Deerfield said. "There's no deal."

"Bullshit, there's no deal," Reacher said. "There's always a deal."

Silence again. It lasted minutes. Then Blake shrugged.

"Well, you want to cooperate, we could compromise," he said. "We could call Lamarr a suicide, grieving about her father, tormented she couldn't save her sister."

"And you could keep your big mouth shut," Deerfield said. "You could tell nobody nothing, except what we want them told."

Silence again.

"Why should I?" Reacher said.

"Because you're a smart guy," Deerfield said. "Don't forget, there's absolutely nothing on Lamarr. You know that. She was way too smart. Sure, you could dig around a couple of years, if you had a million dollars for lawyer bills. You could come up with a little meaningless circumstantial stuff, but what's a jury going to do with that? A big man hates a small woman? He's a bum, she's a federal agent? He breaks her neck, and then he blames her for it? Some fantastic story about hypnosis? Forget about it."

"So face it, OK?" Blake said. "You're *ours*, now."

There was silence. Then Reacher shook his head.

"No," he said. "I think I'll pass on that."

"Then you go to jail."

"Just one question, first," Reacher said.

"Which is?"

"Did I kill Lorraine Stanley?"

Blake shook his head. "No, you didn't."

"How do you know?"

"You know how we know. We had you tailed, all that week."

"And you gave a copy of the surveillance report to my lawyer, right?"

"Right."

"OK," Reacher said.

"OK what, smart guy?"

"OK nuts to you, is what," Reacher said.

"You want to expand on that?"

Reacher shook his head. "You figure it out."

The room went quiet.

"What?" Blake said.

Reacher smiled at him. "Think about strategy. Maybe you can lock me up for Lamarr, but you can't ever claim I'm also the guy who killed the women, because my lawyer has got your own report proving that I'm not. So what are you going to do then?"

"What does that matter to you?" Blake said. "You're locked up anyway."

"Think about the future," Reacher said. "You've told

the world it's not me, and you're swearing blind it's not Lamarr, so you've got to be seen to keep on looking, right? You can't ever stop, not without people wondering why. Think about the negative headlines. *Elite FBI unit gets nowhere, tenth year of search.* You'd just have to swallow them. And you'd have to keep the guards in place, you'd have to work around the clock, more and more manpower, more and more effort, more and more budget, year after year, searching for the guy. Are you going to do that?"

Silence in the room.

"No, you're not going to do that," Reacher said. "And not doing that is the same thing as admitting you know the truth. Lamarr is dead, the search has stopped, it wasn't me, therefore Lamarr was the killer. So it's all or nothing now, for you guys. It's make-your-mind-up time. If you *don't* admit it was Lamarr, then you use up all your resources for the rest of history, pretending to look for a guy you know for sure doesn't exist. And if you *do* admit it was Lamarr, then you can't lock me up for killing her, because in the circumstances it was absolutely justifiable."

Silence again.

"So, nuts to you," Reacher said.

There was silence. Reacher smiled.

"So now what?" he asked.

They were quiet for a long moment. Then they recovered.

"We're the Bureau," Deerfield said. "We can make your life very difficult."

Reacher shook his head.

"My life's already very difficult," he said. "Nothing

you guys can do to make it any harder. But you can stop with the threats, anyway. Because I'll keep your secret."

"You will?"

Reacher nodded. "I'll have to, won't I? Because if I don't, it'll all just come back on Rita Scimeca. She's the only living witness. She'll get pestered to death, prosecutors, police, newspapers, television. All the sordid details, how she was raped, how she was naked in the tub with the paint. It'll hurt her. And I don't want that to happen."

Silence again.

"So, your secret is safe with me," Reacher said.

Blake stared at the tabletop. Then he nodded.

"OK," he said. "I'll buy that."

"But we'll be watching you," Deerfield said. "Always. Never forget that."

Reacher smiled again.

"Well, don't let me catch you at it," he said. "Because you should remember what happened to Petrosian. You guys never forget *that*, OK?"

IT FINISHED LIKE that as a tie, as a wary stalemate. Nothing more was said. Reacher stood up and threaded his way around the table and out of the room. He found an elevator and made it down to street level. Nobody came after him. There were double doors, scarred oak and wired glass. He pushed them open and stepped out into the chill of some dark deserted Portland street in the middle of the night. Stood on the edge of the sidewalk, looking at nothing in particular.

"Hey, Reacher," Harper called.

She was behind him in the shadow of a pillar flanking

the entrance. He turned and saw the gleam of her hair and a stripe of white where her shirt showed at the front of her jacket.

"Hey yourself," he said. "You OK?"

She stepped across to him.

"I will be," she said. "I'm going to ask for a transfer. Maybe over here. I like it."

"Will they let you?"

She nodded. "Sure they will. They're not going to rock any boats as long as the budget hearings are on. This is going to be the quietest thing that ever happened."

"It never happened at all," he said. "That's how we left it, upstairs."

"So you're OK with them?"

"As OK as I ever was."

"I'd have stood up for you," she said. "Whatever it took."

He nodded. "I know you would. There should be more like you."

"Take this," she said.

She held out a slip of flimsy paper. It was a travel voucher, issued by the desk back at Quantico.

"It'll get you to New York," she said.

"What about you?" he asked.

"I'll say I lost it. They'll wire me another one."

She stepped close and kissed his cheek. Stepped away and started walking.

"Good luck," she called.

"To you too," he called back.

He walked to the airport, twelve miles on the shoulders of roads built for automobiles. It took him three hours.

He exchanged the FBI voucher for a plane ticket and waited another hour for the first flight out. Slept through four hours in the air and three hours of time zones and touched down at La Guardia at one o'clock in the afternoon.

He used the last of his cash on a bus to the subway and the subway into Manhattan. Got out at Canal Street and walked south to Wall Street. He was in the lobby of Jodie's office building a few minutes after two o'clock, borne along by sixty floors of workers returning from lunch. Her firm's reception area was deserted. Nobody at the counter. He stepped through an open door and wandered down a corridor lined with lawbooks on oak shelves. Left and right of him were empty offices. There were papers on desks and jackets over the backs of chairs, but no people anywhere.

He came to a set of double doors and heard the heavy buzz of conversation on the other side. The chink of glass on glass. Laughter. He pulled the right-hand door and the noise burst out at him and he saw a conference room jammed full of people. They were in dark suits and snowy white shirts and suspenders and quiet ties, and severe dark dresses and black nylon. There was a wall of blinding windows and a long table under a heavy white cloth loaded with ranks of sparkling glasses and a hundred bottles of champagne. Two bartenders were pouring the foamy golden wine as fast as they could. People were drinking it and toasting with it and looking at Jodie.

She was rippling through the crowd like a magnet. Wherever she walked, people stepped up and formed a crowd around her. There was a constantly changing sequence of small excited circles with her at every center. She turned left and right, smiling, clinking glasses, and then moved on randomly like a pinball into new acclaim. She saw him at the door at the same moment he saw himself reflected in the glass over a Renoir drawing on the wall. He was unshaven and dressed in a crumpled khaki shirt dried stiff with random green stains. She was in a thousand-dollar dress fresh from the closet. A hundred faces turned with hers and the room fell silent. She hesitated for a beat, like she was making a decision. Then she fought forward through the crowd and flung her arms around his neck, champagne glass and all.

"The partnership party," he said. "You got it."

"I sure did," she said.

"Well, congratulations, babe," he said. "And I'm sorry I'm late."

She drew him into the crowd and people closed around them. He shook hands with a hundred lawyers the way he used to with generals from foreign armies. *Don't mess with me and I won't mess with you.* The top boy was an old red-and-gray-faced man of about sixty-five, the son of one of the names on the brass plaque in reception. His suit must have cost more than all the clothes Reacher had ever worn in his life. But the mood of the party meant there was no edge in the old guy's attitude. He looked like he would have been delighted to shake hands with Jodie's elevator man.

"She's a big, big star," he said. "And I'm gratified she accepted our offer."

"Smartest lawyer I ever met," Reacher said over the noise.

"Will you go with her?"

"Go with her where?"

"To London," the old guy said. "Didn't she explain? First tour of duty for a new partner is running the European operation for a couple of years."

Then she was back at his side, smiling, drawing him away. The crowd was settling into small groups, and conversation was turning to work matters and quiet gossip. She led him to a space by the window. There was a yard-wide view of the harbor, framed by sheer buildings on either side.

"I called the FBI uptown," she said. "I was worried about you, and technically I'm still your lawyer. I spoke with Alan Deerfield's office."

"When?"

"Two hours ago. They wouldn't tell me anything."

"Nothing to tell. They're straight with me, I'm straight with them."

She nodded. "So you delivered, finally."

Then she paused.

"Will you be called as a witness?" she asked. "Is there going to be a trial?"

He shook his head. "No trial."

She nodded. "Just a funeral, right?"

He shrugged. "There are no relatives left. That was the point."

She paused again, like there was an important question coming up.

"How do you feel about it?" she asked. "One-word answer?"

"Calm," he said.

"Would you do it again? Same circumstances?"

He paused in turn.

"Same circumstances?" he said. "In a heartbeat."

"I have to go to work in London," she said. "Two years."

"I know," he said. "The old guy told me. When do you go?"

"End of the month."

"You don't want me to come with you," he said.

"It'll be very busy. It's a small staff with a big workload."

"And it's a civilized city."

She nodded. "Yes, it is. Would you *want* to come?"

"Two straight years?" he said. "No. But maybe I could visit, time to time."

She smiled, vaguely. "That would be good."

He said nothing.

"This is awful," she said. "Fifteen years I couldn't live without you, and now I find I can't live *with* you."

"I know," he said. "Totally my fault."

"Do you feel the same way?"

He looked at her.

"I guess I do," he lied.

"We've got until the end of the month," she said.

He nodded.

"More than most people get," he said. "Can you take the afternoon off?"

"Sure I can. I'm a partner now. I can do what I want."

"So let's go."

They left their empty glasses on the window ledge and threaded their way through the knots of people. Everybody watched them to the door, and then turned back to their quiet speculations.

If you enjoyed *Running Blind*, you won't
want to miss *Echo Burning*, another thrilling
Jack Reacher novel from Lee Child.
Here's a brief excerpt . . .

Look for

Echo Burning
in bookstores now from Jove.

THERE WERE THREE watchers, two men and a boy. They were using telescopes, not field glasses. It was a question of distance. They were almost a mile from their target area, because of the terrain. There was no closer cover. It was low, undulating country, burned khaki by the sun, grass and rock and sandy soil alike. The nearest safe concealment was the broad dip they were in, a bone-dry gulch scraped out a million years ago by a different climate, when there had been rain and ferns and rushing rivers.

The men lay prone in the dust with the early heat on their backs, their telescopes at their eyes. The boy scuttled around on his knees, fetching water from the cooler, watching for waking rattlesnakes, logging comments in a notebook. They had arrived before first light in a dusty pick-up truck, the long way around, across the empty land from the west. They had thrown a dirty tarpaulin over the truck and pegged it down with rocks. They had eased forward to the rim of the dip and settled in, raising their telescopes as the low morning sun dawned to the east behind the red house almost a mile away. This was Friday, their fifth consecutive morning, and they were low on conversation.

"Time?" one of the men asked. His voice was nasal, the effect of keeping one eye open and the other eye shut.

The boy checked his watch.

"Six-fifty," he answered.

"Any moment now," the man with the telescope said.

The boy opened his book and prepared to make the same notes he had made four times before.

"Kitchen light on," the man said.

The boy wrote it down. *Six-fifty, kitchen light on.* The kitchen faced them, looking west away from the morning sun, so it stayed dark even after dawn.

"On her own?" the boy asked.

"Same as always," the second man said, squinting.

Maid prepares breakfast, the boy wrote. *Target still in bed.* The sun rose, inch by inch. It jacked itself higher into the sky and pulled the shadows shorter and shorter. The red house had a tall chimney coming out of the kitchen wing like the finger on a sundial. The shadow it made swung and shortened and the heat on the watchers' shoulders built higher. Seven o'clock in the morning, and it was already hot. By eight, it would be burning. By nine, it would be fearsome. And they were there all day, until dark, when they could slip away unseen.

"Bedroom drapes opening," the second man said. "She's up and about."

The boy wrote it down. *Seven oh-four, bedroom drapes open.*

"Now listen," the first man said.

They heard the well pump kick in, very faintly from almost a mile away. A quiet mechanical click, and then a steady low drone.

"She's showering," the man said.

The boy wrote it down. *Seven oh-six, target starts to shower.*

The men rested their eyes. Nothing was going to happen while she was in the shower. How could it? They lowered their telescopes and blinked against the brassy sun in their eyes. The well pump clicked off after six minutes. The silence sounded louder than the faint noise had. The boy wrote *seven-twelve, target out of shower.* The men raised their telescopes again.

"She's dressing, I guess," the first man said.

The boy giggled. "Can you see her naked?"

The second man was triangulated twenty feet to the south. He had the better view of the back of the house, where her bedroom window was.

"You're disgusting," he said. "You know that?"

The boy wrote *seven-fifteen, probably dressing.* Then: *seven-twenty, probably downstairs, probably eating breakfast.*

"She'll go back up, clean her teeth," he said.

The man on the left shifted on his elbows.

"For sure," he said. "Prissy little thing like that."

"She's closing her drapes again," the man on the right said.

It was standard practice in the west of Texas, in the summer, especially if your bedroom faced south, like this one did. Unless you wanted to sleep the next night in a room hotter than a pizza oven.

"Stand by," the man said. "A buck gets ten she goes out to the barn now."

It was a wager that nobody took, because so far four times out of four she had done exactly that, and watchers are paid to notice patterns.

"Kitchen door's open."

The boy wrote *seven twenty-seven, kitchen door opens.*

"Here she comes."

She came out, dressed in a blue gingham dress which reached to her knees and left her shoulders bare. Her hair was tied back behind her head. It was still damp from the shower.

"What do you call that sort of a dress?" the boy asked.

"Halter," the man on the left said.

Seven twenty-eight, comes out, blue halter dress, goes to barn, the boy wrote.

She walked across the yard, short hesitant steps against the uneven ruts in the baked earth, maybe seventy yards. She heaved the barn door open and disappeared in the gloom inside.

The boy wrote *seven twenty-nine, target in barn.*

"How hot is it?" the man on the left asked.

"Maybe a hundred degrees," the boy said.

"There'll be a storm soon. Heat like this, there has to be."

"Here comes her ride," the man on the right said.

Miles to the south, there was a dust cloud on the road. A vehicle, making slow and steady progress north.

"She's coming back," the man on the right said.

Seven thirty-two, target comes out of barn, the boy wrote.

"Maid's at the door," the man said.

The target stopped at the kitchen door and took her lunch box from the maid. It was bright blue plastic with a cartoon picture on the side. She paused for a second. Her skin was pink and damp from the heat. She leaned down to adjust her socks and then trotted out to the gate, through the gate, to the shoulder of the road. The school bus slowed and stopped and the door opened with a sound the watchers heard clearly over the faint rattle of the idling engine. The chrome handrails flashed once in the sun. The diesel exhaust hung and drifted in the hot still air. The target heaved her lunch box onto the step and grasped the bright rails and clambered up after it. The door closed again and the watchers saw her corn-colored head bobbing along level with the base of the windows. Then the engine noise deepened and the gears caught and the bus moved away with a new cone of dust kicking up behind it.

Seven thirty-six, target on bus to school, the boy wrote.

The road north was dead straight and he turned his head and watched the bus all the way until the heat on the horizon broke it up into a shimmering yellow mirage. Then he closed his notebook and secured it with a rubber band. Back at the red house, the maid stepped inside and closed the kitchen door. Nearly a mile away, the watchers lowered their telescopes and turned their collars up for protection from the sun.

Seven thirty-seven, Friday morning.

Seven thirty-eight.

SEVEN THIRTY-NINE. MORE than three hundred miles to the north and east, Jack Reacher climbed out of his motel room window. One minute earlier, he had been in the bathroom, brushing his teeth. One minute before that, he had opened the door of his room to check the morning temperature. He had left it open, and the closet just inside the entrance passageway was faced with mirrored glass, and there was a shaving mirror in the bathroom on a cantilevered arm, and by a freak of optical chance he caught sight of four men getting out of a car and walking toward the motel office. Pure luck, but a guy as vigilant as Jack Reacher gets lucky more times than the average.

The car was a police cruiser. It had a shield on the door, and because of the bright sunlight and the double reflection he could read it clearly. At the top it said CITY POLICE, and then there was a fancy medallion in the middle with LUBBOCK, TEXAS written underneath. All four men who got out were in uniform. They had bulky belts with guns and radios and nightsticks and handcuffs. Three of the men he had never seen before, but the fourth guy was familiar. The fourth guy was a tall heavyweight with a gelled, blond brush cut above a meaty red face. This morning the meaty red face was partially obscured by a glinting aluminum splint carefully taped over a shattered nose. His right hand was similarly bound up with a splint and bandages protecting a broken forefinger.

The guy had neither injury the night before. And

Reacher had no idea the guy was a cop. He just looked like some idiot in a bar. Reacher had gone there because he heard the music was good, but it wasn't, so he had backed away from the band and ended up on a bar stool watching ESPN on a muted television fixed high on a wall. The place was crowded and noisy and he was wedged in a space with a woman on his right and the heavyweight guy with the brush cut on his left. He got bored with the sports and turned around to watch the room. As he turned, he saw how the guy was eating.

The guy was wearing a white tank-top shirt and he was eating chicken wings. The wings were greasy and the guy was a slob. He was dripping chicken fat off his chin and off his fingers onto his shirt. There was a dark teardrop shape right between his pecs. It was growing and spreading into an impressive stain. But the best barroom etiquette doesn't let you linger on such a sight, and the guy caught Reacher staring.

"Who you looking at?" he said.

It was said low and aggressively, but Reacher ignored it.

"Who you looking at?" the guy said again.

Reacher's experience was, they say it once, maybe nothing's going to happen. But they say it twice, then trouble's on the way. Fundamental problem is, they take a lack of response as evidence that you're worried. That they're winning. But then, they won't let you answer, anyway.

"You looking at me?" the guy said.

"No," Reacher answered.

"Don't you be looking at me, boy," the guy said.

The way he said *boy* made Reacher think he was maybe

a foreman in a lumber mill or a cotton operation. Whatever muscle work was done around Lubbock. Some kind
of a traditional trade passed down through the generations. Certainly the word *cop* never came to his mind.
But then, he was relatively new to Texas.

"Don't you look at me," the guy said.

Reacher turned his head and looked at him. Not really to antagonize the guy. Just to size him up. Life is
endlessly capable of surprises, so he knew one day he
would come face-to-face with his physical equal. With
somebody who might worry him. But he looked and
saw this wasn't the day. So he just smiled and looked
away again.

Then the guy jabbed him with his finger.

"I told you not to look at me," he said, and jabbed.

It was a meaty forefinger and it was covered in grease.
It left a definite mark on Reacher's shirt.

"Don't do that," Reacher said.

The guy jabbed again.

"Or what?" he said. "You want to make something
out of it?"

Reacher looked down. Now there were two marks.
The guy jabbed again. Three jabs, three marks. Reacher
clamped his teeth. What were three greasy marks on a
shirt? He started a slow count to ten. Then the guy
jabbed again, before he even reached eight.

"You deaf?" Reacher said. "I told you not to do that."

"You want to do something about it?"

"No," Reacher said. "I really don't. I just want you to
stop doing it, is all."

The guy smiled. "Then you're a yellow-bellied piece
of shit."

"Whatever," Reacher said. "Just keep your hands off me."

"Or what? What you going to do?"

Reacher restarted his count. *Eight, nine.*

"You want to take this outside?" the guy asked.

Ten.

"Touch me again and you'll find out," Reacher said. "I warned you four times."

The guy paused a second. Then, of course, he went for it again. Reacher caught the finger on the way in and snapped it at the first knuckle. Just folded it upward like he was turning a door handle. Then because he was irritated he leaned forward and head-butted the guy full in the face. It was a smooth move, well-delivered, but it was backed off to maybe a half of what it might have been. No need to put a guy in a coma, over four grease marks on a shirt. He moved a pace to give the man room to fall, and backed into the woman on his right.

"Excuse me, ma'am," he said.

The woman nodded vaguely, disoriented by the noise, concentrating on her drink, unaware of what was happening. The big guy thumped silently on the floorboards and Reacher used the sole of his shoe to roll him half onto his front. Then he nudged him under the chin with his toe to pull his head back and straighten his airway. The recovery position, paramedics call it. Stops you choking while you're out.

Then he paid for his drinks and walked back to his motel, and didn't give the guy another thought until he was at the bathroom mirror and saw him out and about in a cop's uniform. Then he thought hard, and as fast as he could.

He spent the first second calculating reflected angles and figuring *if I can see him, does that mean he can see me?* The answer was yes, of course he can. If he was looking the right way, which he wasn't yet. He spent the next second mad at himself. He should have picked up the signs. They had been there. Who else would be poking at a guy built like him, except somebody with some kind of protected status? Some kind of imagined invulnerability? He should have picked up on it.

So what to do? The guy was a cop on his own turf. And Reacher was an easily recognizable target. Apart from anything else he still had the four grease spots on his shirt, and a brand-new bruise on his forehead. There were probably forensics people who could match its shape to the bones in the guy's nose.

So what to do? An angry cop bent on revenge could cause trouble. A lot of trouble. A noisy public arrest, for sure, maybe some wild gunshots, definitely some four-on-one fun and games in an empty out-of-the-way cell down at the station house, where you can't fight back without multiplying your original legal problem. Then all kinds of difficult questions, because Reacher habitually carried no ID and nothing else at all except his toothbrush and a couple of thousand dollars cash in his pants pocket. So he would be regarded as a suspicious character. Almost certainly he'd be charged with attacking a law officer. That was probably a big deal in Texas. All kinds of witnesses would materialize to swear it was malicious and completely unprovoked. He could end up convicted and in the penitentiary, easy as anything. He could end up with seven-to-ten in some tough establishment. Which was definitely not number one on his wish list.

So discretion was going to be the better part of valor. He put his toothbrush in his pocket and walked through the room and opened the window. Unclipped the screen and dropped it to the ground. Climbed out and closed the window and rested the screen back in its frame and walked away across a vacant lot to the nearest street. Turned right and kept on walking until he was hidden by a low building. He looked for buses. There weren't any. He looked for taxis. Nothing doing. So he stuck out his thumb. He figured he had ten minutes to find a ride before they finished at the motels and started cruising the streets. Ten minutes, maybe fifteen at the outside.

Which meant it wasn't going to work. It couldn't work. Seven thirty-nine in the morning, the temperature was already over a hundred degrees. It was going to be impossible to get a ride at all. In heat like that no driver on the planet would open their door long enough for him to slide right in, never mind for any long prior discussions about destinations. So finding a getaway in time was going to be impossible. Absolutely impossible. He started planning alternatives, because he was so sure of it. But it turned out he was wrong. It turned out his whole day was a series of surprises.

Jack Reacher returns in

Make Me

Available in paperback from Dell
Turn the page for a special preview
of the first two chapters

1

MOVING A GUY as big as Keever wasn't easy. It was like trying to wrestle a king-size mattress off a waterbed. So they buried him close to the house. Which made sense anyway. The harvest was still a month away, and a disturbance in a field would show up from the air. And they would use the air, for a guy like Keever. They would use search planes, and helicopters, and maybe even drones.

They started at midnight, which they thought was safe enough. They were in the middle of ten thousand acres of nothingness, and the only man-made structure their side of any horizon was the railroad track to the east, but midnight was five hours after the evening train and seven hours before the morning train. Therefore, no prying eyes. Their backhoe had four spotlights on a bar above the cab, the same way kids pimped their pick-up trucks, and together the four beams made a wide pool of halogen brightness. Therefore, visibility was not a problem either. They started the hole in the hog pen, which was a permanent disturbance all by itself. Each hog weighed two hundred pounds, and each hog had four feet. The dirt was always chewed up. Nothing to see from the air, not even with a thermal camera. The picture would white out instantly, from the steaming animals themselves, and their steaming piles and pools of waste.

Safe enough.

Hogs were rooting animals, so they made sure the hole was deep. Which was not a problem either. Their backhoe's arm was long, and it bit rhythmically, in fluent articulated seven-foot scoops, the hydraulic rams glinting in the electric light, the engine straining and roaring and pausing, the cab falling and rising, as each bucketload was dumped aside. When the hole was done they backed the machine up and turned it around and used the front bucket to push Keever into his grave, scraping him, rolling him, covering his body with dirt, until finally it fell over the lip and thumped down into the electric shadows.

Only one thing went wrong, and it happened right then.

The evening train came through five hours late. The next morning they heard on the AM station that a broken locomotive had caused a jam a hundred miles south. But they didn't know that at the time. All they heard was the mournful whistle at the distant crossing, and then all they could do was turn and stare, at the long lit cars rumbling past in the middle distance, one after the other, like a vision in a dream, seemingly forever. But eventually the train was gone, and the rails sang for a minute more, and then the tail light was swallowed by the midnight darkness, and they turned back to their task.

Twenty miles north the train slowed, and slowed, and then eased to a hissing stop, and the doors sucked open, and Jack Reacher stepped down to a concrete ramp in front of a grain elevator as big as an apartment house. To his left were four more elevators, all of them bigger than the first, and to his right was an enormous metal shed the size of an airplane hangar. There were vapor lights on poles, set at regular intervals, and they cut cones of yellow in the darkness. There was mist in the nighttime air, like a note on a calendar. The end of summer was coming. Fall was on its way.

Reacher stood still and behind him the train moved away without him, straining, grinding, settling to a slow rat-a-tat rhythm, and then accelerating, its building slipstream pulling at his clothes. He was the only passenger who had gotten out. Which was not surprising. The place was no kind of a commuter hub. It was all agricultural. What token passenger facilities it had were wedged between the last elevator and the huge shed, and were limited to a compact building, which seemed to have both a ticket window and benches for waiting. It was built in a traditional railroad style, and it looked like a child's toy, temporarily set down between two shiny oil drums.

But on a sign board running its whole length was written the reason Reacher was there: *Mother's Rest*. Which he had seen on a map, and which he thought was a great name for a railroad stop. He figured the line must cross an ancient wagon train trail, right there, where something had happened long ago. Maybe a young pregnant woman went into labor. The jostling could not have helped. Maybe the wagon train stopped for a couple of weeks. Or a month. Maybe someone remembered the place years later. A descendant, perhaps. A family legend. Maybe there was a one-room museum.

Or perhaps there was a sadder interpretation. Maybe they had buried a woman there. Too old to make it. In which case there would be a commemorative stone.

Either way Reacher figured he might as well find out. He had no place to go, and all the time in the world to get there, so detours cost him nothing. Which is why he got out of the train. To a sense of disappointment, initially. His expectations had been way off base. He had pictured a couple of dusty houses, and a lonely one-horse corral. And the one-room museum, maybe run part-time and volunteer by an old guy from one of the houses. Or the headstone, maybe marble, behind a square wrought-iron fence.

He had not expected the immense agricultural infrastructure. He should have, he supposed. Grain, meet the railroad. It had to be loaded somewhere. Billions of bushels and millions of tons each year. He stepped left and looked through a gap between structures. The view was dark, but he could sense a rough semicircle of habitation. Houses, obviously, for the depot workers. He could see lights, which he hoped were a motel, or a diner, or both.

He walked to the exit, skirting the pools of vapor light purely out of habit, but he saw that the last lamp was unavoidable, because it was set directly above the exit gate. So he saved himself a further perimeter diversion by walking through the next-to-last pool of light, too.

At which point a woman stepped out of the shadows.

She came toward him with a distinctive burst of energy, two fast paces, eager, like she was pleased to see him. Her body language was all about relief.

Then it wasn't. Then it was all about disappointment. She stopped dead, and she said, "Oh."

She was Asian. But not petite. Five-nine, maybe, or even five-ten. And built to match. Not a bone in sight. No kind of a willowy waif. She was about forty, Reacher guessed, with black hair worn long, jeans and a T-shirt under a short cotton coat. She had lace-up shoes on her feet.

He said, "Good evening, ma'am."

She was looking past his shoulder.

He said, "I'm the only passenger."

She looked him in the eye.

He said, "No one else got out of the train. So I guess your friend isn't coming."

"My friend?" she said. A neutral kind of accent. Regular American. The kind he heard everywhere.

He said, "Why else would a person be here, except to meet the train? No point in coming otherwise. I guess normally there would be nothing to see at midnight."

She didn't answer.

He said, "Don't tell me you've been waiting here since seven o'clock."

"I didn't know the train was late," she said. "There's no cell signal here. And no one from the railroad, to tell you anything. And I guess the Pony Express is out sick today."

"He wasn't in my car. Or the next two, either."

"Who wasn't?"

"Your friend."

"You don't know what he looks like."

"He's a big guy," Reacher said. "That's why you jumped out when you saw me. You thought I was him. For a second, anyway. And there were no big guys in my car. Or the next two."

"When is the next train?"

"Seven in the morning."

She said, "Who are you and why have you come here?"

"I'm just a guy passing through."

"The train passed through. Not you. You got out."

"You know anything about this place?"

"Not a thing."

"Have you seen a museum or a gravestone?"

"Why are you here?"

"Who's asking?"

She paused a beat, and said, "Nobody."

Reacher said, "Is there a motel in town?"

"I'm staying there."

"How is it?"

"It's a motel."

"Works for me," Reacher said. "Does it have vacancies?"

"I'd be amazed if it didn't."

"OK, you can show me the way. Don't wait here all night. I'll be up by first light. I'll knock on your door as I leave. Hopefully your friend will be here in the morning."

The woman said nothing. She just glanced at the silent rails one more time, and then turned around and led the way through the exit gate.

2

THE MOTEL WAS bigger than Reacher expected. It was a two-story horseshoe, a total of thirty rooms, with plenty of parking. But not many slots were occupied. The place was more than half empty. It was plainly built of stuccoed blocks, painted beige, with iron stairs and railings, painted brown. Nothing special. But it looked clean and well kept. All the light bulbs worked. Not the worst place Reacher had ever seen.

The office was the first door on the left, on the ground floor. There was a clerk behind the desk. He was a short old guy with a big belly and what looked like a glass eye. He gave the woman the key for room 214, and she walked out without another word. Reacher asked him for a rate, and the guy said, "Sixty bucks."

Reacher said, "A week?"

"A night."

"I've been around."

"What's that supposed to mean?"

"I've been in plenty of motels."

"So?"

"I don't see anything here worth sixty bucks. Twenty, maybe."

"Can't do twenty. Those rooms are expensive."

"Which rooms?"

"Upstairs."

"I'm happy with downstairs."

"Don't you need to be near her?"

"Near who?"

"Your lady friend."

"No," Reacher said. "I don't need to be near her."

"Forty dollars downstairs."

"Twenty. You're more than half empty. Practically out of business. Better to make twenty bucks than nothing at all."

"Thirty."

"Twenty."

"Twenty-five."

"Deal," Reacher said. He took his roll of cash out of his pocket and separated a ten, and two fives, and five singles. He laid them on the counter and the one-eyed guy swapped them for a key on a wooden fob marked 106, taken from a drawer, with a triumphant flourish.

"In the back corner," the guy said. "Near the stairs."

Which were metal, and which would make a clanging noise when people went up and down. Not the best room in the place. Petty revenge. But Reacher didn't care. He figured his would be the last head to hit the pillow that night. He didn't foresee any other late arrivals. He expected to be undisturbed, all the way through the silent plains night.

He said, "Thank you," and walked out, carrying his key.

THE ONE-EYED GUY waited thirty seconds, and then dialed his desk phone, and when it was answered he said, "She met a guy off the train. It was late. She waited five hours for it. She brought the guy here and he took a room."

There was the plastic crackle of a question, and the one-eyed clerk said, "Another big guy. A mean son of a bitch. He busted my balls on the room rate. I gave him 106, in the back corner."

Another crackling question, and another answer: "Not from here. I'm in the office."

Another crackle, but this time a different tone and a different cadence. An instruction, not a question.

The one-eyed guy said, "OK."

And he put the phone down and struggled to his feet, and stepped out of the office, and took the lawn chair from outside 102, which was empty, and dragged it to a spot on the blacktop where he could see his own door and 106's equally. *Can you see his room from there?* had been the question, and *Move your ass somewhere you can watch him all night* had been the instruction, and the one-eyed guy always obeyed instructions, if sometimes a little reluctantly, as at that point, as he adjusted his angle and dumped his bulk down on the uncomfortable plastic. Outside, in the nighttime air. Not his preferred way of doing things.

FROM INSIDE HIS room Reacher heard the lawn chair scrape across the blacktop, but he paid no attention. Just a random nighttime sound, nothing dangerous, not a shotgun jacking a round, not the hiss of a blade on a sheath, nothing for his lizard brain to worry about. And the only non-lizard possibilities were a lace-up footstep on the sidewalk outside, and a knock on the door, because the woman from the railroad seemed like a person with a lot of questions, and also some kind of expectation that they should be answered. *Who are you and why have you come here?*

But it was a scrape, not a footstep or a knock, so Reacher paid no attention. He folded his pants and laid them flat under the mattress, and then he showered away the grime of the day, and climbed under the bedcovers. He set the alarm in his head for six o'clock in the morning, stretched once, yawned once, and fell asleep.

THE DAWN CAME up entirely gold, with no hint of pink or purple. The sky was a rinsed blue, like an old shirt washed a thousand times. Reacher showered again and dressed, and stepped out to the new day. He saw the lawn chair, empty, oddly placed in the traffic lane, but he thought nothing of it. He went up the metal stairs as quietly as he could, reducing the likely clang to a duller pulsing boom, by placing his feet very carefully. He found 214 and knocked on its door, firmly but discreetly, like he imagined a bellboy would, in a fine hotel. *Your wake-up call, ma'am.* She had about forty minutes. Ten to get going, ten to shower, ten to stroll up to the railroad again. She would be there well ahead of the morning train.

Reacher crept back down the stairs and headed out to the street, which was wide enough at that point to qualify as a plaza. For farm trucks, he guessed, slow and clumsy, turning and maneuvering, lining up ahead of the weighbridges and the receiving offices and the grain elevators themselves. There were train tracks embedded in the blacktop. It was a whole big operation. Some kind of a hub facility, presumably, serving the locality, which in that part of America could have meant a two-hundred-mile radius. Which explained the large motel. Farmers would come in from far and wide, and spend the night before or after a train ride to some distant city. Maybe they would all come at once, at certain times of the year. When futures were for sale, maybe, in faraway Chicago. Hence the thirty bedrooms.

The wide street or the plaza or whatever it was ran basically south to north, with the railroad track and the shiny infrastructure defining the eastern limit, on the right, and what amounted to a kind of Main Street defining the western limit, on the left. The motel was there, and a diner, and a general store. Behind those establishments the town spread out in a loose westward semicircle. Low density. Sprawl, country style. A thousand people, maybe less.

Reacher headed north on the wide street, looking for the wagon train trail. He figured it would come in across his path, from east to west, which had been the whole point of wagon trains. *Go west, young man*. Exciting times. He saw a crossing fifty yards ahead, after the last of the elevators. A road, perpendicular, exactly east to west. On the right it was bright with the morning sun, and on the left it was long with shadows.

The crossing had no barriers. Just red lights. Reacher stood on the tracks and gazed back south, the way he had come. There were no other crossings for at least a mile, which was about as far as he could see, in the pale light. There were no other crossings for at least a mile to the north, either. Which meant that if Mother's Rest laid claim to its own east–west thoroughfare, he was standing on it.

It was reasonably wide, and slightly humped, built up with dirt taken from shallow ditches dug either side. It was covered with thick blacktop, grayed with age, split here and there by weather, and random like frozen lava on the edges. It was dead straight, from one horizon to the other.

A possibility. Wagon trains went dead straight when they could. Why wouldn't they? No one put in extra miles just for the fun of it. The lead driver would steer by a distant landmark, and the others would follow, and a year later some new party would find the ruts, and a year after that someone would make a mark on a map. And a hundred years later some state highway department would come by with trucks full of asphalt.

There was nothing to see in the east. No one-room museum, no marble headstone. Just the road, between infinite fields of nearly ripe wheat. But in the other direction, west of the tracks, the road ran through the town, more or less dead center, built up on both sides for about six low-rise blocks. The corner lot on the right had expanded northward about a hundred yards. Like a football field. It was a farm equipment dealership. Weird tractors and huge machines, all brand-new and shiny. On the left was a veterinary supply business, in a small building that must have started out as an ordinary residential dwelling.

Reacher made the turn and walked on the old trail, due west through the town, the morning sun faintly warm on his back.

IN THE MOTEL office the one-eyed clerk dialed the phone, and when it was answered he said, "She went back to the railroad again. Now she's meeting the morning train, too. How many guys are these people sending?"

He was answered by a long plastic crackle, not a question, but not an instruction either. Softer in tone. Encour-

agement, maybe. Or reassurance. The one-eyed guy said,
"OK, sure," and hung up.

REACHER WALKED SIX blocks down and six blocks back,
and he saw plenty of stuff. He saw houses still lived in,
and houses converted to offices, for seed merchants and
fertilizer dealers and a large-animal veterinarian. He saw
a one-room law office. He saw a gas station one block north,
and a pool hall, and a store selling beer and ice, and another
selling nothing but rubber boots and rubber aprons. He
saw a laundromat, and a tire bay, and a place for stick-on
boot soles.

He didn't see a museum, or a monument.

Which might be OK. They wouldn't have put either
thing right on the shoulder. Back a block or two, probably,
for a sense of reverence, and to stay out of harm's way.

He stepped off the wagon train trail into a side street.
The town was laid out on a grid, even though it had
grown up semicircular. Some lots were more desirable
than others. As if the giant elevators had a gravitational
system all their own. The furthest reaches were undevel-
oped. Closer to the apex, buildings were shoulder to
shoulder. The block behind the trail had one-room apart-
ments that might have started out as barns or garages,
and what looked like pop-up market stalls, for folks who
had given over an acre or two to fruits and vegetables.
There was a store that did Western Union and Money-
Gram and faxing and photocopying and FedEx and UPS
and DHL. There was a CPA's office next to it, but it looked
abandoned.

No museum, and no monument.

He quartered the blocks, one after another, past low shacks, past diesel engine repair, past vacant lots full of weeds as fine as hair. He came out at the far end of the wide street. He had covered half the town. No museum, and no monument.

He saw the morning train pull in. It looked hot and bothered and impatient about stopping. It was impossible to see whether anyone got out. Too much infrastructure in the way.

He was hungry.

He walked straight ahead through the plaza, almost all the way back to where he had started, past the general store, and into the diner.

AT WHICH POINT the motel keeper's twelve-year-old grandson ducked into the general store, to the pay phone on the wall just inside the door. He dumped his coins and dialed a number, and when it was answered he said, "He's searching the town. I followed him everywhere. He's looking all over. He's doing it block by block."

Ready to find
your next great read?

Let us help.

Visit prh.com/nextread